JOHN D. MacDONALD

"It is not at all startling to discover that Mr. MacDonald can create a series character just as well as he does everything else in the suspense field. . . . The adventures are admirably plotted and suspenseful, and give MacDonald ample opportunity to picture and comment upon our society and mores, which he does probably better than anyone else in the crime field. . . ."

—THE NEW YORK TIMES BOOK REVIEW

"I automatically buy every John D. MacDonald as it comes out, and not even MacDonald's invention of a serial character, with all the dangers which I personally know so well, will deter me from continuing to do so."

—IAN FLEMING

"John D. MacDonald is the great American storyteller. McGee is for me."

—RICHARD CONDON

"With his exceptional talents as a storyteller, there's no problem he can't handle and handle well."

—REX STOUT

"A truly gifted and imaginative novelist."

—TAYLOR CALDWELL

JOHN D. MacDONALD

DRESS HER IN INDIGO

A FAWCETT GOLD MEDAL BOOK
Fawcett Publications, Inc., Greenwich, Conn.
Member of American Book Publishers Council, Inc.

"*He that leaveth nothing to chance will do few things ill, but he will do very few things.*"

—GEORGE SAVILE, MARQUIS OF HALIFAX

DRESS HER IN INDIGO

ONE

On that early afternoon in late August, Meyer and I walked through the canvas tunnel at Miami International and boarded a big bird belonging to Aeronaves de Mexico for the straight shot to Mexico City. We were going first class because it was all a private and personal and saddening mission at the behest of a very sick and fairly rich man.

We had the bulkhead seats on the port side because I am enough inches beyond six feet to cherish the extra knee room.

Tourist cards in order, cash in the moneybelts, underseat luggage only. And the unfamiliarly sedate wardrobes of the airborne businessman because there is a constant flow of them back and forth, the systems analysts and the plant location experts, the engineers and the salesmen, importers and exporters, con men and investment specialists.

The Mexican peso is rock solid, the economy roaring, and the population zooming past fifty million. So it is protective coloration to join the flock, as most trips combine business and pleasure, and the pure tourist is fair game for every hustle in the book.

But in one respect we were not entirely plausible. We'd spent the last few weeks aboard my houseboat, *The Busted Flush,* puttering around Florida Bay and the Keys with a small, convivial, and very active group of old and new friends aboard. When you get your clock adjusted to the routines of anchoring off shore, you keep the same hours as the sea birds, and the long hot bright days of summer had been full of fishing and swimming, walking the empty beaches of the off-shore keys, exploring in the dinghy rigged for sail, diving the reefs. So we were both baked to the deep red-bronze that comes from the new deep burn atop the years of deep-water tan, hair baked pale on my skull, salt-dried and wind-parched, the skin sea-toughened. Even Meyer's heavy black pelt had been bleached a little and now looked slightly red when the light hit it the right way.

So if we were of the business breed, it was something to do with engineering and the out-of-doors, like pipelines and irrigation projects.

He had the window seat. We sat in the sweltering heat of the tin bird until finally they unsnapped the umbilical tunnel, swung the door shut, and taxied us out toward takeoff. Then the warm air that had been rushing out of the overhead vents turned to cool, and white shirts began to come unstuck.

Meyer shrugged and smiled in a weary way and said, "That poor, sad son of a bitch."

No need to draw a picture. The memory of my short visit with Mr. T. Harlan Bowie was recent and vivid. Maybe any complex and demanding life in our highly structured culture is like that old juggling routine in which a line of flexible wands as long as pool cues is fastened to a long narrow table and the juggler-clown goes down the line, starting a big white dinner plate spinning atop each one, accelerating the spin by waggling the wand. By the time he gets the last one spinning, the first one has slowed to a dangerous, sloppy wobble, and so he races back and waggles the wand frantically and gets it up to speed. Then the third one needs attention, then the second, the fifth, the eighth, and the little man runs back and forth staring up in horrid anxiety, keeping them all going, and always on the verge of progressive disaster.

So Mr. Bowie's white spinning plates had been labeled Vice President and Trust Officer of a large Miami bank,

8

Homeowner, Pillar of the Community, Husband of Liz, Director of This and That, Board Member of The Other, Father of Beatrice known as Bix, the lovely daughter and only child.

He kept the plates spinning nicely, and I imagine he expected to eventually take them off the wands and put them down, with each deletion simplifying the task that remained, until maybe there would be just one plate called Sunset Years, placidly spinning.

But somehow life is arranged so that if one plate wobbles too much and slips off the wand tip and smashes, the rest of them start to go also, as if the sudden clumsiness were a contagion.

One morning Liz had asked him if he had time for another cup of candy. She became furious when he couldn't seem to understand what she meant, and she got the steaming pot and poured another cup and said, "Candy!" She hesitated, frowning, and said, "Coffee? Of course it's coffee! What did I call it?"

By the time she was scheduled for all the neurological tests at the Baltimore clinic, she had lost the differentiation between genders, using he and she so interchangeably she had a fifty percent chance of being right at any given time, and she had admitted to having had sudden and severe headaches for several months, but had paid as little attention to them as possible, because she had never believed in babying herself. They took the top of her skull off like a lid and got some of it but knew they could not get all, and stuck a cobalt bead in there for luck, even knowing she had no luck left. She kept talking for half the time it took to die, but the words didn't go together in any pattern anyone could translate. It took five months to kill her, if you start counting the morning she poured her beloved husband a cup of candy. It was hideously expensive and, to Harl Bowie, hideously incomprehensible. She died on Columbus Day. Daughter Bix had spent the summer at home and had stayed on, of course, rather than going back in September for her senior year at Wellesley.

After Liz died, Bix told her daddy she would probably go back at mid-term.

He was not paying much attention, not only because he was stunned by the loss of his wife, but also because there had been a merger of certain banks, and there was a new imperative computer system for the handling of trust account investments, and Harl Bowie had to keep running up to Atlanta for a week at a time to try to find out what the hell the quiet young men who had been posted in the trust department were talking about.

But he paid a lot of attention when she told him right after Christmas that she had decided not to go back. She had decided to go to Mexico for a while "with some kids I know." He had tried every bit of leverage he could think of, and he couldn't move her an inch. He couldn't even get any display of emotion out of her. She reminded him gently that she would become twenty-two in another month, and there was the twenty thousand left her by her mother, and said it would be nice if he could stop being so manic about it because she was going, with or without approval.

So she went, and he got some infrequent postcards, and in April he was driving through thunder to the airport for another bout with the systems analysis people in Atlanta, and a big semi coming the other way got a big blast of wind and lost it, and came piling and jackknifing across the medial strip into heavy oncoming traffic. They said it was a miracle half a dozen or more people weren't killed, instead of just one man seriously injured, a local bank executive.

T. Harlan Bowie had to be prybarred and torch-cut out of his squashed Buick, and there was so much blood the rescue people were in a big hurry. As it turned out, they would have done a lot better taking it slow and easy rather than turning him and twisting him and working him in muscular style out of the metal carapace. Nobody could prove anything afterward. The lacerations were superficial. But there was a fracture of the spine, and between the second and third lumbar vertebrae the unprotected

10

cord had been pinched, ground, bruised, torn, and all but severed. Nobody could ever say whether the accident had done it, or the rescue efforts.

And it killed him—from the fracture point on down to his toes. Meanwhile the fates were laughing dirtily in the wings at another aspect of the treatment they were giving the poor, sad, sorry son of a bitch. T. Harlan Bowie had always been both shrewd and lucky with what Liz used to call "Harlie's funny little stocks." He liked to put his eggs in a couple of baskets and watch the baskets like an eagle. The day they told him they wanted to take the top of Liz's skull off, he stopped watching the baskets. They were a couple of little technology companies. He had about an eighty thousand investment in them, evenly split. It was not savings, because bank officers don't make enough to save money like that after taxes. It was the pyramided gains of a dozen years of those funny little stocks.

His personal broker would call once in a while and try to report what was going on, but Harl didn't want to talk about it or hear about it or even know about it. After Liz died, he was too upset about being so damned alone, and about Bix, to have even the slightest stir of curiosity about his two little dog stocks. Then, of course, there were the weeks in the hospital, and by early July they moved him from the hospital to an elegant place that was a combination rest home and therapy center. When he found out that the tab was running seventy-five a day plus extras, it stimulated the money-nerve and he began to check things out. An old and good friend had emptied out the house on Cricket Bayou, the redwood and coquina stone house Liz had loved so, had stored Harl's personal stuff, and had gotten a very good price for the house the day after it was listed. The personal accident and disability and major disaster insurance was paying off handsomely. His attorney had negotiated a surprisingly fat settlement from the company which handled the trucker's liability insurance. The premature retirement benefit and the bank insurance

11

disability income clause were spewing more money diligently.

So he called his broker finally and heard the awed, hushed and respectful tone, and finally comprehended that the two funny little technology stocks had both come out with a couple of earnings quarters of a fantastic richness, that they had valuable patents in areas Harl had never even heard of, that one was listed on the big board and the other one had applied, and the stock of both of them had been generously split a couple of times. So in one of them, what had cost him six dollars was worth two hundred and fifty, and the laggard had gone only from eight dollars to a hundred and twenty. So there was upwards of two million two, or an aftertax one million six.

He laughed after he found that out; he laughed himself sick. He had his broker arrange a negotiated sale through the floor specialists, and he put the tax money aside in treasury bills, and he stuffed the rest of it into tax-free municipals, and there he was all of a sudden with a tax-free income coming in on the basis of like two hundred and forty dollars a day forever, and it was money he didn't have to touch because what was coming in from all other sources was more than sufficient to his needs, even in Garden Suite Number Five in Tropicana Grove Retreat.

His lawyers had been trying to locate Bix in Mexico to tell her that daddy had been badly injured. But the last plate had to smash and did so when a man with a polite and careful voice tracked T. Harlan Bowie down by long distance from the State Department to tell him that Miss Beatrice Tracy Bowie had been killed near Oaxaca when the vehicle in which she had been riding had gone off a mountain road, and the Mexican authorities wanted to know where the body was to be shipped and who would arrange and pay for the shipment.

Poor sick sorry rich and sad son of a bitch.

All you can say is: Well, that's the way it goes sometimes. It goes very bad sometimes because they give you the bad in great big indigestible wads. As if they want to

12

write you off in a hurry. As if the idea is to tear down your whole scene and sow the area with salt and acid, and be off looking for the next fellow who happens to be standing and smiling and thinking that life is pretty good lately.

So only-daughter was airfreighted back to eternal rest beside mother Liz in one of those happy-vale places were the markers are flush with the ground level, the walks and gates have names, and stereotaped organ music comes wafting out of the pole-mounted guaranteed weatherproof high-compliance speaker systems.

Nobody knew whether she had enjoyed Mexico.

So three days ago T. Harlan Bowie got Meyer on the phone and they had a long talk, and then Meyer said I should accompany him to Miami and talk to a friend of his. I said I did not want to talk to anybody about anything, because it had been a very nice cruise and I wanted to slob around and savor it in full measure.

Meyer then reminded me that I had met Bix Bowie, and that last year, a week or so after her mother's funeral, he had brought her around and we had gone with her and some other people on the *Flush* up the waterway, and the girl had seemed to have a good time, but it was hard to tell. He explained that he had been a sort of unofficial godfather to the girl when she was smaller, before she had gone away to school.

It stirred my memory, but I could not get a clear image of the girl herself. The world seems overful of quiet pretty blondes lately, and the trouble is that when they are silent and withdrawn one no longer knows whether it is shyness, total disinterest, or a concealed and contemptuous churl-ishness.

But I could see that it had racked my friend Meyer, and that if I continued to drag my feet, he was going to say please, and then I would be unable to help myself, so I agreed before he had a chance to say the magic word friends should not have to use on one another.

On the way down he talked a little about how Liz used to ask him to show up at school when there had been

13

some kind of bring-a-parent situation and Harlan Bowie was too tied up to make it. He thought Bix was glad he would show, but he could never be certain. He had never been able to reach through to her. She had extraordinary composure and control. He and Liz had attended her high school graduation together, because Harl had an appointment in Tallahassee that day.

I said I thought a father should be able to manage at least a graduation for an only child and only daughter. And Meyer said it had often seemed so to him, too.

So we drove on down to Tropicana Grove Retreat, and Meyer was so troubled, I found myself getting emotionally hung on this blonde I couldn't remember. By God, anybody who cruises with McGee deserves better treatment than the fates, or her father, had apparently given her.

The establishment was in a quiet area in Coral Gables, with low buildings, a lot of very handsome old banyans, lots of plantings, summer birdsongs, and old parties being wheelchaired along curved walks. They made a phone call from the office. A stocky woman in a gray and white uniform appeared and introduced herself as Mrs. Kreiger and smiled in pleasant recognition at Meyer, and led us back through garden walks to Garden Suite Five. T. Harlan Bowie sat in a wheelchair in the air-conditioned, carpeted living room, watching a cable television picture of the changing prices on a brokerage house board, while a man was talking about the rails confirming the Dow. He turned it off with the remote control.

Tall thin frail man. His handshake was fragile and tentative. His eyes had that look. It is not so much a haunted look or a hollow-eyed look. It is a look of constant and thoughtful appraisal that keeps going on and on in spite of all conversations, all diversions. Any man who outgrows the myths of childhood is ninety-nine percent aware and convinced of his own mortality. But then comes the chilly breath on the nape of the neck, a stirring of the air by the wings of the bleak angel. When a man becomes one hundred percent certain of his inevitable death, he gets The Look.

14

He had a long face, high forehead, the fine-bodied white hair of the erstwhile blond. Mrs. Kreiger told him she would be back in an hour to take him to therapy. She had broad pale lips, lovely eyes, a tidy muscularity in the way she moved. She told us happily, in a little more than a trace of German accent, that Mr. Bowie had moved the toes on his right foot.

He flushed. Part irritation. Part Aw shucks, it was nothin', guys.

He looked at the door she closed behind her and said, "Und soon, Herr Bowie, ve vill haff you running races, nein?" He asked us to sit. He said to Meyer, "Did you tell Mr. McGee what we discussed?"

"Some of the background, Harl. Not what you want done."

He turned the chair slightly to face me more directly. "Mr. McGee, I know damned little about what my daughter, Bix, felt and thought and believed. I've had a lot of time to think. And a lot of the thinking has been painful. Appraisal of myself as a father—very, very poor. I know that when she was a toddler we were close. She adored me. That was the good part of it. Our only chick. Liz had had a bad time. Couldn't have more. You know, Bix never went through any ugly period at all. Beautiful baby, lovely little girl, handsome teenager. No acne, no braces, no gawky period. Liz and I were too aware of her being an only child, I guess. And awed by how damned pretty she was, and upset at all the admiration she got. So we were too harsh with her. Two against one. United front. She had to strain like hell to get our approval, and we were too chinchy about giving it out. We made her obedient and docile and sweet, and we probably made her unsure of herself. But how can you tell? How many chances do you get to raise a child? I was very, very busy. So I wasn't paying attention, not to Bix as a person. She was an object. Beautiful child.

"Then when Liz ... got sick, Bix came down. She stayed with her mother right through it. And it wasn't pretty. Bix was a rock. I took her for granted. I took her strength for granted. God only knows how badly it tore her up. She never let me know. Without Liz I was a zombie. I went through the motions. It should have been the two of us then. Father and daughter. But each of us was alone in a private way. I had my own hell. I don't know where she was spending her time. She was just ... around."

He gave me a despairing look, and made an empty gesture with his hands. "I'm dithering. I'm not saying it Look. I don't even know how she lived when she was here with me in Miami. I'd find her in the house with friends. Pretty oddball-looking kids. I'd go through and they'd stare at me as if I came from Mars, as if my house were a bus station and I were some strange type in transit. Empty eyes, loud music. She went to Mexico in early January this year. Seven months later she was dead. I want to know ... what it was like. I want to know—Oh God help me—I just want to know if she was having a good time." His voice broke and he put his hand across his eyes.

Meyer said, "Harl had an agency do a little investigating. But the reports are facts without any flavor. He'd follow the back trail himself, if he could. He tried to think of somebody who could get away, somebody without a regular job or a family and he thought of me. When we talked about it, I said you were the man for the job. He wants us both to go. All expenses. Take our time and do it right and come back and tell him how it was for her."

"And find out," Bowie said, "what kind of people she was running around with—find out if they could have played ... some kind of cruel game."

I questioned him, and he explained. After he had had word of his daughter's fatal accident, he had received a letter that had been written and mailed at least a week before she had died, but had been sent to the house that had been sold and had taken a long time in transit. He took it out of the drawer and handed it to me.

Ordinary mail. Sent from Oaxaca in July, with a date stamp so blurred it could have been the 23rd or the 28th. Cheap envelope, cheap paper. Blue ballpoint. It was small untidy writing, half script, half printed, with no clue to the sex of whoever wrote it. No salutation or date or signature.

You want Bix to come back ever, or ever want to come back even, you better come after her or send somebody pretty quick because she doesn't have any idea what's happening to her lately.

"My daughter always knew exactly what was happening," Bowie said. "Somebody was trying to create a problem for her. I don't know why. A cruel little game of some kind. The part about her not wanting to come back certainly means that this note has no relationship to the accident."

So we had talked a little longer, but by then I knew it was for no other reason than to have us report on the end of the short and happy life of Miss Bowie. But he did not look as if he really wanted to hear anything too ugly.

Maybe it wasn't very pretty for Bix Bowie.

Maybe it was a dingy way to die.

So we had the brief reports from the investigation agency, and we had the translation of the Mexican police report of the death, and we had some duplicate prints made from a negative Harlan Bowie had given us. The picture did not restore my memory of her. Full face, half a smile. A flash picture taken the last Christmas the family was intact. Home from school. Without a schoolgirl look. Mature woman. Long creamy spill and fall of thick, ivory-blond hair. Watchful eyes. Meyer told me they were dark, dark blue. Mouth curved with secrets untold. The expression was contradictory. She looked bland and reserved, almost content. But the slant of the flashbulb light picked up a little bulge at the corner of the jaw, a little knot of muscle, a look of tension held under the clench of teeth, under iron control.

The tin bird whoofed down the runway and lifted sharply, while everybody played the habitual game of total indifference which hides the shallow breathing and contracted sphincters of the Air Age.

17

I looked across the blue bay at the fantasy known as Miami Beach. Cubes of maple sugar. Candy minarets. Special low summer rates. We were off to start at the end of her life and work back.

TWO

The two Mexican stewardesses in first class were tidy, handsome, efficient, and very polite. It was restful to find they had apparently not been programmed to smile constantly. The drink cart was well stocked, and it stopped as often as you wanted it to. Lunch was late, fairly heavy, and though no gourmet feast, was served in a manner which had more of the illusion of permanence than is created by the disposable plastics of the domestic airlines in the states.

The plates were heavy cream-colored china with a gold band. Tablecloth and napkins were thick linen. The cutlery was massive silver plate, and the cream, sugar, salt, and pepper came in chunky, permanent, cut-glass containers.

Meyer found the whole thing pleasantly inconsistent. "The jet aircraft is a limited life-support system. It hangs up here, above the thunderheads, heated, pressurized, ventilated, with food and water and waste disposal. The duration of the system depends on the fuel supply. So, if one comes down at the wrong place at the wrong speed for the wrong reasons, the logical debris should be of disposable items. Travis, the mind boggles at visions of a wooded hill littered with broken pieces of dinner plates, cups, saucers and silver tableware. As if a dining room fell out of the sky. Those horrid little plastic compartmented plates and cardboard shotglasses for the cream and salad dressing are more apt for scenes of disaster. So the whole

19

bit is an affirmation that it can't possibly fall out of the sky. Subtle and interesting. Now if they could cover these jukebox plastic bulkheads with a very thin layer of teak or library oak . . ."

"Mighty guru, take your bulging brain off the psychology of air travel and put it on your old buddy, T. Harlan Bowie. He did not ring loud and clear. There is a crack in the bell somewhere."

Meyer shrugged. "Sure."

"What is that supposed to mean?"

"He rings true enough, as what he is. What you sense is that his concern seems a little faked. It isn't. It's limited by his own limitations. He's using us to buy a kind of emotional respectability. He's using us to pat his image back into shape. Oh, he adored her when she was a toddler. Tiny girls are cute and huggable, like puppies and kittens. Lots of people adore kittens, and when they get to be cats they take them for a nice ride and dump them out in the country somewhere and imagine them living in a nice barn, catching mice. McGee, the world is full of reasonably nice guys like Harl. They go through all the motions of home and family, but there is no genuine love or emotion involved. There is an imitation kind. They are unconscious practicing hypocrites. They're stunted in a way they don't and can't recognize. If I had to nail it down, I'd say that people like Harl go around with the unspoken, unrealized conviction that nobody else in the world exists, really, except as . . . bits of stage dressing in the life role that they are playing. So wife and child and job and home are part of the image, and he kept it burnished and tidy, but without any deep involvement with anybody but T. Harlan Bowie. Now he's studying his way into his new role. Tragic, crippled figure. So the dramatics are off key, just a little. And the tears are not quite real. Our mission is part of the new image. But don't fault him. He believes he is really in the midst of life and always has been. He doesn't know any better, because he's never known anything else. What a limited man believes is emotional reality is indeed *his* emotional reality."

"Doesn't everybody fake a little in their own way?"

"Sure. And you're aware of it when you do, aren't you?"

"Uncomfortably."

"But he isn't. And that's the difference."

I thought it over. "Question answered, Meyer. What was his wife like?"

"A nice woman. Comfortable. Adjusted."

"Would Bix have been able to understand what you've told me about him?"

"She would have known it existed. Whether or not she understood it is something else. Maybe she thought it is what people mean when they talk these days about the generation gap. I imagine it would have given her the feeling that no matter how hard she tried, she could never really please him. She would believe, maybe, that there was some well of warmth and understanding and love that she couldn't ever reach, without realizing that she couldn't reach it because it wasn't there, not for her, not for anybody."

I retrieved the investigation reports from the inside pocket of my jacket and studied them carefully, looking for any lead I might have missed the other times I had gone over them.

The group had left Miami on January third, five of them traveling in a blue heavy-duty Chevrolet pick-up truck, two years old, Florida license, registered in the name of Walter Rockland, who, up until Christmas, had been a swimming pool attendant at the Sultana Hotel on Miami Beach. A few days before Christmas Miss Beatrice Bowie had withdrawn eight thousand dollars from her savings account, leaving a balance of thirteen thousand two hundred and eleven dollars and sixty cents, twelve thousand of which had been part of the twenty thousand from her mother's estate. She had purchased a new camper body for the truck, and the group had purchased a great deal of camping equipment and supplies—sleeping bags. a shelter tent, hatchets, camp stove, netting, gasoline lanterns, flashlights, first-aid kits.

They had shown up on January 10th in the public records at Brownsville, Texas, where they had applied for and received tourist cards good for six months. The other three members of the group were Minda McLeen, age twenty, occupation student, address Box 80, Coral Gables, Florida; Carl Sessions, age twenty-two, occupation musician, listed at the same address as Miss McLeen; and Jerome Nesta, age twenty-six, occupation sculptor, home address Box 2130, Key West, Florida.

The agency had come up with only a few additional facts about the quintet. Miss McLeen had stopped going to classes at the University of Miami in May of the previous year. Walter Rockland had been fired by the Sultana Hotel, and though the personnel manager would not state why, there was reason to believe that the hotel management thought he was implicated in some way in a series of robberies of the winter guests at the hotel. Jerome Nesta had been arrested three and a half years previously at Marathon, Florida, in a narcotics raid, had been charged with and had pleaded not guilty to possession of marijuana. When the case came to trial, there was insufficient proof that the marked and tagged container presented in court was in fact the same container taken from him when he was taken into custody, and a defense motion to dismiss was granted by the judge.

And that, of course, is the tragic flaw in the narcotics laws—that possession of marijuana is a felony. Regardless of whether it is as harmless as some believe, or as evil and vicious as others believe, savage and uncompromising law is bad law, and the good and humane judge will jump at any technicality that will keep him from imposing a penalty so barbaric and so cruel. The self-righteous pillars of church and society demand that "the drug traffic be stamped out" and think that making possession a felony will do the trick. Their ignorance of the roots of the drug traffic is as extensive as their ignorance of the law.

Let's say a kid in Florida, a college kid eighteen years old, is picked up with a couple of joints on him. He is convicted of possession, which is an automatic felony, and given a suspended sentence. What has he lost? The judge who imposes sentence knows the kid has lost the right to vote, the right to own a gun, the right to run for public office. He can never become a doctor, dentist, C.P.A., engineer, lawyer, architect, realtor, osteopath, physical therapist, private detective, pharmacist, school teacher, barber, funeral director, masseur, or stock broker. He can never get any job where he has to be bonded or licensed. He can't work for the city, county, or federal governments. He can't get into West Point, Annapolis, or the Air Force Academy. He can enlist in the military, but will be denied his choice of service, and probably be assigned to a labor battalion.

It is too rough. It slams too many doors. It effectively destroys the kid's life. It is too harsh a penalty for a little faddist experimentation. The judge knows it. So he looks for any out, and then nothing at all happens to the kid. Too many times harsh law ends up being, in effect, no law at all. All automatic felony laws are, without exception, bad law, from the Sullivan Act in New York State, to the hit and run in California. They destroy the wisdom and discretion of the Court, and defeat the purposes they are meant to serve.

I wondered if Jerry Nesta, sculptor, knew how close he had come to the edge. I wondered if it had marked him in any way. And I wondered if I'd ever get a chance to ask him.

So they had crossed over into Matamoros, Mexico, on January 10th, and some seven months later, on August third, a Sunday, according to the translation of the police report, Miss Beatrice Bowie, twenty-two years old, American tourist, had been driving at dusk down State Highway 175, heading southwest toward Oaxaca. At a steep and dangerous part of the highway, the vehicle left the road at a spot fifteen miles from the city. A bus driver on a switchback on the opposite side of a valley saw the bloom of flame and reported it when he reached the bus station in Oaxaca. As night had fallen, the police were unable to locate the automobile until the following morning. She had

23

been alone. The car was a British Ford with State of Oaxaca plates, owned by a resident American named Bruce Bundy, age 44, of 81 Calle las Artes, Oaxaca.

He stated that on Saturday afternoon he had loaned his car to a young man, an American tourist, known to him only as George. He did not know why there was a girl alone in the car, or why she had been on that road. Police could find no identification. On Monday afternoon a woman came to the funeral parlor and made a positive identification of the body as that of Beatrice Bowie. She made a statement to the effect that Miss Bowie and Miss McLeen had been staying in the guest apartment at her winter home on Avenida de las Mariposas in the section known as La Colonia. The woman, a French national, Madame Eva Vitrier, told the police that several days earlier her guests had evidently quarreled, and Miss McLeen had left for Mexico City. She said that Miss Bowie had seemed upset and depressed. When she did not return to the guest apartment on Sunday night, and when on Monday she heard of the recovery of the body of the unidentified woman, she had thought it might be Miss Bowie, and discovered that indeed it was. She knew Mr. Bundy, but did not believe that Miss Bowie knew him. The name George did not mean anything to her. But it was probable that Miss Bowie knew him. All the young American tourists seemed to become known to one another.

The police had returned to Mrs. Vitrier's home with her and had there picked up Miss Bowie's personal effects, including her purse and her tourist card which, on the day of her death, was almost a month overdue for renewal. Their search for the young man known only as George had been unsuccessful.

As I put the papers away again, Meyer said, "Anything new?"

"Just more questions. When did she send for that bank draft to clean out her account?"

"Harl said it was in late March."

I had the address where they had sent it. She had been at Los Tres Rios Trailer Park at Culiacán, over in the

24

State of Sinaloa, on the Gulf of California, and it had been made out to her, payable at the Culiacán branch of the Banco Nacional.

"My question right now, Meyer, has something to do with it being one hell of a trip from Brownsville to Culiacán, and another hell of a trip from Culiacán down to Oaxaca. And did they all go, and did they go in that camper, and where and when and how did they split up? And the Mexicans are very touchy about people getting their vehicles back to the border in six months. You can renew and go back in again, but don't get cute about overstaying your tourist card deadline. Why did she want the money, all of it, and why did she overstay her permit?"

"Shut up," said Meyer, "and look out at the nice volcano, McGee. I mean at the three nice volcanos. No, by God, there are four of them."

"Citlaltepetl, Malinche, Ixtaccihuatl and Popocatépetl."

"Travis, do you have something caught in your throat?"

"If you want to cheat a little, you can call that one over there Orizaba instead of Citlaltepetl."

"I did not know you had any expertise on Mexico's snow-capped peaks."

"Once upon a time there was a roof garden in Puebla, and a little tile stairway going up to it, and the biggest mesh hammock you ever saw in your life, old friend. And when the moonlight was right and the night balmy, a fellow could go padding up the tile stairs and stretch out in that hammock, and one Maria Amparo Celestina Rodriguez de la Vega would take up her warm one third of said hammock and make a fellow name each volcano and name it right."

"Is that where you got your pidgin Mexican, señor?"

"It helped."

So fasten seat belts, and, in the late afternoon, head down and into that misty, poisonous, saffron smutch that

25

fills the mountain bowl of that great city half full. Better than six million of the fifty million Mexicans live on that swampy plateau seven thousand five hundred feet high. An inaccurate comparison would be twenty-four million Americans living in Denver. Mountains rim the Mexico plateau, enclosing and holding the exhaust fumes of uncounted thousands of trucks and buses ranging from brand new to items so ancient they have a sidelong, clattering shamble, steaming and groaning. And the exhaust of a bedazzling number of Volkswagens. A big new plant on the Puebla highway stamps them out like production-line tacos, and every boulevard is a combination scrambling road rally, dodgit game, and demonstration of machismo. Add the smoke of a few hundred thousand little charcoal cooking fires, and the city is in an unending haze, saffron-gold on the sunny days, purple-brown when it is cloudy.

Our cab driver was a large, loud, jolly type with a dashboard covered with religious statuary and medallions. With graceful little flourishes of hand and wrist on the wheel, he slid through openings that opened just as he got there, closed just as he got through. He said we were very lucky it was not yet five o'clock, because we would make the trip to the Hotel Camino Real in perhaps twenty minutes, and a half hour later it might take an hour and twenty minutes. I translated for Meyer. Meyer sat with his eyes shut and said he would have preferred the hour and twenty minute version.

Once he got to the Paseo de la Reforma heading out toward Chapultepec, he was able to play the chicken game at each traffic circle—at Colón, Cuauhtémoc, Independencia, Diana. To play the game properly, you get into five-abreast traffic and accelerate to fifty as you enter the traffic circle, then all go screaming and swaying around the monument in the middle and find room to peel off and out of the group and exit from the circle at the street you want.

Meyer had opened his eyes. They were too far open. I tried to take his mind off the chicken game by telling him

26

bits of lore—such as the fact that Chapultepec means Grasshopper Hill. But all he could say, watching the traffic inches away, was a barely audible "Dear kindly Jesus." He said it several times.

We popped out of the flow at Diana, sped across the bow of several buses, and gradually slowed down as we went along Mariano Escobedo. The driver turned into the hotel entrance, stopped abruptly, hitched around to face us, looked at his watch, and with a big grin said in semi-English, "Twenny-toos minootis!"

"I'll just sit right here for a while," Meyer said.

But a large young man garbed like an Ecuadorian admiral handed us out and got us and our luggage into the incoming flow. My first look at the Camino Real. Twenty-five million dollars worth of it. Seven connected buildings, the tallest only five stories. Entrance lobby the size of a football field, paved with little oblongs of gleaming hardwood, each piece smaller than the end of a pack of cigarettes. Bold colors, daring architecture, startling vistas, all of it a maze of shops and bars and lounges, fountains and pools and restaurants, stairways and corridors and carpeted luxury. Seven hundred and something rooms and suites.

The reservation was in order, the bellhops brisk, and after a very short elevator ride and a very long walk, we were deposited in a pair of interconnecting singles on the third floor of a bedroom wing. Drinks came swiftly. I unpacked. I heard Meyer's voice raised in sonorous melody, and wandered into his place and found him in his giant tub, his drink on the broad marble encircling slab, the black pelt on chest and shoulders foamed with soap.

"About those last lions," he said. "Too damned fat and sleepy and indifferent. Send the boys out to get some lean and hungry lions. How can we put the fear of God into those Christians unless we use faster lions?"

"Anything else?"

"Who catered that last orgy? There were only three dancing girls apiece. An austere orgy is no orgy at all."

"I'll make a note of it."

"And get me my fiddle."

"So soon? We haven't put out the last fire yet."

He hoisted his glass. "Here's to primitive, backward Mexico. Here's to hardship."

I left him there, paddling happily, soaping and singing, and went back into my room and looked up Ron Townsend's number in the oversized phone book. The hotel operator told me I could dial direct. There was a little gadget on the phone. Push the gadget and dial.

A girl answered and I asked for Ron.

She had a good voice, husky and very personal. She got my name and came back and said, "Hang in there while waterboy gets the soap out of his eyes, friend."

He came on the line, properly enthusiastic. He is a young partner in a Miami advertising firm. He was born and partially raised in Cuba. He is the agency expert in Mexico and doing well. I had made a good recovery for them some time ago when a secretary, unbonded, took off with enough cash out of the safe to sting them pretty good. He was delighted to learn Meyer was with me, and apologetic about having a date he couldn't break. But he said he could stop off on the way, so in thirty minutes or so he joined us at the bar in the Camino Real which he favored, named Azulejos, bringing with him the voice on his phone, a young girl at least five ten, suitably spectacular, and clad in mini-leather fastened with big brass chains and galoshes snaps. Her name was Miranda Dale and she had just finished a bit part in a West German motion picture they had shot at Mazatlán, on Mexico's west coast.

I told Ron our problem, and the girl listened to it with a pretty and sympathetic show of interest. I asked him if he could recommend a useful and influential contact in Oaxaca, and he came up with one named Enelio Fuentes and wrote it on the back of his business card and slid it across to me. He said Enelio was an old friend, had a big VW agency and other business interests scattered around the State of Oaxaca. But he couldn't help with a name in

28

Culiacán. He said he would phone Fuentes and tell him to take care of me if I had to look him up.

Then I asked him how he would go about checking on the Chevrolet truck and camper with Florida plates, registered to a Walter Rockland, and he said he wouldn't even try. In theory you get car papers at the border, and they keep a copy at the place where you enter, and if you leave at some other border town, the stamped papers are supposed to go back to the place where you entered, and then the set is supposed to be sent to Mexico City and filed somewhere, possibly by some branch of the Mexican Tourist Bureau. But that was only theory.

I said we'd be back in Mexico City sooner or later, but right now the most useful thing to do was get down to Oaxaca while there was still a good chance that friends of Miss Bix might be around.

They had to leave. Went across the dim and crowded room. Those long, sweet, taffy-sleek legs, from boot leather to mini-leather, seemed to gather available light and reflect it. Three mariachi types were on the stand, one singing a ballad, and he inserted an improvisation I could not catch. Ron turned, grinning, and called something to the musicians, and there was laughter and applause.

Meyer and I stayed on. He had discovered that *tequila añejo commemorativo,* with *sangrita* on the side, is one of the world's more pleasant drinks. The añejo—the "j" pronounced like a gutteral cough—means old. The commemorativo means a very special distillation. It is drunk straight, pale amber in color, strong, smooth, and clean. The chaser's full name is *sangrita de la viuda,* which means for some reason I have yet to learn, "little blood of the widow." It is tomato juice, citrus juices, with several varieties of pepper and spices. It changes the taste buds, readies them for the next sip of the tequila. Meyer crooned and beamed and ordered more.

But later his mood changed. "Vulgarity can be many things," he said. "It can be having a good time while en route to where the daughter of an old friend died. Dead young women are a pitiful waste."

29

We had finished a late dinner. "Tequila shouldn't make you morose," I told him.

"Without it, I would probably be crying," he said.

THREE

We were reserved on an early Mexicana flight. It was an elderly Douglas with four genuine propellers and a full load of passengers. Noisy engines, with oil stains on the housings, littered floor, some popped rivets, lots of vibration. My turn at the window seat. Went roaring and clattering down the runway and lifted off. You get conditioned to that steep upward slant of the jets. This thing lifted off and seemed to hang there, fighting for every slow foot of altitude. Lots of time to look down into the streets. At seventy-five hundred feet as a starting place, and with a full load, we did a lot of clawing before we finally came up out of the last of the bright morning smutch and made a long slow turn.

A very plump stewardess in a soiled uniform served us paper cups of coffee and sweet rolls, and she did a lot of bantering with the customers. Then we went between Popo and his sleeping lady, Ixtaccihuatl. The blazing white summits of the dead volcanoes were easily a thousand feet above us, and vivid against the indigo sky. We were close enough to see snow plumes trailing off the cliffs of Ixta in the morning winds.

Then down along the torn and crumpled country, old stone spilled from the spine of the Sierra Madre. A day so clear you could see tiny villages, see the pale narrow marks of burro paths along the ridges. Too harsh a land to sustain life, but it does. Spaniards could never have taken it from the Indios without all those cute political tricks, turning them against each other. Travel-worn old DC grinding slowly down the side of the rocky world, a tin impertinence making its rackety noise across the stone indifference of the volcanic land. So eat the sweet roll and look down at the world of a thousand years ago. Mexicana Airlines sells tickets on a time machine.

So we came down into the valley of Oaxaca—pronounced wuh-HOCK-ah—beginning the descent at the upper end of the valley, some twenty miles from the airfield. Green valley encircled by old burned brown rounded hills. It is a plateau valley, five thousand feet high, in the Sierra Madre del Sur, and the Pacific is not far away. Skimmed lower. Saw a broken, abandoned, stone church amid cornfields. Saw a man scratching a groove in brown soil with a wooden plow pulled by slow oxen. Saw village children, bright as spilled flowers. And our pilot set the old crock down with such precise and loving delicacy that there was but one small yelp of rubber, and not the slightest jar.

A neat little terminal, wine warm air, a confusion of greetings and luggage and taxis and hotel vehicles. The man from our hotel made himself known by pacing through confusion, calling "Veeeek Tory Aaaah! Veeeek Tory Aaaah!"

So soon we were off in a VW bus, the other passengers two stone-faced ladies with blue hair, large satchels, and guidebooks in German, and one young Mexican couple. The girl was in a smart travel suit of painful newness. The boy looked everywhere except at her. New gold rings gleamed.

We passed a sign as we approached the city, asserting that there were eighty thousand people therein. We skirted an edge of it, and climbed steep grades, then, in lowest low, ground up the long, steep, divided driveway to the parking area at the top, and the portico over the entrance to the Hotel Victoria.

The modern hotel, five stories tall, stretched along the top of a ridge, looking out across all of the city. Down the slope, in random array, beyond a huge swimming pool, were individual bungalows, each with carport, each land-scaped with brilliant flowers and flowering vines. Rough stone steps and walks and stone driveways wound down through the bungalow community, all of it behind a guarded security fence.

The bungalows had girl-names instead of numbers, and they put us in Alicia. There was one large, tiled, plain room, simply furnished, two double beds, a bath, a dressing room, and a small porch in front overlooking the panorama—a porch with a tin table and poolside chairs. Alicia was two hundred and fifty pesos a day for two. Twenty dollars. I had explained to Meyer the quick easy McGee system for keeping track of the pesos. A fifty-peso bill is a four-dollar bill. A ten-peso bill is an eighty-cent bill.

Meyer stood on the porch and looked at the city and the mountains and the blue, blue sky. He looked at the flowers. He sniffed the flavors of the summery air. Then he turned to me and said, "I would have this handy little magic wand and I would take one little pass at you. Kazam! Suddenly you are Miranda Dale, looking at me like she looked at Ron Townsend."

"Didn't all those legs make you feel insecure?"

"And so did the age of the child. But this is the sort of place where I could try to overcome minor obstacles."

"You are a hairy, over-educated, lecherous old man."

"Flattery will get you nowhere, McGee. It's eleven-fifteen. What now?"

"Our wheels." We took a cab down into the city. The Hertz office was on a side street near the *zocalo*—the public square. The man was pleasant enough, but had absolutely no record of any reservation. He would have a lot of nice cars soon. Maybe in a week. He said he felt desolated by being unable to serve me. I said I would like to give him a four-dollar bill to ease his desolation. It was not to spur him to greater effort on my behalf, I said, because I was certain he would give me every possible help. It was a token of my understanding. He said there was, in truth, a car, but it would be a pity to rent it to me,

33

because I obviously was used to better, and deserved better. It had been many, many *kilometros* and needed small repairs and was unclean. A boy with a Le Mans psychosis brought it around.

It was a Ford Falcon, from the Guadalajara assembly plant. Made in Mexico by Mexicans. Pale green. Four doors. Standard shift. It had been thirty-five thousand kilometers, and had been grooved on both sides by near disaster. And it had been traveling some very dusty roads. I signed for it. I took it on a test run, with Meyer copiloting, using the street map they had given us at the airport. Either the Ford engineers have decided Mexicans are a smaller race, or the cars shrink in the dry climate. With the seat as far back as it would go, my knees were on either side of the edge of the steering wheel, and unless I remembered to swing the right knee out of the way, each time I shifted into high I gave myself a sharp and painful rap on the inside edge of the kneecap. When we hit the first potholes I found the front shocks were gone. The front end hit the frame with a metallic thunk, and then a rumbling chatter.

So I asked directions, and found the Ford garage about seven blocks west of the zocalo. It was then a little past noon. The boss man took it for a turn around the block and came back shaking his head, and said I could have it at four.

We walked to the central square, along narrow sidewalks on narrow streets. The plaster-over-stone fronts of the two-story residences and shops formed a solid wall along the walkway, and they had been painted and re-painted with pure strong pigments. One blue wall brought Meyer to a stop. Maybe it had been painted and patched fifty times. Layers had cracked, peeled, faded. It was all the shades of blue there are.

"Fix that with transparent epoxy," he said, "peel off a rectangle eight feet long and five feet high, frame it in rough-cut cypress with a white stain, and take it to any decent gallery—"

34

"And somebody will tell you their little daughter could do it better."

"The creative act is in selecting *which* rectangle to frame. It is very damned beautiful, Travis. And that talented daughter is a rotten kid."

Buses, trucks, cars, bicycles, and the ubiquitous popping and snorting of the Mexican plague—the motor scooter. So we went out of the sun heat into the cool shade of the gigantic trees of a splendid zocalo. It had its ornate circular bandstand in the middle, a criss-cross of wide walkways and a perimeter walk past gaudy riots of flowerbeds. Traffic circled it counterclockwise. There were men, women, children selling serapes, shoeshines, chewing gum, straw baskets and straw animals, black pottery, fresh flowers and wilted flowers, serapes, cigarettes, fake Indian relics, silver jewelry, junk jewelry, firecrackers, aprons, serapes, ice cream, soft drinks, and hot tacos stuffed with God only knows what kind of meat. And serapes.

There was evident poverty, beggars with twisted limbs, sick children, stray mongrels, but there was a sense of great life and vitality, of enduring laughter. We found an empty bench. Meyer sat and saw everything, soaked it up, and smiled and smiled. And it was Meyer who spotted a little group on one of the diagonal paths, carrying purchases from the public market, walking toward the largest hotel that fronted on the zocalo, an old ornate stone and plaster structure with a sign proclaiming it as the Hotel Marqués del Valle. There was a long, narrow roofed porch across the front of it, a couple of steps up from sidewalk level. Fat cement columns supported arches that held up the overhanging bulk of the hotel. The porch was two tables wide and about thirty tables long, about half of them occupied, with white-coated waiters hustling drinks and food.

It was a group of four young men and three girls. The college-age men were wearing faded Mexican work shirts, bleached khakis. Two of the men and one of the girls were barefoot, and the others wore Mexican sandals. The girls wore shorts with bright cotton Indian blouses, and the

35

boys were extravagantly bearded, long-haired. This, as Meyer pointed out, was clear indication they had been in Mexico for a long time. The government had long since closed the border to what were called "heepees," so the shorn locks and whiskers had to be regrown south of the border.

We got up and followed along. The waiters pushed two tables together for them. Meyer and I took a table about twenty feet from them, which was as close as we could get. The tempo of the public square was diminishing visibly. Shops were closing. It was siesta time, and not until two-thirty or three would the town begin to stir again. Only the serape salesmen along the sidewalk stayed in business, holding up the rough-woven gaudy wools, trying to catch the tourist eye, the tourist interest. And a dirty, big-eyed child roamed from table to table, trying dispiritedly to vend her "cheeeklets."

The young seven were a closed circle, totally indifferent to everything and everyone around them, relating and responding to one another. Too many for any initial contact. So I looked at the menu. Meyer had to trust me. The waiter was very patient with my verbless Spanish, and I was equally patient with his rudimentary English. So I managed to find a good solution—chicken enchiladas covered with Chihuahua cheese and baked. He said they had no Dos Equis, but if we wanted a dark beer, Negro Modelo might please us. And it did, and we were into the second bottle before the enchiladas came, bubbling hot in oval steel dishes.

After some thoughtful mastication, tempered with the dark beer, Meyer said, "Offhand, what are the immigration laws?"

"I'll just leave you here, and you can take your chances."

"I'll send you a card every Christmas."

Another student couple had appeared, a huge boy with a small head and a sensitive delicate face, and the blond silky hair and beard style of the Christus. He was with a small wiry black girl with a skin tone like dusty slate,

36

sporting an African blouse and a tall tightly kinked African hairstyle through which she had bleached several startling amber-gold streaks.

"Wish me luck," I told Meyer, and with beer in hand went ambling over to their table. There was one extra chair.

"Join you for a couple of minutes?"

They looked up at me with a quick, identical wariness, and looked away again, and kept talking as if I was not there. Bad tactics. Should have asked the stranger to go away.

So I sat down, smiling blandly, and cut into their conversation, saying, "I am not on vacation, kids. I am not looking for fun and games. I am not drunk. I am not fuzz."

She stared at me with a hot, dark-eyed hostility and said, "Did you catch the strange word, darling? This fellow seems to have some sort of in-group syndrome."

"Fuzz," the boy said thoughtfully. "Wasn't there some sort of quip about that we never understood, Della?" Boston accent.

"I don't recall at the moment, dear."

He put on a minstrel show, end-man accent, doing the Sambo thing very badly. "Hey, you all hear 'bout what happen to Jemima?"

"No!" she said. "Whut happen to ol' Jemima?"

"Got herself picked up by the fuzz."

"Lordy me! That sure musta stung."

"Hyuck, hyuck, hyuck," I said, unsmiling.

"Just go away," Della said. "Be cooperative. Go back to your friend."

"If you had to make a guess, why would you say I came over here?"

They glanced at each other. The boy shrugged. "I guess the most likely thing would be one of those little speeches about tolerance and miscegenation and all that, so that you can pretend to be so terribly understanding and get some queasy little kick out of it, and get some barroom conversational gambits back wherever you come from, and

37

also, let's see, delude yourself into believing that there is something so awfully swinging about you that you can bridge the communications gap."

I laughed. I couldn't help it. He was bright. He was so damned right and so damned wrong, all at once. I rocked the chair back and laughed. They looked startled, then angry, then they fought the temptation to smile, and then they were laughing. She had a piercing giggle, and he had a deep, rhythmic bray. We were being stared at. Finally, when I could get my breath, I said, "My name is Travis McGee. Fort Lauderdale, Florida."

"Della Davis," he said. "I'm Mike Barrington." His was a large, hard, muscular hand.

"Equal time?" I asked. He nodded. She had the hiccups. "I'm loaded with a lot of kinds of tolerance and intolerance, and the only time I get defensive is when I identify some kind of tolerance or intolerance I didn't know I had, or thought was something else. The only people who need queasy kicks are the ones with the sex hangups, and I think I was a little hung up when I was twelve years old, but not lately. I don't need a new supply of small talk. And if I did, I wouldn't look for the raw material on a hotel veranda. Anybody who gives it any thought knows that there has always been a communication gap between everybody. If any two people could ever really get inside each other's head, it would scare the pee out of both of them. I don't want to share your hopes and dreams, Mike. I just want to communicate in a very limited way, politely, with no stress on anybody."

"I guess they aren't with the mining company after all," Della said to him. She turned to me. "We noticed you two and decided you weren't tourists. There's a mine up in the hills northeast of the city. Okay, Mister McGee, let's communicate in our limited fashion."

"If you two haven't been here a month, communication ends."

"We got here ... the second of something. May or June, dear?" she asked.

"May," said Mike, "and I change my guess. You're

38

looking for somebody's baby darling, so in your nice, personable, reasonable way you can talk baby darling into coming back home to daddy. Or maybe that's daddy you were sitting with over there. And you locate her—or him—and lay on the tickets, the kind you can't cash in."

"Closer. But that isn't daddy over there. Daddy is back in Florida because he got nearly, but not quite, torn in half. And baby darling went home already. From here. In a box, early this month."

"Oh sure. The one with the country-day-school nickname. What was it they called her, Del?"

"Hmmm. Dox? Nax? Bax? . . . Bix!"

I put one of the prints on the table, facing Della Davis. She pulled it closer. "That one?" I asked.

" 'Tis she," said Della. "We saw her around. You know. Stay here a while and you see everybody. Nod and smile. Didn't socialize. The group she was in, or better the groups she ran with, we don't make those scenes. I've got nothing for or against, you understand. Freedom is being left alone to do your own thing. Mike is a painter."

"Wants to be a painter," he corrected.

"And he doesn't want to talk about it. He gets up early and he works all day and he goes to bed. And I prowl around driving hard bargains for tortillas and beans and rice and thinking up new ways to cook them. So today I got a little check from my sister in Detroit. So we're living it up. I mean we aren't here much, so we don't keep good track. Anyway, she's dead. What are you after?"

Mike Barrington said, "If old dads wondered if somebody pushed his baby darling off the mountain, he might send somebody like Mr. McGee to come and snuff around."

"'Oh, he doesn't doubt that it was an accident. It was a pretty good police report. They were out of touch since last January, when she came to Mexico. He wants to know what the last six months of her life were like. How she lived and what she thought and how she died."

"And," said Della with an acid sweetness, "I suppose she was always a very good girl."

39

"Kept her room neat," I said, "got good grades, remembered names, thanked the hostess, brushed her teeth, and said her prayers. I guess he'd like to know who the hell she was."

"None of them know who we are," Mike said. "Or care much, really. Hang in there with an image they can live with, and they love it. You don't know who they are, and they don't know who you are."

"So who was Bix Bowie?"

"A girl who died young," Della Davis said.

"If I had to guess why," Mike said, "and understand I'm not knocking her, I'd say she was probably turned way on. She was high and she was flying, and she was coming down the mountain without knowing if she was there or she was dreaming it, and it turned out she wasn't dreaming it. In a dream, when you hit bottom, you wake up. The thing about Mexico, the stuff that's on prescription in the states, here you can buy it in any drugstore. All you have to know is the name of what you want. Little lists circulate. The right names for Thorazine, Compazine, oral Demerol, Doriden, reserpine, Mardil, Benzedrine, other amphetamines. And in the public market, at the herb stalls, you can buy a kilo brick of very good, strong pot. It's all a big lunch counter. You mix them up in brand new ways and wait and see where and how it hits you. If you like it, you try to find the same combination again."

She put her wiry black hand on his and said, "That *used* to be the name of your game, sweetheart."

"There's a better high," he said, smiling into her eyes. "I don't ever have to come down off this one."

She gave me a bawdy wink, which somehow was not bawdy at all, and said, "Like the old saying, man, I changed his luck."

"It needed changing," Mike said.

"Was she any kind of hooked?" I asked them.

"I wouldn't know," Mike said. "I didn't know her. It's unfair to make guesses. Maybe one of those damned cows came clumping onto the road and she swerved and lost the

40

car. But it's fair to say she was some kind of user, because it was users she was with, mostly, but I don't know how much or how often, or even what."

"Those seven over there at that table. Would any of them know more about her?"

Della leaned back and made a careful inspection. "I just don't know. If any of them, it would be the girl facing this way, with the round face and the reddish hair and the big sunglasses, and the skinny fellow sitting on her left. I think they've been here the longest."

"Got a name for either of them?"

"Mike, isn't that the girl they call Backspin?"

"Yes. God knows why."

I used my little notebook to refresh my memory. "Here are the names of the ones she came into the country with back in January. Stop me if I come to anyone you know. Carl Sessions? Jerry Nesta? Minda McLeen?"

"Whoa," Della Davis said. "Little bit of a dark-haired girl. She and that Bix were usually together. Strange-acting girl. Haven't seen her around lately. But that doesn't mean anything. Mike, darling, that horrible bore of a man with the funny hat. Wasn't his name . . . ?"

"McLeen. I went to the public market last week with Del and he introduced himself. Said he was looking for his daughter."

"He still around?"

"I have no idea."

"Walter Rockland?"

They both looked blank, both shrugged.

"They came down in a Chevy pickup, blue, with a new camper body on it."

She looked at Mike. "Rocko?" she asked.

"He says the name is Rockland, and the truck fits. Mr. McGee, is he a little older than the rest of the bunch? Husky?"

"That fits."

"Then Miss Bix came down here in bad company if she came with that one," Della said. "That one is one mean

41

honkey son of a bitch. That one is a smart ass and a hustler. When did we have that fuss with him, honey?"

"About the fourth of July, I think. The day after the fourth." They took turns telling me about it. They'd gone to visit a couple they knew, who were living in a travel trailer at the trailer park over near the Plaza de la Danza. Rocko's camper was in a nearby site. Evidently someone had pried open a little door in the side of the camper and stolen his little tank of bottle gas. He came over to the travel trailer in an ugly mood, acting as if it was the fault of the friends of Mike and Della for not seeing it happen. Mike told him to take it easy. Rocko looked the situation over and told Mike he didn't need any advice from him *or* his spade chick. They were standing outside the travel trailer. Mike swung on Rocko and missed, and Rocko tagged him as he lunged forward off balance.

"And," said Della, "Mike was out of it right then. And that mean bastard knew it, but he hit him three more times before he could fall down, and then kicked him in the side. I jumped on his back and reached around to claw his face, and he bucked me off right into the side of the trailer. It sprained my neck and I went around for a week with my head way over on the side like this."

"Is he still there?"

"Our friends left not long after that. We had no reason to go back. Maybe he's still there." They told me how to find it. It was on the west side of town. It was near a street carnival. It was near a school. It had an iron fence around it. It was near the Ford garage. Oh. And called Los Pájaros Trailer Court.

With considerable animation, Della said, "We've got a crazy pad, built like into a corner of a walled garden where there used to be some kind of tourist home that burned. We met such a sweet guy in Mexico City at the art school, and we were running out of money, and he said we could stay there. Outdoor plumbing, and a well with a pump that Mike fixed, and all the tame flowers have gone wild. It's about a mile along the Coyotepec road. You ought to come and see us and . . ."

She froze, and her eyes changed and narrowed. "You are some kind of sneak, man. What the hell am I saying? Who knows you?"

"We know him, honey," Mike said gently. "You have to go along with your own reaction. We can't keep all the walls up all the time. We can't demand credentials."

"Easier for you," she said obliquely. "The man can be so dear, and then his partner takes over and raps you on your kinky haid until your ears bleed, and then the dear man takes his turn with sweet talk."

"Come and see us if you get a chance. On the left on the way to the airport," Mike said. "Look for an old red jeep parked under the trees by the wall."

"I'm sorry," Della Davis said.

"I'll stop by and say hello. Thanks for the invitation. One thing I forgot to ask. The man who owned the car she drove off the road. Bruce Bundy. Know him? Or the woman who identified the body, the French woman, Mrs. Vitrier?"

They did not know them. Mike said, "There are some eerie people living in these little resort spots in Mexico. Here and in Cuernavaca and Taxco and San Miguel. Some are loaded and some are just making it. And the summer is hunting time, both ways. All the kids come flooding down, and there are weirdo types who stalk the kids, and hard kids that stalk the resident crazies. I used to make that scene. Now I don't need it. I can't use it. Depending on what hangups you run into it can go all the way from laughs and kicks to nightmares you couldn't believe."

Their waiter came with the tab. I made a foolish move to pay it, and nearly lost both of them. I relinquished it to Mike, saying, "It was going to be a deductible contribution to the fine arts."

They softened, their pride undamaged.

We said good-by, see you around, see you soon, and I went back to Meyer.

FOUR

Just as I was finishing my factual summary report to Meyer, four departed from the group of seven. One of the girls and three of the boys took off and headed slowly along one of the shady walks that angled across the zocalo, in the somnolence of the warm siesta afternoon. Only a half dozen tables on the porch were occupied. The sun was slanting in. The three who were left—the round-faced redhead with the curious nickname, the very skinny boy, and a muscular girl with a tight cap of brown curls and sunglasses with blue lenses—moved back to an empty inside table out of the sun. A yawning waiter went over to them.

A red jeep went by, with Mike driving. Della was talking to him, gesturing with little chopping strokes of a slender black hand. The windshield was down, and the breeze of passage streamed back his silky hair and beard.

Our waiter brought us more Negro Modelo, and when I glanced again at the three of them, I saw that after the departure of their four friends, they were no longer turned inward upon themselves, making their own closed world of talk, but were now aware of what was around them. They had become interested in us. The redhead, staring at us, said something inaudible to the others. The boy laughed and laughed. The big-shouldered girl in the blue glasses did not react. It was idle interest, and we were fair game. Business types. Establishment. She was pretty good at her little jokes. She kept the boy laughing, never taking

44

her eyes off me. The quite obvious intent was to make me uncomfortable, and if they could get a reaction it would improve the game. So I provided the reaction.

I gave Meyer a warning wink, and got up and walked over to them, properly stuffy and irritated, and said, "Something seems to be very, very funny. How about letting me in on it?"

They were delighted. The victim had walked right up to the gun. The skinny boy took it. He said, "Think maybe big tourist fella like to make bang-bang with nice clean American college girl? This one here name Jeanie. Nice big strong girl. Three hundred pesos maybe? Take her up to your room right now, big fella. She give you a good time. She likes you. Right, Jeanie? You like the big fella, sweetie?"

The girl's head turned very slowly and I could not see her eyes behind the blue lenses as she looked up at me. I pulled the extra chair out and sat down. The skinny boy and the redhead waited in mildly pleasurable anticipation for the shocked reaction. This was called blowing the mind of the random member of the establishment. I let my mouth sag in stupefaction as I appraised them, looking for clues to the best approach. At such close range they were far less attractive than at a distance. The bigger girl looked less muscular, more suety, and smelled slightly rancid. There was grime in the creases of the redhead's neck, and stains on the front of her Indian shirt. The dark boy's hands were filthy. The two pair of eyes I could see were not quite right. They were subtly out of focus, with that slightly glassy and benign look of the mind behind the eyes being skewed a degree or two off center.

There were several ways to go with it. I picked the one I thought might sting the most. I shoved my chair around so that I could call to Meyer and at the same time keep the edge of my eye on the trio.

"Hey, Charley!" I called to Meyer.

"What do you want?" he yelled.

I said to the trio, "My buddy is a little hard of hearing." I raised my voice to a pitch that startled the serape

45

sellers. "Charley, there's nothing here worth fooling around with. The big one with the blue shades he wants twenty-four bucks for. The redhead would maybe go for thirty. But, honest to God, Charley, they're both of them so damn dirty it would turn your stomick. The redhead has spilled food down her shirt, and you should see her neck."

"Knock it off!" the boy said in a pinched little voice.

"Charley, the big one here is named Jeanie, and she doesn't take baths. And all three of them are stoned out of their skulls on something. The kid has got the dirtiest hands I ever seen. Scrawny little bastard. If you ever could get him cleaned up, I don't think even old Crazy Eddie would grope him."

"Get away from us! Get away from us! Get away from us!" It was the redhead, in a dismayed little whine. All the waiters were wide awake. Pedestrians had stopped to admire the volume of sound. Some tourist tables were staring, eyes bulging slightly. Out of the corner of my eye I saw the boy make the move, snatch at the bottle. So I gave him full attention, snapped my hand up and let the bottle slap into the palm. I twisted it away and put it carefully back on the table and gave him a wolf-smile and said, "That's lousy manners, sonny."

I stood up and said, "Charley, maybe a couple of years ago these fatso broads would have been worth a free jump, but now they're so far over the hill ... Charley! Can you hear me, Charley?"

"Just barely," he roared.

"Even if they were cleaned up and dressed nice, they couldn't even make expenses at a hardware convention in Duluth."

I dropped all the way back to merely a hearty conversational tone and smiled down at them and said, "Thanks anyway, kids. You got any slim clean pretty little friends who need more vacation money, send them on up to the Victoria and tell them to ask for McGee. But don't send any turned-on slobs like you two sorry girls. Fun is fun,

46

but a man likes to keep his self respect. Right? See you around."

I went back to Meyer. He rolled his eyes when I sat down with him. I slid down in the chair, ankles crossed, thumbs hooked in my belt, and smiled amiably at the three.

They tried to brass it out for a little while. But the redhead started snuffling and choking. They gathered up their market bundles and took the route that got them around the nearest corner and out of sight.

Meyer sighed. "In a queasy kind of way, I think I enjoyed it. Did you?"

"The target was the redhead."

"And?"

"She won't be able to leave it alone, Meyer. She'll have to pick at it. She's not as far gone as the other two. She can't endure anybody having that reaction to her. They have to be wrong. So she'll have to tell me how wrong I am. Ruptured pride. And then I can ask about Nesta, Rockland, and company. What if I'd asked them today?"

He nodded. "I keep forgetting how devious you are at times. McGee, it was one of your better performances. You were in good voice. But . . . it was brutal."

"Because it was too close to the truth. Let's go."

The car was ready when we got back to the Ford garage. The shift still whammed me on the knee bone, but everything else was fine. I found a place to park it not far from the Ford place, and we walked over to the street carnival area and then located the Los Pájaros trailer park. There was a spiked iron fence around it, crumbling stone pillars. There were big old trees with dusty leaves shading unkempt flower beds. Paths had worn the grass away, and nobody had picked up the scraps of litter in a long, long time.

The bossman was a jolly fat little type in a ragged blue work shirt and paint-spotted khakis. He had a big gold-toothed grin, and more English than I had Spanish. We went into his little office-store and he looked the information up in his registration notebook. When he pronounced Rockland, it came out "Roak-lawn."

"Ah, yes. The Señor Roak-lawn, on place *número* seexteen, from ... ah ... twenny-four of Abreel to ... ah ... twenny-three in Zhuly? Yes. Tree month. He was having a camper here, was Chevrolet trock of Florida, color .. how you say? ... *azul*."

"Blue."

"Ah, yes. Blue!" Suddenly his smile dwindled. "Ah! Yes, it was *that* one. You his fren?"

"No. I am not his friend, señor."

"Then I say. Many, many people here. Nice American *turista* people. That one, that Roak-o, the only one I must ask to leaving when the month is up. Too much the fights and noise. Too many times he called me bad words. This is not right, that is not right. Nothing is right for him. I have to get *policía* to make sure he is going."

"Where did he go from here?"

"Who knows? Away from Oaxaca, for surely."

"Who was with him when he left?"

"Who knows. Different people live with him here the two month. One two three four. Different girls sometimes. Boys and girls. I have no names, nothing. It is nothing to me. So, he is going now for ... wan month and six day." The grin was broad as he said, "I am not missing him moch, you bet. One other señor was asking the same things, maybe it is two weeks ago, I think. And he is asking about his daughter."

"Was his name McLeen?"

"Ah, yes. Señor McLeen. But I do not know of the girl nothing. To me, señor, a father is never letting his daughter go off far away in these times. All is changing, no? Some of these young American, they are very nice and good. But there are the ones such like Roak-o, doing bad things."

"Are there any young people here who were friendly with Rockland?"

"Some would know him, I think maybe. Some are here

48

many month. Perhaps the young ones, the señor and señora . . . I cannot say. Here, look, is the name."

Mr. and Mrs. Benjamin Knighton, of Kerrville, Texas.

They were in space number twenty. It was a travel trailer with canvas rigged to make an extra area of living space. But whatever towed the trailer was not there, and the trailer was locked. Happy Fats explained that the young man was an amateur archeologist who was writing a novel about the Zapotecan civilization in pre-Columbian Mexico, and said that the couple went on a lot of field trips in their "Lawn Roover."

"Very young. Very nice. Very hoppy."

So it was then a little past five on that twenty-ninth day of August, and I asked Meyer if it might not be a good time to chat with that expatriate American, Bruce Bundy, who had loaned his car to some unknown named George, who had loaned it to Bix, who had died in it, or near it.

"I used to be young and nice and hoppy," Meyer said wistfully.

"So now you are old, and nice, and hoppy. And you don't listen. Bundy. Bruce Bundy. Now?"

"Why sure."

I studied the map and found Las Artes, a short street about ten blocks north of the zocalo, toward our hotel. I parked at the end of the street and locked up, and we went looking for number eighty-one.

It was a very narrow two-story house squeezed between its bulkier neighbors. Its plaster front was painted in a faded hue of raspberry. Grilled iron doors were locked across the arched entrance, but the inner doors were open. We could see down a long shadowy corridor to the sun-bright flowers of the rear courtyard. I tugged a woven leather thong and a bell hanging in the archway clanged. A man, slender in silhouette, appeared and came swiftly along the corridor, and then slowed as he saw us, and stopped, frowning, in the edge of daylight, one long step inside the doorway.

"Are you looking for someone?" he asked.

"For a Mr. Bruce Bundy."

49

"I am he," he said, and it surprised me because he looked no more than thirty-four, and the police report had said he was forty-four. "What do you wish to see me about?"

"It's about the fatal accident involving your vehicle on the third of this month."

He shook his head and sighed. "Oh dear Lord, will I *never* come to the end of the bloody red tape. I have answered *endless* questions, and have filled out *endless* reports. What is your part in it?"

"This is my associate, Mr. Meyer. My name is McGee. I'm sorry to bother you, but this is a necessary part of the insurance investigation. Could we come in."

"Now *really*! Are you men trying to be terribly tricky or something? The whole matter has been settled. And I must say that it was terribly unfair. I should have gotten full value for my marvelous little car, but they kept talking about my not putting that fellow, George, on the list of people authorized to drive it. Actually, I shall never loan *anyone* a car, ever again, no matter how nicely they ask."

"Insurance," I said, "on the life of the deceased, Miss Beatrice Bowie of Miami, Florida. There is an accidental death clause in the policy."

"And you came here from *Florida*!"

"A large sum of money is involved, Mr. Bundy."

"And I'm sure it's all terribly important to you and your company and the beneficiary and all that, and I suppose you are here to practically lunge at any hint that the pretty child killed herself so that you can save great wads of money, which I suppose is what you are paid to do, but I am expecting guests, and I was just about to make my famous salad dressing. So why don't you plan to come back tomorrow, Mr. McGoo? But I won't be able to tell you a thing, actually. I did meet those girls, but I knew them so slightly I had the names mixed up. I thought it was the little dark one they called Bix, and I was surprised to find it was the tall, quiet blond one."

"It will only take a couple of minutes."

"Sorry. Tomorrow would be far more convenient. Come at about . . . eleven-thirty in the morning, please."

He turned away and had gone two steps before I tried my hunch. "From talking to Rocko, I thought you'd be more cooperative, Bruce."

He stopped in his tracks and turned very slowly. "To whom?"

"Walter Rockland."

He moved closer to the gate and looked up at me, his head tilted, lips sucked flat. He wore a coarse cotton hand-woven shirt, off-white, with full sleeves and silver buttons on the tight cuffs. He wore a yellow silk ascot, and snug lime-green slacks, and strap sandals the color of oiled walnut. He had brown-gray bangs, a slender tanned face, eyes of pale amber brown.

"Now where would you have encountered *that* creature?"

"If we could come in for a few moments."

"What did he say about me?"

"I promise we won't take too much of your time."

He unlocked the gate. I followed Meyer in. Bundy locked the gate and told us to go straight ahead to the garden and he would be along in a few moments. He said he wanted to make the dressing and get the woman started on the main course. He told us to help ourselves to a drink.

There was a high wall around the small courtyard, a fountain in one corner. The courtyard was paved in a green stone, and the flowers and shrubs were in huge earthen pots. The furniture was of dark heavy wood upholstered in bright canvas. There were bright birds in bamboo cages.

I poured some of his Bengal gin onto ice. As Meyer fixed himself a whiskey soda he said, "From whence came that inspiration, Mr. McGoo?"

"I'd rather not try to find out. I might not get any more inspirations if I knew."

I dug through the back of my wallet and found one of my Central General Insurance cards and showed it to

Meyer so he would at least know who we were working for.

Bundy came into the courtyard carrying a glass of wine. He sat on a low stone bench and looked at me. It was a look familiar to any veteran poker player, when someone is debating whether or not you have the gall to check and raise.

"I think you'd better tell me, Mr. McGoo—"

"McGee."

"Oh. Terribly sorry. McGee, then. Tell me just when and where you saw Charles Rockland."

"*Walter* Rockland."

"Terribly sorry. Charles didn't sound quite right, did it? Rocko suits him better than either, of course."

"We saw him in Mexico City the day before yesterday, Mr. Bundy."

"Really?"

"Just routine. After all, he *did* own the Chevy truck and camper that entered Mexico last January tenth, and Miss Bowie was one of the group. Miss Bowie, Miss Minda McLeen, Carl Sessions, and Jerome Nesta. He wrote to a friend in Miami and gave his Mexico City address. So we looked him up, of course."

"Naturally. Part of your investigation. Go on."

It was turning sour. You can take only so many chances. But when it does turn sour, at least you know at what point it started to go bad, and that can be useful. "Go on with what?"

"With what he said to you about me, of course."

"Just that if you seemed uncooperative, to mention his name."

He finished the wine, licked his finger, ran it around and around the edge of the wine glass until he created a thin, high musical note.

He smiled at me. It was a mocking and flirtatious smile. "Bullshit," he said softly.

I smiled back. "At least I gave it a try, Bruce."

"Dear fellow, little games of intrigue, little fabrics of deception, they're too much a part of my scene. I had

52

years of stage design in New York, and years of set design on the Coast. I'll give you one little gold star for your forehead, though. You are a *little* more subtle than you look. Your type, all huge and hearty and outdoorsy, I expect just a kind of clumsy blundering about. Rocko, for example. Dear God, if at this stage of my life I hadn't learned how to protect myself from anything any piece of rough trade could dream up, I'd be terribly vulnerable and innocent, wouldn't I? Don't you think you'd best leave now?"

"Never argue with the umpire. Come on, Meyer."

He walked us out to the gate. As he unlocked it he said, "I suppose that if you are really what you claim to be, and you really want to know whether it was an accident or suicide, I'd think that that little brunette friend of the Bowie girl's would give you the most clues. Actually, her father is clomping all over town trying to locate her. A perfectly dreadful, dreary man from one of those ghastly midwest states that begin with a vowel. Product of Kiwanis and Dale Carnegie, and once he affixes himself to you, you have to pry him off as if he were a fat little pilot fish."

As I thanked him his two guests arrived, spectacularly, in a little custom Lotus Elan convertible in bubblegum pink with black upholstery. The woman came out from under the wheel, leggy, slender, tall, nimble, in light-blue linen sheath dress to mid-thigh, sleeveless. She had a wild and riotous ruff of wind-spilled lion-mane hair, high-heeled sandals and purse to match the car. For just an instant she was twenty something, but then in the light across her face she was thirty-something, with a twenty-odd body. The boy was in his early twenties, in white shirt open at the throat, crisp khakis, and a powder blue jacket that was a precise match with the lady's dress. He was brick-red from the sun. His hair was cropped to a copper bristle. He had a sullen face, heavy features, and he moved with the indolent indifferent, grace, and ease of one of the big hunting cats, or one of the many imitations of Brando.

"Brucey!" she cried in joyous greeting.

"Becky darling!" he cried.

Giving us a sidelong questing glance, she ran to embrace the host, saying in a British accent, "David had the most fascinating day at the dig. They came upon a whole pocket of tiny beads of bone and jade, and the poor darling had to spend practically the entire day on his knees in the bottom of a monstrous hole, brushing the dust away and picking them up with tweezers. He desperately needs a huge whiskey, don't you, darling?"

The sunbaked boy grunted, and Bruce tried to move them inside. We had gone a half dozen steps when Becky gave that upperclass commanding caw. "You! I say, you two! Wait up a moment! Bruce? Dearheart, why must one set of guests leave when the next arrives? Your house is rather small, I grant that. But not *that* small."

I saw the way it might go, and came back as he murmured protestations to her. I said, "It really wasn't a social call, ma'am. In fact we wouldn't have even got inside the gate if I hadn't tried a little doubletalk. But it only worked for a little while. Mr. Bundy called my bluff. So I don't believe he'd be very happy about having us come back in as guests."

She measured me with vivid emerald wicked-gleam-of-mischief eyes through the rough spill of the red-blond-gold-russet hair and made up her impulsive mind and cried, "Nonsense! We are just too terribly inbred around here. One says the same old things to the same old faces in the same old places year without end. Bruce, dear, these gentlemen would make it a more lively evening."

"But Becky, they are *insurance* types, from Florida. And it's all a very dull bit about the dead girl, the Bowie girl, and they know she traveled here with that Rockland boy. Apparently there was some sort of policy on the girl's life."

"But Brucey, what if they *are* assurance types? Does that mean we have to sit about talking about premiums? Let us widen our horizons a bit, dear."

He hesitated and then, from the little lift and fall of his

shoulders, I could see that he had given up. He said to us, "Lady Rebecca Divin-Harrison is one of our most attractive local institutions, and she has, as you may have detected, a whim of iron. Becky, may I present Mr. McGee and Mr. Meyer. Gentlemen, please come back into my home as my invited guests."

"Bravo!" said Becky. "That was really gracious, Bruce. Like a child taking medicine. Mr. McGee, I am Becky and you are . . ."

"Travis. And Meyer is Meyer."

"And this is David Saunders, who is down here on a grant, grubbing about in the ruins. Bruce, dear, are you going to keep me out here on the street? I'm beginning to feel like Apple Mary."

So we went back in, with Meyer giving me an amused little wink, a little nod of approval. We went out onto the twilight patio, sweet with the evening song of the birds, heavy with the scent of flowers that were just opening for the hours of the night, with fleshy pink petals, and a smell something like jasmine.

Each little group of strangers establishes its own set of balances and unspoken agreements. Tentative relationships are made and broken until the ones are found which are durable enough to last the evening, at least. From long habit, Meyer and I could talk on one level while maintaining an elliptical kind of communication on a level inaccessible to the other three. Bruce and Becky were doing the same thing, wherein innocent expression had subterranean values.

Bruce bustled about, happily hostessing, making drinks, lighting the patio lanterns, summoning a solemn little Mexican woman to present the trays of hors d'oeuvres, with Bruce anxiously awaiting our verdicts on each delicacy.

Becky was all animation, in constant movement, making wry and bawdy judgements, with hoots of harsh laughter. In her evident maturity, she was still totally girl, that special kind of girl who does not have any self-conscious awareness of herself, but can fling herself about,

55

leggy and lithe, laugh with an open throat, comb her casual hair back with splayed fingers, scratch herself, kick off her sandals, stand ugly, lick crumbs from her fingertips. She was teeming and burning with endless and remarkable energies, with taut slender vibrating health. One could not imagine her ever being bored. Her drink was a pale Spanish sherry, in an old-fashioned glass with a single cube of ice, and she seemed able to make one last indefinitely.

David Saunders was a familiar type, muscular, burly yet feline. He moved with languid grace. He sat immobile, thighs bulging the khaki slacks, apparently in total disinterest and indifference to anyone and anything about him. It was that special arrogance which relieves the possessor of any responsibility to communicate with anyone or please anyone. He could have been in a bus station, waiting for an overdue bus. But he did not become inconspicuous or invisible. There was a surly presence, an assurance, that made people try to please him, to bring him into the conversation. His drink, to Bundy's apparent dismay, was bourbon and Coke, and he knocked them back with stolid, metronomic efficiency.

I decided that I could risk, for the sake of possible returns, casting a large doubt on our insurance story, and Bruce's statement of having done stage design in New York and set design in California gave me the opening. So at a handy opening, using that-reminds-me, I brought up a Famous Female Name in the Industry.

"*That* wretched bitch!" Bruce said. "The most self-important little slut in the world, believe me. I did one totally commercial job for her. One of those period piece things, where they wrapped her little ass in crinoline, and had her bang her way through half the Confederate Army. I went a little camp with the decor, not to cut the picture, but to make a little gentle fun that only the cognoscenti would catch. So she raised stinking hell about my color patterns being wrong for her. She wants to act, direct, produce, write the script, and design the sets, and she doesn't know thing one about her own trade. The only acting she does that seems authentic is when they have her horizontal. She is one of the reasons, dears, why I tucked away all their abundant bread into very good little securities, and when I had enough to live nicely on for the rest of my years, I told them all what they could kiss." He paused and looked at me with a suspicious glint. "But don't tell me *she* was buying her insurance in Florida."

"It was something else, Bruce. She partied on a sun deck with a mixed bare-ass group, and somebody with a good telephoto lens tried to get rich quick."

He nodded. "I remember a rumor that she was in that kind of trouble, but nothing happened."

"I got lucky."

"But why would you get involved in something like that, Travis?"

"Because she came around and asked me."

"Why would she come to you?"

"Because I solved another kind of problem for someone she knew."

"Then you aren't really in the insurance business?"

I smiled upon him. "Hell, I don't know. I guess that lady would be willing to say it was a kind of insurance."

"But what are you trying to do here? Who are you . . . trying to insure, Mr. McGee?"

"I think that if I had gone around telling people what I was trying to do for the actress, it wouldn't have worked out as well as it did."

Meyer broke in and said, "We just go around helping people, Bruce. I think it's some kind of guilt syndrome. Trouble with those windmills, you stick a lance into one in a good wind, and it will purely toss the hell out of you."

Bundy, after a few moments of narrow-eyed consideration, dropped it. And soon he began moving in on David Saunders' blind side. But first there was a little exchange between Bruce and Becky that went over David's sullen head.

Bruce said, "Becky, darling, Larry told me last week that you practically *gave* him that marvelous ceremonial mask from Juchatengo."

I saw her eyes go blank and her mouth purse, and though she recovered in a sparkling instant, I felt reasonably convinced that there was no mask, perhaps not even anyone named Larry.

"He seemed to want it."

"It upset him a little. I mean he knew how terribly acquisitive you had felt about it when you first got it, and he didn't want to take advantage of your friendship."

"How silly!" she said. "I was cleaning out my little gallery and I remembered that he seemed to admire it, so I took it over and asked him if he'd like it. My word, had I wanted to keep it, would I have taken it to him?"

"I guess he wanted to be certain it was not just an impulse you'd regret later."

"When you see him, tell him not to worry his little head. Actually, you know, I was very fair with him. I told him when I took it over there that it was really not as first class as I had thought at first. It's very primitive, of course, and quite authentic, but it's just one of those things you tire of seeing every day, I suppose because it hasn't much subtlety."

"It's probably more Larry's sort of thing than yours."

"Very probably. I sensed that, I suppose."

Transfer accomplished, in good faith. And so Bundy engaged Meyer in amateur archeological talk, saying, finally, "I just cannot *imagine* how those priest types could bring the Indian peasants into this terribly inhospitable and certainly waterless countryside and establish a whole culture without losing untold thousands of them."

And that hooked Saunders into his first conversation of the evening. "From what we know now, the system was to send out a large party of specialists, carrying water supplies, just before the rainy season. If they couldn't find reliable wells or springs, they would dig giant cisterns deep in the earth, wide at the bottom and narrow at the top, like gigantic bottles made of stone and waterproofed with clay. Then around the top of the bottle, they'd make a hard surface, round, fifty or sixty feet across, and sloping toward the mouth of the bottle. The rains would fill the bottle and they'd put a big clay stopper in place to prevent evaporation. Next they would bring in the Indian families with grain and fowl and tools and tell them where to build the village and where to plant the grain."

Bruce cried that the information fascinated him. How clever those ancient peoples were! And how clever the ones who were now so carefully reconstructing all that lost marvelous history!

And he kept him going a little while until it was time for dinner. I said we had to leave just to see how much he would protest. And he did, with an earnest vehemence, because it was obvious that if there were just the three of them, he couldn't focus on David.

So we, with show of reluctance, accepted the warm invitation.

FIVE

The food was excellent. Candles flared and flickered in the night breeze. He served a good and heady Greek wine.

A round table. Superb silverware, table linen, glassware, pottery. Muted music from a good tape system somewhere in the house. Bundy had Lady Rebecca at his right, David at his left, with me at Becky's right, and Meyer between me and David.

Rebecca had begun to make an elegant presentation of herself to me, managing in her casual careless way of handling herself, to artfully establish all the sensory awarenesses—of vision, of scent, of apparently inadvertant touch. But more importantly, she knew well that most important ingredient of all charm, all seduction, the art of so listening and responding that she made me feel as if I were the most exciting and rewarding and important man she had met in untold years, that if I had not come along, her life would have continued in its drab and dreary pattern. It requires not only the ability to listen so carefully no word, no nuance, is missed, but also the ability to sense when a contrary opinion will further the growing sense of closeness. I knew what she was doing and knew some of the devices she was using, but that awareness did not prevent my growing feeling that this was, indeed, one hell of a lot of extraordinary woman and nice to be with and worth arranging any further closeness possible.

Bruce Bundy, in another way and on another level, was targeting in on David Saunders. And it was interesting to see how much more masculine Bruce had become, in voice, gesture and opinion. And both Bruce and Becky were using Meyer as that necessary little dilution factor to mask their acquisitive intensity, directing questions and comment to him in much the same way the stage magician makes a great show of letting you look up his sleeves and into his top hat.

Their eyes gleamed in the candlelight, and their faces were smooth and youthful and animated, and their voices were clever, articulate, and amusing. The pretty predators, using their tested skills for the newest stalk.

David Saunders seemed to make, at table, a slightly porcine prey. He would dip his head almost to the plate, shovel in a heaping forkful, chew heavily with rolling bulge of muscle at the jaw corners, and then slosh it down with a gulp of wine, the throat bulging and shifting with the bulky swallow.

So, half in self-defense, half in the interest of moving ahead with the mission, I found a hole in the conversation and ran it off at a new angle. "I'd like to meet and talk to Eva Vitrier. Can you arrange it, Bruce? Becky?"

An instant of wary stillness, such as might happen to the smaller scavengers when they hear the carnivore coming back through the jungle toward the kill.

"Oh, it would have to be Bruce. He seems to get along quite smashingly with the creature. And by the way, dear, her first name rhymes with favor rather than with fever. Shockingly rich, that one. And she doesn't, as we say, mingle."

Bundy said, "I really don't see very much of her. She comes and goes without much warning—I should say with *no* warning. She's not a very social animal. Even were she here, Travis, it would be quite a feat to arrange an introduction. But I understand she left right after identifying that ghastly body. I could hardly blame her for wanting a change of scene."

"Where would she have gone?"

"She's never given me any other address," he said.

"But," said Becky, "it's rumored she has several of her

61

little fortresses scattered about the world. The woman has this secrecy thing. Absolutely barmy."

"But she had those two girls at her place as house guests," I said. "Seems like a sort of friendly sociable act."

"On the same order, one might say," said Becky, "as that touching friendliness and sociability in a dinner invitation from the Borgias."

"Wear the big ring," said Meyer, in nostalgic tribute to Lenny Bruce. It drew blank looks.

I took a sneak shot at Bundy. "Didn't you say you had to protect yourself from something Rocko dreamed up?"

He pressed his gray-brown bangs with the palm of his hand. A ring fashioned of gold mesh gleamed in the candlelight.

"Why do you strain so hard to be clever, McGee?" he asked.

"Answer a question with a question," I said, "and you buy time to sort things out."

"I used the name Rocko in a generic rather than a particular sense. The Rockos of the world are always scheming, aren't they? Just as you were when you first arrived. I merely said that I feel competent to protect myself against the schemes of ... the Rockos and the McGees."

"But you met the girl, didn't you? Bix Bowie?"

"Should I have?"

"Through Rocko or through Eva Vitrier, one or the other. Why not?"

He smiled. "I went through deep analysis *ages* ago, my dear man, with a very fashionable New York shrink. He had this quaint trick of trying to stir up guilt by asking questions in *exactly* that manner. One *does* lie to one's psychiatrist, you know. The truth is so utterly rancid sometimes. One wants to look better. But with all that endless talking, it is terribly difficult to remember what one might have said a dozen afternoons ago. No, I did not meet the lass. Nor do I see any reason why I should be expected to have met her, or have any memory of her if I did. What are you *really* looking for?"

"All the reasons why the girl drove off the mountain in your car, Bruce."

"I shall never never forgive the little bitch. That was a marvelous little car. Very loyal and dependable."

David Saunders yawned, belched, reached for the wine bottle.

"See?" Becky cried. "We're *boring* poor David. A lovely meal, Bruce. Do you have any of that marvelous brandy? The kind I like? I can't remember the name. Good! Just a tiny bit, no more than a tablespoon. And can we leave table? Thank you, darling."

As we got up, Meyer said, "Mr. Bundy, I appreciate your hospitality and your kindness, but I think that I am beginning to feel unwell. The altitude and the wine, I think. The best thing for me would be a walk in the fresh air. I can walk down to the plaza and take a cab back up the hill to the hotel. No, Travis. Don't bother. I'll be fine."

Gracefully and shrewdly done, old friend. After he left the brandy was served, and I noticed that Bruce gave David Saunders the opportunity to pour his own, and a snifter that gave him enough scope to be foolhardy. They went off into the house. Bruce wanted to show David some of the artifacts he had collected.

Becky and I went into a far corner of the patio, sat together on a stone bench near a small, persistent fountain.

"You were very naughty, Travis, really."

"What did I do?"

"Ah! Such innocence. It was a lovely little party and then you made poor Bruce so awfully uncomfortable and nervous. He was terribly upset by that whole Rockland affair. Actually, it's the last thing he wants to have mentioned."

"And you know all about it?"

"He talks over his problems with me. He asks my advice. He's not a bad sort, you know. Sometimes he is quite foolish and impulsive and he encounters . . . problems that are typical of the world he lives in. I think that

63

because I never condemn him, we've been able to become friends."

"Such good friends you brought him a little gift."

"A gift?"

"One husky, sunburned young archeologist."

"Of course, ducks! We are frightfully nasty degenerates who go about handing our discards to our chums. And I imagine that quite puts you off, doesn't it?"

"I don't know enough about it. Or about you."

"Me? I am just a wicked old woman with a ravenous appetite for strong young men. They are generally sweet and touching and grateful. But this chap was ... out of focus somehow. He fancies himself as some sort of overwhelming stud. But he has that talent for little bits of brutality that betrays him for what he really is. I had begun to suspect him, and then he told me a horrid little story about beating up homosexuals and taking their money when he was at school. Such chaps are usually hiding their own tendencies from themselves. I had decided to cut him loose because he is really dull. He has no sense of fun. But I had described him to Bruce, and Bruce said that were I to bring him around, he could quickly tell me if my suspicion was correct. After ten minutes Bruce knew and let me know. So ... it might be rather nice for Bruce after such a fiasco with that Rockland person. Bruce is quite lonely this year. The chap who used to stay with him drowned last year in the surf at Acapulco when they were down visiting friends. It was a terrible shock to Bruce. Do I sound as if I were pleading for forgiveness and understanding? Hardly! After all, I did not exactly bash him upon the head and gift wrap him and put him on the doorstep did I?"

"What did happen with Rockland?"

"My dear, you are very, very nice. But, my word, you are tiresome at times! Here we are, quite alone, both of us with that marvelous knowledge that we would be awfully, awfully good in bed together, and all you seem to want from me is a long tiresome story—far too long to tell here. I *know* you respond to me. We're becoming quite deliciously aware of each other. Shouldn't you be trying to bundle me off into my lonely bed instead of leaving the advances to me? I am quite sick of the young, young men. They are in endless supply, and unlike poor David, they are terrible sweet and earnest and dear. But too sweet. Like endless desserts. They cloy. But one accepts, because the mature ones with any style and presence are usually married. And I have a rule about that. It is too much like theft."

"But what about my wife and five kids?"

"You lie, sir! A woman leaves her mark, her scent, her shape upon what is hers, whether it is her furs, her underthings, or her man. You are not married, and I doubt you ever have been. Though I was once, several centuries ago."

"Here I come again, tiresome as ever. How do I find out about Rockland?"

"Why, I should imagine that you would have to sit down with Bruce and have him tell you, dearie."

"Correction. How do I find out about Rockland from you?"

"Let me see now. You are asking me to betray a confidence. That means that I would have to have some good reason for breaking faith. I should have to know exactly why you wish to know all this, and understand your motives. And, of course, I would have to believe you. That is the tricky part, because you lie so much. And you lie so *well*! No woman ever knows a man, or ever really trusts him until they have made love. Then, of course, she often discovers she has trusted some absolute scoundrel. But then it would be too late, would it not?"

"Let me see. You picked me off the sidewalk in front of this place. You have not had enough booze to cloud the mind of a mouse. You are damned attractive, Becky. And I am sitting here on a fag's patio in lovely Oaxaca letting you put a ring in my nose so you can lead me off to the sack. Such things don't happen."

"Such a horrid, suspicious, nasty little mind. You are a

towering chap, showing signs of rough use, and I find you monstrously attractive. Your pale eyes and your big hands and the way your lips are made and the way your voice sounds, all these things have just made me terribly randy. So I choose not to blush and simper and flirt, because men are horribly anxious to protect their pride and quite often never make the attempt for fear of failure. And life is awfully short, and each day it is shorter by one day. And there is something else about me which I might or might not tell you later. It depends."

"All right. Such things happen."

"But in case you feel overwhelmed or anything, we don't have to make it definite, not at this moment. I can provide a nightcap and we can cast ballots or something. But let's find those two dear boys and say goodnight."

When we were halfway across the patio, David and Bruce appeared in the corridor, walking toward us. Bruce had hold of David's arm. David Saunders was staggering, mumbling, making sweeping gestures, tripping on the irregularities of the tiles.

"Whas'm never'n standa menshunenny."

He peered at us, feet planted wide, and wrenched his arm out of Bruce's grasp. He started to say something incomprehensible and made another big gesture which swung him off balance. He melted down onto the tile and sagged over onto his back and began to snore.

"I think he drank a little too much," Bruce said.

"Would it be too much of an imposition for you to put him up for the night, dear?"

"Gracious, no!"

"Want me to help you with him?" I asked.

"Thanks, I can manage. Becky, the gate is on the latch. When you shut it, give it a try to be sure it's locked, will you?"

"Of course," she said. We thanked him for the dinner. He acknowledged it in absentminded fashion. He sat on his heels, worked one arm under David's shoulders, another under his thighs, poised for a moment, and then came up smartly with the slack meaty burden. The head

66

lolled and an arm swung limply. In sleep the sullenness was gone. David was a large dreaming child. His burned features looked more delicate. Bruce's feat had been impressive and I suspected it had been done for my benefit. He could indeed feel quite able to take care of himself.

We went in her Lotus. She said my rented car would be quite safe where it was parked. She drove through the dark streets alertly and competently, sitting tall, chin up, hands solid on the wheel, through the rush of wind, past dark buildings.

She said her place was in La Colonia. Wider streets. High walls. Gates. She swung in and stopped, the headlights shining on an iron gate. She gave me the keys, indicating the one for the gate. I unlocked it and swung it open. She drove in and waited while I closed and locked the gate. Then along a curving drive paved with white gravel. Night lights on in the house. Left the car in front. Went through large formal rooms and out into a walled area in back. She turned on lights, little spots and floods and the lights below the water level of a large curved pool.

"I know," she said. "It left rather a bad taste. But Brucey will not be sordid about it. He'll undress poor David and tuck him into a big bed and leave him quite alone. In the morning he'll be tearful and terribly upset and accuse poor David of all manner of amorous aggression, and claim he is going to register a bitter complaint with me. Poor David will be beside himself with shock and fright and shame. And sometime tomorrow they will kiss and forgive, and I expect that after the weekend David will be moving in, and in a few months he will have rather a pretty little lisp. He might become a much nicer person, actually. Just stop looking so broody and accusing about it, darling. Open that cupboard door and you'll find ice and all kinds of liquor. Cheer up, dammit!"

So I made my drink. She refused one. She sat beside me for some silent moments, then got up from the chaise and walked to the far end of the pool. Without posing, posturing, or artifice, she kicked her shoes off, pulled the mini-dress off, floated a wisp of brassiere onto the pile, stepped out of sheer pants, hooked her bare toes over the curbing. Her figure was riper than I would have guessed, but solid, smooth and firm as that of a circus girl, tumbler, or ballerina.

"Goes with the nightcap or not," she called to me. "Whatever you choose, my good man."

And in she went, in a flat sleek slapping racing dive.

Well, you came down here, fella, to find out about Bix Bowie. And, by God, no sacrifice is too great once a fella gives his solemn word, right? And the way you get to know a country is by getting to know the people, right? And even though there's a pretty good size to that pool, what with the pool lights and all, you ought to be able to catch her sooner or later. So I think the answer ought to be that if it really goes with the nightcap, then . . .

But I discovered I was already trying to pull the trousers off with the shoes still on, so I sat down again and untied the shoes, thus solving that problem with hardly any trouble at all.

She clung, sweat-misted, still breathing deeply, and ground the scratchy ruff of her tawn-crisp hair into the side of my laboring throat; she gave her small crow-caw of delighted laughter.

"You *do* have to say something, you know," said Lady Becky. "Some observation. Some passing comment. I rather like to remember the better ones."

"Okay. Passing comment: Quote. Holy Mackerel. Close quote."

She rolled up onto an elbow. "I think you are very nice, McGee. I think I will tell you what you just enjoyed."

"I wouldn't want to try to describe it myself."

"I have to confess how ancient I am, darling. I am terribly old. I was married before the Battle of Britain. I was in London for the whole bit. Dreadfully earnest and devoted and valiant. Family tradition. All heroes. Volunteer nursing service. Stiff uppper lip. So my beloved husband was in Spits, and they pranged him early on. And the others went, bit by bit. The chums and brothers, the family and the sister. Stiff upper lip, lass. Strive on. So it ended, you know. And peace came, and two days later some damned delayed action thing went off, and it was my last duty call. Collapsed a row of flats and they burned. And I held two screaming tots, one after the other, on my lap, charred little things, trying to pop morphine into them before they died. Managed with one and didn't with the other. Dreadful stench. Total pointlessness. Walked all night, said odd things. They put me off to rest. I was expected to pick up the loose ends of my life and start over, somehow. Do good works. But there were no loose ends, lamb. And I had a bellyful of good works.

"So one makes an accounting of sorts. I had, God knows, money enough, and time, and a strong body. And I was in a world that charred tots, and I wanted no more of it. What I had most adored with Robin was all the lovely free marital fornication. Never could get enough. He used to say I had great natural talent. So I vowed solemnly, ducks, to become the jolly best piece of Anglo-Saxon ass in all Christendom. It is sad and remarkable that people really know so little about it. They sort of fumble about and trust to luck. I knew that all I had to work with was my body. I had to keep it as enticing as possible, because one must arouse intense desire, or the game is lost before it is begun, what? I haven't changed an inch or a pound in twenty years, my dear. I stay on the most strict routine of diet and exercise. And I go twice a year to a Swiss clinic for hormone balance, and there is a clever little Japanese doctor in your California who does clever little operations when they're needed. To know how to use the body, one must go to Yoga. God, how I labored, and then suddenly it fell into place. I have absolute and independent control now of every muscle in my body, even all those reactions that are supposed to be involuntary responses to erotic stimulus. And all this time, my dear, I was studying all the books on the arts of love that I could find. Hindu, Arabic, Ancient Egyptian. I am now a repository of all that learning and skill. And I know some astonishing things, luv. It is a responsibility, actually. I had to learn a great deal about anatomy, neurology, glandular functions, all that. So you see what's in store, my good man? You've had a taste. And now I shall destroy you, bit by delicious bit. Because you shall respond again and again after you are quite certain you are finished. I need merely do some odd thing like . . . this?"

And as I was tumbled back into my role of awed participant in the second strenuous, virtuoso performance, I realized I had come upon a prime example of that uniquely English phenomenon, the true eccentric. Some of them build cathedrals out of bits of matchstick. Some of them count the number of stalks of hay in the average haystack. Some write a hundred letters a week to the London *Times*. Some catalogue all the birds in fifty meadows. They are all quite mad, but do not know that they are mad, since they find a socially acceptable outlet for their monomania. This woman had been driven mad in a mad war, and had retained one little ledge of sanity and built the rest of the structure of her life upon it. But I could not carry my realizations any further, because something hitherto unknown had begun to happen, and it felt as if my head were starting to fry at the hair roots. I thought I heard her laughing, but then all I could hear in some far corner of the most primitive part of my mind, was myself roaring, atavistic and lonely.

There was another time of respite when, halfheartedly, I asked about Bruce Bundy and Rockland. She told me that they had met on the veranda of the Marqués del Valle many weeks ago, and that Bruce knew Rockland had let himself be picked up. Bruce had told her that Rockland was not exactly inexperienced. He had then begun to ask Bruce to lend him money. Some large amount. Ten or fifteen thousand. It was to be some sort of investment scheme. Rockland had hinted that it was illegal but quite safe. He would double Bruce's money. He then got very surly when Bruce said he would not cash in perfectly good securities in order to lend money to an animal off the streets. Then apparently Rocko had to leave the trailer park. Bruce let him bring the truck and camper and put it in the shed beyond his wall where Bruce garaged his little English Ford. There was room for both. He had moved into Bruce's house on an apparently permanent basis. But he had spent Thursday, the last day of July, away from the house all day and a good part of the evening. When he came back he had asked Bruce to lend him a smaller amount. Three thousand or even two. When Bruce refused, Rockland had accepted it too calmly. In the small hours of Friday morning, Bruce had heard the distant sound of Rocko trying to start his truck. Bruce put his robe on and hurried out. She said Bruce had taken something out of the motor and hidden it. Rocko got out of the truck and tried to hit Bruce. But Bruce had won some sort of belt for some sort of way of fighting, and he kept in splendid shape, and so he had hit Rocko and knocked him unconscious, but when he fell he had hit his nose on the stone floor and bled, and it had made Bruce ill. When Rocko could walk, feeling very weak and shaky, Bruce had helped him into the house and into bed, and then he had gone back and searched the truck and found his little Picasso bronzes, and the solid gold amulets from Yucatan, and the prints and drawings by famous Mexican artists, and some of his better silverware.

Out of an increasingly hazy state, I interrupted her at this point in her narrative to ask her what she was doing.

"Dearest, don't tighten up like that. Trust your Becky. There. Turn just a little bit more this way. That's a dear. This will rest and relax you. It's something Japanese women used to know, thousands of years ago. Just don't think about me. Don't think about anything. Just let your mind drift."

So, though curious, it was restful, relaxing, soothing. It was indeed. For quite a while. And then it began to have quite another effect. And when that effect was sufficiently and unmistakably evident, Lady Rebecca Divin-Harrison swung triumphantly and exuberantly aboard, with spurs, whip, checkrein, and posted tirelessly and happily across the endless moors.

I lay dead, yet managed to say, "Then what happened?"

"Weren't you paying attention?"

"I mean to Bruce and Rockland."

"No, dear, I've told you much too much. No more for now. I shouldn't have told you a bloody thing, you know."

"Then I think I am going to sleep."

"Really? Really? . . . Really?"

"Cut it out, Becky. Whatever ancient rite that happens to be, cut it out. Because it is not going to do any good. Look. I am not ashamed to admit I'm finished. All done. I haven't got any desire at all to set any records. And I don't feel any childish urge to prove anything to anybody. Okay? I *have* to go to sleep, Becky."

"Yes, darling. I agree. Utterly. I've quite finished you off, poor darling."

"Then stop."

"Don't writhe away from me like that. It is awfully impolite. Travis, darling, let me just prove to both of us that we are both absolutely correct, that there is nothing more you can possibly contribute to the evening."

"It's been proven."

So she hummed to herself. She kept busy. Adjust spark and coil. Hop out and run around to the radiator and try the hand crank. Thumb out of the way in case of backfire. Back to spark, coil, mixture. Prime carburetor. Crank again. What the hell is she humming? For God's sake, *Roll Out the Barrel*. Should be humming *Bless 'em All*. Ancient engine catches, sputters, stops, catches again. And then, by God, settles into a deep-gutted roar. Hop behind the wheel, kick it into gear. And I once again enwrapped all that hot limber skill, endured her delighted chuckling, romped her onto her spring-steel spine, and tried in my endless, mindless, idiot frenzy to hammer her down through the damn silk sheets, down through the

72

foam and springs, down through the carpeting and the tile and the beams and down into the deep black Mexican soil under the lovely and formal old house, where I could be buried without fanfare and sleep forever and ever and ever.

SIX

Meyer was gone when I woke up at ten o'clock Saturday morning. When I came out of the shower he was sitting on his bed with a bright red flower tucked behind his ear, beaming at me.

"I heard you come in," he said. "Just after daylight. I think I should say I heard you come *tottering* in. I never heard so much heavy sighing. You sounded like a leaky truck tire."

I pulled my shorts up and turned and said, "I never noticed what really nasty little blue eyes you have, pal."

"What happened after I left?"

"Poor David passed out and was promoted to the status of houseguest."

"Make a note that I am not astonished."

"And I went to Lady Rebecca's house with her for a nightcap."

"Again, no surprise. And then?"

I sat on my bed to rest up a little. "I gathered a few bits of information about Rockland which I shall shortly impart to you, Meyer. I do not make a practice of discussing a lady. I just wish to tell you that the few bits of information were *earned*."

Bland astonishment. "Really, old chap? Why, to look at the lydy, I should have thought her a jolly amusing romp, what? All slap and tickle. Good earthy sport, what?"

"If I had the strength, I swear, I would reach over and hit you right in the mouth, dear friend."

He faked sudden comprehension. "Aha! Oh! Like that, eh? It wasn't because it was distasteful, eh? You mean that she was tasteful and somewhat on the demanding side, old man?"

"Meyer, believe me, I will never try to explain it to you or describe it to you. I do not want to think about it. Here is what you do for me. Some day, two or three years from now, hire the most luscious, unprincipled, hot-blooded wench you can find. Have her strip down and sneak aboard the *Flush* and climb into the master's bunk with the sleeping master. Then you wait outside. If you hear an ungodly thump, it will be her girlish rump bouncing off the deck after I kick her out of bed. When you hear that thump, take the girl away, wait a year, and try again."

"Is this the McGee talking?"

"McGee, the misogynist. From now on, buddy, every broad in the world is going to look as enticing as a rubber duck. I would rather have one handful of cold mashed potato than two handsful of warm young mammalian overdevelopment."

"Did you get too much sun yesterday?"

"Just help me through the day, Meyer. Help me and shut up. Catch me when I start to wobble. Keep me out of drafts. Order me good nourishing food and get me to bed early. Now get me up that hill to the dining room."

At breakfast I told him about the Rocko-Brucey affair, as much as I knew of it. We agreed it fit with Bruce Bundy's asking us in when I used Rockland's name on him. He had to know if Rockland had devised some way to make him unhappy and had sent us around to set him up.

Meyer worried at it, hairy dog with an old meatless bone. "Then we go another step. Bundy had to believe Rocko *could* make trouble."

"It begins to look," I said, "as if Rockland knew just how to make trouble for people. I think the hotel covered up the ugly truth with those hints about theft. I think he was scavenging the older lonely ones. Hustling them. Set-

75

ting them up with pot, hustling them with sex, male and female, and then putting the squeeze on."

"So a type like that comes to Mexico in a truck and camper? Roughing it?"

"Bix drew out part of the money before they left. She drew out the balance from Mexico. Twenty isn't a bad score."

"If he knew she had it," Meyer said.

"And he could lever it out of her easier out of the country. But we have to find one of the others to find out what went on, dammit. Either Rockland himself or the musician or the sculptor or the other girl."

At this stage of the game it seemed to be a good idea to split up. Meyer acquires people as easily as a hairy dog picks up burrs. He smiles and listens carefully, and the little blue eyes gleam with good humor and personal interest. He says the right things at the right time, and surprisingly often the random stranger tells him things he wouldn't tell a blood relative or a psychiatrist. No bore, no matter how classic, ever manages to bore Meyer. It is a great talent, to be forever interested in everyone.

We agreed that the best thing to do would be for me to drop Meyer downtown and then go off and see what I could learn at Eva Vitrier's place. I got lost twice in the Colonia district before I located Avenida de las Mariposas. A man driving a delivery truck helped me locate the home of Eva Vitrier.

It was an estate, enclosed by a high stone wall. The morning sun shone through the shards of glass of the ten thousand broken bottles cemented into the top of the wall. I found a vehicle gate, double-chained and locked. I rattled the gate and hollered, to no effect. I could look through the bars at a curve of driveway paved with brick, disappearing into the trees and plantings, but I could see no part of any building inside the compound. I located the main pedestrian entrance, a solid and massive door of ancient wood, iron-studded. There was a bell button set into the recessed stone beside the door. No one answered.

Around the corner, on a narrower street, I found a

smaller wooden door and, beyond it, a double door which could open wide enough for a good-sized truck. I pushed another bell button by the smaller door and heard a distant ringing. As I was trying it for the third and last time, a hinged square set into the door swung open and a broad, bronze, impassive Indio face looked out at me.

I asked for the señora. He said she was not there. I asked when she would be back. He said he could not know. Tomorrow? Oh, no. Maybe many weeks, many months, maybe a year. Where is she, then? One does not know. Who *does* know? One must ask el Señor Gaona. Who is he? He is the lawyer of the señora. Where is he? In his office, doubtless. Where is his office. It is in the city. In this city? Where else? On what street is his office? It is on Avenida Independencia. What number? One cannot say. It is near the corner of Avenida Cinco de Mayo.

As I started to thank him, he slammed the little opening. It startled me. A rude Mexican is a great rarity.

I had to wait fifteen minutes before Señor Alfredo Gaona y Navares could see me. I waited on a rump-polished wooden bench in a musty ten-by-ten office dominated by a large old lady at a large old typing desk, operating a machine that looked as if Mark Twain had invented it. At last two women in black came out of the inner office, arms around each other, sobbing softly. I was directed to go in.

Señor Gaona was elderly. He had a small pale face and an expression of weary distaste. He did not get up or extend a hand. Complex aluminum crutches leaned against the wall behind him.

"What is your reason for wishing to see Señora Vitrier?" The English was precise, unaccented, with a delivery that sounded like a programmed computer.

"I wanted to talk to her about the two American girls who were staying with her as her guests."

"With what purpose?"

"Señor Gaona, I am doing a personal favor for the Bowie girl's father. He was injured in an automobile

77

accident, or he would be here himself. He was out of touch with his daughter for seven months. He is curious about how she lived here, where she lived, what kind of life it was for her."

"Señora Vitrier would not care to discuss it."

"What makes you so sure?"

He hesitated. "I do not have to explain, but I will. Out of her generous heart she offered the two young women lodging when they had no place they could go. This was not a wise thing to do. One cannot judge by appearances. The young women might have been of a kind one does not want in the home. After they quarreled and one departed, the other one was killed, as you must know, in an accident in the mountains. Señora Vitrier appeared and performed the duty of identifying the dead young woman, and turned over her possessions to the police. It was a very ugly experience for her. I am quite certain she would not care to be reminded of it, or to discuss it."

"Couldn't you let her decide that? Where can I get in touch with her?"

"She is a very, very wealthy woman. The house she maintains here is one of several in various parts of the world. I am retained by her to keep her from being approached by strangers, and also to keep her house here in good order so that she can return, unannounced, and begin living here at any time."

"What would happen if I were to write her a letter?"

"It would come here to this office and I would open it and read it and decide if it is a matter which she would wish to know about. If I so decided, I would mail it to her bank in Zurich and they would forward it to whatever address she is using at the time."

"What would you do if her house here burned down?"

"So advise Zurich."

"And my letter would not get past you?"

"Assuredly not, sir. She gave explicit instructions to me that she did not want to hear any more of this affair, not even if the surviving young lady attempted to reach her by letter."

"And has she tried?"

"No."

"Has anyone else tried, I mean in relation to the death of the girl?"

"I have explained the situation to you, sir, in more detail than is my habit. There is no way you can approach Señora Vitrier, no way whatsoever. So we must consider the matter closed. Good day."

And indeed it was good day. The old lady had entered behind me, unheard, and she startled me when she said, "Theees way ow." I was on the sidewalk nine seconds later. And ten minutes after that I was in a briskly modern office where mini-skirted darlings came beaming in and out, emptying the "out" baskets and putting documents in the "in" baskets, and I was shaking hands with Ron Townsend's friend in the local power structure, Enelio Fuentes. A glass panel in a wall overlooked, from about a thirty-foot height, about two acres of concrete shop space where bug-swarms of Volkswagens were being tuned, inspected, and repaired.

Enelio was thirty, or a little over, ruggedly handsome, with a yard of shoulders, a contrived casual lock of black hair across the forehead, a narrow waist, a big friendly grin, a massive and powerful handshake.

"Ol' Ron phoned me about you. Hey, sit down. How you like our town? How about that bird Ron has got himself? You meet her? That big Miranda. Fonny goddam thing. Ron spend half his life running like hell every time any bird looks at him with that marriage look. This big Miranda, she doesn't want not any part of it, and he wants it so bad he can't breathe deep. That one is some batch of girl, I tell you. Hey, you want a bloody mary? Good. Hey you, Esperanza, go make bloody marys for Mister Travis McGee, here, and me, and stop making the hot eye at him and waving that little butt around. Mr. McGee isn't interested in short, ugly little girls." She was a lovely little thing, and she went running out, giggling. "Soch a one that is," he said fondly. "Can't type, can't file, can't run the switchboard. But she can make any

79

drink you ever heard of, man. My old man says, 'Nelio, why the hell did I waste my money sending you to the Graduate School of Business at Stanford University, all you do is hire pretty girls all the hell over the place?' Me, I don't say a word, just give him the quarterly breakdown, show the profit we're turning, ask him if he'd rather give it back to his brother, my oncle, hired women looked like dogmeat, worked their ass off on overtime, and sometimes didn't even break even. Now my oncle is crapping around with the little feeder airline we bought las' year, Aeronaves Fuentes, and from the way the books look, I got to pretty soon go shake things up over there. Hey, here she is. Try that, Travis McGee. Delicious? Don' stand around bugging the boss fellas, girl. Go file something in the wrong place so nobody ever finds it again." He looked out through the glass wall and suddenly stiffened, the smile gone. He pressed the bar on a call box and bent toward it, and the Spanish was much too fast for me to follow. I looked out at the shop area and suddenly saw a man in a white jacket heading at a half run toward a couple standing helplessly beside an old black Volkswagen.

Enelio grinned and stretched. "Chrissake, tell them five million times anybody comes in, you find out what the hell they want right away. Quick. Then you tell them how long it takes and how much it costs. And you do it in the time you say, and you charge what you say, and get them out on the street fast." I saw something I had overlooked. The big grin did not change the eyes. They remained cool and shrewd and appraising.

A tall solemn girl came in with letters for signature. He nodded and motioned her closer. He read the letters swiftly, scrawled his big signature on each and handed them to the girl, then slapped her smartly across the seat of her skirt as she turned. She yelped and jumped, and he said something in swift, slurred Spanish. She spoke in tones of protest. He spoke again. She smiled and flushed and walked swiftly out.

"That one," he explained, "that Rosita, she had the

unhoppy love affair and now she has the long face. I told her I wanted to see if there was any feeling left in the back side. She told me I should have more respect. Then I said something, it doesn't translate. But it made her face hot and it made the smile, no? Hey, anything you want, just say what it is. Okay?"

I briefed him on the situation, and on what we were trying to do, and showed him Bix's photo. He caught on quickly. He understood the father's need to have all the blanks filled in.

He looked in the phone book and gave his switchboard a number to call. In a few moments his desk phone rang. He picked it up and, after a few minutes wait, got through to somebody he called Roberto. I could make out a word here, a phrase there. He asked some questions and then thanked the man and hung up.

"The sergeant who did the investigation has no English at all. *Nada.* Here is how it will go. At two o'clock today he will come over to the Marqués del Valle. We close this place at noon today. I will come over in my car. You and your friend and the sergeant, we will go up into the mountains and he will show us the place and I will tell you what he says."

"I don't want to put you to—"

"Silencio, gringo! How do you know it doesn't give me the chance to get out of something I didn't want to do, eh?"

"Okay. Next problem. How do I get to talk to Mrs. Eva Vitrier?"

"That one is one rich lady. I remember it was maybe eight, nine years ago, that place was sold. Nearly two million pesos. And then a lot more to fix it up. All the other ricos out in the Colonia, they can't wait to find out who the owner is. They think there will be entertaining. They want to see how the house has been fixed. All of a sudden they find out the owner is there, this Frenchwoman. They go calling. She will not see them. They leave cards. Nothing. Oh, she has guests come in sometimes, very few, from far away. Sometimes she is seen in the

81

city. She shops, and has servants with her to carry packages to the car, and a man to drive the car. People say crazy things. Maybe she is the mistress of a king. Maybe she is a political refugee. Maybe it is stolen money. I think it is easy, man. I think the lady wants to be left the hell alone."

"What does she look like? Have you seen her?"

He leaned back, eyes half closed, a gentle smile on his lips. "She has no age. She could be thirty. She could be fifty. No difference. She looks like that queen of Egypt, you know. The one with the nose."

"Nefertiti?"

"That one. Very proud. Head high. Very hot eye. One day, three or four years past, I walked behind her from one jewelry store to her car. Black hair. Cool day. Had on a dark red wool dress. She walked slow, like music, man Long narrow back, narrow little shoulders. Not much in front, but one truly fantastic ass. Firm, round, heavy but not too heavy. Wide but not too wide. It moved just right when she walked. Nothing under that dress, man. She had some great kind of perfume. It came floating back. You know, she got in that car and it drove away, and what I wanted to do, I wanted to lean against a building and pant like a dog. Hell, I tried to meet her. She was worth a good try. Twenty good tries. I never got to first base. First base! I never found the road to the ball park. I tell you, one long look at her, and that Miranda bird of Ron's looks like somebody's brother."

"So there's no friend of hers here who could put me in direct touch?"

"She has some friends, I think. I don't know exactly. Those friends would not be my friends. People I think who tuck their lives behind walls here, like she does. Because here they are left alone, and it is a freedom for them. I know that Gaona won't help you. That is one tough old man. Long ago there was an election when there were strong feelings. He wanted to be a politico. Somebody shot him in the spine. He dragged himself home in the night. Four miles. Took him all night. Wore his hands to ribbons. Would not say who shot him. If I had to trust a secret to any lawyer in the world, it would be Alfredo Gaona."

"About Mrs. Vitrier's friends. One of them would be Bruce Bundy?"

He looked startled, then impressed. "Yes, it was his car. He loaned it to someone who loaned it to the Bowie girl. I know Bundy by sight. Three or four years he's been here. There's a little group of them here. Nobody pays much attention, if they stay out of trouble. But if one of them starts taking little boys from the public market home, then the police will make their life very ogly. To find out so soon that Bundy and the French lady are friends, something I did not know, means you are very quick with these things, eh?"

"I tend to go in like a bull, Enelio. Or like a kid busting into a room full of slot machines. I pull levers and kick things and usually end up with pure lemons. So I found that Bundy is a friend of Eva Vitrier, and Bundy is a friend of Lady Rebecca Divin-Harrison, and Lady Becky doesn't like Eva worth a damn."

He looked at me with a speculative appraisal, head cocked slightly, and then a slow grin came and widened and then he threw his head back and laughed and slammed the desk top with a big hand.

When he caught his breath, he said, "So! You do not always have those black circles under the eyes, amigo! And that mark on your neck is not a strawberry birthmark. And maybe your hands do not always tremble a little, eh? My God, you are a rare one, McGee! You and me, we are members of one club now. Goddam, there are plenty members, and I joined—let me see—fifteen years ago, and she looked exactly, I swear, the way she looks today. She had a beautiful car and she asked me if I would like to drive it. I was young. I could conquer anything. Car or woman. Perhaps it is good to learn humility when young. Four days I was not a part of the world. Four days and nights, and then ejected, blinking, weak as a new kitten, dazed, damn near destroyed. Ah,

83

that one is legend, my friend. *Muy guapa.* As much woman as there can be. Too much woman. The club is big, but she selects with great care, believe me. One cannot ask to be a member. One must be invited. Some day, McGee, we will be wheeled into the sunshine with the blanket over our knees, and we will have that memory, and we will smile a nice and dirty-old-man smile. There is an old saying among the Oaxacaños: The most bitter remorse is for the sins one did not commit. She is quite mad, of course. But it is an agreeable madness, no?"

"If I recover, I'll let you know."

"One always recovers. I even wished to see if it had all happened as I remembered, or if I had dreamed portion: of it. But she patted my face and she said, 'Nelio, you are a dear boy and I am very fond of you, but I have turned the page you were written on. It is a very long book, and I do not have time in my life to reread any part of it if I am to finish it.' For a time I was hurt and angry. Then later I understood. She was written in my book too, and by then I was writing a new chapter.

"About Bundy being friends with such total female creatures as Becky and Madame Vitrier, I think it is a common thing among women who do not have tea-party friendships with other women, to have a Bruce Bundy to make girl talk with. And I think he helps them with decorating things in their homes. Look, maybe it is like this. Can Becky have a close friend who is a normal man or normal woman? Bundy is, for her, neutral ground. A relaxment? Bad English. A ... relaxation. I do not pry. How is it now with Becky? Not ended, I would think."

"*She* thinks it isn't. She thinks she told me just enough to keep me on the hook." I told him about Walter Rockland moving in with Bundy, trying to hit him up for a large loan, and then trying to clean out Bundy's little store of art treasures and getting a quick education in karate.

I said, "She told me I'd made Brucey very nervous, but there isn't enough there, in her story, to make him nervous, so the best part is yet to come. So I am supposed to drop in, alone, for drinks and dinner tonight. And be spoon-fed another little fragment. By the time I know it all, she'll be able to bury me at the foot of her garden, so it will be less wearing to find out what color belt Brucey earned from Brucey himself. Anyway, I'm imposing. I'm taking up too much of your time."

"No. There are some small things I must do here, then it is enough for this day. Let me say one thing. In the picture you showed me, that is one lovely little chicken. I have respect for what you do, Travis. A father should know more of how such a one came to die. He will never understand why. But to know a little—not too much—will help."

SEVEN

Most of the tables on the hotel porch were full when I got there. I spotted Meyer at the far end, sitting at a table with a portly man wearing a pale tan suit and a yellow sports shirt.

While the waiter was hustling me a chair, Meyer introduced him as Wally McLeen from Youngstown, Ohio. Mr. McLeen's handshake was moist and unemphatic. His hazel eyes were magnified by the thick lenses of glasses with thick black frames. There were steel-wool tufts of hair on his sunburned skull.

Meyer said that Wally had sold out his business and had been in Oaxaca since August first, looking for his daughter, Minda.

"It's more than just looking for her, Mr. McGee. It's trying to understand more about what the young people are looking for. Way back in January she wrote me that she was going to go to Mexico with some friends. Just like that. Well, I wrote airmail special to the University of Miami asking them if she left any forwarding address or anything like that, and they wrote back that she'd stopped going to classes way back last year, before summer started. She came on home last summer for about ten days and then went back. She told me she was doing extra work over the summer. I sent my little girl money every month. Then I just didn't know where to send it, or where she was or anything.

"You know, I got to thinking, Mr. McGee. I had four

establishments, located real good in nice shopping centers, turning a nice profit. I worked hard all my life. Connie died three years ago. We had one other daughter, older than Minda, but she died in infancy. I got to wondering just what the hell I was working for. My little girl came home and didn't have much to say. She acted sour, sort of. It was like lying to me, her not telling me she'd already dropped out of college. Once I decided, it took me a long time to make the right deal on the stores. I figured this way. The only thing I've got in this world is my daughter, Minda. And if I can't communicate with her, then there's no point in anything. If I kept working we'd be in two different worlds. She couldn't or wouldn't move into mine, so what I have to do is move into hers. It's the only way I'll be able to talk to her when I find her."

"You expect to find her soon, Mr. McLeen?"

"Wally, please. Yes, I've got it pretty well pinned down that sooner or later she's coming back down here. I'm right in this hotel, right in the center of things. Room number twelve, on the second floor, looking out over the zocalo. When she gets back, I'll be here."

"Where is she?"

"Someplace in Mexico City, but there's six million people in that city. . . . What do people call you?"

"Travis. Trav."

"Trav, you're one hell of a lot younger than I am, but you're older than these kids. I don't know what you think about them. But I've been talking to them now for a long time, and I've changed a lot of my ideas, like I was telling Meyer. It used to make me so damn irritated just to look at those young boys with all the long hair and beards and beads. I figured them for fanatics and dope addicts and degenerates. I can't stand that rock music and those songs about freedom. All right. Some of them are nuts, so far gone on pills and drugs, they're dirty, dumb, sick, and dangerous as wild animals. But most of them are damned good kids. They care about things. They've taken a good long look at our world and they don't like it. They don't like the corruption, and the way the power structure takes care of its own, and the way we're all being hammered down into being a bunch of numbers in a whole country full of computers. They believe that each individual person is getting so insignificant you can't really change anything by voting for a change. You get the same old crap. So what they want to do is get away from all the machinery that makes Vietnams and makes slums and discrimination and legalized theft and murder. How do you get away? Well, you have to go against the establishment in visible ways, so nobody will have any chance of ever thinking you are a part of it. And so you can identify the other people who don't want any part of it either. You pick ways to dress and act and look that turn the establishment people off. You're against the idea of accumulating money and things, so you cut life down to the simplest kind of food and shelter you can scrounge. Because establishment morality is a lot of hypocrisy, like Lenny Bruce pointed out, you say and you write the words that shock the establishment, and you turn sex into something simple and natural and easy. The art and the music—everything has to be something the establishment can't stand. Because, little by little, or maybe in one big fire, you're going to tear all the false fronts down and start everything over again, in a lot simpler and more decent way, without a lot of hangups about money and race and sex and war. I didn't see where pot and pills and LSD fitted in for a while, but I think I do now. They want to turn on because they believe every person has the right to do anything to himself that doesn't harm others. Society makes laws about that because society doesn't want people to make themselves unuseable to the power structure. If everybody turned on every day, what would happen to industry? They're saying this, Trav. They're saying, 'I don't want any part of things the way they are, man. So don't tell me I'm ruining my life because I'm ruining just that part of me that you'd want to use up if you had a chance. The rest of me belongs to me to do what I want with. And what I want is everything you despise. So don't make a lot of value judgements about a scene you can't dig. You are all caught in the machinery, and you want everybody else to get caught in it, too. I make you uncomfortable, old man, because I get more out of every week of my life than you ever got out of a whole year of yours.'

"You know, they *will* talk to me about these things once they find out I'm not just trying to tell them the same old crap they've always heard. When they find out I want to *learn* what this is all about, then they'll talk about it. And I'll tell them how I feel about my life. What was so great about my life up till now? Mortgage payments, inventories, worries, sickness . . . and so damned many *things*! Color television and the new car every two years, and a lawn mower to ride on. Your friends die and you die, and what's the point of any of it? Who ever misses you? Yes sir, like I've been telling Meyer, when I see my Minda again, I'll be able to talk to her like I never could before. I talk too much about all this, and I guess I bore people, but I have the idea I want to spread the word about these kids. I want to be a sort of . . . a messenger." He looked at me with a goggle-eyed earnestness. "Do you understand what I'm saying?"

"Sure, Wally," I said, comfortingly. "We dig you."

He smiled. "Jesus! When I think of how the guys back in Youngstown would take it, I get the idea nobody over twenty-five can understand what I'm trying to say."

"Wally, I understand you've been trying to locate Walter Rockland too."

"To see if he knew anything about Minda. She was with that group for a while. The groups that travel together keep changing. People split and new ones join. I told Meyer that my Minda and the girl that was killed, Bix something, they left at the same time and took a cheap room at the Hotel Ruiz. That's over there, diagonally across the zocalo on Guerrero. They moved in sometime late in May. I saw the room. It's on the second floor in the back. There's a bath down the hall. There's four kids living in that room right now. But only one was there when Minda and Bix moved in. One from the present group, I mean. He thinks there were six or seven kids there in the room while Minda and Bix were there, and as he remembers it, they left at the end of June or early July when Mrs. Vitrier invited them to stay in her guest house. Such a small room, and pretty beat up. You try to give your girl the best of everything. It hurts to think of her living like that. But what can you do? They just don't want the things you can give them. Not this new bunch of kids. They've turned their backs on the whole thing." He shook his head slowly. "Maybe it wouldn't be nice for you men to go back and tell Bix's father about things like that little room in the Hotel Ruiz. It could give him the same feeling I had, thinking of my daughter there at night, in some dirty sleeping bag in a dark corner, and some boy with a dirty beard laying her, and the others sleeping so close, or hearing it happening. Maybe he should think it is all like the posters and the travel ads. . . . A daughter is not like a son."

Meyer tried him on the other names. Carl Sessions, musician. Jerry Nesta, sculptor.

Wally McLeen said he might have met them and talked to them, but he didn't remember those names. He had asked everyone about Minda. He had shown them her picture. And he had added up the little crumbs of information. She had gone alone to Mexico City. She would be back one day. He would wait. If, instead, she showed up in Youngstown, a friend would cable him. He looked at his watch. Some of his new young friends were expecting him. He said he would look us up and let us know if he learned anything interesting, anything that might make that poor girl's father feel better.

Enelio Fuentes appeared promptly at two, and he had Sergeant Carlos Martinez with him. Martinez, a squat, broad man with very dark skin and several gold teeth, was in civilian uniform. We all got into Enelio's car, a new Volkswagen squareback sedan, custom-painted a strange metallic purple. Enelio took the wheel. Meyer and the sergeant sat in the back. Siesta traffic was light, and Enelio wasted no time scooting north to Route 190, the Pan

American Highway, where he turned right on the road toward Mitla. About a mile beyond the city limits he turned left on State of Oaxaca Route 175, and began streaking across the flats at astonishing speed toward the lift of the high brown mountains.

"I didn't know these things had so much snap," I said, speaking loudly over the sound of wind and engine.

"They don't. We put a Porsche engine in this one, race tuned, man. Heavy duty springs and shocks. Disc brakes. I can make Mexico City from Oaxaca in five and a half hours. Hey, how do you like it? See? One eighty kilometros which is . . . a hundred and ten."

When we hit the first curves and began climbing, I was able to relax. Roaring along the straights proves nothing. On the curves he proved the nice mating of man and machine. He found the right track around every curve. He was showing off and enjoying himself, and it was a pleasure to watch. But it certainly was one hell of a road. It was very narrow asphalt and the climb grew steeper and steeper, with switchbacks, cuts, and no banking on the turns, and not a sign of a guardpost. Ahead I would get glimpses of our road halfway up the next mountain, a little man-made ledge with a rock wall on one side and mountain air on the other. Sometimes I could see where we had been, and it was like an aerial view of a road.

We met two buses hurtling down the mountains, and passed one old truck grinding its way up in low-low-low, radiator steaming. The sergeant told Enelio we were getting very near the place. Enelio slowed down and soon found a place to pull off the road, on the outside of a curve where the car was visible from both directions. We got out and chunked the doors shut. The silence was enormous, the air thin, chilly and very pure.

We followed the sergeant about a hundred and fifty yards further up the road to the next curve. He sat on his heels and pointed at a black rubber skidmark on the asphalt. The mark ran off the asphalt and he pointed to some small bushes with broken branches. The branches dangled and the leaves had turned brown. It was easy to

91

see where the car had come back onto the asphalt. We walked back down the slope and saw where she had gone across into the wrong lane and off the road. He pointed to the yellow paint marks on the rock wall and, a hundred feet further, to some oddly shaped skid marks on the road, like gigantic commas. He made a fast circular gesture with his hand, fingers down, like somebody stirring something in a bowl. Then he made a thrusting gesture with his hand toward the precipice indicating how it had shot out over the edge. Giving me a broad golden grin, he said, "Too fassss!"

Yes indeed. It was vivid. She lost it on a downhill curve to the left, maybe because the curve was sharper than she had anticipated. She fought for control but went across at a long angle and hit the stone cliff, bounced off it into a spin, and shot backwards or forwards—it didn't matter which—over the edge at maybe a forty-five degree angle, and maybe a hundred feet short of the next curve, also left-hand, where the purple tiger was parked.

The sergeant led me to the brink and pointed down. I could not see what he was pointing at. He spoke to Enelio. Enelio shaded his eyes and looked. "Hey, I see it. Travis, you see those three little bushes that grow out of the edge of shale down there, near that round rock? Okay, now about ten feet to the right of the three bushes, and a little way back up the slope . . ."

I saw it. A few smears of yellow paint on sharp edges of rock, and a twinkling of broken glass among the rocks, and a gleaming piece of twisted chrome trim. So that's where it hit first, but the next bounce had to take it out of sight of where we were.

The sergeant walked us down past the purple car, and pointed down at an angle toward the valley floor. From there it was easy to spot the car, or what had been a car. If you took one of those matchbox toy cars and put it on top of the charcoal and cooked steaks for a whole party, then retrieved the little car and stepped on it with your heel, you'd have a pretty good imitation of what was lying in the valley.

"How did they ever get the body?"

"They came down from the other side. There's our road over there. That's where the bus was when they saw the flame when she hit. You can see from here it's not as steep to get down, or as far."

"How was identification made?"

"By Madame Vitrier."

"That's in the report, Enelio. I mean what condition was the body in?"

He questioned the sergeant. Finally he turned back to me and swallowed in a sickly way and said, "She was half in and half out of the car, charred from the waist up, and chopped up pretty bad, man. There was a silver chain on her ankle Madame Vitrier identified, and a red shoe that was hers, fifty feet maybe from where they found the car and the body. Didn't find the other shoe."

"Why was she way up in these mountains? Enelio, this damned road must climb four thousand feet in fifteen miles."

He turned and pointed. Through a notch in the hills we could see the far valley and the smoke-misted shimmer of the city. "Five thousand feet above the sea. Up here we are ... maybe eight thousand and a half? Yes. Ten, twelve kilometers more and we are at the top. The puerto, like the gate or the pass. At Relon. Ten thousand, two hundred and seven. I remember from the sign. Little houses here and there. Mountain people. Very sweet. Very cruel. Ah, this is one evil road, Travis. Every year two, three, four vehicles go over. Most of the time everyone dead. Six years ago a bus with eighteen persons. Why would she come up here? Maybe for the same reasons when I was ... seventeen? Yes. On an English motorcycle. Early, early in the morning, I went down this crazy road, man. I was yelling. It was a great excitement. It was speed and death and terror. It was a rhythm, Travis McGee. Lean into one curve, lean into the other. *Fantástico!* Like when it is the very best of sex, like the mountains are all parts of the body of a great brooding woman. Way down, near the bottom, somehow the wind got under

93

the goggles, blew them crooked, one eye covered, one eye in the wind, so the tears were running. I think there was a little stone I did not see. Zam! I am turning in the air. Smash into trees. Fall. Broke this wrist. See? It is never quite straight again. Blood running out of my hair. Hey, I walked down the road, holding this broken wrist like so. I walked with a big grin and I was singing, and they came out of the huts and stared at the crazy fellow. I had been to visit death, my friend, and had a taste of it and I was alive and I would live forever, and finally see death again and say, 'Remember me! You had me once, old woman, and you let me go!' " He grinned, picked up a stone, threw it over the edge. A truck came grinding and popping and grunting by us, and he waited until it went up around the corner Bix had missed and he could be heard again. "I think it was something like that for the girl. When you are young you drive up the mountains and you drive back down again."

He turned and questioned the sergeant, listened and then interpreted. I had caught about half of it. "He went on up the road and asked the people about the yellow car. He found a boy who would talk about it. The boy was herding two burros back to the little farm. He'd been in the woods that Sunday, cutting wood and making two big loads for the burros. The yellow car was parked off the road in the late afternoon, about a kilometer this side of Guelatao. The pavement stops there. Beyond that it is gravel and stone all the way to Papaloapan, and from there paved again until it ends on Route 140 on the Gulf of Mexico, south of Veracruz. It can be driven in a Rover or a Jeep or a good truck. No matter. The boy said a big foreigner was leaning against the yellow car, and a young foreign woman was sitting on a stone. He said they spoke greetings and he replied. Because of what the boy said, the sergeant came back with a dozen men and they searched every inch of the slope to be certain the man had not been with her and been thrown clear. They looked in the tops of trees to see if he was wedged there. There was no sign of him."

"Ask him if he got any description of the man from the boy."

After the sergeant replied, Enelio shrugged and said, "The boy told him that all foreign people looked exactly the same to him, as identical as kernels of dried corn."

"Did anybody else see them?"

"Perhaps. Who knows? These mountain people. They say very little to anyone from the valley, and they say nothing to the police. Look over there. See that place where the top of the smaller mountain seems to be flattened?"

"What is it?"

"In this light you can see faint lines running across, below the flat part, like terraces. If we went up there, Travis, and dug where those lines are we would find old, old walls. We would find shards of Zapotecan pottery, maybe splinters of obsidian. Under the soil of the flat top will be stone paving. There could be tombs there, but if there are they will be broken open, because that site is easy to spot. It overlooks the valley. Maybe it was an outpost for soldiers, maybe a place of the priests. There are maybe twenty thousand archeological sites in Mexico. Some say fifty thousand. Maybe five hundred have been investigated by the professionals. Here is how it was. Five, six, seven hundred years ago, these mountain people, who had been led into this place by the priests and the soldiers, they climbed to that place you see, and they made offerings of food, and they worshipped. They built the temples, dug the wells, carried the stones, made the pottery, cut the thatch. But the priests got too far away from the people. They thought they owned the people forever. They lost common understanding. So one day the people went up to the high places and killed the priests and killed the guards and pulled down the temples and never went back. They did not talk about it. They did not have elections. They just got tired of slave life, of catering to the demands of the priests for food and women and children to train, and tired of work that became more meaningless to them. They went up and killed them and

95

put an end to it, and did not talk about it, or make legends, or write about the revolution. These are hard, enduring people. I am proud to have this Indian blood in me. Do you know the kind of men who come out of these valleys? Benito Juárez! Porfirio Díaz! This small place of Oaxaca breeds great men who dream big dreams and then act on them. Hey! Sorry, I am not teaching school here. But listen to the silences here! They never shout, these mountain people. The greeting is adios, said so softly city ears can hardly hear it. Shall we go?"

And so we went back down that insane road, with Enelio driving conservatively, automatically, far away somewhere in thought and memory. Down to the flats and across to the intersection of the main road. There was a small industry on the right, where men baked adobe brick in rough ovens, then stacked them in the sun, in shades ranging from brown-orange to yellow-gold.

"Ask him if the American students cause him many problems," Meyer said. The sergeant talked at considerable length.

Enelio translated. "Martinez says that as a group they are like all people. Most of them create no problems. But there are always the very few who get drunk and break things, and there are the ones who live foolishly and become sick and require help. Some go into the wrong places with valuable things and become the victims of thieves. Some take drugs and act irrationally. Some act in a very improper way, which upsets the simple people."

"Improper how?" Meyer asked.

"A boy standing in the zocalo, fondling and kissing a half-dressed girl in front of a hundred Mexicans who have come in from the villages for a market day upsets them. But suppose you take some bearded, ragged, dirty kid, loaded with pot, digging the village scene, just floating and smiling, the village people will treat him with great gentleness and courtesy and consideration. Know why? It is tradition to be very nice to all madmen. The ancient gods have put a spell on them, and to be mad is to have been touched by the gods."

"Does he get requests to find specific students?" Meyer asked.

"He says that the American Embassy makes the request of the Federal Police, and then the information is sent down here. Then the registration list at every hotel and motel and trailer court is checked. If the student is found, he is told to get in touch with the Embassy in Mexico City. If he is not found, then that is reported."

"Do they keep a list?"

I congratulated Meyer for clear thinking. In the city, Sergeant Martinez brought a stack of papers out to the car. It was not a list, but rather a sheaf of faintly imprinted carbon copies of the Embassy requests, about forty of them.

"He says it is for all of this year up until now," Enelio explained.

Meyer went through them swiftly, with minor pauses, and then stopped at one and showed it to me. *Request to locate Carl Sessions, age 22, five foot eleven, one hundred and forty pounds, fair complexion, blond hair. Request contact Mr. Lord at the American Embassy, Extension 818.* It was dated the ninth of June. There were some notations and numbers written on it in red ink. Enelio asked the sergeant to explain the notations, then interpreted for us.

"They couldn't find this boy and they made a routine report. Okay, on July seventh, on a Monday morning, the boy is found dead in a doorway on Arteaga Street, in a bad section over beyond the public market. There wasn't anything left in his pockets, probably taken by kids who thought he was drunk. If his clothes hadn't been so ragged and dirty, they would have taken those too. A doctor took a blood sample. There were needle marks on his arms and thighs. Some were infected. He was badly undernourished. The cause of death was an overdose of an opiate. They found out he had been sleeping in a little place he had made out of cardboard boxes in the back of one of the market stalls. The owner of the stall had locked some of the boy's stuff up for safekeeping. There was a

97

guitar case with a guitar and some personal papers in it. They found his name from the papers."

He asked Martinez another question, listened, and then said, "A lieutenant called the Embassy in Mexico City and reported it. An embassy employee flew down and took care of the details. The body was sent by air freight to the boy's sister in Atlanta, Georgia."

I was suddenly aware of the way I was being studied by Sergeant Carlos Martinez. It was the cop look, flat, narrow, hard, and thoughtful. I didn't need any translator for that one. We showed an interest in two young travelers, and both of them were dead. Cops do not believe in coincidence. It offends their sense of orderliness. They find it hard to believe, for example, that every DWI they arrest has had exactly two beers.

We all thanked him for his time. Enelio shook his hand in that special way which inconspicuously transfers a folded bill from pocket to hand to hand to pocket.

As we drove away I said I wanted to replace the gift.

"Hey, you are pretty fonny, McGee. What time is it? Five o'clock already! Hey, Meyer and me will leave you off at the car, and by the time you get up to the Hotel Victoria, hombre, you will find us sitting at a shady table by the swimming pool looking at the lovely little birds in their wet little bikinis, and you will be one drink behind."

EIGHT

There were indeed some delicious little morsels making energetic use of the giant pool, getting the last of sun and water and squealing games of tag before the shadows of the mountains moved in and the evening chill began.

The drinks were good, and Enelio was sufficiently well known to get very earnest service. For a time Meyer scribbled on the back of an envelope, pausing to squint into the distance and think. When I asked him what he was doing he said he would show me in a couple of minutes.

Finally he handed it to me and said, "Timetable. If I screwed up anything, let me know." I held it so Enelio could read it also.

Jan. 10   Five cross into Mexico at Matamoros in camper.

Mar. 25   (*approx*) $13,000 + sent to Bix in Culiacán, Sinaloa.

Apr. 24   Rocko w/camper checks into Los Pájaros.

May 25   (*approx*) Bix & Minda move from Los Pájaros to room in Hotel Ruiz.

June 9   Official request to locate Sessions.

June 30   (*approx*) Bix and Minda move to Mrs. Vitrier's guest house.

July 5   Rocko beats up Mike Barrington.

July 7   Sessions found dead.

July 10   Camper permit & tourist cards run out.

July 23	Rocko leaves Los Pájaros, by request, moves in with Bruce Bundy.
July 30	(*approx*) Bix & Minda quarrel & Minda goes to Mexico City.
Aug. 1	Before dawn, Bundy stops Rocko from leaving with loot.
Aug. 1	Minda's father arrives, looking for her.
Aug. 2	Bundy lends his yellow British Ford to unknown person called George.
Aug. 3	Bix killed.
Aug. 4	Mrs. Vitrier identifies body.

I said, "Meyer, it makes it look a lot neater and more orderly than it is."

Enelio took the envelope and frowned at the timetable, and then said, "No sense to one thing here, men."

"Such as?"

"He couldn't have stayed in the trailer park after the permit and cards ran out. You have to show your car papers when you check into any trailer park. They put the date and so forth on their records. The police are very fussy about car permits. They check the books. So then their papers were still good on July twenty-three ... which means this first date is wrong, when they came in."

"No, Enelio. It was pretty well checked."

"Okay. Then sometime before April twenty-four, they went up to the border and got everything new again. New car papers, new tourist cards. I think ... maybe seven days from the border down here to Oaxaca. So the date on everything could be April seventeen, eh? Good until October sixteen. You can look in the office at Los Pájaros. They will have the permit number and the place of entry. It is not so necessary to go to the border to get the tourist card new. It is not supposed to be done, but it can be newed ... *re*newed in Mexico City, if there is a little gift to the right clerk. But not for a vehicle. One *must* go to the border. Where were they? Culiacán? Shortest way is up to Nogales." He grinned at us. "And I know why they went there. Pretty stupid thing to do."

100

"How could you know?" Meyer asked.

He tapped the side of his head. "Very smart fellow, this Enelio Fuentes. Sessions died from drugs. Okay. Sonora has a lot of poppies growing. The crude opium—it's called *goma*—is sold in one ton lots to the little factories where they reduce it to heroin. I think the biggest operations are in Sinaloa. And some very rich men there in fine houses, you believe me. What was stupid was having money sent to Culiacán. But maybe not. How was it sent?"

"Bank draft."

"Dumb stupid, man! A few years ago, okay. Now the Mexican Narcotics Bureau is pretty smart. They find out who is making a deal. Then they tip their people on our side of the line. So they get searched and, okay, suppose there's four kilos of heroin. Tell them they are going to be tossed into a Mexican jail for ninety-nine years. Scare them all to hell. Then take three kilos, and a big bribe to let them keep one, then tip the customs men on your side of the line. They get ... what's the damned word ... saw-hammered?"

"Whipsawed."

"So a bank draft is like hanging out a sign. I wonder what the hell happened."

Meyer said, "I can't see Bix Bowie as a smuggler of narcotics."

"So? That sister probably couldn't see little brother Carl stone cold dead in the market, man, full of old needle holes."

I asked him, "Could anybody go to Culiacán and buy heroin?"

He shrugged. "For double the going price, and never seeing the face you buy it from. Why not? Double the going price is maybe one tenth the wholesale price in the states. One hundred and thirty thousand dollars, U.S., is ... one million, six hundred twenty-five thousand pesos."

"In a very dirty business," Meyer said.

Enelio laughed. "Sure. But don't you know how the whole world thinks about dirty business? Everybody says,

101

'Oh, I know it is a bad, bad thing. But it is going to happen anyway. I can't stop it all by myself. So as long as *somebody* is going to do it, it might as well be me.' Meyer, I like you. You could not do bad things. Me, I do terrible things, believe me."

"Oh, so do I, Enelio. Unspeakable things."

Enelio made a sad face. "But for me, instead of involving money, always it involves women. That is my burden."

He looked at his watch. He said he had to go and change and go out. We thanked him for everything. He said he would phone us tomorrow, and maybe we could find something amusing to do.

The pool was shadowed, and most of the birds had flown. A batch of American youngsters in their late teens came whooping down from the hotel, smack-diving into the pool. Brown little girls, rangy boys, firm young flesh.

"You have to understand that all these kids are in revolt against the establishment," Meyer said in earnest imitation of Wally McLeen.

"Oh for chrissake, Meyer!"

"I found Wally quite touchingly simplistic. And that *is* a very funny tourist hat he wears."

I yawned. "And they translate ancient tablets inscribed three thousand years before Christ and find out that way back then the young were disobedient, had no respect for the old ways, and everything was going to hell in a handbasket."

"Spoken like a true member of the establishment."

"Old friend, there are people—young and old—that I like, and people that I do not like. The former are always in short supply. I am turned off by humorless fanaticism, whether it's revolutionary mumbo-jumbo by a young one, or loud lessons from the scripture by an old one. We are all comical, touching, slapstick animals, walking on our hind legs, trying to make it a noble journey from womb to tomb, and the people who can't see it all that way bore hell out of me."

"You're snarling, McGee. So it is either the effects of

the altitude, or postcoital depression. Or nervousness at round two coming up."

"Or frustration. I want to know where Rocko is. I want to know who was up on that mountain with Bix. I want to find Jerry Nesta. I want to talk to Minda McLeen. I want to talk to Mrs. Vitrier. I can scratch Carl Sessions. Thin blond guitarists shouldn't live in cardboard boxes and use dirty needles. And I want to bounce the rest of Brucey's story out of him."

"And you should be busy prettying yourself up for Lady Rebecca."

"I keep thinking of all the other people who would have been so happy to come to Mexico with me. You're getting so nervous about my date, I better make a phone call. Don't move."

I walked down and put the call through from our cottage.

"Darling McGee person!" she said, breathy and husky. "God, I feel so overall delicious! I'm humming and tingling and I hardly touch the floor when I walk. I ache for you so terribly, I feel hollow. Hurry, hurry, hurry! Please!"

"Becky, I'm afraid there has to be a change of plans."

"You monster! I can't *endure* it!"

"A chance has come up to move ahead a little, to get some more questions asked and answered. And I realize it was unfair of me to try to get you to tell me things told you in confidence by a friend. That was the wrong way to go about it. I won't pester you that way any more."

After a pause she said, "You are precisely what I need, you know. The young, young men would come to me at a dead run. Maybe that's what cloys. Having such total control over them. One gets so accustomed to getting exactly what one wants, right on schedule. Darling, I bow to your sense of responsibility. I shall wait here very, very patiently, if I must. And when you are finished with your chores, come to me no matter what hour it is."

"If it's possible at all."

"What are you trying to *do* to me? Could it be that I

103

was just a bit too mischievous last night? Darling, you *were* a challenge, you know. What is that silly thing they shout when great trees fall? Timber! Then they stand aside, smiling. Suppose I make a solemn vow not to be aggressive, and even teach you some special ways to absolutely destroy *me*? Fair is fair. Now will you promise to come here?"

"If I knew exactly what was going to happen, I'd promise. But I don't know how long it will take me to do the things I have to do."

"Could another woman be involved in all this work, dear?"

"It might turn out that way."

"If it does, kindly do not bother to come here. Is that quite clear?"

"From the tone of voice, Becky, abundantly."

"You're trying to spoil things. I'm not accustomed to that."

"All change is beneficial, honey. Take care."

I heard her start to say something as I hung up. I felt slightly weak in the knee. Say you are driving through on a green light and out of the corner of your eye you see a crazy running the red, about to hit you broadside. So you step on it hard and your car jumps ahead far enough so there is just a little clink as he ticks the rear bumper on his way past. So you drive three blocks and park carefully and get out. And the knees feel strange.

So we drove down into the center of the city. The military band was playing marches on the ornate stand in the center of the plaza, and people were walking slowly around and around the perimeter walkways. The traffic sounds, roar of conversations on the veranda, motor scooters, and vendors hawking everything salable overpowered the band, reducing it to an occasional cymbal-clash, an oompah now and then.

It was so crowded we had to take a table at the far end, near the jewelry-store corner. By the time we'd put a drink order in, and I was about to bounce my Bundy-plan

104

off Meyer's more temperate outlook, the Backspin redhead came out of nowhere and plumped down at Meyer's left and glowered across the square table at me.

"You put on a great rap, you sneaky bastard!"

"*Well* now! All fresh and clean and pretty as a picture. See, Meyer? Her eyes focus and her neck is clean. Carrying a little too much weight, but trim her down and she could cut it at anybody's convention."

"Mark was making a joke. That's all. I want to tell you I didn't appreciate the floor show you put on."

I smiled at her. "What were we supposed to do, honey? Sit there and let three heads think that the laughing was a great put-on? Should I have plucked that scarecrow stud out of the chair and booted his scrawny tail out into the traffic? Should we have ignored you and spoiled your fun? Should we have gotten up and walked away? Name it."

"We had some Mardil caps with a Coke was all."

"All for Jeanie?"

"That's something else again."

"Yes indeed. She is long gone. It looks like barbs to me. What's she using to come back? Speed? Is she popping it or eating it?"

"She is *not* long gone. She'll be okay."

"Get her when she's leveled off, kid, halfway between, give her a little kiss, and say goodby."

"You know so *damned* much, don't you?"

"I tried to sweat the whole thing out once upon a time with a very dandy little girl named Mary Catherine. She went onto reds and blues. Tuinal. They used to hate to see her coming, because the ward nurses hate the barbiturate addicts worse than the drunks or the ones on horse. Took her up to North Carolina to a cabin to get her once and for all clean. I'd go in for groceries and come back and find her gone away on some kind of high. Sneaked back and watched through a window. Draining gas out of the lantern, heating it and sniffing it. Lovely sweet faraway smile. Busted in. Tears, promises. Never again. Then she took off. Couldn't find her. Pretended to look. Pretended I had the broken heart. But you know, Red, that look on her face had killed it. I was the most relieved lover in contemporary history. I have no idea what Jeanie is to you."

"My best friend. My roommate at school."

"Take my word. She'll never make it back. Not from where she is."

"So what if she doesn't? It's her life, isn't it?"

"If you want to call it living."

"Hah! That big act of yours, mister. It so happens I found out you're nothing but some kind of rotten private fuzz, both of you. Private pigs for the establishment, down here to make trouble for people. That's some kind of living, isn't it?"

Meyer hitched around and leaned toward her. "Listen to me, my dear. And believe me. We came here as an act of friendship to find out how a lovely girl died. Just that. Nothing more. It seems like such a waste. Your friend Jeanie seems like a tragic waste to me. And to you too, I think. You are being very defensive and impertinent because you are very troubled. I think more has happened than you can handle. If I can help you, privately, personally, no strings attached, if I can help you in any way, just tell me what you need."

She shook her head. "Oh, for chrissake. You kill me. Honest to God, *me* need help from *you*!" And she began to laugh. Very merry. Very young and jolly. Ha ha ho. Meyer sat looking at her. Very patient. No change in the concerned, benign expression. And the laughter took on a thinner edge, a shrillness that suddenly broke into a sob. She slumped, face in her hands, crying quietly. I opened my mouth to speak. Meyer gave me a warning look, a quick lift of the hand. She was straining for control, trying to smother the crying, trying not to be conspicuous.

"What do you need?" he asked.

She reached blindly, head bowed, chin against her chest. She grasped his bulky forearm with both hands. "Can you ... can you get us out of here? Jeanie and me. Please. ... Tickets. I can ... pay you back."

"Where to, dear?"

"Oklahoma City."

"Where are your people?"

"In Europe with my youngest brother, traveling."

"How soon do you want to get out of here?"

"Now! Tomorrow!"

He borrowed a blank sheet from my pocket notebook, and put it and his pen in front of her. "Write your names and addresses."

She hunched over the paper, snuffling. She gave it to Meyer. He said he'd be back in a few minutes.

She wiped her eyes with a paper napkin and sat up and sighed deeply and made a wry mouth. "He isn't kidding?" she asked in a small voice.

"No. Not Meyer."

"I have run into so many lousy rotten people."

"Who briefed you on me?"

"Oh, there was a man around like an hour ago, maybe even two hours. Sort of handsome and elegant and faggotty. He was speaking real good Mexican to one of the waiters and he came over to the table with the waiter and the waiter pointed me out. So he asked me to come back to his table for a minute. So what the hell, why not?"

"Brown-gray hair, good tan, bangs, gold mesh ring."

"Yes, that's him. He lives here. He described you and, boy, did I ever remember *you*! He said he found out there was some kind of scene and wanted to know what went on. I asked why, and he said that a girl had died accidentally, the Bowie girl, and I knew about that, of course. Everybody who was here knew about that. And he said you were an investigator trying to turn it into a murder or something so you could make more money off her parents, and you were trying to make trouble for innocent people who live here. So I told him that what happened had nothing to do with anything like that. He wanted to know who else you talked to, and I said you had talked to the big fellow named Mike, with the Jesus beard, the one who paints, and the black girl named Della who's living with him, but I didn't know what you talked about to them. And that was all."

107

Meyer returned and gave her a pat on the back of her hand and said, "You can pick up two air tickets at the travel desk in the lobby after eleven tomorrow morning, dear. For your protection more than mine, I'm arranging it so that they can't be turned in for cash."

She nodded. "I think that's the best way. I . . . I won't believe it until I've got the tickets in my hand."

"You leave here at two tomorrow afternoon. You'll have three hours in Mexico City, so you better stay in the airport."

She tried, almost successfully, to smile. "Is there anybody you want killed? . . . Sorry. I guess that isn't very funny."

"You might be able to help us with one little problem. We're looking for three people Bix Bowie traveled with. There were five all together, but the Sessions boy died. We'd like to find Minda McLeen and Walter Rockland, known as Rocko, and Jerry Nesta."

"Those last two, Rocko and Jerry, if anybody wants to kill those two, I'll help. They are rotten human beings, especially Rocko. Look, I'm not going into any details about it. A bunch of us went back to that camper with those two, for like a fun party for one evening. So that Rocko gave me something that ran me up the walls. It ended up a girlfriend of mine named Gillian and me, we were there for I think it was three days. It taught me why the blond and the little dark one split and lived in that crummy hotel room. Mostly that lousy Rocko had me. He is strong as a bull. I mean I knew that if I went there I might end up getting balled, and that it would be taking that risk, right? Look, there are things you say you won't do. You know. Stopping points. But when people keep hurting you and hurting you, then it's easier to do any sick thing than keep getting hurt. It was all rotten. The kids who should have gotten us away from those two didn't do a damn thing. They just left us there. Jerry wasn't so bad. Gillian had the idea he'd be all right if he'd get away from Rocko. Jerry has this fantastic black beard. It's the biggest, blackest beard I ever saw. All that shows are his eyes

108

and a little bit of cheekbone and the end of his nose. I saw her in the market two or three days ago and she said they'd been out to Mitla and she saw Jerry walking along with a kind of ugly little Mexican woman walking behind him, so she made Ricky stop the car and she went back, but he was very strange. He didn't want to talk to her at all. He's living out there someplace, but he wouldn't say where. I haven't any idea where Rocko went, and I couldn't care less. I heard that the dark one—Minda?— yes, Minda. She's supposed to be up in Mexico City and her father is here waiting for her to come back. So that's all I know."

She got up and smiled good-by and said she couldn't say thank you or she'd start crying again. But she bent over and kissed Meyer in a very quick, shy, small-girl way. And fled.

"How did you know she'd grab at it?"

He shrugged. "I didn't. But sometimes you can smell despair. Besides, all generosity is selfish. It made me feel good all over."

Quickly I told him about Bruce Bundy's quest. It was logical, Meyer agreed, that Bundy would have a good contact among the waiter staff, because it would be useful to know what was going on at all times.

"But," asked Meyer, "what is he so damned jumpy about?"

"That is what we now go to find out."

He looked doleful. "A minute ago I felt good all over."

NINE

So I left the car at the end of the block and once again, this time by night, we walked along Calle las Artes, to the narrow front of number eighty-one.

Hundreds of years of dedicated and diligent theft have made Mexican homes very hard to crack. They grill everything you can reach. They put that busted glass into the tops of their patio walls. And they listen for thieves all the time without knowing they are listening. Thievery is a recognized, though not highly respected, profession. Artists use a limber length of bamboo with a hook at the end to snag the tourist trousers and pull them through the bars of the bedroom window.

There was a light upstairs, and the patio area, seen through the entrance corridor, was lighted. We stood in the shadowed darkness across the narrow street, and I said in a low tone, "I do not think we can talk our way through the gate. He won't buy a drunk act. He won't be bluffed, and he won't be hustled. And it would take a trampoline or a Tarzan act to pop in there uninvited."

"I'm still afraid you'll think of something, Travis."

I was afraid I wouldn't. And then luck took a hand. If you sit still, you don't give that lady much of a chance to operate—for or against you. But if you move around, she can get into the act oftener. She sent the tired old clattering cab down the street to pull up in front of Bruce's house. When the back door opened the dome light went on. Bruce got out. David Saunders was in the back seat.

Bruce went a few steps and looked back and then came back to the cab. He leaned in. The rough idle of the motor made it impossible to hear what he was saying. But his expression, seen through smeared glass, was animated, amused, coaxing. He made little shrugs and hand gestures. And at last David hitched himself along the seat. Bruce reached in and lifted a large suitcase out, put it down, paid the driver. The cab drove away. They moved toward the gate, Bruce carrying the suitcase. They talked outside the gate in low tones. Bruce unlocked the gate and swung it open. He began to lead David through the gate, with a quieting, comforting arm across David's back in such a way that it reminded me of that classic, *The Specialty of the House*, when the plump customer is being taken into the restaurant kitchens.

So I was on my toes with good knee action, angling across, hoping Meyer was reasonably close behind me. When Bundy spun, hearing the sudden unexpected sound, I was coming through the gate full out, shoulder already dipped, and a tenth of a second from impact.

Karate, judo, boxing, jiujitsu, wrestling—not one of the formal schools of unarmed combat prepares a man for the special problem of suddenly catching a sack of bricks that has fallen out of a third story window. It was a driving, rolling block coming in from the blind side, and the impact was impressive. It took us both ten yards down that tiled corridor, right to the end of it where it opened up onto the patio. We picked up a small table en route, along with some decorative crockery that had been on it. I rolled up onto my feet, my back toward him, and spun and was bemused and disconcerted to see him bounce up in a springy way and land in the dangerous balance of the expert, hands low and slightly forward. I did not want him to start that business of *Hah!* and *Huh!* The table was on the corridor floor between us, the three remaining legs aimed toward me. So I punted it at him, getting a lot of leg into it, and getting a nice lift on it. He got his hands up in time, and as the table fell away, I was right there to pop him with a short overhand right, slightly off target,

111

and correct the error when he came back off the wall. He had been obliging enough to wear a leather thong as a belt for his vermilion stretch slacks, and I yanked it loose, rolled him onto his face and took two fast turns around the wrists and two fast hitches that would hold long enough for me to go solve Meyer's problem, even if Bruce woke up right now, which didn't seem plausible.

I came upon the Mexican woman standing crouched in terror, wringing her hands. I smiled broadly and told her that it was a game Americans play. Don't worry, señora. We are all very happy.

Meyer was between the gate and the entrance to the central corridor. He was clumping around in a small circle, taking quick steps to the side now and again to catch his balance. He was shaking his big head and muttering to himself. David Saunders sat spraddled like a chunky little kid. He was swaying from side to side, cradling something against the lower part of his big chest and making a small thin keening sound. He looked like he was rocking a little dolly, and he couldn't carry a tune in a basket.

I got the gate shut and latched. I caught Meyer as he came around his circle. He stopped and shook his head violently and knuckled his eyes.

"Violence is vulgar," he said. "It offends me."

"You won, didn't you?"

"By giving him a frightful blow on the fist with my forehead. The expression is, 'I ducked into it.' "

I helped Saunders up and walked him past Bundy into the bright area of the walled court and eased him into a white iron armchair. I pulled the hand away from his chest. It was beginning to puff. Broken hands are unpredictable. There are ten thousand nerve bundles, and if the break doesn't involve them, you don't feel a thing until later on. But if the broken bone or bones grind into the right nerves, it is an agony that prevents you from thinking about anything else in the world, and keeps you right on the twilight edge of a faint.

I plucked Brucey off the floor and put him on a purple

112

chaise, rolled him onto his side and neatened the thong. The maid stood staring at us. I smiled at her. Meyer smiled at her. After a few moments she smiled back and scuttled away.

Bruce lifted his head, coming awake all at once. He swung his feet to the floor and sat up. He worked his jaw from side to side and licked his lips and looked at me and said in a totally masculine manner, "You are pretty goddam impressive, McGee. Men your size are supposed to be slower." He looked at David and frowned. "What's the matter with him?"

"He broke his hand hitting me on the head," Meyer said. "Terribly sorry about that."

"But he's in *agony*!" Bruce said. "He's *terribly* hurt. He needs medical attention immediately. *Look* at his poor hand!"

"He'll get it, after we have a little chat."

"What in the world do we have in common worth talking about, McGee?"

"The subject of discussion is what makes you so nervous about my asking questions about Walter Rockland and the Bowie girl."

"Am I nervous?"

"Nervous enough to talk to that redhead earlier tonight and tell her I was trying to make something out of nothing."

"Aren't you?"

I kicked a chair closer and sat facing him, about four feet away. "Brucey, the trouble with playing games is that you never know how much the other party knows. Rocko moved in here with you at your invitation, and put the camper in the shed out in back, and tried to hit you for a large loan, and then he tried to make off with a lot of valuable little goodies, but you'd read him right and disabled the truck. Took the rotor, probably. He jumped you and you black-belted him pretty good."

He tossed his head to throw the bangs back. He turned pale under his golden tan, and the odd brown eyes turned to dingy little slits. At that moment he looked his age.

"I shall *never, never, never* forgive that treacherous, rotten British bitch." He continued at some length. He had a truly poisonous mouth.

"All through? So why are you so edgy about it?"

"I can't afford to get involved in anything."

"What is there to get involved in, Bundy?"

He hesitated. "What if I happened to know that someone saw Walter Rockland and the Bowie girl together just a week ago? Ah ... at the airport, getting on a flight to Acapulco."

Misdirection. Nice footwork. Toss in a thought that warps the mind. Maybe it was true. So how to test it?

It took me quite a segment of silence to come up with the leverage. "You are a clever man, Bruce. Look at it this way. Nobody knows where Rocko is. It wouldn't be hard to prove he lived here with you. You are very nervous about the whole thing. I can get the information to Sergeant Martinez that you fought with Rockland. I can tell him that he can find traces of human blood on the stone floor of the shed out behind this place. I can tell him your story about Rockland going to Acapulco, and I guess they could check that out and see if he did. Then I would suggest that they take this place apart looking for a body and take you apart to see what you know about it."

"You are *such* a cruel son of a bitch."

"So?"

"All right! All right! All right! I nearly moved away from here after the first four months. I had a stupid mishap with the car I had then. A drunken old fool on a bicycle ran right into the side of the car. And so I ... enjoyed the hospitality of the local prison. My dear friend Freddy, now deceased, tried frantically to get me out, but they managed to hold me there five days. Police the world over seem to have this compulsion to mistreat men of my particular sexual pattern. They treated me with contempt. I did not mind that. I considered the source. The brutality from the jailors could be endured. But each night I was locked into a very large cell with the very dregs of Mexico, who had been informed, of course, of what I was.

114

And so I was used and abused. They degraded me. It put me into a depression that lasted for months. Freddy talked me out of leaving Mexico. He said it would be the same anywhere in the world. That is a valid observation. We have no recourse in the law, really. And Walter Rockland knew that when he tried to make off with some very valuable things. He knew that I would not report the theft, that I would not dare report it for fear they'd think of some pretext for locking me up again. I don't think I could endure that a second time. If you understand that, Mr. McGee, and understand my absolute terror, then I can tell you what happened."

He told us that Walter, as he called him, had stayed in bed all day Friday, and had said on Saturday morning that he still felt unwell, but begged to be allowed to leave. Bruce told him to rest. At noon on Saturday while Bruce was in the kitchen fixing something for a light lunch, he had been struck from behind and knocked unconscious. When he regained consciousness, Walter was gone. So were his car keys, a couple of hundred pesos from his wallet, and his yellow English Ford. At first he had been afraid Walter had broken in and taken the valuables which he had locked up after the first attempt, but they were still there. He had no intention of reporting it as a theft. He still had the truck and camper, and they were worth more than the car Walter had taken.

On Monday, in the middle of the morning, the police had come to see him. They had asked him about his car, asked him where it was. He had thought they had picked Walter up, and he remembered Walter's hints about needing the money for some illegal act. He could not be tied in with any illegality, so he had invented the fictitious young American named George, and had described him in a way that would fit half the young Americans in Mexico on summer vacation. Only after they had made him go over the story several times did they tell him that an unidentified girl had gone off the mountain road, that his car was a total loss and the girl was dead.

Later that day, before learning that Eva Vitrier had

115

identified the body, Bruce had gone to Becky and told her the whole story and had asked her what she thought he should do. He was frightened that Walter was involved somehow in the girl's death, and that if they picked up Walter he would manage to involve Bruce somehow.

Becky thought it was logical that Walter Rockland would come back after his truck, and that Bruce should leave the shed unlocked and leave the keys in it, and replace the rotor. Maybe somebody would steal it, or Rocko would retrieve it. And if neither happened, she would help him get rid of it some dark night, follow in her car while he parked it somewhere else in the city, and bring him back. In the small hours of the night, at a little after two o'clock on Tuesday morning, he heard the truck start, heard the backing and filling in the narrow alleyway, heard it speed away, the drone fading into the normal night sounds. And he did not care whether Rocko had taken it or a thief had taken it. He thought he was out of it.

"So weeks later," he said bitterly, "you show up at my door, telling your lies about insurance. I had to let you in, because I had to be certain Rocko hadn't sent you on some kind of blackmail project. But you didn't say the right things because you had no way of knowing."

"Like I have no way of knowing that all this is true."

"It *is* true. And the Bowie girl is dead. Eva telephoned me to say good-by. She said she did not know when she would be back."

"Where did she go?"

"She never says. I have no idea. I know she was very upset. It was unlike her to . . . identify the body. I think she had to be certain in her own mind that it was the blond girl, and she was too impatient to wait for them to identify her in some other way. I think it was quite a strong and unusual infatuation for poor Eva."

"Infatuation?"

"You aren't as aware as I thought, McGee. It seemed to me that Becky made it obvious last night that Eva and I are opposite sides of a very old coin. But the approach is

116

not the same. She is very rich and quite impersonal about her ... requirements. When she arrives here she will usually have a personal maid with her, never the same one. Girls of a certain type. Bovine, Nordic, bursting with health, quite young, tailored drab uniforms, terribly submissive and polite and humble. Northern Europeans. I suppose it is a great deal more efficient and less wearing than forming emotional attachments, and of course she can afford it without pain. I must say I did get a certain dirty satisfaction out of hearing how distressed she was, and realizing she is just as human and vulnerable as the rest of us. My hands are getting awfully numb. And poor David is in misery. And I have told you the whole thing."

I looked over at Meyer. He had several small purple knuckle-lumps on his forehead. "Do you buy it?" I asked him.

"I buy it."

"How terribly kind!" Bruce said acidly.

"Meyer, I would not like to untie him and have him start making out like we are pine boards and cinder blocks and going into that yelling and grunting bit. So why don't you just take that same walk again, and take a cab from the square to the hotel, and if I'm not there by the time you think I should be ..."

So I gave him five minutes and then untied Bruce. He flexed his hands and went at once to David, turned and asked me where my car was and would I please bring it to the front.

They sat in the back. I heard Bruce coaching him in what to say at the hospital. Bruce told me the turns to take. They talked in low tones. I heard Bruce say at one point, "But *really*! Somebody is going to have to wait on you hand and foot, and shouldn't I have that right? Besides, Davey, it was all settled, wasn't it? And your things are at my place, aren't they? Be *practical*, darling!"

They got out. Bruce said he could manage from there on, thank you. He gave me an absent nod, and walked David slowly toward the ambulance entrance.

I managed to get lost and end up back in town rather

117

than out on the Mitla Road. I got lost because my mind was too busy trying to make order out of too many fragments. I went up the hotel hill and around past the lobby entrance and down the cobblestone drive to the cottage carport.

Meyer hadn't left any lights on. I stumbled on the steps to the front porch of the cottage, and I heard the legs of the metal porch chair scrape on the cement as he moved. I groped for the other chair and sat down, feeling a few twinges from the tumble along the tile, and wondering if they would turn into morning aches.

"Hoo, boy," I said. "Dandy little village they've got here. These sweet kindly folk tear me up, they really do. I'm even beginning to wonder about Enelio Fuentes. He'll probably turn out to be a retired female wrestler going around in drag."

"Never fear," said Lady Becky from the neighboring chair. "Enelio is *muy hombre*. I can so certify."

"How the hell did *you* get here?"

"That's what I like, dearest. A warm welcome."

"Where is Meyer?"

"He's really a dear man. Did you know that? Oh, I packed him off. I expect he's settling down for the night in one of the other cottages. Things are thinning out, you know. We had a nice little visit, and he went puddling off carrying his little kit. He's marvelously tactful and understanding."

"And treacherous."

"I was driving around and about looking for you, darling, and saw him walking toward the zocalo, so I gave him a lift back here. Thought you might spot my car and turn into a ninny and drive away again. So I parked it discreetly. Travis dear, such a lot of nuisance and nonsense for you to hammer poor Bruce about. All you had to do was come to me. I should have told you all the rest of it."

"If I lived long enough to hear it all."

"But darling, you'll want to hear it from me too, to see if it all matches up, won't you? So doesn't it come out to

118

the same thing? You *do* struggle so. One would think I was quite sickeningly ugly or a horrid bore."

"If you would kindly be ugly or boring, I would be very grateful."

"But I shall be both soon enough! Any day now one ghastly wrinkle will appear, and all of a sudden I shall be ... Doriana Gray? Or like that carriage one of your sentimental poets wrote about. Quite suddenly I shall dwindle into a scruffy little old lady in tennis shoes, peering through bifocals, fussing with her hearing aid, who, in a quavery little old voice, will bore everyone with her memories of lovemaking. I am here because I forgave you."

"Thank you very much, Lady Rebecca. But you see, I wrote you down in one of the pages of my life, and now the pages have been turned, and we cannot go back and reread them because ... because ..."

"Because the book is very long and life is very short. Nice try, ducks. But *I* did the writing, and all I wrote was a preface. I told you. I was being a horrible show-offy person. I shan't be like that at all. Promise. Besides, you would be cheating me dreadfully. I granted myself a few little moments of climax, dear, but then I nipped the poor struggling things in the bud because, should I let one get truly started, it goes on and on and on, quite unendurably. It is so terribly lasting and intense and exhausting that I have to ration myself carefully. Even so, I go dragging about for days, looking quite puffy and done in. It would be wicked at this stage to deprive me."

I stood up slowly and made a wide circuit of her chair to reach the door. "It may be wicked, Becky. It may be unforgivable. It might even be a shocking lack of courtesy. But I am going to deprive the hell out of both of us, and I am going to get a long night's sleep, alone. Sorry about your pride and all that. Someday I may think back and kick myself. Sorry. Go drive that bubblegum car home. Good night, Lady Rebecca. Bug off, please."

I opened the screen door and reached in and found the switches for the room lights and porch lights and clicked everything on. She stood up and turned to face me, eyes sparkling green through the sheepdog ruff, mouth broadened in a delighted bawdy grin.

"You know, I *thought* you might be stuffy and stand-offish and difficult. So one does what one can to make it a *fait accompli*, what?"

She wore a wine red hotel blanket gathered closely around her. She laughed and said, "It would take you *hours* to find where I hid my clothing, dearest."

She dropped the blanket to the porch floor. "What is that quaint Americanism you people use? Peekaboob?"

I flapped a weak and frantic hand at the switches until I hit them back the way they were and we were in darkness. Well, shucks. And puh-shaw, fellas.

"That's right," I said, as she found me, locked on, and strained close. "Exactly right. Peekaboob. Very quaint old saying."

TEN

I sat out on the cottage porch in the Sunday-morning clang-bang of church bells and rooster announcements. Blue-gray smoke of breakfast fires hazed the morning bowl of the city.

Meyer came tentatively around the corner and looked up at me on the porch. Dopp-kit dangled from one hairy finger.

"Yoo-hoo," he said.

"Yoo-hoo to you, too, my good man."

"I didn't see her car, so I thought . . ."

"Come on up. You live here, Meyer. Remember?" So he came up onto the porch, started to say something, and changed his mind and went silently into the cottage. He came out in a few minutes and sat in the other chair.

"McGee, I thought that you had gotten back and somehow managed to send her on her way, implausible as that may seem. But I can see from the . . . the wear and tear . . . that she stayed for a while."

"She went tottering out of here about forty minutes ago, Meyer. She claimed she could walk to her car unaided."

"But . . . how do *you* feel?"

"Vibrant, alive, regenerated, recharged."

"I . . . I'm sorry I let her talk me into moving out for the night, Travis. But I guess you know you can't argue with that woman. She doesn't listen. And after all, it was your personal problem and—"

121

"Stop apologizing, my good man. No trouble at all. Quite a pleasant night. Active, but pleasant. Now if you would pick me up and take me up to breakfast, we can begin the long day."

We went back to Los Pájaros Trailer Park. The office and store were closed and locked. We left the rented car outside the gates and walked in. In the space numbered twenty, a Land Rover was parked under a tree with dusty leaves, near the travel trailer of Mr. and Mrs. Benjamin Knighton. The Rover was battleship gray, dusty and road-worn, with tools and gas cans strapped aboard.

He was sitting at an old table, typing with two fingers at respectable speed, apparently copying from yellow hand-written sheets. She was hanging some kahki shirts on a line to dry. They both stopped working as we approached, staring with an air of expectant caution. They could have been brother and sister, slat-thin young people, deeply sun-weathered, small statured, with colorless eyes, mouse hair, that elusive pinched and underprivileged look around the mouth that seems typical of slum people, swamp people, coal mine people, and mountain people. He wore steel-rimmed glasses, and she had a plastic clothespin in her mouth.

"Good morning!" I said.

He took off the glasses and she took out the clothespin. "Howdy," he said, in a voice more appropriate to a seven foot cowboy. " 'Morning," she murmured.

"Sorry to bother you. My name is Travis McGee. This is my friend Meyer. The manager said you were acquainted with a man who stayed here for a while, right over there in number seventeen. His name is Rockland."

"Why do you want to talk to me about him?"

"I thought you might have some information that would help us locate him, Mr. Knighton."

"Why do you want to find him?"

"To ask him about a girl who came into Mexico with him."

"Afraid you're wasting time, Mister McGee, covering ground already covered. I think he should have told you he was already here over two weeks ago."

"Who was here?"

"That girl's father. What was his name, hon?"

"McLeen," she answered softly.

"This isn't about the McLeen girl. This is the girl we're asking about." I moved over to the table and handed him the picture.

He looked at it, tilting his head, squinting one eye. "I don't want to tell you something that isn't true. Maybe could you tell me this one's name?"

"Bowie. Beatrice Bowie. She was called Bix."

He was quick. "*Was* called. Then I wouldn't be breaking news, would I? You know she's dead."

"Yes."

"But you want to ask about her? You related to her?"

"No. Friends of her father. He's unable to travel. He wants to know what things were like for her down here, before she died. They were out of touch."

His wife had hung up the shirts. She came over to the table to look at the photograph. "Never knew she'd been such a pretty one," said Mrs. Knighton.

"We don't want to interrupt your work," Meyer said.

Knighton studied us in turn. He shrugged and stood up, hand out. "I'm Ben. This here is Laura. Hon, you want to bring us out some of that coffee?"

"Surely," she said. "We take it black with a little sugar." We both nodded acceptance, and she responded with a thin smile and went into the travel trailer. The three of us moved over to the cement picnic table and benches that were, with the fireplace, part of the permanent installation at each site.

"Set," Ben Knighton said. His wife brought coffee, poured it and sat with us. They were comfortable people. He explained that he was on a sabbatical year from Texas Central University, and it was nearly over, and they had to leave in a few days.

He was obviously fond of young people, and he was also well acquainted with the drug scene on campus. It was natural that they would be curious about the five young people who had arrived in the camper back in April.

"Some of them dabble a little, without knowing the least damn thing about what the direct effects and the side effects might be. And some of them turn into heavy users. So you give them what help you can, what help they'll take from you. After a while you learn the categories. There's the predators who get their kicks out of turning the weaker kids on and taking monetary advantage or sexual advantage of them, or both. And some of the kids are such victims natural born, they seem to be looking for their personal predator. You can tell when a kid is so susceptible he is too far gone before you can manage to get to him. There's a faculty expression. D.T.O.D. Down The Old Drain. Black humor, but so true. They slip through your fingers. I watched them, those five. Rocko is a predator, and one merciless son of a bitch."

"Ben!" she said.

He smiled at her. "Honey, I've been writing this novel for a year. I have to talk like a novelist, don't I?"

"But you don't have to sound like the dean of men."

"Rocko seemed clean as far as I could tell. He hit the bottle sometimes, which is a good indication he was clean. And he is one mean drunk. Jerry, the one with the black beard, I'd label a semi-predator. He was on something, and getting closer to getting hooked on it every week. That's the way the predators turn into victims. The guitar player, Carl, was already way down the old drain. The blond girl, Bix, didn't look much like her picture any more. She wasn't too many steps behind Carl. The McLeen girl seemed to be on stimulants of some kind. She was burning herself up."

Mrs. Knighton shuddered. "That Carl used to sit over there under that tree and think he was playing the guitar. But there weren't any strings on it. And when the wind was from that direction, you could hear his long dirty fingernails rattling on the wood where the strings should have been."

"Cats tire of crippled mice that can't scamper any more," Ben said. "Sessions left, and then one day the girls were gone. But there was a fresh supply available in town and they used to bring them back. They'd stay three or four days sometimes and then they'd leave. Rocko and Jerry weren't a pair anybody'd want a permanent home with. Rocko was mostly bluff though. See those two tanks fastened there to the yoke of our house trailer? Gas tanks. Cooking gas. Twenty gallons each. That camper had been jacked off the truck and was on blocks. One day after Jerry had left, too, and Rocko was there alone, he drove back from town and found out somebody had pried open a little locked hatch in the back of the camper and stolen his bottled gas. He went storming around to all the sites, fussing about whether anybody saw the theft. He came over here, ugly, loud and mean. I was adjusting the fan belt on the Rover. I kept working and told him I didn't know a thing about it. I guess he thought I should stand at attention when spoken to. So he grabbed my shoulder and pulled me up and spun me around, and I came right around with the lug wrench I was using, and rang it off the top of his skull."

"Ben doesn't like people grabbing hold of him," Mrs. Knighton explained with a little air of pride.

"He walked back on his heels with his hands clapped on top of his head. Then he shook himself like a wet dog, and I knew from his eyes he was going to make a try for me, so I walked into him while he was getting organized and popped him again the same way but harder. He went down onto one knee and I told him to stay off my site from then on. I could tell from his color it had made him sick to his stomach. He looked at me and knew I meant it. He went away and I went back to tightening the nuts under the hood. Then he pulled out about two weeks later because Tomas wouldn't rent to him for another month."

125

"How bad off was the Bowie girl?" Meyer asked him.

"Bad. Passive, dirty, confused. Disoriented."

Laura Knighton said, "She seemed withdrawn and dull and listless. Stringy hair and a puffy face and bad color. I'd say she looked fifteen years older than that picture you've got. One of the retired couples hitched up and moved out because of her. She had . . . a habit they didn't take to."

"Don't get so fastidious, darling, nobody knows what you're trying to say. If that girl was walking slowly across that site over there and had an urge to pee, she'd pull up her skirt and squat wherever she was, unconscious as a dog in a cemetery."

"Then," said Laura, "there was that one day she had a blouse on and forgot her skirt or pants or whatever she was going to wear. And the little dark girl came running out and got her by the hand and tugged her back and got her inside and got her dressed the rest of the way. The poor lost thing is dead now, and I can't help saying it. I think it's for the best, just as I think the guitar player is better off dead, no matter what sorrow his folks may be feeling for him. They'd have no way of knowing how bad off he got toward the end."

I said, "It would be a help if you knew how we could locate any of the others, Rocko or Jerry or Miss McLeen."

"I wish we could help you," Ben said.

"I *did* see that truck and the camper that day, dear," she said.

"You *maybe* saw a blue truck with an aluminum camper body."

"That is *exactly* what I saw!"

He went into the trailer and brought out a large map of the State of Oaxaca, and also brought along his work journal to pin down the date. In one part of the historical novel he was finishing, a young Mixtec priest from Mitla flees all the way down the long slope of the Sierra Madre del Sur to the Pacific coast a hundred and fifty miles away. He had decided the imaginary priest would follow the dry bed of the Rio Miahuatlán, and so on Tuesday, August 5th, over three weeks ago, they had driven the Rover south along the road to Puerto Angel as far as Ocotlán, and then headed east on a road that was barely more than a dusty trace. Where it was blocked by a rock fall, they had gone ahead on foot. They had climbed a ledge and surveyed the country to the east with a pair of seven power binoculars. When he had gone wandering off, she had picked up a dust swirl far to the east, appearing and disappearing across rolling country. She had steadied the glasses and identified it as a blue truck with an aluminum truck body or camper on it.

"I was terribly curious about it because it was going so *fast*," she explained earnestly. "Mexicans will drive like maniacs on paved roads, but when they get onto dirt roads they positively creep, because if they break springs or anything in the holes or on the rocks it is so terribly expensive to replace them. And tourists in this country drive very carefully when they get off the paved roads. And anyway, what would there be over there to attract a tourist. I mean it was just so unusual I was interested and I wondered about it. I decided the driver was drunk or it was some terrible emergency."

He showed us on the map about where the road had to be, but there was not even a dotted line on the map. It had been headed south, Mrs. Knighton said. It had to be some road that turned south off 190 somewhere beyond Mitla, maybe as far as the village of Totolapán. Distances, he said, were very deceptive in the dry, high air. "But the chance of it being Rockland?" He shrugged.

We thanked them for the good coffee and the talk. He talked a little bit about his book. We wished him luck.

As we walked out, Tomas, the manager, was unlocking the store and the office. He was delighted to serve us by looking up the date he had copied from the vehicle papers on Rockland's truck. Yes indeed, the permit had been issued at Nogales on April 10th, and was thus good for yet another month and a half.

As we drove away Meyer made listless agreement with

my observation that the Knightons seemed like nice people. He seemed dejected. I knew what was wrong with him. The picture they had given us of Bix Bowie had been vivid, ugly, and depressing. I could not get him to talk. He did not feel like going to Mitla to look for Jerry Nesta. He seemed to want to go back to the cottage at the Victoria, so I skirted the center of town, drove up there. He plumped himself into a porch chair, sighing. I put on swim pants and walked up through the noon sun and swam slow lengths of the big handsome pool, staying out of the way of the young'uns who came squealing down off the diving tower. I dried off in the sun on a towel spread on the fitted stones of the poolside paving. The high altitude sun had a deep stinging bite to it that went all the way down through all the old layers of Gulfstream tan.

I opened small gates and let the immediate sensory memories of Becky flow into my mind. By rights I should have felt even more surfeited and exhausted than before. But though this weariness was deep, it seemed more gentle, with a spice of male arrogance, of satisfaction, of knowledge of satisfaction given in full measure.

She had been simpler, softer, more feminine somehow. She had been involved more with herself and her own reactions and timings. Before, we had used me, and this time we had used her, first in partial measures and at last in a final full measure which had been, she said, more than she had wanted to spend.

Later we had talked in a sleepy way of half sentences, and the sound of her shower had awakened me. I slept again, and was awakened by the kiss that was good morning and good-by, sat up to see her standing tall and smiling nicely, dressed in orange linen, white leather hatbox in her hand.

"You were very wicked, darling. I am utter ruin. It will take a week to mend my puffy old face. But I feel buttery delicious. And you are very dear. Afterward, remember, we chuckled together at nothing. Just at feeling nice. That is rare and *very* nice."

"And now you turn the page, Becky?"

"Yes. But I shall turn the corner down. One of the special pages that I go back and look at sometimes. Take good care, lamb."

When she got to the door I said, "You are . . ."

She turned, waiting for the rest of it. "Yes?"

But how to tell her she had achieved her aim in life? And wouldn't she be aware of it anyway? "You are completely Becky."

"Hmm. Rather nice that. Some are totally barmy. And I am completely Becky. Really no other way to say it, is there? Keep well, luv." She waggled her fingers at me, slammed the door smartly, and soon thereafter rammed the Lotus up the slope with thunderous verve.

I walked back to the cottage. Meyer said, "Would it be possible for you to stop smirking?"

"You have a foul manner today, Meyer."

"Let's give up on the whole thing, Trav. What the hell good are we doing? We can't tell Harl any of this. She was on a gay adventure, full of plans and excitement and fun. Until the tragic accident. Let's rehearse it. I don't want to know any more about it. I *knew* that girl. She was a quiet, calm, decent kid. So she tripped and fell into this damned septic tank, and we don't have to follow her any further into it, do we?"

"Can I tell you one thing I want to know?"

"You get compulsive about these things."

"The sergeant found a boy who saw a man that afternoon back up in those mountains with Bix. Everything we've learned thus far tells us she was in no shape to drive down a six-lane highway across Kansas at high noon. But somebody let her bring a car down that mountain, or try to, at dusk. Is it any different than pushing her off a bridge? And with Harl, which would fester the longest— pure accident, self-destruction, or contrived murder. I think it's something we ought to know before we leave this place."

129

I watched him work it out. Finally he grunted and rubbed his eyes.

"So, I won't get off just yet. I'll ride to the next stop. But I don't think I'll like it any better than the whole ride up till now."

ELEVEN

After a hotel lunch, a few miles out of the city on the Mitla road we came upon El Tule, and Meyer said that he wanted to be a tourist for a few minutes, and look at the biggest tree in the world.

It was not far from the highway, a hundred yards perhaps. It dwarfed the old church nearby. I was astonished to see how rich and vital and green it was. Seemed to be of the banyan family. Elephant-gray bark. Glossy dark leaves. There was a low iron fence all the way around it. The trunk was maybe a hundred and fifty feet in circumference. It made better than an acre of shade.

Meyer stood absolutely still, staring up into the cool green shadowy places beyond the giant lower limbs. When he turned smiling toward me, I knew that the tree had restored his nerves and composure.

"At the time of Christ," he said, "nobody was giving this tree a second look. It was just an ordinary little tree."

"It looks as if it has decided to stay around awhile."

"And I am going to come back here," he said, "and I am going to paint myself blue, and I am going to live up there in the top of that tree forever."

"Come on, Meyer. Ya vamonos."

The knowledge of the huge black beard on Jerome Nesta simplified the search.

"El americano con una barba negra y grande. Un escultor."

Ah, yes. I have seen him. Yes, he goes often to the

131

ruins. Also to the Museo de Arte Zapoteca, near the plaza and central market. No, I do not know where he lives.

We found an American student at the small museum. He was an archeology major from the University of New Mexico, an exchange student working on the continuing excavation and restoration program at the Mitla ruins. His name was Burt Koontz, and he was out in the rear courtyard, carefully washing and brushing the fragile shards of an old broken vase. He was burned to the rough red shade of roof tiles. He wore a white T-shirt, khaki shorts, and G.I. boots.

"I know Jerry. I mean as much as I guess you can get to know him. They let him come in and make sketches. He's been sketching some of the old stone heads. I haven't seen him around the last few days though. Maybe even a week. I couldn't say for sure."

He told us, as he worked, that he had been curious about Nesta. He was big and he moved carefully, as if he were convalescing from a serious illness. A Mexican girl always came with him. Young, but not pretty. One of those broad stocky ones with the same kind of Indio face you see in the old carvings. She would sit with infinite patience under one of the trees and wait for him, then get up when he came out, and follow him, a few steps behind, usually carrying one of those baskets they take to the market.

He had the impression that Nesta was living over toward the south side of town, up one of those steep dirt streets to the left of the main road as you come in.

So Meyer and I trudged up and down a lot of steep little streets, and met with varying degrees of suspicion, indifference, and secret amusement. But with the help of pesos and persistence, we finally found the place, on Calle Alivera, halfway up the hill. There was a pink house that seemed to be crumbling away. There was a walled courtyard with a broken gate. In the courtyard were mounds of litter, a couple of dozen small noisy children, and some women squatting around a pump, several of them nursing the future members of the gang.

We had a twelve-year-old businessman who led us across to a room in a far corner with a door that opened onto the roofed gallery that extended along the side of the courtyard. It was a dark little room. There was a cement and plaster fireplace-stove built into one corner. There was a raised platform along the opposite wall, where pallets could be placed for sleeping. The little room was entirely empty. I could not get it through the boy's head that I wanted him to speak slowly and clearly. So I had to make him repeat everything over and over until I thought I had the general idea.

The wife of the Americano was Luz. They had lived here many weeks. Then they had gone away. Three days ago. Four. Maybe they were married, maybe not. It was the same. They were poor. For marriage the priests and the government charge too much money, so one waits. The Americano had little Spanish. Luz had been married to a baker and had three sons. The baker and the three sons had died of enormous pain in the belly. Luz had the pain but had not died. The Americano seemed often sick. The room was five pesos a week. Maybe the Americano had sold his . . . I could not understand what it was that Nesta was supposed to have sold. He said it so many times he was getting discouraged and angry before I caught on. It was a gigantic head made of wood, taller than a man. The señor worked on it each day. It was a very curious thing. It was very ugly.

As near as I could tell, the giant head had been carried away by the señor and another big Americano, with great difficulty. And the tools and the cooking pots and the clothing and the beds. They all went away in a heap-di-row. In a what? Heap-di-row. What? Heap-di-row! Again, please? Heap-di-row! Heap-di-row!

He was close to tears with frustration. So I brightened his face with pesos. Once again as we crossed the court-yard the children fell silent, stopped all movement, and stared at us. The women pulled the edges of serapes together to hide the sleepy suck of small mouths.

And then, twenty-four miles back to Oaxaca, feeling

133

glazed and unreal. When you stack into one day the biggest oldest tree in the world, a gigantic ugly wooden head, a magical disappearance in a heap-di-row, and a page with the corner turned down in the Book of Becky, it is time to start searching the hedgerows for Alice and that well-known rabbit.

I had been counting on a therapeutic Sunday siesta, one which might have lasted right through to Monday breakfast. But when we got back to the hotel, there was a message to call Enelio Fuentes and a number where he could be reached. He was at a party at something that sounded less than interesting, called the Commercial Club. I tried to beg off but he insisted. It was atop a great big new farm equipment agency building set back off the Oaxaca-Puebla highway a mile or so beyond the city limits. He had said to drive around in back and go up the stairs in back. The cars were varied and impressive, parked back there.

When we walked out onto the gigantic roof, I saw why he had insisted. That part of it was called the Beach Club. There was a gigantic swimming pool with some kind of infernal device that created pretty good waves which broke on a realistic slope of sand beach. The high wall beyond the pool was painted to resemble a seascape. There were areas of lawn, small trees, fountains, cement sculpture, big bright beach umbrellas. There were several bars, and there were waiters in red coats, and there was a good trio working hard in the waning day. There were tennis courts and badminton courts, and the whole happy busy place was aswarm with jolly tanned Mexican businessmen with the same stamp of success as Enelio, but generally smaller and heavier, and the entire scene was bubbling and dancing with platoons of the vivid young girls that Enelio variously described as either cheeklets or crumpets. There seemed to be a difference, but I could not identify it.

"Just a simple, warm, primitive people," Meyer muttered.

Enelio found us and took us to his table. He had been

134

playing tennis. Pretty soon he would change. He recommended the tall sour rum drink he was having. He said, "An old friend, Ramón, he put up this dull building here, and one day we realize here is this hell of a big roof, and we can have the storage floor underneath too. So we made the initiation big, and big dues, because where else can they go, and we brought down a crazy man from Mexico City, told him to go ahead, make a place to have fun. Three million pesos! By God, you find out everybody uses the club to get back the fun for the money. Hey now, over here, you *pollitas*. These soaking wet crumpets, they are here on vacation from Guadalajara. This one, she is Lita, short for Carmelita, and has very little English so she is with me, okay? And these two here in pink, they are the sisters del Vega, the tall one Elena, the not so tall one Margarita. Darlings, this big ogly one is Señor Travis McGee, and this round hairy one is Meyer. They are my friends, so they are evil dangerous fellows, eh? Now we sit. Elena, you are to be with this McGee, and Margarita, here, dear, between me and Meyer. Now smile and greet my friends."

Elena was spectacular. "Yam ver' please to knowing you, Meester McGee," she said with a five hundred watt smile.

"You will have one little drink with us now, and then you will run away and play in the pool, while we make man talk, and we will summon you when we want you back. Waiter! And you will not make friends with any sly fellows or never, never, never again will Enelio Fuentes fly his little airplane to Guadalajara and bring you here for such a nice vacation from that insurance company office."

They had their drink, and they giggled, and then they went trotting off in their little sopping bikinis back to the artificial waves breaking on the artificial beach.

So we gave Enelio the full report of our activities. Meyer and I took turns filling him in on the details. He was particularly interested in the information about the truck being seen by Mrs. Knighton, heading south on a distant road at high speed.

"Yes, it fits the time," he said. "It is taken from Bundy's place before dawn on the fifth, that same day. Tuesday. I know those little roads. I used to hunt there. I used to kill small things in that burned country. One day I said, Who are you, Fuentes, killing things that breathe the same air, walk the same earth? What gives you the right? Who said you are more important, and other life is just for your sport? So I stopped. No matter. Those roads do not go to anyplace. Interesting. I think it would be nice, we go down there in my jeep. Not tomorrow. Some damn engineers are coming in to spoil my day. Tuesday, eh? Maybe in the morning. I will phone to you. Now I am wondering what things can be true and maybe not so true in the story Bundy tells you. I think you were great fools to do what you did, but it worked, eh? A man like that, it is easy for him to twist things a little, change things a little, the way a woman can do."

I said, "It's exactly the same story he told Lady Becky."

He looked puzzled. "But, my friend, I do not understand. You talked with Becky *before* you got all the story from Bruce."

"Well . . . I talked to her last night again."

"You are some kind of man to go visiting Becky again."

"Well . . . she visited me. By the time I got back from the hospital, she was at the cottage and Meyer was gone. Nice fellow when you get to know him, this Meyer."

He shook his head slowly and then he began to grin. "Oh boy. And how did you feel when you meet Elena, eh? Strong, young, handsome girl, eh? Look, I am not the kind of man who hands you out a sure-thing cheeklet, man. Just only a nice girl who if she decides she likes you, and if you make the struggle to be nice to her, then there she is, without teasing. Oh boy. One time in California on television I saw a contest, many men at tables eating apple pies as fast as they could. An ugly scene, truly. The winner, I don't know, eight or nine whole pies maybe. He walks careful. When he is getting the prize, the poor fellow looks sick. So here you are, McGee. You win the contest. So here I come with your prize, eh? Know what it is? Piece of apple pie. This is very, very fonny."

"Look at McGee chortling," Meyer said.

"Pretty girls are nice to be with," I said. "You are a very considerate man, Enelio. We will have drinks and we will have dinner, and they will brighten the table and the hours. And I will make excuses and slip away and you two can work things out."

"Just a minute!" Meyer said. "That girl is just a child!"

Enelio and I agreed she looked grown up. We reconfirmed the Tuesday date. Enelio went to shower and change, and when he came back the Guadalajara girls were with us, and Margarita was studying Meyer's palm and telling his fortune, and Meyer, so help me, was blushing.

So off went the girls from Guadalajara and they came back in their vivid little shifts and high-heeled sandals and with their big handbags and fun-sparkle eyes, all golden sun-glowing in the blue dusk under the festive lights strung across the roofed dining areas and umbrellaed bar areas. The trio had become a quartet with the addition of a muted trumpet of great clarity and passion, and they played a lot of Augustin Larra's romantic ballads. Meyer was the light-footed tireless dancing bear, and Enelio Fuentes was the good and amusing host. The world of Bundy, of Rockland, of Carl's stringless guitar, of plane tickets to Oklahoma City that Meyer had arranged in the early morning—all were far from the elegant roof where they had stopped the wavemaking machine and the colors of the lights striped the still water of the giant pool.

I, too, had my fortune told. Elena studied for a long time, biting at her lip, and then looked at me, head cocked to the side, unexpectedly solemn.

"I do not know how to say. Bad things happening. You are smile but you are sad. It is a . . . a evil time for you in your lifetime, Trrrravis."

137

TWELVE

Monday was hiatus. A quiet day, useful as a compress on an ugly bruise. Meyer was up early by prearrangement and braved the traffic in our rental to go down to the Hotel Marqués del Valle and pick up Lita, Elena, and Margarita, who were staying there, and take them all the way out to visit the ruins at Mitla, stopping on the way to admire, once again, the great tree in which he had vowed he would one day live.

I slept so deeply that when I awoke I had that rare and strange feeling of not only being unable to figure out where I was, or what month and year it was, but even who I was. The dregs of dreams were all of childhood, and in the morning mirror I looked at the raw, gaunt, knobbly stranger, at the weals and the pits and the white tracks of scar tissue across the deepwater brown of the leathery useful body, and marveled that childhood should turn into this—into the pale-eyed, scruff-headed, bony stranger who looked so lazily competent, yet, on the inside, felt such frequent waves of *Weltschmerz*, of lingering nostalgia for the lives he had never lived.

After long showering, I went up the hill and sat out on the high deck of the hotel and ate enough breakfast for any three people, then sat in delightful digestive stupor, making the pots of coffee last. When I began to wonder how the waiters would react if I went over and did a handstand on the wide cement railing, I realized that I felt very, very good indeed, felt better than I deserved to feel,

138

felt as if I had a sudden dividend of youth, available for the misspending. Then I decided, for like the ten thousandth time, that I was one rotten contradictory fellow, that my talent for dissipation should have long since turned me into a slack, wheezing, puffy ruin, had it not been combined with that iron Calvinistic conscience which, upon noting too much progressive decay, would drive me into the kind of training the decathlon boys seem to enjoy, punishing myself back into the kind of fitness that makes you feel as if no maniac could dent you with a sledge hammer.

Meyer arrived at one-thirty with the three crumpets, complete with swim togs. While they changed in our cottage, he explained to me that a crumpet was a cheeklet with a warm muffiny heart, whereas a cheeklet was a crumpet with a talent for creating special problems. I told him that was worth knowing, certainly. He told me his tree was fine, and he had driven with raceway verve, and he could understand why the Mixtecs took Mitla away from the Zapotecs. He said that he had checked with the girl at the hotel, and that the redhead had picked up the two tickets and had made the flight.

We lolled the long afternoon, with sunshine, hamburgers, beers, and pleasant, sidelong, inconspicuous admiration of the tender textures of the maidens of Guadalajara. Enelio arrived at rum-time, full of such fury at the arrogance and ignorance of visiting engineers that he had to swim a dozen thrashing laps before he could get the scowl off his forehead. Before he left, taking Lita with him, he brought a map from his car to the lighted cottage and spread it out and showed me, by drawing a pencil line, the road which the Chevy truck had probably been on when Laura Knighton had seen it.

On Tuesday morning at a little before eleven, Meyer and I were standing out in front of the lobby entrance to the Victoria when Enelio, in a yellow jeep, came roaring in low gear up the steep hotel driveway. It was the earliest

139

he could get away from the agency. Enelio looked very elegant and dashing in his white-hunter hat. He came to a flashing grinning stop within a few feet of us. The jeep had those special fat low-pressure tires useful for traversing open country full of stone and sand.

As we clambered in, two little Mexican boys who had been vigorously rubbing a tourist sedan with greasy rags came trotting over to examine the vehicle with their quick, bright obsidian eyes. They looked at the gas can racks and the power takeoff winch and the big spotlight.

One asked the other one a question, and got the authoritative answer, in the slightly contemptuous tone of all authority, *"Es un heep especial, seguro."*

Enelio spun it in a tight turn and went charging down the hill. He stopped at the bottom to wait for truck traffic on the highway. The word had been echoing in my head.

"Wait a minute," I said. "Please wait right here a minute."

Enelio turned and looked back at me. "Forget something?"

"Remember something. Any 'j' is pronounced like an 'h.' Jalisco. Jugar. And so, by God, we are riding in a heep."

"Very fonny joke. But very old," Enelio said.

"I know what he's getting at," Meyer said. "That kid at Mitla. You couldn't understand that thing he was saying."

"Heap-di-row. Jeep de rojo. Jeep de color rojo."

"Yes indeed," said Enelio. "A red jeep. And this is a yellow one. Is the game over?"

Meyer had hitched almost all the way around so as to look directly at me. "A painter and a sculptor. Why not? What's Mike's last name? Barrington?"

"And Della Davis."

"Too much sun at this altitude," Enelio said, "and the brain gets cooked and people don't make sense."

"Enelio, what's the name of the road toward the airport?"

"The Coyotepec Road."

140

"And about a mile out, is there some kind of a tourist place that burned?"

"I know the place. It burned a long time ago."

"Can we go out there?" I asked. "I went to check something out."

I leaned forward and hollered the explanations over the wind roar and tire whine as Enelio pushed the jeep hard.

The place had been surrounded by a thick high adobe wall, enclosing about an acre of land. There were shade trees inside and outside the wall, but the land around it was bare and flat, and planted with parched and scraggly corn. Over the wall, which began back about a hundred yards from the highway, I could see the broken and sooty stone walls of the structure, open to the sky, with an angle of charred, leaning beam that had rank green vines clinging to it. The old red jeep was parked close to the wall over at the left, under the shade trees. Several little groups of people sat and squatted in the shade, at respectful distances, looking toward the wall. Two police cars were parked with their noses toward the red jeep, and at an angle to each other, as though snuffing it.

"Something bad is going on here," Enelio said. "Those are people who have stopped working the fields to come and wait and watch. They don't do that for a small thing. Something very bad, I think."

Both doors of the entrance gate in the side wall stood open. A very shiny black Mercedes sedan was parked inside the compound. An adobe cottage was built into the corner of the compound, so that the encircling wall formed two walls of the cottage. Two wooden sheds had been attached to it, one on either side, braced against the wall.

A big young man sat in the sunlight on a scarred wooden bench. He was hunched forward, elbows on his knees, face in his hands, shoulders thrust high. He wore dirty gray denim work pants and a clean white shirt. He was barefoot. The fringe of a huge glossy black beard curled inward around the edges of the hands he held against his face. A bald man in a black suit was standing in front of him. Three uniformed policemen stood off to one side. Our acquaintance, Sergeant Martinez, in civilian clothes, stood a couple of paces behind the bald man.

All except the man on the bench looked toward us as we came through the open gate. I saw a startled look cross the sergeant's face, immediately replaced by that cop look I had seen before, but this time considerably reinforced by this new coincidence.

The bald man said, "Enelio! Using you for speaking here, maybe?"

He came several steps to meet us. Enelio introduced us to Doctor Francisco Martel and then the doctor launched into such rapid Spanish I gave up trying to catch the meaning of any part of it. He did much gesturing and pointing, and spoke with dramatic emphasis. The sergeant joined them and there was discussion for a time, then Enelio came and told us what had happened.

An hour ago a man had run out and waved a city-bound bus down and told the driver people were dying behind the wall. The driver stopped at the first telephone and reported it. The police sedan had arrived just before the ambulance. The young black girl was just inside the gate, sprawled in the dust, killed with a single blow that had apparently come from behind, and had so ruined her skull that brain tissue had made a spatter pattern in the dust. The big blond bearded American youth had been over beyond the shed, the whole upper left side of his forehead smashed inward. There was a heartbeat but it had stopped before they could load him into the ambulance. Near him lay the Mexican woman, dead of a similar single stupendous blow over the left ear, eyes bulged and staring by the force of the hydraulic pressure created within the brain case. And the black-bearded one was sitting on the ground with her head in his lap, weeping. He claimed he had arrived minutes before the police, and found them like that.

"Have they identified him?"

The sergeant brought the tourist card over. It was sweat-stained and dog-eared. The ink on the signature had run. He was Jerome Nesta. Enelio said, "Martinez knows he's guilty of being in Mexico illegally. The card has run out. Guilty of one thing, guilty of everything. That's how the official mind works, eh? So I have the permission to ask some questions. Come listen. Maybe you two think of some, help me out a little."

Enelio sat on his heels in front of Nesta. "Jerry?" he said softly. "Hey, you. Jerry!"

The head lifted from the hands. The eyes did not match the virility and vitality of the great black beard. They were gray-blue, hesitant, uncertain. And reddened by tears.

"How you making it, boy?" Enelio asked.

"All ... all three of them. Jesus! All three of them. I just can't ... can't start to believe it's true."

"Who did it, Jerry?"

"I don't *know*! There wasn't anybody here. I didn't see anybody. I came in, calling Della on account of I wanted to know where to put the stuff."

"What stuff?"

"The stuff I brought back from town. It was my turn to go in. Nobody felt like coming along. Luz was doing washing, and Mike was going good on a painting, and Della had a headache."

"You drove the jeep to town?"

"Yes, sir."

"What time did you leave here?"

"I don't know. Maybe a little before ten. I bought fruit and radishes and beans, and a kilo of masa for Luz to make tortillas. I guess I was gone most of an hour probably."

"How soon after you got back did the police come?"

"I don't know. Like two minutes."

"Jerry, can you think of any way we could pin it down, what time you got back here, man?"

"I don't know how I can."

Enelio got up and went over and spoke to the doctor

143

for a little while. They walked over near one of the sheds and the doctor indicated a dark stain on the dust and stones. Enelio came back and sat on the bench beside Nesta. "Did you see anything unusual or hear anything unusual on your way out of town or on the highway?"

"I can't remember anything."

"Nothing interesting at all?"

"Oh, wait a minute. There was something. Right near the edge of town, where the railroad tracks are, there was an old truck pulled over and the engine was on fire, and people were running around yelling, and they were throwing dirt on it and a man was beating at it with a blanket."

Enelio said, "You are one lucky fellow. The cops saw it too and stopped for a minute. They were just putting the fire out. So they were, like you said, a minute or two behind you."

"What difference does it make?"

"This wasn't robbers, Jerry. Nobody touched a pocket or a purse. From the blood over there, it had to have happened at least twenty minutes before the police got here, according to the doctor here."

Jerry stared at Enelio. "Would these damn fools think I'd kill my friends?"

"That's what most people kill. Their family or their friends. Very few people kill strangers. I got to tell what you said to the sergeant."

I sat where Enelio had been. "How come you and Luz moved in here with Mike and Della?"

He looked at me, puzzled. "Who are you?"

"My name is McGee. I've been trying to locate you. I found where you had been living, out at Mitla."

"Why have you been looking for me?"

"Just to see what you might know about Bix Bowie."

"Bix got killed in an accident."

"I know. And Carl Sessions died of an overdose. So the only ones left to talk to are you and Minda and Rocko."

"Why should anybody know anything about Bix? Minda, maybe. It happened after everybody had split."

144

"A girl named Gillian saw you in Mitla and told a friend. Gillian talked to you and she said you weren't very friendly. She asked you where Rocko was and you said you didn't know."

"I didn't and I don't. I was the last one to split. I had to get the hell away from Rocko. I got pretty sick there. I had to try to get clean. I'm not in real good shape yet. I get this ringing in my ears, and I get shaky, and my eyes blur sometimes. I have real bad nightmares, but I don't hallucinate any more. Luz took care of me when I was real, real bad. I don't even know how I got to Mitla. It was all part of a bad trip. She pulled me out of a ditch and got some friends to help her get me under a roof. I had the idea Rocko was trying to kill me, you know, like paranoia, and I had to cut out. Jesus! Why would anybody kill Luz? You know she had a beautiful smile? When she smiled . . . I tell you it was something else."

"Was it better here than it was in Mitla?"

"Oh sure. I ran into Mike out at the ruins and we started talking, and I took him back to the place and showed him the big timber head I've been working on. So he came out to see it and he liked it. I mean there are too many people around just *talking* about doing something. I told him I was trying like hell to work, because it had been too long. I leveled with him. I said I had been on things that didn't do me much good, but now I was clean and I was going to stay clean. I said it was lonely, me not being able to talk much of Luz's language, and he told me about his free place, and how there was room, and Della might like having another woman around to share the scut work. So why not? We got a guy to help and we loaded the big head on his jeep and packed and came here. Luz was pretty weird about Della for a little while, until she got used to her. Then they started to get along. But . . . they haven't . . . didn't have much time to get acquainted. Oh goddammit all anyway! It's such a lousy waste. Della was pregnant. That's why she was having headaches."

Enelio sauntered back and said, "Jerry, they want to

investigate further, but because the time you got back checks out and because they can't find any kind of a weapon, you ought to be okay."

"One of them was looking at one of my sculptor's mallets."

"And he would like to cry because it was such a nice thing for somebody to use, but there would have to be blood. Blood and skin and hair. And fantastic strength. But they have to take you in anyway."

"Why?"

"Your tourist card is no good. Got money to get home?"

"Hell no."

"So they hold you and ask the American Embassy to make arrangements."

"Look, I forgot the card ran out! I didn't even think about it. I don't want to sit in any Mexican jail."

"Nobody sitting in one wants to be there."

I took Enelio aside. "I want to talk to this kid, alone and in the right relaxing surroundings. Any way to keep him out?"

"Want to pay for his trip to the States?"

"If it'll help."

"Want to give a little gift to the police welfare fund?"

"Like?"

"Five hundred pesos?"

"Sure."

"Then let them keep him overnight and we'll see what we can do tomorrow. Tomorrow they are maybe going to be happy to get rid of any little problems. Newspaper people will be here today from Mexico City. This will be one big stink. The Tourist Bureau will be very ugly about it. This is supposed to be such a nice safe country, eh? But always there are damn fools going off into primitive places where los Indios are still damn savage. No Spanish at all. Cruel land and cruel people. Canoe trips. Hiking. Go see the interesting Indios and get your interested throat cut, and get thrown naked into an interesting river, man. So that is one thing, and that is something else. One

146

and a half million cars cross the border and stay for a time. God knows how many more go over into border towns for the day. It is big industry. Come to beautiful Oaxaca and get a big hit on the head. Travis, my friend, to get this bearded boy with the sad eyes loose, I must make some little kind of guarantee all will be well. You think everything will go well?"

"I'll know better after I talk to him. If I don't like the vibrations, he better go back in."

Meyer came over to us and said, "Come take a look at something." He took us over to a space against the adobe wall beyond a wooden shed. The wooden sculpture stood there. A head five feet high, carved and gouged and scraped out of old gray beams that had been bolted together. It was the same sort of Zapotecan face of the ancient carvings in stone. It had the same cruel, brooding look of lost centuries and forgotten myths. It was the size and weight and texture of the old timbers that gave it impact. There was no neck. It sat solidly on the great hard width of jaw. It could have been just a kind of self-conscious trick, but somehow he had given it a presence that made you want to speak softly.

"Son of a bitch," Enelio said slowly.

Jerry Nesta came up behind us, a man in uniform with him. He said, "I had to find hunks of metal and make the tools. I kept them sharp by rubbing them on stone. I kept thinking of the whole figure, and the way he would stand, so the head would carry the look of the whole figure. I thought of it as being something that would stand at the corner of an old temple, looking out. Not a priest or a soldier, but one of the laborers that built all these ruins and died building them. Like maybe the priests decided those unknown people should have a statue, but not out of stone. Mike thought it was . . . said it was . . ."

He turned away. Pretty soon they put him in a car and took him in. They left a car and two men to keep watch over the place. As we drove away, the silent people were still under the trees, looking toward the place of murder.

THIRTEEN

The hours spent on the Coyotepec Road had taken too big a piece out of Enelio Fuentes' available time, and he said we would have to delay the exploration of the unmarked road until later.

He drove us into the center of town. The girls from Guadalajara had planned to spend the morning shopping and have a late lunch on the veranda at the Marqués, where we were to join them if we got back in time. Otherwise we would see them after the siesta time. But it was too early for lunch. Enelio said he might as well clean off another square foot of his desk and see us later. We let Meyer off near the big camera store on Hidalgo and Enelio took me around the zocalo to drop me in front of the hotel. There was, by some freak of chance, a parking space available, so he braked and swung in.

"*Momentito*, my friend." He sat with his big hands on the wheel, looking straight ahead, frowning. "One thing I did not know. I did not know I would be so busy, so many things would happen to keep me busy. So what I have done, I have made you two hombres into tourist guides and taxi drivers for the three little crumpets. I had been telling my conscience, why not? What man could not have pleasure to be with the tiny little flock of bright birds? But I forget. You are here on a sad and serious kind of business, eh? My God, that blood on that dusty ground is enough to wake me up. What I am saying, if they are a burden, arrangements can be made."

"No burden, amigo. They are a good contrast."

"You are certain? Good!" He grinned and winked. "I tell you, those sisters they are ver' pozzled by you two. I am old and good friends with Lita a long time. They tell her the pozzlement and she whispers it to me. These girl on vacations, McGee, they are having a beautiful time. But what soch pretty ones want on a vacation is the chance to say yes or say no. They do not know what it will be. Much depends on the asking, eh? But they look back on a vacation, they can say, well, I am sorry or I am glad I said yes, or I am sorry or I am glad I said no. Margarita thinks Meyer is one of the great men of our time, and Elena is beginning to think maybe she is ogly, or she is using the wrong toothpowder. I tell you one thing, with these girl, if you do not know the new Mexican working girl, maybe you are afraid they are wanting a permanent thing, hunting for keeps. Forget it. This is a vacation. They take care of themself pretty good, and they were upset with me I should find dates with Americans before they met you, because the Americans they meet, they are too much interested in one thing only. Do as you please. I just say they are pozzled. But if you ask, if they say yes, I tell you it will be one hell of a distraction from this serious matter you are doing here. No, I do not want answers or conversation, please. See you later on, my friend."

And he went swinging out, putting the fear of the hereafter into a bevy of bicycles and motor scooters. I claimed a table for four on the hotel porch. Though it was nearing the busiest time of day, it was not as crowded as usual. There were far fewer of the college young. It was time to head home, sort the gear, and head back to school. I could overhear the tourist conversations, and quite a few of them were exchanging very lurid and distorted versions of sudden death on the Coyotepec Road. One beflowered matron was explaining loudly to her friends as she walked by that some hippie had shoved a knife into five fellow drug addicts and had been killed resisting arrest.

Suddenly Wally McLeen scurried up and plopped into one of the empty chairs. "Remember me, Travis? Wally McLeen? God, wasn't that a terrible thing that happened! Did you hear about it? Two wonderful kids were killed this morning . . ."

"Mike Barrington and Della Davis. And a Mexican girl."

"Their skulls were crushed. Absolutely crushed. I knew those two kids. Not well, of course, because they didn't come into town often. They knew my Minda, just casually. They were very nice to me, actually, because they knew I was trying sincerely and honestly to keep from making any emotional judgements about a white boy and a black girl living together. I mean it is rough enough for any young couple to make it, even when they have the same heritage, isn't it? But you have to respect genuine emotion wherever you find it, I say. No one could be with them without seeing that they were in love and were so terribly anxious to make it work. Now the difference in race doesn't seem important at all, does it? Dying is the same for everyone. I understand that they think a boy named Jerry Nesta did it while deranged by narcotics. Do you remember when either you or Meyer asked me about Jerry Nesta and Carl Sessions? I since found out that they were in the same little group that came down together, that my Minda was in! Did you know the Sessions boy died?"

"We heard about it."

"From drugs, I understand. Well, if they were using drugs, I'm certain that's the reason Minda left the group the first good chance she had. Even if we couldn't communicate, I know she respected her body too much to abuse it with narcotics, but I will have to accept the very real possibility that she uses marijuana and probably LSD. I've been trying them from time to time, without really very much effect. But I have had some periods of a new kind of self-awareness, a sort of spiritual feeling of kinship with all living things and all of history. Knowing the effects gives me a better chance to relate to Minda when she comes back here, I think. I thought that Jerry Nesta might have known when she was coming back or where to get in touch with her, so I'd been looking everywhere for him. Do you know, I rode my Honda right past that place twice this morning, where it happened, once on my way to the airport and once on the way back!" His eyes looked goggly behind the thick lenses.

"Wally, Wally. A Honda yet."

"I got one, a rental, as soon as I got here. It was pretty hairy for a while, those trucks and buses, but now I'm getting quite confident with it."

"And those beads, Wally?"

"Well . . . they're from the market. They're made of the vertebrae from the backbones of little fish, stained with vegetable coloring."

"And that is, or will be, a goatee?"

He laughed unhappily and felt his chin. "Guilty. I don't know what the boys would say back home. But it's like . . . a protective coloration, Trav. These kids, if they peg you as a square, they are absolutely cruel and merciless. That's the part I don't understand yet—the cruelty. The very first evening I was here a boy made an absolute ass of me, just for sport, I guess. I'd been up and down this veranda all day and all over the zocalo and the market, asking every kid I saw if they knew Minda McLeen. I had just flown down from Mexico City that morning, a Thursday morning. And this young man asked me if I was the one looking for Minda, and he took me back into that bar lounge there, to one of those circular booths. The place was absolutely empty. He was very mysterious about it and very cautious. He said he might know Minda and he might know where she was, and she might be in some kind of a jam, and so what was it worth to me to have him see what he could do to get her out of the mess she was in and turn her over to me. I must say I was suspicious. We finally made a deal that if he'd bring me some proof, like a note from her, I would give him five thousand dollars, and then give him five thousand more when he brought Minda to me. But he just never showed

151

up again. It was a game, a story to tell about how he blew my mind. It's hard to forgive him, but I think I can."

"So the beads and the Honda and the goatee are just a disguise, so they won't try so hard to put you on?"

"Oh no! It's more sincere than that. I mean they'd see through that in a minute. Why, last night there must have been thirty or forty kids milling around this porch at midnight having a good-by party. Most of them went out this morning. And I was genuinely part of it, Trav. They talked to me freely. They knew I was trying to find Jerry Nesta, and one girl told me that he was in bad shape and living in some Mexican hovel in Mitla, hitting up the tourists for money to live on. But I thought he might have *some* crumb of information about where my Minda is and what day she planned to come back here. Do you think they would let me talk to him at the jail?"

"Why not?"

"But isn't he in isolation or anything?"

"No. He was able to prove he was here in town when it happened. He came back in the jeep and found the three of them dead."

"Then why would he be in jail? Answer that, will you."

"Because his tourist card ran out and he's an indigent, Wally."

"Oh. Then what everybody is saying about him—"

"Is inaccurate."

"How do you know so much about it, McGee?"

"I dropped in. A social visit, but I got there too late."

"Oh. Well, I suppose I better try to see Nesta then. Well . . . thanks again." He got up. "And if you happen to hear anything about my Minda, anything at all, I'm right here in the hotel. Room twelve. You can leave a note in my box. I would appreciate it so much."

He'd been gone maybe two minutes when Meyer, with a straw bag full of little gift-wrapped items, sat down at the table and said, "Guess who nearly ran me down?"

"Wally McLeen on his Honda."

"If I didn't like you, McGee, I'd find it very easy to

152

hate you. So you saw him. Okay, what struck me about him? What item?"

I tried the beads, then the goatee, but he smugly said no. "The best thing, the unforgettable thing was what I saw as he thundered by, jaw clamped. They glittered in the sun. Old-fashioned bicycle clips, by God, with his trousers neatly furled and held in place thereby."

"I envy you that vision," I said. I reported our conversation. I found that Meyer wanted to know more than I thought worth telling. He made me go back twice to the fellow who had conned Wally with the wild tale about Minda, and try to tell it in Wally's words.

"Whoa! Let me up, or at least tell me what you're after."

He gave me his most infuriatingly smug Buddha smile. "I would hate to think that a certain lady of noble blood romped you into permanent semi-consciousness, old friend. Nor would I like to believe that yesterday's lazy sun cooked the protein in your head. So why don't you take it from the top all by yourself, with one little clue. Just imagine that the fellow who wanted to peddle Minda to her father was named Rockland." And when he spoke again, several minutes later, he said, "Your face is all aglow with a look of rudimentary intelligence. Now try it out loud."

"McLeen said he'd been here since the first. So he could have arrived on the last day of July. That was a Thursday. It was the day that Rockland stayed away from the little nest on Calle las Artes all day long and part of the evening, and came back and asked for a loan of three thousand and made Bruce Bundy suspicious by not being sour about being turned down. So all of Rockland's troops had deserted him, and he had been tossed out of the trailer park, and he was trying to hustle a sizable piece of money anywhere he could find it. So maybe he spent a lot of time that same Thursday trying to establish contact with Minda McLeen. He would know where she was, but that house is a fortress, the Vitrier house. And neither girl would be very anxious to see Rockland for any reason, I'd assume. But let's say he did get in touch, or find out how he could get in touch later."

"You're recovering nicely," Meyer said.

"So Rockland had written off Bruce Bundy, at least as far as any willing donation is concerned. So he decides to leave with the things that look most valuable, going on the basis that the Bundys of this world seldom blow the whistle. They would rather write off the loss than make it police business. But Bundy was too cute. And when Rockland tried to jump him, Bundy was too rough. Rockland got black-belted all to hell. It probably made him pretty sick. But he had to get out of there on Saturday to meet Minda."

"What would he be most worried about?" Meyer asked.

"I guess he would realize that if Wally McLeen located his daughter, that would end any chance of selling the information and delivering the girl to him for a price."

"So we have a gap in the sequence. Better than twenty-four hours, and we have Bix and an American up on that mountain Sunday afternoon, parked and both out of the car and talking. Because it was Bundy's yellow car, we can assume it was Walter Rockland with Bix. He had to have a way to get down off the mountain. He could walk it after dark. But it would be full daylight before he could get down to the valley floor."

"Or somebody picked him up, by arrangement."

"He'd run out of people," Meyer said. "And if it was by arrangement, then there would have to be the assumption that he knew she would take off with the car and wouldn't make it all the way down. How could he be sure she wouldn't? What would the motive be?"

"Then there's the next gap until Tuesday morning, when he took the camper out of Bundy's shed."

Meyer shook his head. "It doesn't fit together. None of it. We just don't have enough of the missing pieces to even be able to guess how many other pieces are missing. Unless Jerome Nesta is willing to talk freely, we might as well go home. And maybe even if he does talk it won't be helpful."

154

Just then the Guadalajara sisters came clattering and squealing down upon us, laden with purchases, and there was much arrangement of girls and packages. They were still avid with the lust and fury of shopping, and they made expensive burlesques of total exhaustion, then dived into the bags and bundles to open the small ones for the reassurance of our admiration, and pluck open the corners of the big ones to show the pattern and texture of bright fabric.

And where is Lita? Ah, there was someone here in this city she had to call, an old couple who were friends of her mother, and she had been putting it off, so at last she called and they had asked her to come to have lunch with them, and it seemed as good a time as any, so she had phoned Enelio and informed him and had gone to meet the old couple. So Enelio would not join us either.

The sisters were both thirsty and famished, so as soon as a drink came they ordered lunch, and then went chattering on up to their little hotel suite to drop their purchases and freshen up.

They had made crackling inquisition of the waiter, and so we had ordered what they had ordered. It was very, very good indeed, and not at all heavy.

After lunch Margarita, the one with the best command of English, said, "Meyer, I wish to ask of you one great favor, a very selfish thing, a very dull thing for you. I am silly. You can say no, please."

"I say yes. Okay."

"Without knowing, even! You remember at the place coming into Mitla at the right side, how I saw the mos' lovely color shawl and cried out to all to look? There is *no* such color in the market here. I must have, Meyer. I must go and buy it in Mitla or it will be gone forever and never, never will I see another one."

"So we will all go to Mitla. Right, Travis? No problem, ladies."

"Please, wissout Elena," said Elena. She put the back of her fist in front of a gigantic yawn. "You three are going. I am sitting and then up above sleeping, I think."

155

"Okay," I said. "Wissout McGee too, if you don't mind."

They didn't mind. They took a cab up the hill to the hotel after I told Meyer to look for the Falcon keys on my bureau. We watched the people, few and slow-moving in the time of siesta.

"Asking one favor too? Okay?"

"Sure, Elena."

"Maybe one little swimming in the so beautiful pool as before we were?"

I agreed. She went up and came down quickly with a little blue airline bag. We strolled over to the cab row on the post-office street and took a cab up to the hotel. She changed first in our cottage named Alicia, and came out in a narrow bikini that was a froth of rows of crisp horizontal white ruffles, and by the time I got up to the pool she was swimming, wearing a swim cap covered with vivid plastic daisies. People were baking in the sun, and except for some children in the shallow end, we had the pool to ourselves. She was an unskilled and earnest swimmer, rolling and thrashing too much, expending too much effort and trying to hold her head too high. I told her a few things that would help, and swam beside her. She learned quickly and was very pleased with herself and kept at it until she was winded and gasping. We climbed out and she pulled the cap off and said, "Now enough I think. Okay?"

We walked back down to Alicia, among the cottages below and beyond the pool, and I unlocked the door for her and sat on the porch while she went in to change. I heard the clatter as she closed the blinds.

"Tuh . . . rrrravis? *Por favor, ayudarme*? Thees dombo theeng is es-stock."

So if something is es-stock, one must go in and un-es-stock it for the lady. She was between beds and bath, back toward me, still in bikini, and she looked over her shoulder and indicated the snap or fastening or whatever at the back of the bikini top was es-stock.

So I went to her. She pulled her long dark hair forward

156

and stood with head bowed. She held the bikini top against her breasts with her hands. There were two snaps hidden by ruffles. I put a thumbnail under one and it popped. I put a thumbnail under the other and it popped and the two straps fell, dangling down the side of her rib cage. She stood without moving. It was a lithe and lovely back. Droplets of water stood on her back and shoulders. Crease down the soft brown back. Pale down, paler than her skin, heaviest near the vertical furrow. The bikini bottom came around her just a little above the widest part of her hips, leaving bare that lovely duplicated tender concavity of the girl-waist, leaving bare two dimples in the sun-honeyed brown, half a handspan apart, below the base of her spine.

So the response is an acceptance, a dedication, a tenderness expressed by very slowly, very precisely, very carefully placing the male hands upon the slenderest part of the waist, thumbs resting against the back, aimed upward, parallel to the center division of the back, edges of the hands resting against that soft shelf where the hips begin to bloom. She shivered at the touch, then lifted her head and leaned back against me. I bent and kissed the top of her shoulder, close to her throat, felt the dampness of some tendrils of hair which the swim cap had not completely protected. She was breathing very steadily, audibly, deeply, and her eyes were heavy and almost closed when I turned her around and kissed her on the mouth.

"But . . . they might come back here," I said.

She gave a little shake of her head and spoke through soft blurred lips. "No, no. She will taking Meyer to the Marqués to see dresses she bought. She trying them on for him, no hurry. Ah, she bought one hell of a lot of dresses, that sister mine."

So you go over and bolt the door, and the room is golden with the sun through the tiny cracks of the closed slats. She wants to be looked at, yet is at the same time shy. She is avid and timorous. She is experienced to a small degree, yet unsure. There is a musky-sweet, pungent scent of herself in her heat, distinctively her own. She has a secret inward smile when the pleasure is good for her. She has a long strong belly and rubbery-powerful hips and thighs, yet there are no feats of astonishing muscle control, no researched ancient trickeries, and that is a sweet and simple relief. Approaching climax her body heats and her breasts swell and her mouth sags. She deepens her strong and heavy beat and her eyes roll wild in the dim room, as if in panic, and she rolls her head from side to side and has the look of listening, and of being afraid of what is rolling up out of the depths of her, and then she is into all of it, making a very small and very sweet whimpering, and holding tight, like a child on a high scary place.

Siesta is sweet when the light is gold, and when the vivid young face on the pillow looks into yours, beside her, inches away, and smiles the woman-smile older than time, her exhalations warm against your mouth, as with slow fingers she traces your brows, lips, and the shape of cheek and jaw. There is nothing more es-stock. It has all been unfastened, all turned loose, with a guile that was so sweetly planned it could not be denied, even had there been any thought of denying it. Elena, you are the Mexican afternoons forever.

FOURTEEN

At eleven on Wednesday morning Enelio Fuentes brought Jerome Nesta to our cottage at the Hotel Victoria. Nesta acted sullen, uncommunicative. He wore the same clothes, but otherwise I would not have recognized him.

Enelio said, "They gave him a choice with the big bushy beard. Take it off himself, or they'd strap him down and take it off with a dull knife. The haircut was done by a jailor with no talent, eh?"

"Have your laughs," Nesta mumbled. The area where the beard had been was blue-white and nicked in a half dozen places. His scalp shone pale through a half inch of black bristle. Without the beard he looked older. I remembered he was twenty-six. He looked thirty. There were deep lines bracketing his mouth. Also, without the beard he looked almost frail. His hands were big and heavily calloused from the work with the mallet.

"One thing they forgot," Enelio said. "Out in the open if you stay upwind from him, it's not bad. In the car you keep the window open and stay close to it, very important. In this room, this size, he is impossible. It cannot be endured."

"Screw yourself," Nesta muttered, eyes downcast.

I went into the dressing-room closet and picked some tan slacks I'd never liked much, and the white sports shirt that had been, despite all instructions, starched, and some laundered jockey shorts and socks which had seen dutiful valiant service. I handed him the bundle and said, "Go in and scrub."

"Screw yourself," he said again.

"Enelio," I said, "can you give this thing back to the law, or don't they want him either?"

"As a favor to me, they'll give him his same cell back."

"Then take him along. Thanks for your trouble. I don't need to talk to him. Not right now. Not this way. When they fly him into Miami, I'll have him picked up there."

"For what?" Nesta asked.

"We'll think of something," I said.

"How about air pollution?" Meyer asked.

"Dade County loans able-bodied prisoners to Collier County for road work," I said. "Sheriff Doug Hendry's people give a short course in manners and personal hygiene."

Nesta looked at me, then at Enelio. It was a quick, flickering glance of appraisal. Without the beard he had the con look, the loser look. He had been there before, and knew he would be back there again, and it didn't make too much difference whether it was going to be a valid rap. He had the cronkey look, that flavor of upcoming trouble that alerts any cop anywhere. I don't know what it is. It is a combination of facial expression, posture, gesture—and the experience of the cop who sees the stranger and sees that indefinable thing he has seen so many times before. The animal behavior experts report that something similar exists in those wild animals who have some form of community culture. Certain individuals will be run off by the others, will be killed, or will be left to roam alone.

He picked the clean clothing off the floor and went into the bathroom and slammed the door.

Enelio said, "The shock yesterday opened him up. He talked pretty good, remember? So now he closed the doors and locked them. I don't know if he'll talk to you. I know damn well he won't talk if I'm here. The chemistry is not good. I better go. You know, one funny thing. You types from the Estados Unidos, too many talk about dirty Mex-

160

icans, right? Okay. Those little huts over there on that hill. Poor people. Carry water a hell of a distance. And take a bath every day, and the women wash that long hair every day. Clean, clean, clean. So we talk about dirty heepies. There is an old dirty heepie in there, showering. But I have had the pleasure of knowing some of your little heepie crumpets, and they have been, my friend, deliciously fresh and sweet and clean. Clean and shining as the beards on some of their boyfriends. So, big conclusion. There are dirty Mexicans and dirty heepies. But it is not a characteristic, hey?"

"Thanks for getting him out."

"Use your judgment. If there's a chance he'll make trouble, we better stick him back inside fast. He looks to me as if he wants to take off."

"The bathroom window has bars on it too."

"I noticed. If you decide he's trouble, take him in yourself and give him to Sergeant Martinez, okay?"

We thanked him and he left. Room service, as a concession to the standard issue American tourist, has hamburgers with everything all day long. I phoned up for two for Nesta, and a pot of coffee. He showered for a long time. At last he came out. My stuff was big for him, except around the waist. He had to turn the bottoms of the slacks up. He had wadded his old clothes up. Meyer told him to stuff them into the wastebasket and put the wastebasket out on the porch. Nesta looked guarded and self-conscious. Before he had come out, anticipating problems, I had told Meyer we had better go into the good-guy bad-guy routine if he seemed too uncooperative.

"Sit down, Jerry," I said. "I want you to start at the beginning. How did the five of you get together originally and decide to come to Mexico?"

"Maybe we answered an ad."

I glanced at Meyer. We'd have to try the routine. The hotel waiter arrived with the tray, and that gave me my opening.

"Did you order this stuff, Meyer? For him?"

"When you walked out with Enelio. Yes."

"Out of the goodness of your heart? Your motherly instinct? You want gratitude from this dreary bastard?"

"I don't imagine he got much to eat in jail, Travis."

"That's one part of the hotel bill we don't split down the middle. That little gesture is all yours."

Nesta took a small, tentative bite, and then wolfed the two hamburgers down. He was taking a gulp of the coffee when I asked him the same question again.

"Maybe we had this real great travel agent," Nesta said.

I waited until he set the cup down, then took a long reach and backhanded him across the chops. It was quick and substantial. It rocked his head and emptied his eyes.

Meyer jumped up and yelled at me. "What are you trying to do? You've got no right to do that! Give him a little time. He'll explain it all."

"I know he'll explain it all. Because somewhere along the line the message is going to get through to him. He's going to talk it all out or I am going to keep bending him until something breaks. And he is going to tell it straight because he doesn't know how many ways I have to check it all out. I know this slob beat a possession indictment three years ago. I know he was inside the Bowie house at Cricket Bayou on several occasions. I know they all crossed in on the tenth, from Brownsville into Matamoros, and I know exactly when the Bowie girl got the money in Culiacán, and exactly how much. And I know a lot of other things that better match with what he says, and if they don't match, you'd better take a long walk, Meyer, because there are some things you don't like to watch. They upset your stomach."

"That's no way to talk to him!" Meyer said.

"Look at him! Look at the expression. It's the only way to talk to this pot head."

"I think you better take the walk, McGee," Meyer said.

"I'll be right on the porch, because you're going to need me, my friend."

I slammed the door. I sat in one of the porch chairs and put my heels up on the brick railing. Meyer would take it as far as he could, and then it would be my turn, and

162

between the two of us we had a chance of whipsawing him.

From the porch I could hear the tone of their voices without being able to hear the words. I heard Meyer mostly, and then I began to hear more and more of Nesta's voice. It was the Meyer magic at work. I looked through the window. Nesta sat on the end of Meyer's bed, leaning over on one elbow. Meyer had turned the desk chair around and he sat facing Nesta.

They say that only a small portion of personal communication is verbal, and that the rest of it is posture, expression, gesture, those physical aspects of man which antedate his ability to speak. Meyer constructs somehow a small safe world, a place where anything can be said, anything can be understood, and all can be forgiven. We are all, every one, condemned to believe that if we could ever make another human understand everything that went into any act, we could be forgiven. The act of understanding bestows importance and meaning, encouraging confession.

After a half hour I knew he was going to get all of it, and so I went for the walk. I went up to the hotel and picked up a cold beer at the bar, which had just opened, and carried it out onto the porch overlooking all the cottages and the summer city beyond. The scent of flowers was heavy. Gardeners were working on the green lawns. Sprinkler heads were clicking their big slow circles, and birds hopped and preened in the falling mist. A lithe lass, deeply sunbrowned and wearing a vivid orange bikini, stood alone on the diving tower, using the railing to practice the standard exercises of ballet. She was moist with her efforts, smooth skin gleaming in the sun. Her hair was tucked into a plastic swim cap clustered with plastic daisies.

The cold dark beer stopped halfway to my lips, and even before I could make the mental association—yes, that is the kind of swim cap Elena wore yesterday—there was such a violent surge of desire for the girl from Guadalajara that it startled me. Becky diminished need. Elena compounded it. Elena had, with a splendid earthiness spiced with innocent wonder, so emphatically superimposed herself on the memories of Becky, I would have to carry those memories into a bright light to see who the hell they were about. After those dedicated decades striving to become the very best, thinking she had attained it, it would have crushed her to find out a sweet Latin amateur was, in the light of memory, by far the better of the two, more stirring, more fulfilling, and far more sensuous.

So make a note, McGee. There are some things which practice does not enhance. Thunderstorms never practice. Surf does not take graduate lessons in hydraulics. Deer and rabbits do not measure how high they have jumped and go back and try again. Violinists must work at it and study. And ballerinas. And goalies and shortstops and wingbacks and acrobats. But that business of acquiring expertise in screwing turns it into something it wasn't meant to be.

Beer finished, I went back to the cottage to see how Meyer was doing. I was amused at Meyer and at myself. We were very formal with each other today. Remote, thoughtful, and formal. I had bought Elena a late dinner the night before at the hotel and sent her home in a cab—at her insistence on not being a nuisance. Meyer had arrived as I was getting ready for bed. Yes, he had eaten in town. Not bad, actually. Car had run fine. Margarita had found the shawl. Sleep well. Good night.

I looked through the window. Nesta had a hand over his eyes. Meyer waved me away.

Back up the hill. Drifted around. Watched the happy vacationers at play. Kept out of the line of people taking happy pictures of each other. Admired shrubbery clipped into the shapes of animals. Elephant. Ostrich. Donkey. Tried to remember the name for that particular art form. Couldn't.

Sat on a stone bench and tried to bring back some specific memory of Bix Bowie the day Meyer brought her aboard the *Flush*. Couldn't. Brain apparently failing along with everything else. Premature instant senility. But Meyer had the vivid memories of the girl. Vivid and now painful. And some more painful images to put on top of the heap.

Finally went back. Meyer was on the porch, sitting in a kind of slack, dumpy solemnity. I looked through the window. Nesta was sprawled on Meyer's bed, with a blanket over him.

I sat down beside Meyer. "So?"

"I feel sick."

"That bad?"

"Bad. Yes. And . . . pointless. Wasteful."

"Did you get all of it?"

"I don't see how there could be anything more. He's exhausted, physically and emotionally. And he's not alone."

"How did the group get together?"

"Bix had some friends at the University of Miami, kids she went to public school with in Miami. After her mother died, she looked them up. She met Carl Sessions at a party. They started going around together. Carl knew Jerry Nesta. Jerry was Carl's connection for marijuana. Jerry was living with Minda McLeen. And he also made deliveries out to the Beach, to Walter Rockland, as a go-between. He and Rockland talked about some way to make a big score someday. The four of them, Carl, Bix, Jerry and Minda began running around together. Rockland found out Bix had some money from her mother's will. Rockland talked Nesta into helping him promote the Mexico trip. Sessions had already turned Bix on to pot, and she obviously took to it all too well, as some will. Rockland claimed to have a good contact in Mexico where they could buy pure heroin at Mexican wholesale prices. The idea was to get Bix down there, talk her into financing it, smuggle it across the line and peddle it to a wholesaler in Los Angeles. So Nesta helped Rocko develop some enthusiasm among the other three to take a Mexican vacation. Bix was willing to buy the camper and the supplies and pay expenses. She did not seem to care about the money one way or another, or really care much whether she went or stayed. So when Rocko was fired, they moved the timetable up and got ready and left, and there was absolutely nothing Harl Bowie could do about stopping her."

"But she didn't know the real reason."

"Not until later. And by then I guess you could say it was too late for her to do anything about it. You see, Rockland was the only one of the five who was not a user of anything at all. In fact, not even liquor except very rarely and then too much. No cigarettes. A physical culture type. But he had a couple of mimeographed sheets he'd paid five dollars for in Miami. They give the trade and generic name of a list of pharmaceuticals available in the states on prescription only, but available over the counter in Mexico. Opposite each was the Spanish name and the phonetic pronunciation. They bought good strong pot the minute they were over the border, and at Monterrey they loaded up with items off the list. Rockland was in charge, ostensibly to keep people from taking too much when they were too stoned to know what they were taking. He kept the drugs locked in the tool compartment of the truck, but the pot was available at any time. Rocko set a slow pace across Mexico. It was the cold season. He and Nesta shared the driving. When they found a good place to camp, they would stay two or three days. They went from Monterrey to Torreón to Durango to Mazatlán. Nesta doesn't know how long it took. He said it could have been a year or a week. He said it was all pretty blurred. Rockland would dole them out a mixed bag of opiates and stimulants, barbiturates and mescaline, and he said you didn't know what kind of a high you were going into until you were there, and some of them were bad."

"It's a wonder he didn't kill somebody."

"I know. In the beginning Bix was paired off with Carl Sessions, and Minda McLeen with Jerry Nesta. Those relationships fragmented. It didn't turn into some kind of orgy, even though repeating what he told me makes it sound that way. Apparently the first deviation was when

Rocko made love to Bix. Carl was angry and upset about it at first, but he got over it when Minda slept with him because she felt sorry for him. Then Jerry Nesta fought with Minda, and then got even with her by sleeping with Bix. Except for the tension in the beginning, it seemed to all iron out into a kind of casual and, except for Rocko, infrequent thing. Nesta told me that Bix was totally placid and submissive. It didn't matter to her which of the three had her. She seemed to accept and endure, with no evidence of either pleasure or displeasure. Once when Carl was still reasonably lucid Nesta asked him if Bix had ever been passionate with him, and Carl said no. By then Minda was taking care of Bix. Unless prodded and helped she wouldn't wash, brush her teeth, blow her nose, change her clothing. It was a process of disintegration for all of them. Except Rocko. Each was hooked in his or her own way. Rocko was the ground control. Sessions apparently became ever more hopelessly addicted to methadone, moving in a fumbling, stumbling, hazy dream, losing all sexual drive. Nesta was on pot and mescaline. Minda McLeen was on stimulants, amphetamine and dexedrine compounds, getting ever more shaky and thin and nervous, and becoming ever more physically dependent on Rockland. Do you see the pattern, Travis?"

"In the kingdom of the blind, the one-eyed man is king. And a five way split is a lot of ways to split it."

"But Nesta apparently didn't suspect. As they neared Culiacán, Rocko took Bix's indispensible pot away from her, and so she behaved exactly as directed, sent for the money, cashed the draft, turned the money over to Rocko, and was rewarded with a half-dozen joints and swiftly sucked her way back into her waking dream. Rockland's contact had been reliable. They got pure heroin in full quantity. Rocko, working alone, transferred it into small sacks made of thick transparent plastic tied with nylon cord, and took an inside panel off the camper and stowed it in the shallow space between the inside and outside skin. He was nervous on the way up to Nogales. Sessions got on his nerves, playing the same chords over and over and over on the guitar, until one evening Rocko took the tin snips out of the tool box and cut the strings off. But Sessions kept playing as if nothing had happened. All they could hear were his fingernails on the frets and the box. Ten miles out of Nogales, Rocko decided that it had all been too easy. He decided to make a dry run. So he tied all the little bags up in a raincoat and buried it in the dirt near a flowering bush. He took Bix with him to the border, taking her off pot for a full day first. He left the three others with the supply of pills and pot in a cheap motel, with orders to wait until they crossed back in. They came back four days later. He had new papers on the truck and camper, and new tourist cards for himself and Bix. But Rocko was savagely angry. The sellers had apparently tipped the customs people. The total search took fifteen hours, and they had to reassemble the truck and camper when it was over. The border people knew the names of the five of them, said they knew they had made a large buy, and said that no matter how they tried to bring it back across, they would be nailed, all together, or one at a time."

"Very thorough."

"They went back down Route Fifteen and recovered the heroin. Rocko concealed it in the camper. They made camp well off the road by a dry stream bed another ten or twenty miles down the road. Rocko was in a foul mood. Minda, humming and burning with energy, was doing the cooking, washing, laundry, mending, housekeeping, and taking care of Bix, her hair and her person. During the second day at that place, she began complaining to Rocko that they were nearly out of cooking gas, that the gauge was way down. When would he get it filled? She was sick of having to make fires with sticks when they were out of gas. He paid no attention. And then she said that at least the border people hadn't let the gas out of the tank, and she should be grateful for that much. He jumped up and ran and examined the tank. The fill valve and the outlet valve were part of the brass assembly that was fastened onto the top of the tank. They drove south and at Hermosillo he bought two small pipe wrenches and got the whole assembly off. The orifice was just large enough so that by rolling the plastic bags between his palms he could make them small enough to drop into the tank. He put one in the tank and had it refilled at Hermosillo. Three days later he let the gas escape and, with some difficulty apparently, got the bag out. It looked and tasted fresh and unharmed, so he loaded the bags into the tank and got it filled again. Nesta thought he would start for the border right away. But Rocko was unexpectedly relaxed and unhurried. There was a pretty good piece of Bix's money left. They might as well see the country. He became very charming."

"Life of the party."

"Sure. He even had a special little treat for Carl Sessions. On the way south in Ciudad Obregon he picked up a hypo and some distilled water, some cotton swabs and some alcohol, and he fixed his good friend Sessions a nice little pop and injected it under the skin on the underside of his forearm. Sessions got very sick from it. But Rocko kept helping him out until finally Carl could inject himself and feel very good. Then when he had worked up to injecting it directly into the blood stream and felt very, very good, Rocko talked him into sharing his new talent with Bix."

"I know why you said you feel sick."

"That Walter Rockland is a real charmer. All heart. So our little caravan came wandering through the mountains on down here to Oaxaca. And the flavor changed, or, I might say, the alignment. Minda got sick. Nesta was appointed by Rocko to look after Bix. When he refused, Rocko beat the hell out of him. He said he got to sort of like it after a while, scrubbing her and washing her hair. But he'd lost any physical desire for her. She and Carl Sessions had gone off into some country of their own, nodding and popping. Minda, scared by being sick, was stubbornly taking herself off the stimulants. I suppose as they are habituating rather than addicting, a person with enough will could do it. And she apparently, as if compensating, became ever more infatuated with Rocko in a purely physical way. After they were here a while, Rocko started to cut off the supply to Carl and Bix. He would let them get sick before he would dole out a very small amount. One day Nesta took Bix off somewhere on some errand. He had wanted to get out of Rocko's way because Rocko was on one of his rare drunks, when he was inclined to get violent and nasty. When he came back, Carl wasn't there. Rocko was asleep, snoring loudly. Minda was in some kind of shock. For a long time Nesta couldn't find out what happened. Then he learned that Carl had come pleading and begging to Rocko. Rocko, in Minda's presence, had asked Carl if he would do anything in the world for a fix. Carl said he would. And after he had stripped down, as Rocko asked, Rocko boosted him up into the double bed over the cab and climbed up in there with him, and Minda went running out. She heard Carl crying. That apparently finished it for Minda. A few days later she left and took Bix with her. Nesta said Rocko seemed perfectly content to have them gone for good, all three of them. Nesta stayed on. But he began to have the feeling that Rocko was watching him and planning how to kill him. It could have been an induced paranoid hallucination. But he took off, by then in very bad shape, and gradually came out of it in Mitla, with the woman Luz taking care of him just the way he had taken care of Bix."

"So now we know," I said, "why Rocko reacted the way he did to having somebody pry that little door open and take that tank of gas. He knew it had to be taken by somebody who knew what was hidden in it. The first guess would be Sessions. So he would go looking for him."

Meyer nodded. "Let's say he didn't find him. Sessions was found dead on the morning of the seventh. He could have stolen it, emptied it, hidden the stuff away, and died of an overdose."

"Or once he found him, maybe he was satisfied Carl knew nothing about it. And it would be fair to assume

170

Rocko had enough left on hand to stick much too much into Sessions."

Meyer thought that over. Then he shook his head. "I can't buy that, Travis. I can't buy the idea that Rocko would kill anybody. Not then. Not at that time. Maybe now. Maybe he has been coming closer and closer. I think he gave it a lot of thought after he discovered a hiding place the border search had overlooked on the dry run. He knew that if he tried to cross with the whole group, five minutes of interrogation would crack any one of the other four, and the five of them would be busted. So they camped out, in wild areas. He knew that alone he could make it. Maybe he had plans of marketing it at ten times his cost, hiding the cash in the same place, crossing back with it, and running another batch over again, for the big final score. I think he must have thought of the obvious way out. Chunk them on the head and bury them out in the wastelands. It's so completely efficient, he *had* to think about it. And if he didn't do it, it is because he couldn't bring himself to do it."

"Because he is such a nice guy."

"Because he decided they would destroy themselves if he nudged them in the right direction. And check his track record so far. Carl and Bix are gone. We don't know about Minda McLeen. We know he's batting five hundred. It could be seven fifty."

"So who stole the little gas tank, Meyer?"

"You force me to guess? I would say that Carl Sessions talked about the Americano with a fortune in junk in the bottled gas tank, and I would guess that his addiction would put him into contact with some very rough local types, and it would be natural for them to check it out. And easy enough. So then Rocko would be compelled to pick up another stake, so he could go make another buy, hide it in another tank, and take it across alone. So he went cruising, and he let Bruce Bundy pick him up, but it didn't work out the way he planned it. When he saw he wasn't going to con any cash out of Bundy, he went cruising again, and came up with Minda's father, Wally

171

McLeen. So he would have heard by then that Bix and Minda were guests of Eva Vitrier."

We were both silent, trying to appraise the possibilities. I said, "Remember? The girls quarreled. Minda left for Mexico City. So Rocko couldn't contact her. Assume that when he took the Bundy car, he went right to the Vitrier place in La Colonia. And the next thing we know, it's Sunday afternoon and he and Bix and the yellow car are way the hell up in those mountains."

"It would be nice to talk to Eva Vitrier," Meyer said.

"It would indeed. A total recluse, using a hell of a lot of money to buy total privacy, to build big walls. And she's gone. Try and find out where."

"Somebody could get into her place and look around."

"Like me?"

"Well, any large, curious, agile fellow, let's say."

"And I get slapped into a cell out in that Zimatlán jail."

Meyer shrugged. "I'll be there every visitors' day. Speaking of jail, what about our friend in there?"

"You're in the best position to decide."

"I just don't know. He seems docile. I might take the risk if I had to take the blame, too. But if I make a bad guess, then Enelio is in trouble. It's just a hunch, my friend. I sense a kind of animal wildness, a potential for unpredictability. Talking to him, even when he wept, was like sitting in a zoo. I didn't want to make any sudden motions. I would have felt better with bars between us."

"So, I go with your instinct, Meyer. Your average is too good. We can get in touch with Enelio and find out if he wants us to take the package back to the store."

We got up. Meyer went through the door first. The blanket was thrown back. The bathroom door was closed. I could hear water running. No reason at all why I shouldn't accept that obvious conclusion, that Nesta had gotten up and gone into the bathroom. I did accept it, and in a sudden surge of adrenalin, rejected it a microsecond later, rejected it as I was in motion, going through the doorway. To reverse motion meant vulnerable stasis for

172

too long an instant, so I dived forward, and just as my palms hit Meyer in the middle of the back, knocking him onto and over the nearest double bed, something chunked very solidly and painfully into the meat of my back, just under the right shoulder blade. I used the leverage of Meyer's solidity to thrust myself to the right, and the momentum took me across the tile floor, scrabbling on all fours for balance, and simultaneously trying to turn so I would be facing the doorway when I came back up. I made it and saw Nesta going by the windows. He was out on the porch and moving fast.

I caught him on the road, about seventy yards up the hill. He was in no shape for uphill running. He turned, gasping and gagging, and swung some kind of dark club at my head so off balance I had time to step back and let it go by. It carried him halfway around. So, in that tiny interval of time when he was almost motionless, trying to reverse direction, I hit him a very nice right hand shot right on the point of the shoulder. It is that ancient and effective torture of schoolyards and playgrounds. The nerves run over the bone of the arm socket right at that point. He dropped the weapon. Something inside a sock. It made a metallic thud. His arm hung slack, dead and useless and he cupped his shoulder in his big left hand and looked at me with the twisted face of a child fighting tears, chest heaving from the effort of running.

"Naughty, naughty!" I said and reached out quickly, caught the end of his nose between thumb and the bent knuckle of the forefinger, and gave a long hard pull downhill, stepping aside and releasing him. He ran a half dozen jolting steps and stopped, his back toward me. I picked up the improvised weapon and gave him a gentle push. It got him in motion and he walked the rest of the way to the cottage, up onto the porch, and into the room, not looking at Meyer as he passed him. Meyer stood outside the door, fingers laced across the nape of his neck, grimacing as he turned his big head from side to side.

"Whiplash, maybe," he said.

"Officer, he stopped dead right in front of me." I spread

the opening of the dark sock which belonged to Meyer and peered down into it and said, "Tsk tsk tsk! Little present for you."

He took it, reached down into it, and pulled out his sturdy little travel alarm. Sturdy no longer. The case had burst open and there were a lot of little loose parts down in the toe of the sock.

He dumped them out on the metal top of the porch table, quite sadly. "McGee, I have to assume you reacted first. It will never cease to make me feel insecure, the way you do that. What alerted you, dammit?"

"I haven't any idea. Something subliminal. Something smelled or heard or seen, on an unconscious level."

"And if I were a more primitive organism, I could perform such feats also?"

"Flattery won't help."

We went in. Nesta sat on the foot of Meyer's bed. His right arm was cradled in his lap and he was looking down at it, slowly flexing the fingers.

"They'll be interested in knowing you like to pop people on the skull," I said to him.

He did not raise his eyes. "The law likes to get cases off the books. It takes the heat off them. I thought I better get going before I got elected," he said.

"You're going back inside."

"So?" he said in a toneless voice.

"I can tell them about your little try here, or I can keep it between us."

It brought a quick and wary glance before the eyes dropped again. "What'll it take?" he asked.

"Something important that you maybe left out of your confession hour with Meyer. We think there's a good chance Rockland could have set Bix up to kill herself trying to drive down the mountain alone at dusk."

"I didn't even know about that until just the other day, when Mike and Della told me about it. I didn't even know she was dead."

"How did you feel when you heard it?"

"I didn't feel much of anything. A long time ago she

was something else. That was one pretty girl and that was one hell of a body. I was willing to trade off Minda for the chance to start balling her. But it was like nothing. Like one of those plastic things in a store window. All you had to do was lead her into the bushes or take her into the camper and she'd lay down on her back. Then a long time later when she'd lost a lot of her looks, and nobody was hacking her any more, I sort of got to like taking care of her. I don't know why. Making her look a little better, making her eat, making her walk around. But she was gone anyway. She was dead before she was dead. Even pot took her too far out of her tree. When Carl turned her on with horse it was too late to make any difference one way or another. What did I feel? Nothing, I guess. Nothing at all."

"Would Rockland want her dead?"

"Why would he? She didn't know who the hell she was or where she was or who we were. Her memory was shot. The way she was just . . . around, like a lump, used to get on Rocko's nerves. He used to try to get some kind of rise out of her. One time . . . I don't know where it was, I think maybe someplace south of Puebla, outside one of those little towns, some Mexicans came around in the evening, mean-looking bastards in those white pajama suits and straw hats, one with a shiny new rifle, and the others with machetes, a dozen I guess. They had eyes for Bix. So Rocko started laughing and grabbed her by the wrist and grabbed a blanket and took her over into the cornfield and peddled her ass for two pesos a trick, and came back with her and told me the banker's daughter had earned herself thirty-two pesos. He gave me the money and told me to buy her some penicillin in the next town. Why would he kill her? She was less than nothing. Good Christ, by then she looked forty years old."

"When you left you were giving up your share of the Los Angeles loot?"

"I didn't even think about it, man. I was hallucinating bad. I could shut my eyes and feel my hands melting and dripping off my wrists. Rats were running around under my clothes, eating me. Hairy red spiders as big as airdales kept jumping out and jumping back in any direction I tried to walk. And Rocko had sicked them on me and he was making my hands melt, and I just had to get the hell out of there. And I did. I wish I could help you with something. But I don't know anything I didn't already tell."

"What would you have done if you'd nailed me with that clock when I came in the door?"

"Hit him next. Take your money and your car keys and get onto one ninety and head southwest, because they'd expect me to head for Mexico City. My best bet would be to try to get to Vera Cruz and stow away aboard some crock heading across the Gulf."

"And if you hit us hard enough to kill?"

"I start running. It looks like I killed the others, so what difference would it make?"

"It might make a little difference to you," Meyer said softly.

"To me? Well . . . yes. A little difference, I guess. But not a hell of a lot."

I sat on the bed and phoned Enelio. I said, "We don't want to take any chances with this one. He got cute, and he'll get cute again."

Enelio said that Chief Alberto Tielma of the Zimatlán jail would give me a nice official receipt for him. He asked me if we got anything out of Nesta, and I said we got a history of the little Mexican hayride those five took that would gag a weasel, but nothing that helped with the primary problem of how come the girl drove off the mountain.

"So," he said, "when something pozzles me, I find out anything I can find out, and I still see no reason under God for anybody to drive a camper going like hell down into that lousy country down there, except somebody wants to get rid of a camper, which is a large object. If, God forbid, I wanted to get rid of a large object on wheels, I mean without selling it, which is always possible,

176

no matter what kind of papers you have on it, maybe I would take it down that way."

"So you'd consider going on another expedition with Meyer and McGee?"

"My trouble is I am impulsive. Also I never make the same mistake once. I think. . . . Yes, if it's okay with you, I pick you up maybe at the Marqués tomorrow afternoon?"

It was agreed. We toted Nesta back to jail. He had the contrived indifference of the born loser. He had not a word to say all the way.

FIFTEEN

Meyer and I had just finished a late Wednesday lunch on the veranda of the Marqués del Valle when Enelio Fuentes arrived, by prearrangement, in the jeep. As we went out the Mitla road, Meyer and I, taking turns yelling against the wind, filled Enelio in on the little talk with Nesta, and the subsequent problem of talking him out of leaving.

I said that after due deliberation, and weighing of all factors, I had told the police chief, with gestures, about Nesta's antisocial behavior. I had finked on him.

"Hey, how can an animal like that one," Enelio roared, "carve that strong glorious wooden head? How is it possible?"

"All great artists lead placid, humble, gentle lives," Meyer hollered. "They are all celibates and never drunk or violent. You know. Like your own Diego Rivera was."

Grinning, Enelio took his right hand off the wheel and made that unique and expressive Mexican gesture of consternation, like trying to shake water from the fingertips.

The road he was looking for began about twenty miles beyond Mitla. It was a dirt road that, about four miles from the main road went through a village, and then continued on, dropping perhaps a thousand feet before reaching dry stony flats. Sometimes he could get up to twenty miles an hour before braking, putting it in low, and lurching through rain gulleys and across a moonscape of potholes. Then the road became straighter and smoother, and he was able to make good time. A long high dust plume was kicked up behind us in the windless hot afternoon.

He slowed and stopped and we got out. He took binoculars out of a case and looked west. He said, "Yes, the smaller road out of Ocotlán runs down through those ridges. When I was small we hunted rabbits over there. But not over here. This is the burned land. Sand, rock, cactus. Only by the dry rivers are trees. See. Deep roots. They drink deep only after the rains. You know, it is maybe a little bit too much, those Texas schoolteachers just being there at the right time and looking way over here and just happening to see what she thinks was the camper, and he thinks was not."

"But the dust would draw your attention," Meyer said.

"And this," I explained, "is the kind of coincidence—if she _did_ see it—that is not a coincidence at all. Because the world is jammed with people, and if you talk to enough of them, you usually find that the unseen things were seen by someone. And if they are a little out of the ordinary, like the vehicle she saw going too fast, they stick to the edge of memory. Had it been going slower, she would never have examined it so carefully through the glasses, and she would have forgotten it by the next day. She claimed she saw blue, and saw glintings that could have been the aluminum camper body. But it is a hell of a way over there."

"One hell of a way indeed. And the road goes nowhere," said Enelio. "So what went down it had to come back, or still be somewhat ahead. And the wind blows the sand and dust so there are no tracks."

The road dwindled away to nothing in about six more miles. Enelio told us to hang on. He turned sharply right and soon I realized what he was going to do. He made a big circle around the rocky landscape. It had to be an irregular circle due to the contour. A couple of times he had to back and shorten the diameter of the circle.

When we were two thirds of the way around I tapped Enelio on the shoulder and pointed ahead and to our left,

179

inside the arc of the circle. He drove over and stopped and we got out again. It was a clear and distinct tire track in the lee of an outcropping of red-brown rock. It had run through some kind of crumbled clay, and though some sand had blown into it, it was unmistakable.

Enelio sat on his heels and crumbled the claylike substance between his fingers. *"Animalitos.* Damn, we call them *hormigas.* Some are red. They bite. They make little hills."

"Ants?"

"Yes! The tire went through the middle of this little one and along the edge of this big one. They brought up the dirt from underneath the sand, and it is moist almost."

He stood up and shaded his eyes. "Back there is the last of the road. So draw a line from there to these tracks . . ." We turned and looked, and Meyer suggested we fan out a little and walk it, looking for any clue, not taking any route a vehicle could not take.

After a hundred yards my route ended in impossibility. I backtracked and cut over to the other side, beyond Meyer. Then I came to a place where the earth dropped away. It was a deep meandering crack, perhaps twenty feet across and fifty feet deep, with round boulders and brush at the bottom of it. Enelio shouted. We hurried along the brink to where he stood. He was at the edge of a semicircular bite looking down at where the landslide had choked the bottom of the dry wash. There was an uncommon amount of loose brush on top of the barrier.

Enelio widened his nostrils and sniffed the breeze. He crossed himself and said, "Death." I caught it then, too—the sweet, rotten, sticky smell of decaying meat.

We stumbled and slid down the slant of sandy soil. We pulled the brush away, exposing the upper half of the rear of the camper. It was nose down into the stones, the landslide drifted high around it. The smell was sickeningly strong.

"The McLeen girl?" Meyer asked in church tones.

"Somebody our boy Rocko took a dislike to," I said.

"You get the dirt off the door while I go get something

180

I know about," Enelio said. He went plunging up the loose slope and disappeared. I started digging the door out with my cupped palms, and with Meyer helping me. We heard the sound of the jeep overhead. It stopped. After a few minutes Enelio came sliding back down. He had a thin piece of rag tied around his head so that it came across his upper lip. He had another piece for each of us. The center portion that came across the lip was damp with raw gasoline.

"One time when we had to go into the mountains after bodies from a plane crash, one of the medical people taught me this thing. Gasoline numbs the smelling. It overpowers everything. There was one trouble. For nearly a year afterward, each time I would smell gasoline, I would start gagging. Also it makes a burn on the lip. But it is better than the only other choice, eh?"

The camper body was out of line and the door was jammed. But it was on such a steep angle I could stand on the aluminum beside the door and bend over and take hold of the handle. I yanked it open and let it fall back. There was enough reflected sunlight so that we could see quite clearly into the dark interior. Enelio grunted, spun, jumped down and trotted twenty feet along the bottom of the wash, then bent over and vomited explosively.

"You can move away too," I told Meyer. "I want to make sure."

"I should help you."

"Get going."

"Thanks, Travis."

I took a deep breath and clambered down into the camper. He had been wired up with considerable loving care. Extension cord wire. Spread eagled, on his back on the narrow floor, head down, feet up toward the doorway. Wire snugly knotted to each wrist and ankle and angling off to whatever was sturdy enough and handy enough. Dead mouth crammed with something and taped in place. Bulky roll of the sleeping bag under his back, to keep him arched. I tried not to look too closely at him. I found his trousers against the bulkhead up front. The wallet was in

181

the hip pocket. I turned the identification toward the bright light that streamed down, and got my verification. I put the wallet in my pocket and climbed carefully up to where I could hoist myself up and out with one final effort. Then I took that long close look at him, and left in a hurry. I went up that slope like a giant jackrabbit and hit a prety good stride as I passed the jeep. I stripped the gasoline rag off and dropped it as I ran. I stopped and faced into what little breeze there was and started hyper-ventiliating.

The jeep stopped behind me. Over the motor noise I said, "Make no jokes."

"There is no intention, señor," Enelio said.

I knew they would not want to touch the wallet. I turned and held it so they could read the drivers' license through the yellowed plastic.

"Rockland!" Meyer said loudly. "Rockland?"

"The description matches what . . . what's left."

"Was he shot, or what?" Meyer asked.

"I don't think the question is material. I do not know everything that was done to him. But I think he was tapped on the head and then stripped, spread and wired in place and gagged. Then various things were done to him. The most impressive, perhaps, being a knife line drawn across the belly, then down the tops of the thighs, then across the thighs about six inches above the knees. Then the entire area thus outlined was carefully flayed, skinned like a grouper. I would guess that he was not blinded until a bit later on."

"I would be very grateful if you would not continue this," Enelio said.

"I am glad to stop right here."

I climbed in by going over the back of the jeep, as I sensed they did not want me too close.

Meyer said, "Not even Rockland should be . . ."

"Are you sure of that?" I asked.

Meyer gave it thought. "Not entirely sure. But if we could understand all the formative influences on Walter Rockland—"

"We would learn," I said, "how come he turned out to be a wicked, contemptible, evil son of a bitch."

And by then it was too late for more talk. Enelio wanted to be home. He wanted to be there very badly. He was willing to sacrifice our kidneys, our discs, and our silver fillings to that desirable end.

But near Oaxaca, Enelio suddenly braked, swung over to the curb and cut the motor off. He turned in the seat to address me and Meyer simultaneously. "I am a respected citizen of the State of Oaxaca," he said. "I have a certain amount of influence. I am a happy man. I enjoy my work. I enjoy my friends. I enjoy doing a favor for a friend. McGee, I was glad to welcome you to Oaxaca as a favor to my good American friend Ron Townsend."

"And I appreciate it."

"But I am *not* going to go to the officers of the law and try to explain to them just how we happened to find that body. They look at me strangely already. They look at you even more strangely. I am not a man who has this big thing about killing and bodies and investigation. I am going to be a bad citizen. If you report it, I never heard of this trip today. A dear little crumpet will swear I spent a long, long siesta with her. In fact, it was my plan. In fact I should have been with her. I do not like to throw up. It gives me a severe headache. But you, of course, are at liberty to report it."

"It would be nice if they knew about it," Meyer said.

"I think that tomorrow one of our pilots for our little airline will see a gleam in that arroyo and so advise the police."

"In that case, Don Enelio," I said, "I too have lost my taste for civic duty. I think that sergeant of yours would like to knock my head a little."

"He implied as much. He is known for enjoying such small pleasures."

"What about this wallet?"

"If I had it, I would wipe it off very carefully and put it in the mailbox by the Hotel Marqués del Valle."

"Consider it done, but after I see what's in it."

183

He waited. They did not turn around to watch me. Three hundred and sixty-two pesos, which is twenty-eight dollars and ninety-six cents. A Mexican peso, after it goes from hand to hand in the public market a few times can turn into something that looks like a piece of Kleenex rescued from the bottom of a pot of very stale and very greasy bean soup and then used to patch a manifold in a sloppy garage. Florida driver's license. Truck registration slip, a couple of months overdue for re-registration. Tourist card. A small squashed notebook with a soiled red plastic cover containing addresses, phone numbers, notes to himself. It seemed to be in the order in which he had written the items down. It was better than half filled. I scanned the last few pages and found Bruce Bundy, with address and phone. What they did not know had been there, they would never miss, and it needed longer and more careful study, so I put it in my pocket. I found a Miami Beach health card certification, with thumb print and picture. The picture confirmed a positive identification of the thing suspended in the tipped camper. I found two keys, obviously vehicle keys, probably spares. I found three folded color Polaroid prints quite ancient and faded, and featuring obscene acts so unique, so improbable, that after an instant of surprise, the performers no longer looked obscene or shocking, but looked instead strangely comic and forlorn. Nobody I knew. All strangers, even the sheep dog. I put them back in the wallet with everything except the red book, thinking that the prints might well end up taped on the inside of the door of some local cop's locker. Some daring sociologist should someday publish a collection of the art work found on the insides of locker doors of cops, firemen, ballplayers, and resident golf pros.

So we went roaring ahead again, back to the downtown hotel where he had picked us up. The car was parked over beyond the post office. On the way I felt a stupid smile appearing on my stupid face from time to time. Perhaps more rictus than smile. It is one of the many curious phenomena of reaction. There is a dreadful jolly animal

184

hidden inside us all who keeps reminding us we are alive and somebody else is dead. It kept telling me to remember how deeply the wire had eaten into the wrists of Walter Rockland, impacted there by the spasm of powerful muscles reacting to unspeakable pain.

No more hustling towels for the guests around the pool. No more two hundred percent markup on funny cigarettes. No more decisions, boy. All problems are solved forever.

Fuentes double-parked in front of the hotel and signaled the strolling cop that he would be but a moment by holding up thumb and forefinger a half inch apart, and the cop touched his cap in proper deference to the local power structure.

Enelio said firmly, "You are very nice fellows. You are splendid fellows. Lita tells me that the delicious sisters from Guadalajara have dreamy eyes about you two, and say now that it is the best vacation of all. For that the sisters and I am grateful, and my faith and trust is justified. But no more of death, eh? Maybe I am not a true Mexican. I am not enchanted by death. Do not tell me any more you learn. Do not ask my advice on any such matters, eh? In fact, let us not see each other as planned tonight. In exactly . . . forty minutes I shall be in one big deep hot tub, and pretty soon I will give a big yell and Lita will come scampering in with very, very cold wine because I like it very cold when I am in a hot tub, and she will pour a glass, and when I have drunk it all she will take the big brush and the special soap and scrub my back, and then she will pour me another glass, and soon then maybe I will begin to sing a little. I shall tell her that we are going to stay in, because with a woman in my arms I can stop thinking about death. I know I will live forever. So there is the place at this hotel, and there is the other place at the other hotel, and Lita will stay with me. So I advise you, kind gentlemen, to stay apart, to stay with your loving girls, to lose the stink of death in the sweetness of girls, and have food and drink sent in, which is possible in both places, and make the girls of Guadalajara laugh and also, in time, make them cry, because

185

laughing and crying are very living things. Tomorrow, perhaps, you will hear from me. Adios, amigos."

So he sped off. It was after five. Meyer grabbed a table. I went inside to the men's room and scrubbed my hands and face and neck and arms, and looked at myself in the mirror and saw I was still wearing that stupid smile. It is the smile of the survivor. A man walks away from the pile of tinsel junk that was once an airplane, and which for some unknown reason failed to explode and failed to burn, and he wears that smile. I wiped the wallet off and dropped it into the mail box. Meyer had a cold Negro Modelo waiting on the table for me.

"I'm trying not to think," he said. "I don't want to do any thinking, please."

"So don't."

"But the stinking wheels go around in my head. I keep remembering that day aboard the *Flush*, and trying to say something to Bix that would make it easier for her, somehow, to accept Liz's ugly death, and those beautiful deep blue eyes of hers were absolutely bland and indifferent, no matter what polite thing her mouth was saying. There was a . . . a challenge there. Something like that. I wanted to try to reach her and get some reaction, some genuine reaction, no matter how. To say or do some . . . ugly thing, to shock her awake maybe. Travis, I wonder if there are people in this world who are appointed by the gods to be victims, so that they bring out the worst in everybody they touch. And the perfect victim would have to be surpassingly lovely, of course, to be most effective. I keep wondering if she was the catalyst, not Rockland. And maybe, that day, if I hadn't become irritated at being unable to get any reaction, if I had tried harder."

"Meyer, Meyer, Meyer."

"I know. I have this thing, like the disease of kings. A bleeder. The internal wounds do not clot well. All my life is remorse. If I had done this, if I had done this . . ."

"And if your aunt had wheels she'd have been a tea cart."

"Where *are* we Travis? Just *where* the *hell* are we?"

186

"In Oaxaca The Chamber of Commerce motto is 'Stay One More Day in Oaxaca.'"

"Perhaps I do not care to."

"A pity to spoil a nice girl's vacation just when it is shaping up, Meyer."

"Now Travis."

"My God, when you get the shys you look just like Howland Owl."

"Well ... she is quite young, and ... and, dammit, McGee, anything that pleasurable has to be shameful, sinful, and wicked. I am a lecherous old man, shaken by remorse. We should go home."

"So we can go back to Lauderdale, land of the firm and sandy young rump, home of the franchised high-starch diet, and appraise the cost and the seaworthiness of all the playtoys that churn up and down the waterway, and criticize the way they are being handled. And we can wonder who did what to whom and why, and wonder why we didn't stay just a little bit longer and find out."

"Or *not* find out."

"Somebody wasn't in it for the money. Somebody wasn't worried about little incriminating items in the wallet. So Rockland has been dead in that aluminum hot box since August seventh, and I think maybe whoever did it parked the truck on the rim, worked on him for a long, long time, then rolled it over, pried dirt down on it, piled brush on it, and went away. It was a punishment which somebody devised to fit the crime. It was a very sick mind at work. Very sick and very savage."

"As with Mike Barrington, with Della Davis, with Luz?" Meyer asked. "As with my travel clock which is now junk?"

"Mr. Nesta? You had what we'll call an exploratory session with him. Do you buy him?"

"No. Not for that. Maybe, without the alibi, for what happened on the Coyotepec Road. Hallucination, violence, amnesia. But not what ... was done to Rockland. It's fallacious to try to assess what any human being is capable of, naturally."

187

"You know, Meyer, my friend, what has put us into cerebral shock is knowing that Rockland was probably capable of doing to others just what was done to him. He was the sweet guy who led Bix Bowie out into the cornfield. He was the charmer who did the one thing that would finally destroy Carl Sessions. And he—possibly— set Bix up to fly off the mountain."

Meyer shrugged, massively, slowly, expressively. He wore that inexpressibly mournful look of the giant anthropoid, of the ape who knows there is not one more plantain left in the rain forest.

"There's Bundy," he said without conviction. "We don't know if Bundy told us the whole story, and . . . . Forget it. It was a stranger. It was somebody who took a dislike to him, for some strange reason."

Lady Rebecca Divin-Harrison came up behind me and pressed my shoulder affectionately. "Travis darling! How lovely to see you again, dear." I came to my feet, feeling as clumsy and oppressed as the big-footed kid who has to come into the living room to meet mother's bridge friends. I mumbled the presentation of Meyer. She had a friend with her, a sunburned youth of sufficient inches over six feet to be able to look me right in the eye. He was rawboned, shy, with cropped blond hair and a face and manner from the midwest farm belt.

"I want you to meet Mark Woodenhaus," she said. "Isn't that a precious name?" The boy suddenly looked even more sunburned. "He's been working out in a primitive village doing some kind of sanitation thing with the . . . what is the name of it, dear?"

"The Friends' Service Committee, ma'am."

"And I found him trudging down the highway all hot and dusty and carrying a monstrous dufflebag because he couldn't spare bus fare. It's volunteer work, isn't it, dear?"

"Yes, ma'am."

"And I truly believe that parasites like myself should take every chance to express their deep gratitude to marvelous young men like Mark, don't you, Travis?"

"The best is none too good," I said. I could not see

through the dark lenses of her glasses very well, but thought I saw a significant wink. "Would you like to sit with us?" I asked her.

"Oh, thank you so much, but I think not. We have some errands to do, don't we, Mark darling? Some bits of luxury for those poor young people slaving away out there in the bush. *So* nice to see you, really. Do hope you'll be about for a time, Travis. Come along, Mark."

She looked, as one might well say, smashing. Vibrant and saucy and a-hum with improbable energies. Happily predatory, she scurried along in her lime-yellow slacks beside the gangly, unsuspecting prey, with his plowjockey stride. The solid and shapely behind swung in graceful clench and cadence, and as I watched it disappear down the long aisle between the evening tables, I remembered, out of nowhere, an ancient incident, and remembered the tag line because of its aptness.

I'd been out in the placid Gulf of Mexico off Manasota Key in a small boat with a good and longtime friend named Bill Ward. We were trolling slowly for anything interesting and edible. But there was no action. A gull came winging by, and in the silence, out of boredom, Bill aimed a forefinger at it and said, quietly, "Bang!" At that precise instant the gull, spotting a small meal on the surface, dropped like a stone. Bill, eyes and mouth wide in amazement, turned toward me, inadvertently aiming the lethal finger at me. "Don't aim that thing at me," I told him.

"And there you sit," Meyer said, "steeped in jealous envy."

"Smiling, the boy fell dead."

"Well, he has found a Friend. And the magic word is Service. But it will play hell trying to get back to that primitive village, carrying that dufflebag."

"And on his hands and knees. Where were we? Hell, let's write a finish for it, Meyer, for a bad movie. Harl Bowie is really not confined to a wheelchair. And that German nurse of his got her basic training in concentration camps. So, as a cover story, he suckered us into

189

coming down here openly. He knew the whole story, snuck into town with the German nurse, and took care of Rockland before ever sending us down here."

Meyer smiled and then sobered. "Remember my saying that one shouldn't guess about what people are capable of? I think if Harlan Bowie knew the whole story, he could possibly do that to Rocko."

"So let's write the part for Wally McLeen. Minda didn't make as many bad scenes as Bix, but it wasn't exactly a fond daddy's idea of a nice vacation for dear daughter."

Meyer chuckled. "Poor Wally. What's the word for what he's trying to do? He's trying to get with it. Or maybe that expression is already passé."

"And for a man devoting his whole time to tracking down his daughter, he isn't very well organized. He hadn't even nailed down the names of the original group."

We sat in our silences, watching the people.

Meyer said, "Somebody had a hell of a long and lonely and conspicuous walk back from the place where we found the camper. Unless, of course, they had a rented Honda to offload before running the truck into the dry gulley."

"Come off it, friend. Wally is trying to establish communication. He is a very earnest little guy. Boring, obvious, comical . . . but earnest."

More silence. Then it was my turn. "So he reports a conversation with Rockland. He *says* he didn't know it was Rockland. He *says* the mysterious stranger tried to con him out of money in return for producing darling daughter. It accounts for the two of them being seen together in a public place . . . how long before Rockland had his little misfortune?"

Meyer half-closed his eyes and turned his computer on. "Wally McLeen claimed they talked on the . . . we figured out that it had to be the last day of July. Rockland lived five more days. But could that puffy little man immobilize Rockland long enough to wire him and gag him? Unlikely. And could he have done the mischief on the Coyotepec Road? Three of them?"

So I thought that over and finally said, "Item. Let's say, just for the hell of it, that Wally went into that compound believing that Jerry Nesta was there with the others. He could have taken Mark by surprise, then got the two women before they could run. Then he could have scurried around and found that Jerry wasn't there. Item. He made a point of telling me he had been out on the Coyotepec Road that morning on his rented bike."

Meyer shook his head. "No, Travis. We're playing bad games."

"Agreed. But he *is* a common denominator, and so what we do is get him off the books because if we don't he'll muddy up the logic of the situation. And we get to throw two stones at one bird, because maybe he knows something useful, without knowing how useful it is."

"But we will have to listen to the communication lecture again."

"And admire the progress of the chin whiskers."

Meyer remembered the room number and went and checked and came back and said the key was in the box, so Wally McLeen was out. I took a stroll down the porch and couldn't spot him. I put a note in his box to call me at the Victoria. By then it was five minutes past the time we had all agreed to meet on the veranda. And the sisters appeared, newly and too elegantly coiffed, high heels, gloves, evening bags, dresses more suited to the night life of Guadalajara or Mexico City than to a September night in Oaxaca.

Their festive smiles and dancing eyes dimmed when they saw that Meyer and I were still in the rough dusty clothes of the expedition to the burned land, and they exchanged a meaningful sisterly glance. They came to the table and were seated. I said that I was sorry that we had not yet had time to change. I said that it had been an evil day, and they would have to forgive us if we seemed solemn and tired. I said that Enelio Fuentes was also tired, and that he and Lita had decided not to join us.

Any affront Elena may have felt was erased immediately by the concern in her eyes as she searched my face. She moved her chair closer, laid her hand on my wrist. In a little while I noticed that Meyer and Margarita were gone. I had not seen them leave. I told Elena, in our special clumsy mixture of English and Spanish, that I was sorry she had taken such care to dress for a dinner party. She said she had dressed to please me, and asked me if she did please me. I said there could be no question of that. She said that whatever I wished—*cualquier tu quieres*—that would be the evening that would please her. I said that I wished to go up the hill with her, to have a quiet drink with her, to have food together, and then to have love. She said she had planned on love in any case.

The last angle of the sun before it slipped over the mountains found her face with a single shaft of orange light. She looked at me, her eyes moving back and forth, focusing on each of my eyes in turn, and she wore a small, questioning sensuous frown. Black pupils set in deepest brown, whites of her eyes blue-white with superb health, long fringe of wiry black lashes, long oval face, matte golden skin, microscopic beads of moisture in the down of her upper lip above the broad solid mouth. Then suddenly her eyes looked heavy and her mouth loosened, and her head bowed slightly. She took a deep and shuddering breath and exhaled slowly. Her nostrils flared and the enameled nails bit into my wrist. She smiled and said, "Why we are sitting here so long time, *querido*?"

I could have reported to Enelio—but knew I would not—that a back can be effectively scrubbed in a tiled shower stall, and that there is no real need for a special brush and special soap. Also gin over ice is cold and pleasant and goes with a hot shower in a very Sybaritic way. I could have reported that soon I came to believe that I would live forever, and even sang a little.

Good steaks came down the hill from the hotel, and when we were done we put the cart outside at the end of the porch, turned off the lights and sat comfortably and quietly and had coffee and looked at the stars. Wally had the grace to phone at that time, and I went in and took it in the dark, sitting on the turned-down bed.

"Trav? This is Wally. I just found your note in the box a little while ago. What's it about? Have you ... have you heard something about Minda?"

"I wish I had, Wally. No. This is something else."

"Well, what is it?"

"Meyer and I would like to have a chat with you when it's convenient, Wally."

"What about?"

"We think it's a good idea to pool everything we've all learned up to this point. What do you think?"

"Well ... I guess it couldn't do any harm."

"When would be a good time? Now?"

"Oh, not now. I'm going with a bunch of the kids up to Monte Albán to see the ruins by moonlight again. Say, how about tomorrow morning? Have you ever seen the ruins at Yagul? It's only about ten miles down the Mitla Road, and there's a sign where you turn off to it."

"I saw the sign the last time we were out that way."

"I'm getting turned on pretty good by these ruins. I mean they are sort of timeless, and your own troubles don't seem to mean so much. They don't really know much about Yagul. It's so quiet there, you can sit and ... contemplate things. I was planning to go out early. I'll be there all morning. Why don't you and Meyer come out any time tomorrow morning? It will be a good place to talk. I think a place that is very, very old and peaceful and dead is a good place for really talking, don't you?"

"Sure, Wally. We'll see you there."

As I talked I had heard her close the door and click the night lock. I had heard a tock of heels on tile, then felt a dip of the bed as she sat on the other side. Whisk-whisper of nylons, then slap-pad of bare feet. Zipper-purr, rustle of fabric, click of snaps. Dip of bed again. I hung up. Hand on my shoulder to urge me around and pull me down to a mouth that fastened firmly and well, while a hand plucked at the tied belt of the robe I had put on

193

after showering. Voice making a tuneless little contented *ummming* sound, way back in the strong round throat.

"This you want?" she whispered. "Turn some bad day to good things?"

"This I want."

"This you have, Tuh-rrrravis."

"You are fine."

"Sank you ver' motch. You are doing some thing in Mexico . . . how you say? . . . *peligroso*?"

"Dangerous? I don't know. Maybe, maybe not."

She held me tightly and made a small growling sound in her throat. "Some person hurting you, Elena will fix. Tear out some eyes. Cut out some tongue. Breaking all bones, *verdad*?"

Something came flickering in through the back door of my mind, but by then everybody had become too busy to notice, and so the thought sat patiently out there in the back entryway until somebody had time to notice it.

I got around to noticing it when she lay purring into my throat, tickling weight of long heavy dark hair fanned across my chest. I eased the blanket up over her without awakening her. The thought that had come into the back of my mind was a memory of how the primitive warriors of history dreaded being handed over, alive, to the women of the enemy tribe. There had been a very convincing savagery in Elena's threats about what she would do to whoever harmed me.

Rockland had gone to Eva Vitrier's estate in La Colonia, and he had managed to take Bix Bowie away in Bundy's car. Bundy had been wickedly pleased to learn that Eva could become emotionally involved, infatuated, with a girl she saw on the street and contrive to invite the girl and her friend into her home. The two girls had been her guests for a long time. It would seem plausible that they might tell Eva Vitrier some of the rancid highlights of their vacation in Mexico, the same things Nesta had told Meyer.

So sooner or later Mrs. Vitrier would reveal, calculatingly or accidentally, her desire for the Bowie girl. In view of Bix's passivity about being used in physical ways, perhaps an actual affair had begun. Safe to assume that Minda McLeen would be opposed, and also fair to state there was very little she could do about it. So the note to Harlan Bowie about coming to get Bix may have come from Minda. Perhaps the girls quarreled over Eva's attentions to Bix, Minda demanding that Bix leave, Bix refusing. So Minda left.

Knowing Rockland's past abuse of Bix, knowing Rockland was responsible for her addiction, knowing Rockland was responsible for her death that Sunday evening, what would happen to Rockland if he went back to the Vitrier house? She could very well have mutilated him in exactly the ways I had seen. The flaying and blinding could even be said to be a symbolic expression of her attitude toward male sexuality. And perhaps her wealth enabled her to employ muscle she could trust—muscle that could overpower him, truss him up, leave him alone for her savage attentions, and then dispose of truck, camper, and body in one package.

So then Wally McLeen would be a waste of time. But it was set, so we'd lose nothing by going through with it. I thought of a twelve-second system for opening him up, and knew it would draw a wide dazed blank. He was one of the nice little people you meet on a Honda.

Elena suddenly began to jerk and twitch and make muffled little yelping sounds. I woke her up, and tenderly and gently quieted her down. She said it had been a terrible, terrible dream. I had been broken into tiny bits, and if she could put them together in time I would live. But the little wet pieces kept crawling away in every direction as she tried to reconstruct me.

SIXTEEN

Thursday was another bright, hot, beautiful morning. I had spent the time after driving Elena to town, sitting at the desk in the room and going through Rockland's little red notebook. There were Miami and Miami Beach addesses, and addresses all over the country, presumably people who had stayed at the Sultana and who had subscribed to one of Rockland's services—in one way or another. It would be logical for him to keep such a record.

The notes and reminders were too cryptic to be of any use. Things like "L. 2 Sat aft"; "2 doz, suite 20B"; "$100 Reb in 7th." As they were chronological, I could get enough hints to figure out when notes were made. He didn't make many. There was a notation of the cost of new tires in pesos and dollars, made before they got to Oaxaca. And just a few addresses after that, Bundy, the Vitrier estate, the hotel where Bix and Minda had stayed, and one that read, "I. V. Rivereta, Fiesta D, Mex City." All the rest of the pages were completely blank. On the inside back cover was his social security number.

At breakfast I checked out my twelve-second system with Meyer. "If I start edging up on him, he has time to adjust, assuming he's our nut, which I doubt. So I will drop it on him suddenly and from considerable altitude, and we will watch his throat and his mouth and his eyes like a pair of eagles, and no man living can make a fast

196

enough recovery to hide every part of it, especially when I come on very amiable and kindly and understanding."

I told him the approach. He approved. He had watched me do it before. He had seen it work and seen it fail.

So we drove out to the turnoff to Yagul. We could see it a couple of miles north of the main road as we turned off, old stone patterns atop a rounded hill which bore faint traces of the old horizontal terracing. I drove across flats and then up the steep winding road to a wide paved parking area. There was an old sedan there with Mexican plates, and the small Honda. That was all.

As we got out, a large Mexican family came down the worn path from the ruins and started getting into the sedan, arguing about who would sit where. We went up the path. A gnarled little man came trudging out of a shady spot to collect the small government fee and give us our handsomely printed tickets. He went back to his place in the shade, his back against raw rock. From there he could look out across the valley, with all the ruins behind him.

The morning sky was a deep rich Kodachrome blue. A buzzard wheeled in the updraft from the hill slope, making sounds very like a pig. Tall clumps of cactus with big red blossoms grew out of the stony soil. It was indeed quiet. Two buses moved along the valley floor toward Oaxaca, stolid, silent beetles.

We came upon the traditional ball court, a long sunken rectangle with sloping sides of carefully fitted stone, with the high place where the priests sat and watched, and the lower places for the other spectators. Tricky bounces off those side walls. Iron rings set into the stone at either end, now long rusted away. Archeologists believe that the captain of the winning team was beheaded. It was some sort of honor to strive for. It meant a permanent place in the record books. It would keep a team from running away with the league. Perhaps the same theory as the cellar team getting first draft choice.

We looked at the front of the long temple, at the altars, at the peak of a distant knoll beyond the edge of the

197

temple front wall, and saw, silhouetted against the sky, along with some twisted little trees, a dumpy figure semaphoring its arms at us, and a faint hail came upwind.

We found the stone steps that would lead us up to the temple level. A lot of it was restored. When they restore, they stick pebbles in the mortar between the new courses of stone. The academic mind saying, "See? This is all fake. We stuck it on the way we *think* it used to be."

Behind the temple facade there were small courtyards and unroofed stone walls forming a maze of small rooms and corridors. After we came to two dead ends, I found a toe hold and climbed up and picked out the right route toward Wally's little hill. We came out the back of the temple complex and went up a narrow and winding footpath, puffing a little in the unaccustomed altitude.

Wally McLeen beamed upon us. "Isn't it great? See, from up here you look over into the next valley too. Pretty strategic place. These holes here, these were tombs. The big shots got buried at the highest place. They bust into every one they can find because there's gold jewelry in some of them. Now look back at the whole thing. Gold, sacrifices, underground passages, astronomy, brain surgery, it blows my mind thinking about it."

He wore a market shirt of coarse unbleached cotton, a pale blue beret acquired from God knows where, burgundy-colored walking shorts cinched around his comfortable tummy by a belt with a lot of silver knobs affixed to the leather, and market sandals. His goatee was coming along nicely. He carried a bag woven of yellow fiber, shaped like a two-handled market bag. He had flip-up sunglasses fastened to his thick eyeglasses, and the cycle was turning his previous angry red to a red-brown, with some pink patches on forehead and nose where the early burns had peeled.

"When Minda comes back, I want to show her all these places, Trav, on account of I know she'll flip. I remember when she was a little kid, one summer at the lake she found an arrowhead and I read to her all about the Indians, and you'd be surprised how much she remembered, a little kid like that. Just turned five years old. They can bolt another seat on that Honda and we can travel all over this part of Mexico."

Meyer had moved around into position, so that we were both facing him.

"But that won't work out so good, Wally," I told him.

"*Sure* it will!"

"For a while. But then sooner or later the cops are going to find that village kid that saw you dump the camper into the ravine, and find out what you did to Rocko, and start adding things up and nail you for Mike and Della and the Mexican woman, too. So you better aim that bike for the nearest border crossing, Wally."

It is like that lousy frog routine I had to do in high school biology lab. You hook up the battery and touch the wires to the right place and that slimy dead leg makes jumping motions.

He stared at me and he stared at Meyer. And his mouth hitched up into a weak little smile and then opened into an O. Not a big O. About twice the size of the one you use to whistle. It went through the same pattern again.

"What the hell are you *talking* about?"

"Too long, Wally," Meyer said sadly. "You took too long finding the right way to play it. Too much was happening in your head. You froze. You had too much to add up."

"I . . . I've *got* to wait for Minda! You can understand that. I've got to wait for her to come back here!"

It was hard to believe it, looking at him, even though it had come through as clear as a ten page confession.

"Wally," I said, "I can understand the thing with Rockland, sort of. You're over the edge. You found out too much. Those three—Sessions, Nesta, Rockland—they turned your little girl on, and they banged her, and they degraded her, and something went wrong then in your head, Wally. This is a hell of a long way from the weekly Kiwanis meeting and the shopping center stores. What you did to Rockland means you've been taken sick. It means you've got to go into town and tell people about it and get

199

help, because there was Mike Barrington and there was Della Davis and there was Luz."

"I know. That went wrong. I mean I wouldn't feel bad about it if I got Nesta too, because I thought it might have to be that way. I went in from the back, over the wall. The jeep was there when I went by, but when I came back to look for him I found it was gone. I should have waited for him to come back. But I got scared. I have to get him, you know. And I will. I made a vow. I've been working it all out. Mike and Luz were so close together, I got her before she could take a step, after he went down. But the nigger bitch could run like the wind. If she hadn't stumbled and fallen, she would have been out the gate and gone." His voice was small and thoughtful, the words half lost in a small warm wind that gusted and died.

"What did they do to you . . . or Minda?" Meyer asked.

The shadow of the buzzard angled across the stony earth between us. Silent, awkward tableau. Wally McLeen bent over and picked up a small triangular shard of Zapotecan pottery. He looked at it with care and flipped it aside.

"I like the ones with designs," he said. "I like to think of them out here, hundreds and hundreds of years ago, scratching little designs in the clay to make the pots prettier. Funny thing about that. This morning, maybe an hour ago, over there down the slope of the hill, I found a piece that reminded me of an ashtray Minda made for me in the first or second grade. She made the same kind of wavy lines in the clay. I've got it here in the bag." He opened it and peered down in, reached in.

My alarm system went off too late. He yanked out some kind of a weapon, swinging it so swiftly I could not see what it was. From where he stood, his first choice was a backhand slap at Meyer. He should not have been able to reach him, but he did. There was the sickening solid thonk of a hard object striking the skull. Meyer went down in a bad way—a boneless sloppy tumble. There was no interval, no half-step, no attempt to break the fall. In a

200

fluid continuation of the same motion, McLeen took a forehand shot at me and I sprang back, leaning back at the same time, and even so felt the wind of it across my upper lip, heard its whistling sound. He stood nicely balanced, slightly crouched as I moved back cautiously. Meyer had rolled over twice, down the slope, slowly, but it took him to a steeper slant and he rolled more rapidly for perhaps fifteen feet before the upper half of his body dropped into one of the small open tombs. He was wedged there then, the legs spraddled, toeing in, the substantial bottom turned toward the blue sky.

The weapon was at rest. I could see what it was. He held a hardwood stick about two feet long, gray with age, greased with much handling. A leather thong, heavy, tightly braided, was fastened to the end of the stick. The end of the thong was fastened to a crude metal ring that had somehow been affixed to a stone, round, polished, irregular, a little smaller than a peach.

He came at me with a little rush of quick light steps, bouncy and balanced. I feinted to run down the slope, then dodged and ran uphill, angling away from him. The feint had been a mistake. He missed my head by an inch. I realized I had seen smallish portly men like Wally McLeen moving very lightly and quickly and well on many dance floors in years past. Long-waisted men like Wally, and with the same short, hefty legs.

"I bought this in a stall in the public market," he said. "One of the kids told me it was a fake. But it's just like the soldiers used to use. It's tricky. You have to practice with it. The handle is limber. See? So all you need is good wrist action. I practiced on trees. You have to get the range right."

"Let me go help Meyer. Please, Wally."

"You can't help him. He's dead. Or dying."

When again he came bouncing toward me, I spun and ran up the slope all out, thinking to get far enough away from him so that I could circle around and go down toward the temple. But as I started down the other side I took a quick look back and saw that he was only thirty

201

feet behind me, moving too well. There was a crumbling, unrestored wall to my left and I angled toward it, snatched up a chunk of rock and turned and hurled it at him. He scrambled to the side and it gave me enough leeway to pick up another jagged piece and, in too much haste, overthrow him. He backed away quickly.

With more time, I was able to pick up one of better size and heft. I turned it to fit the hand, and took my best shot. He was fifty to sixty feet away. I put it on a good line, right toward the middle of his face. He moved just his head. He moved it quickly to the side and just as far as was necessary.

A rock fight. Too many years since the last one. I might be able to get away from him, but that wasn't enough. I had to get to Meyer, and I had to get to him soon. I didn't like the choices. If I picked some good rocks and charged him, trying to get close enough to chunk him, he was going to have just as good, or better, a chance to bust my skull as he had with the three in the old compound on the Coyotepec Road. He was too good with that thing, and he could make it whistle.

A madman is curiously deadly. When the strictures and restraints of civilization and conscience are wiped away, the animal can move with ancient shrewdness. Man is a predator.

He stood downhill from me, slowly swinging the stone ball from side to side at the end of the stick, planning what to do next. Stocky little storekeeper in blue beret and new goatee, and just as calmly intent on killing me as a Bengal tiger would have been.

I squatted by my wall and picked up a rock the size of my head and held it in both hands and arched it at him, like taking a shot from the foul line. He squinted up at it and stepped to his right. It hit, bounced and rolled down through coarse grass and brush toward the temple level below. All the ruins were silent. For perhaps the first time in my life I desperately wanted to see a chattering flock of tourists, festooned with Instamatics, leaving a spoor of yellow boxes.

I knew that if I didn't come up with something workable, fat Wally would, and I wouldn't like it.

Misdirection is the name of the game. I couldn't point behind him and yell, "Hey! Tourist!" and hope to bounce a rock off his skull as he turned and stared.

But he had looked up at the big rock, hadn't he? Indeed he had. So I palmed a couple of good small ones, holding them in place against my palm with ring fingers and little fingers, and picked up another big melon of a rock and gave it as much height and distance as I could, and as he looked up at it, I let fly with the first small stone. He glimpsed my movement and looked at me, moving swiftly to his left along the slope. He ducked away from the first small one, had to check the one in the air again to be sure he was out from under it, and moved forward, taking the second small rock high on the forehead and going ass over teacup into a backward somersault as I came bounding down the slope. He peered up at me, on hands and knees, a bright rush of blood on his face. He had lost the ancient fake weapon and the blue beret and his glasses. But he reached and grabbed the weapon and took a blind full-arm swing and got me on the outside of the left thigh, just below the hip bone. It felt to me as if he had smashed the hip. I fell and rolled and got up, surprised to be able to get up. He wiped blood out of his eye and started toward me and I made ready for him, telling myself I would catch that damned rock, catch it in my teeth if I had to, and take it away from him and feed it to him. He hesitated and ran down the slope. I saw him fall and roll and get up and disappear into the maze of walls behind the temple facade. I was trembling with reaction. I picked up the sweaty beret and the eyeglasses with the tilt-shades attached, and saw that one lens was shattered.

I went hobbling on my broken, ground-glass hip to the opened tombs and heard myself saying, "Sorry. Sorry, Meyer. Sorry."

I got him by the belt and pulled him out of the tomb. He seemed very heavy. I rolled him onto his back. He was very loose and sloppy. He had a lump over his ear the size of half an apple. His cheeks and forehead were scratched and torn from rolling down the slope. I put my ear against his chest, and the mighty old heart of Meyer said, reassuringly, "Whup tump, whup tump, whup tump."

So I thumbed an eyelid up, and a blank, sightless, and bright blue eye stared out, stared through and beyond me.

The other one opened, unaided, and slowly the focus came back from ten thousand miles in space, down through all the layers with fancy names, and stared at me. Tongue came out and licked dusty lips. Rusty voice said, "So? So hello."

"Are you dying?"

"The point is debatable. What happened? I saw McLeen way up on the hill. We started up. Here I am. I fell?"

"You got hit on the head with a rock."

A slow hand came up and the fingers touched the lump. "This is part of my head? Way out there?"

"Do you want to sit up?"

"I would like to think about it. We economists have very thick skulls. It is a characteristic. Everybody knows that. But we are happy people with a great sense of rhythm."

"You are talking a lot."

"It keeps my mind off my head. So let's try this sitting up part."

He sat up and spent a little time moaning. And then he stood up, and we started down the slope, very slowly.

"Why are you limping?" he asked.

"I, too, got hit with a rock."

"What do you have there in your hand?"

"A blue beret and a pair of broken glasses. Shut up, Meyer."

"Ask a stupid question and you get . . ."

"Shut up, Meyer."

"Sit up, Meyer. Stand up, Meyer. Walk, Meyer. Shut up, Meyer."

I had been listening for the snoring sound of the Honda

heading down the hill, and I hadn't heard it yet. It made me thoughtful. So I made Meyer sit on a short, wide, restored wall, and hold the beret and glasses. I went over to the side and climbed up onto a high wall. I could see a portion of the parking lot. I could see the Falcon and the cycle. I looked around. I could see the pattern of the maze, but not down into the rooms and corridors.

I dropped down from the wall, and managed not to scream out loud. Just silently, in the brain. I listened for a long time. I moved a few feet and listened again.

With an explosive grunt of effort he came scuttling out of a doorway, blinking and swinging, forgetting that part about the wrist action, and forgetting how tall I am. I stepped inside the arc, so well inside it that the lethal rock which I had expected might wrap around me and splinter a rib, smacked the wall behind me instead. I got one paw on the stick and the flat of my other hand against his chest, pushed and yanked and took away the toy. He ran backward, kept his balance, turned, and kept running. I went after him with no hope of catching him—not on a leg that felt as if I were wearing it backwards—but to see where he was headed, and if there was anyone interested in stopping him.

He came out onto the wide stone plaza that ran along the front of the temple façade. By the time I got to the end of the unroofed corridor and made the turn, he was scooting along toward the nearest set of big steep stone stairs leading down to the lower courtyard level, to the same level as the ball court a hundred yards away.

As I came hitching and galumphing along, I saw him make his turn and slow to go down the stone steps. He tried to take the steps in stride, but he had not slowed quite enough, probably because perceptions of depth and distance were flawed without the thick lenses. So momentum carried him to the outside edge of the stairs. There was no railing. And he flailed his arms to recover balance but momentum took him over, leaning further and further, his feet trying to stay on the edge of the steep stone.

He dropped out of my sight. I heard a single cry which

could have been "Oh!" and which could have been "No!" The sound ended with a whacking, dusty thud. I went down the steps and around and back to where he lay, half in white sunlight, half in black shadow. He lay on his right side in white dust, using a rock for a pillow, left arm curled around the pillow.

I went down onto one knee with some difficulty, and as I placed the pads of three fingers against the big artery in the side of his throat, I could see into his half-open mouth, see the neat gleam of a reasonably new filling. The dentist probably belonged to the same luncheon clubs and called him Wally, told him jokes and told him when to spit. The artery throbbed once, and in about three seconds throbbed again with half the vigor, and then did not ever move again. Escaping air rattled in his throat. All my life I had heard about the death rattle. Thought it was a myth. Now it was confirmed. A classic sample. A collector's item.

I stood up and walked beyond the steps. No tourists. A thousand years worth of silence. Baked rocks. Shards. Dust. A lot of Indio blood had soaked into the soil of Yagul, enough to chill the back of my neck. And I had to go up and get Meyer and did not relish the climb.

But Meyer was sitting up on the stone plaza, his feet on the top stair. His color was pasty.

"I told you to stay put."

"I came to tell you I feel very dizzy. And ... in all truth, a little bit frightened."

I got up those stairs and got him down them, taking a lot of his weight. I then put the blue beret next to the stone pillow, and tucked one bow of the broken glasses under Wally's cheek. I had shoved the wooden handle of the weapon down inside my belt, above the right hand pants pocket, and put the stone ball in the pocket, so that only the braided leather showed.

Walked by the ball court, out along the path. No new visitors. Tourists go to Monte Albán, to Mitla, not often to Yagul. I shouted the gnarled little ticket-taker out of his shady nest, and pointed back in agitation, and then at the

206

Honda, saying in my pidgin Mexican that the man had fallen, the man was hurt. He looked absolutely blank, and then there was sudden comprehension and concern. I said I would have the *ambulancia* come, the *Cruz Rojo, los doctores*. He went trotting to find the dead daddy of the dear daughter, and I wedged Meyer into the Falcon and took off. Before we got to the main highway, he toppled over against the door on his side.

The large modern hospital was on the fringe of La Colonia, toward the city. I was glad I had taken Brucey and Davey there. I left rented rubber on every turn, using one hand to hold Meyer in place when I made turns to the right.

A birdlike little nurse came hurrying out of the emergency entrance. She ignored my linguistics. She looked at Meyer, sucked air audibly as she saw the lump on his head. She directed the attendants who lifted him onto the stretcher and rolled him in. I refused to understand their instructions to get my car out of the way, knowing it was perhaps the quickest way to contact somebody who could speak English.

A big brown man in a white smock appeared and said, "Would you please move your car out of the ambulance gate, sir. You can park it in back."

"My friend and I saw a man fall from in front of the temple at Yagul. While we were hurrying to tell the man who sells the tickets, my friend fell and struck his head. The man who fell was an American tourist, and I think the fall may have killed him, Doctor. What about my friend?"

"He is being examined right now. If you will move your car and then go to the office and help with the admission papers . . ."

"Is he in bad shape?"

"*Please* move your car."

And so I did. Then a large, billowy, benevolent lady in the office helped me interpret their form and put Meyer's name, rank, and serial number in the right spaces. I caught Enelio Fuentes just as he was leaving the agency. I

207

was using the phone on her desk. Enelio came through with that clout and speed that only a certified member of the local establishment can provide. A Doctor Elvara arrived twenty minutes later to be a consultant on the case. He was young, brisk, authoritative, and emotionless. After fifteen minutes he came back to the waiting room and made his report.

"There is no fracture. The patient regained consciousness and seemed rational, and then lapsed again into a comatose condition. It is obvious there is a severe concussion. The question of tissue damage cannot be resolved as yet. Pulse, respiration and pressure are good. It is safe to say there is no major area of hemorrhage in the brain, according to present symptoms. There could be a slow seepage from small blood vessels and torn capillaries. If so, the indication will be a deterioration in pressure, respiration, and pulse. We have no mechanized intensive care installation, and so the procedure here is to use student nurses on one hour shifts, constantly taking the pulse rate and the blood pressure and the rate of respiration and marking them on a special chart form which carries a column for cumulative change. If percentage change exceeds specified limits, she will immediately alert surgery. I will be on call and be here by the time the patient is prepared. The chief resident in surgery will assist me. In almost every instance the seepage is subdural, evident, and readily accessible, with a favorable prognosis. When a deeper area is traumatized, the problem becomes more grave."

"Do you think you'll have to operate?"

"I do not make guesses."

I knew he would make his guess if I could word the question correctly. "Doctor Elvara, if you had ten patients with exactly the same test results as my friend, the same lump on the head, how many do you think would require surgery?"

"Hmmm. Ten is too small a sample. Make it a hundred. At least twenty would require surgery, perhaps as many as forty."

"Out of a hundred operations, given the same conditions thus far, how many wouldn't respond?"

"Perhaps five, perhaps four."

"How long does it usually take before you know whether you have to operate?"

"There will be a deterioration in the first twelve hours. But we would keep close watch for eighteen to be safe, then two more days of observation before the patient would be discharged."

"Thank you, Doctor."

"You are most welcome." He stopped outside the door and turned and looked in at me. "You ... ask very nice questions," he said. It was probably his compliment for the whole calendar year.

So then, three chances out of ten they'll have to open your skull, Meyer, and, if they do, it's twenty to one in your favor. Your friendly neighborhood oddsmaker can thus put up fifty bucks against the dollar you don't make it, and still have a twenty percent edge in his favor. But with your pants showing above the edge of the tomb, you didn't look all that good.

But nothing in the world could keep it from being a very very long twelve hours.

SEVENTEEN

At eleven on Thursday night the twelve hours were up. Enelio, Margarita, and I got in to see him. Small room. Hospital gown. Side bars on the bed up. Blue beard on Meyer's jaws. White compress on the head lump. A squatty little girl in gray and white, skin color like old pennies, was pumping the bulb on the blood pressure gadget and reading the levels.

"Well, well, well," said Meyer.

Fuentes said, "Meyer, if you were a gentleman, you would tell the young lady there is a beetle crawling right across that little nurse cap." When she did not move, Enelio smiled and said, "No English."

"Some day," said Meyer, "kindly tell me what happened. Memory stopped. Travis, you are not limping as much."

"They stuck something in there that works like novocaine."

The girl posted her chart and started taking his pulse, moving her lips as she watched the sweep second on the gold watch pinned to her uniform.

"Meyer," I said, "it now appears that they do not have to open your skull and examine the contents."

His eyes went wide. "They were thinking of it?"

"All day long."

"Too bad," he said, "to deprive them of the chance. Better luck next time."

"Now we're going to the Victoria and celebrate. We'll order drinks for you too and take turns drinking yours."

"Salud, and happy days."

Margarita, however, was not going. She had pulled a chair close to the far side of the bed. The squatty student nurse made querulous objection. Margarita blazed up and exploded several packages of Spanish firecrackers around the girl's head. It backed her up and shut her up, and she soon resumed her testing.

Margarita looked content as a cat on a warm hearth. She held Meyer's hand, and with her free hand, she gave that odd little Mexican good-by wave, which looks more like a summoning than a dismissal.

Meyer gave us an inordinately fatuous smile. I told him I'd be back in the morning. He told me not to put myself out. Elena was waiting in the Falcon. She did not seem at all surprised that her sister had stayed with Meyer. I got the feeling it would have astonished her if Margarita had not stayed. Enelio followed us back to the Victoria. I left Elena off at the main building and told her to wait for me in the lounge. I parked the car there, and concealed the weapon once more, and walked down to the cottage with Enelio. Inside the cottage, with the blinds and draperies closed, Enelio stood and held the handle and let the stone ball swing from side to side, then swung it a few times, cautiously.

"Hey, one hell of a thing. I have seen the *autenticos*, in collections. Very much the same thing. Any weapon, they keep changing it, changing it, until it is as dangerous as they can make it. I think you better throw this thing away, my friend."

"I have that feeling about it too."

"By God, they were a bloody people. A thing like this, there's no halfway. What it does is kill."

I took it and put it in the closet on a shelf. I got out a bottle of genuine bottled-in-Guadalajara House of Lords gin, and phoned up for ice for both of us, and some mix for Señor Fuentes.

211

"What about the camper?"

"Fonny thing. One of our pilots saw something shiny in that arroyo and reported it to the Federales. Maybe they went out today. Maybe in the morning. No talk about it yet. I tell you, Martinez and Tielma are getting damn sick and tired of dead American tourists. Telephone calls come from Mexico City. 'What are you trying to do down there, you *estupidos!* Ruin business?' But I think the little fat man is no problem. Mexico is full of pyramids and temples and they are all of stone, and Mexico is full of tourists, and some of them are feeble and some are careless and some are dronk, and some have bad hearts and faint and fall, so it is not something special, one more little man with a sack full of pieces of pots, eh?"

"If anybody else had shown up, it would have been a different ball game."

"Not so many go to Yagul. Some days probably nobody. Maybe two or three days, nobody."

The ice and mix came. We fixed our own. He give a little lift of his glass and gave that Spanish toast that covers everything there is. "Health, money, love, and time to enjoy them." I've never been able to think of anything it doesn't cover.

"So," said Enelio, "your friend will be all right, and now it is finished, and now you go home and you tell nice pretty little lies to the father, eh?"

"Is it finished? All day I've been worrying about Meyer with half my mind and using the other half to list the questions I would have asked Wally McLeen but didn't get a chance to."

"What do you need to know from some fat little madman?"

"I wanted to know who crazed him. Somebody had to give him enough sordid and factual information to actually arm him like a bomb, to turn him into a deadly weapon."

"You told me he talked to that Rocko?"

"Yes. Apparently on the first night he was here. So he

212

came here knowing who to look for. So I think it's fair to say that somewhere along the line Minda dropped him a letter or a postcard, telling who she was with and their destination. Otherwise, he and Rockland got together too fast. Too big a coincidence. I can see how Rocko would see it as a way to come up with some quick money. That would be his style, to sell a man his own daughter. But there wouldn't be any point in Rocko talking about what shape the girl was in, or talking about what kind of a trip they'd had, or telling him his daughter was hooked on speed."

"Speed?"

"Stimulants. Amphetamines. Dexedrine. People develop a physical tolerance but not a mental tolerance, so they hit it heavier and heavier and they can get pretty nervous and erratic. If they get so dead for sleep they try to balance it off with barbiturates, then the real trouble starts. Look, Enelio, Wally McLeen came here to find his daughter. He went looking for Rockland and found him. So Rockland said that, for a fee, he might be able to produce her. He knew the girls were guests of Eva Vitrier, and we can assume he knew her place is like a fortress. What he would have to do is get to Minda, con her into writing a note to her father, peddle the note for half the money with the balance on delivery of the girl. But according to what Mrs. Vitrier told the police when she identified the body of the Bowie girl, Minda and Bix had quarreled, and Minda had gone to Mexico City a few days earlier. So Rockland went back to Bruce Bundy's house and tried to leave in the middle of the night, but Bundy had different ideas. So he didn't get to leave until Saturday, a little past noon. That leaves the rest of Thursday evening, and all day Friday, and half of Saturday, for Wally McLeen to find out where his daughter might be. I think he could have managed it. I think he could have gotten to the Vitrier estate without any help from Rockland. That's as far as I can take it. It's a point of focus, for Wally McLeen, Minda, Rockland and Bix. So the Frenchwoman must know something that will make sense out of it. What's the name of that little lawyer again, on the crutches?"

"Alfredo Gaona y Navares."

"And I can't get past him to locate Eva Vitrier. Can you?"

"I would think no."

"But he does communicate important things to her."

"Maybe not direct. Anyway, I have told you—I don't want to play very much of these games of yours, McGee."

"What if he can communicate with her directly? Is there anything that anybody could tell him that he'd think important enough to bother her with?"

Enelio got up and fixed a new drink. He shrugged. "I suppose he is responsible for the house here, and the staff. It must always be ready for her at any moment, I understand. I cannot think of any problem of the house he could not take care of without bothering her. Unless it is totally destroyed. You want me to burn it down, no thanks!"

"There must be some way."

"He is a tough old man and he is being paid *not* to bother her, Travis."

"And he is a very sharp-minded old man."

"Very."

He roamed the room, scowling, pausing to sip his drink. He stopped in front of me. "One small idea. No good, maybe. From everywhere in the world it is possible to telephone to Oaxaca. I say possible. Our great *larga distancia* service makes grown men cry. But if he can be in touch with her, he would follow instructions if there was an order from her to him to phone her at once. Then, if somehow you could learn to where the call is placed. . . . But how can we do that? Hide under his desk? Damn!"

"Suppose the message came to him by phone, Enelio."

He looked blank. "So?"

"Long distance connections are frequently bad, aren't they?"

214

"Bad? They are unspeakable sometimes."

"And local lines are out of order sometimes?"

"If it is only once a week, it is a very good week."

"So what if that old lawyer *thought* he was talking to the long distance operator."

"I think I begin to see . . ."

"And she said she had an urgent call for him from Señora Vitrier, person to person, but when she tried to get through his line was not working, and then the long distance call faded before she could get the place of origin of the call and the number. Perhaps, if he had the number, she could try to put the call through to the lady."

A slow smile spread across his face. "Señor McGee, you have a great talent. Of course, you have one loathsome disease, which is the need to know everything. But it is a beautiful talent. I have the correct little girl for this improvisation. Very bright, very lovely, very, very naughty. And to be trusted. . . . Why am *I*, Enelio Fuentes, helping you with this nonsense?"

"Because the disease is contagious."

"And it is also a very Mexican disease, you may have noticed."

So we agreed that I would come to the agency at ten-thirty Friday morning and he would have the girl briefed, and we would see what happened.

In the morning I went to the hospital first. Meyer was sitting up, eating a large bowl of hot oatmeal. The compress had dwindled to a small bandage, and the swelling was down. But his bright blue eyes peered out through two slits in puffed flesh of deep purple and cobalt blue. It made him look less simian—and more like a hairy, dissipated owl. The girls had stopped checking his condition on a continuous basis. He had a dull headache. He said he felt as if he had been rolled downhill in a barrel. He said everyone was being very nice to him. He said that everybody seemed to have the idea that if they were not nice enough to him, the senorita from Guadalajara would say a few little things that would make their hair smoke. She had gone off to the center of town to buy some things for him which she said would make him more comfortable. He had little idea what they might be.

He asked about Elena, and Enelio, and Lita, and I said that last night we had celebrated his thick skull by stopping at Enelio's bachelor penthouse apartment and picking up Lita and a hamper of cheese and fruit and wine, and the four of us had picnicked in the moonlight at the ruins at Monte Albán, and had toasted his health frequently, invented new lyrics to old songs, and identified the constellations. Now, Elena and Lita were resting, having vowed to slay anyone who woke them before noon. He said wistfully he was glad everybody was having such a nice time. Then he wanted to hear about Wally. He still was blacked out by a traumatic amnesia covering that period. I told him he wasn't ready yet. He should rest.

When I got to Enelio's office he was ready and impatient to get started. He closed and locked the office door. The chosen girl was named Amparo. She wore a pink mini-dress, had cropped hair and huge dark eyes and an amused, mocking mouth. She was not the least bit nervous about the chore. She used Enelio's private line, which did not go through the switchboard.

Though her Spanish was faster than I could follow, she had adopted, for the occasion, that flat, impartial, decorous tone of long distance operators the world over, and the overly careful enunciation of all numerals.

She spoke, listened, spoke again, wrote on the pad beside the phone, said something else, then sat for several moments with her palm over the mouthpiece. She then said something which ended in *momentito,* thanked him, and hung up.

Enelio went over and ripped the top sheet off the pad. He bent over the girl and kissed her heartily. She beamed and bridled and went switching out, giving Enelio a solemn wink after she had unlocked the door.

"She is close," Enelio said. "Mexico City. Hotel Camino Real. Extension F.D."

216

We shook hands. Successful conspiracy warms the blood. He told me that the girl had pretended to place the call, and had told him the circuits were busy and she would try again in a little while. So, when Alfredo Gaona did not hear, he would try again, and it would go through normal channels, and there would be a certain amount of confusion and apology.

He checked the schedules and discovered that if I could get to the airport in fifteen minutes, I could be in Mexico City at twenty after twelve. He said he would explain to Elena. I was not dressed for the trip. He ran me back into the suite of bedroom, dressing room, and bath off his office, grabbed some clothes, and jammed them into a small suitcase.

I gave him my car keys and told him where I was parked. He said he would inform Meyer and have the car taken up to the hotel and the keys left at the desk. I changed to his shirt in the car on the wild ride out, and finished putting the necktie on as we got there. I knew the jacket was going to be uncomfortably snug. They were so close to departure they would not have waited for me. But they were all pleasantly glad to do a favor for Señor Fuentes. He slipped a tip into the hand of the stewardess, patted her on her behind, said he would sign inside for my ticket. We got on, and the stairs came up, and she spun the lock, and I got the belt buckled as the aircraft reached the end of the runway and turned for final check and takeoff.

I checked into the Camino Real at five after one on Friday afternoon. No reservation. A single. Any single. Yes sir, of course sir, thank you, sir. Twelve twenty-eight for the gentleman. Enjoy your stay with us, Señor McGee.

I unpacked the assorted garments. I sat on the bed and read the instructions on how to dial other rooms in the hotel. But there was no clue as to how to dial F.D. I tried the operator. With hardly a pause she said, "I am ver'

217

sorreeee, but I am ask to put no calls to that number, Señor."

Hmmm.

Sat at the desk and used the elegant stationery and elegant envelope. *Am very anxious to speak to you on a matter of the greatest importance.* Name and room number. Sealed it. Señora Eva Vitrier. Took it down to the desk. The man checked the indexed list of guests. Handed it back.

"I am sorry, sir. We have no one of that name in the hotel. Perhaps if you check the reservation desk, they might know if she is coming in."

Thank you very much.

Hmmm.

So I went down to the shop near the coffee shop and bought razor, toothbrush, and the other essentials. Went into the coffee shop. Hamburger and coffee. Very tourist-like.

Obviously the lady had built walls here also. She liked walls around her, with broken glass on top.

Big money plus a passion for privacy makes an effective combination. How long since anyone has seen Howard Hughes?

Went back to the lobby area and roamed about until I found a bellhop with a very amiable expression. Laid ten pesos on him to tote my little sack of toiletries up to twelve twenty-eight. It was enough to make him look even more amiable. It established me as a guest. When he came back down I intercepted him again, my hand in my pocket. He looked delighted.

"Say, all these rooms have numbers, but there seems to be phone numbers with letters instead of numbers."

"What, señor? What, please?"

"Suppose a phone number is F.D. Where is that?"

"What, señor? No understands."

"*Si el número de teléfono es effay day, donde está el cuarto?*"

"Oh! Oh, yes, señor. Isss not a room. Isss a suite.

218

Other part of hotel, that way. Effay means is Fiesta Suite. Effay ah. Effay bay. Effay—"

I thrust another ten onto him and told him that was very interesting. And something was nibbling at the frayed edge of my memory. Yes indeed. Fiesta D, in Rockland's little red book. With a name I could not remember. I found a writing desk and made some tries at it. I. V. Rivatera. I. V. Traviata.

Close. But not close enough.

Eva Vitrier. And there is the old game of anagrams. So take out an "i" and a "v," and you have the letters E A V T R I E R. And in three tries they assemble into Rivereta. I. V. Rivereta was exactly right.

New envelope. Same note. Tear open and reseal. Mrs. I. V. Rivereta. Walk to desk.

"Would you please see that this is delivered?"

Checks the index. "Yes sir. Thank you, sir."

"Thank *you*."

Walk back up to room and turn on the television and watch an episode of *Gunsmoke* and wonder how come they all speak Spanish; and wait. And wait. And wait. Start to give up and wonder what the hell to try next.

Quarter to five. Got the phone on the second ring.

"Mister McGee?" A throaty and charming voice, with that strange French bit with the vowels, and the little clickety R's of the Parisian.

"This is he." Grammar reassures.

"I 'ave your note. What is this thing of so much great importance?"

This was a crucial moment. I had the feeling that if I said the wrong thing she would hang up, and that would be the end of it for good and all.

"It concerns Beatrice Bowie, Walter Rockland, Minda McLeen, Walter McLeen and, of course, you."

"Perhaps it is important to you, yes? But not to me."

At least I had not lost her yet. "I want to remind you that it is a matter of record in Oaxaca that Miss McLeen and Miss Bowie were staying with you. It is a matter of record that you identified the body. It is a matter of record that Miss Bowie was under suspicion of complicity in an attempt to smuggle narcotics into the United States."

"This has nothing to do with me. Nothing. I should not have . . . done the kindness of helping them find out who that poor child was, and giving them her possessions to send home to her family. I do not become involved in such matters."

"But the point is you *did* become involved. I agree with you, Mrs. Vitrier. Things should always be handled privately and with discretion. I find myself in an awkward position. I must return to Florida and report to the Bowie girl's father. He wanted to know the circumstances of her death. If I go back to him with a lot of unanswered questions, he has the resources to pursue this matter through diplomatic channels. I have talked to your attorney in Oaxaca, Alfredo Gaona. He refused to give me any help in getting in touch with you. But from talking to him, I think I know how much you value your privacy."

"Do you now have a desire to threaten me in some way, Mister McGee?"

"No. But should Mr. Harlan Bowie pursue this further because I could not give him any answers, I would think that the Mexican government would make a complete and official investigation, as a matter of diplomatic courtesy. And I do not think that you could . . . stay behind your walls under such circumstances."

There was such a long pause I began to be afraid she had hung up very quietly. Then she said, "I have always enjoyed this country. But you see, it is not entirely necessary to me, is it? There is nothing to prevent my leaving tomorrow and never coming back here. What I have would be sold without difficulty."

"I think that would be a very odd thing for you to do."

"I cannot be impressed with what you might think of what I do or do not do."

"I merely meant that it seems like such an extreme reaction to a very simple thing. I just want to fill in the

220

blanks. It would not take much of your time. And then I would leave you alone, and I could make my report to Mr. Bowie. It's that simple."

"I think . . . you are a clever person, Mr. McGee."

"Not particularly."

"To learn the name I use here was a clever thing. Poor Alfredo was dreadfully upset to learn there had been no call from me. So it is to understand you found where I am by tricking that old man. But certainly he did not tell you this name I invented."

"Sometimes there is luck."

"Luck is something one makes for oneself, I think. Mr. McGee, I think I will give you that little time to ask your questions. You will present yourself at this suite at seven promptly?"

"Thank you very much."

"This is done only because I must believe you are a person of some discretion and privacy."

"I will be there at seven."

The wing of the hotel that was given over to the suites had wider and more luxurious corridors, was more deeply carpeted, more boldly decorated. The Fiesta Suites were on the fourth floor. I had gone in and talked to the reservation people about accommodations and had learned that suites were available from forty dollars a day to three hundred dollars a day. The wing was five stories high, and the several Fiesta Suites were duplex, with the living areas on the fourth floor, opening out onto spacious, walled roof gardens, and with two bedrooms and two baths on the fifth floor, and an internal staircase. The reservation girl was friendly, not busy, willing to chat.

She said that the largest suite, the presidential suite, had four bedrooms, a servant's room, a baronial dining room, and, on its larger roof garden, quite large shade trees and a large heated swimming pool. She said that several of the suites were permanently rented, some by businesses, some by individuals who had taken them when the hotel had opened and either lived there most of the year, or used them whenever they visited the city.

I pressed the bronze button by the door. I noticed one of those little peepholes set into the door, a wide angle lens, and I repressed my usual impulse to put my thumb over it.

The door opened six inches, as far as the heavy brass safety chain would let it. Eva Vitrier looked out through the gap at me. Enelio's description had been apt. Her face had all the striking thrusts and angles and slightly vulpine harshness of Nefertiti. Black hair piled high. A long muscular throat, graceful but not delicate. It was as broad as the slender face. The mouth was small and plump and fleshy. Her eyes were set oddly, one more sharply tilted than the other. She was wearing some sort of hostess gown, deep aqua, floor-length, with a wide scooped neck, a metallic golden rope belting it at the natural waistline. She had a look of extraordinary sensuous vitality kept under such exacting control, such practised control, that she was an immediate challenge.

I could see beyond her into a hushed and handsome room, with a high ceiling and glass doors beyond, through which I could see a patio garden so verdant and substantial it was difficult to adjust to being on the fourth floor. Sizable trees, and muscular flagstones winding through heavy plantings.

"You *are* Mr. McGee? I do not care to ask you in, or feel the need to apologize. I am quite alone here. There is no reason why I should even give you this much time. But I was curious to . . . put a face and body with your voice, perhaps."

"I'm what you imagined?"

"Does it matter? I thought you would be a large man, but with more of the American look of softness and baldness and the quick clever eyes behind glasses, the look of the ones who find their way to the money so easily. I would rather you looked like that, because as you look now you disconcert me. To be so muscular and fit and

222

brown, and to have about you a look of laughing at me somewhere inside you, and to look so ... indolent— perhaps it is a part of cleverness to create an illusion of being a faithful dog one can scratch behind the ears, and send bounding off to fetch some object or to kill some animal. Now if you will tell me the blanks I will give you the little words to fill them, and everything will be tidy and proper for your report."

So the day was fading quickly, the room darkening behind her, and I was sorry I could not be reassuringly balding and soft with little shrewd economic eyes so she would be reassured.

"Okay. What day did Minda McLeen leave and go to Mexico City?"

"The twenty-eighth day of July. A Monday."

"What did they quarrel about?"

"I have no idea. She was a tiresome girl, nervous and restless and irritable. She asked me to lend her money so she could leave. I was glad to."

"How much?"

"I do not know exactly. Perhaps two thousand pesos."

"How did she travel?"

"I have no idea. Something was said about someone driving to Mexico City. I did not listen. I was not interested. I do not know if she even came here, nor do I care."

"Why did you invite them to stay with you, when it must have been obvious to you that Miss Bowie was on drugs?"

"I felt sorry for them. One makes certain impulsive gestures from time to time, and usually regrets them. I had room for them, or for a dozen of them, at my Oaxaca home. And servants and money. It was a human impulse. I thought I might help them."

"Did you try to do anything about the Bowie girl's addiction?"

"Of course! I had a discreet doctor fly in and give her a complete physical examination. She was in very bad shape from the addiction, malnutrition, intestinal parasites, several small chronic infections. The McLeen girl needed medical attention too, but mostly rest and nourishing food. Soon she was able to help with the Bowie girl. I gave her much personal care. I have had some practical experience. My first husband was seriously ill for a year and a half before he died, and he would not permit anyone else to care for him. I gave her the prescribed injections to quell the withdrawal symptoms of heroin addiction."

"And you knew what you were taking on?"

"One becomes bored and feels a bit ... unnecessary from time to time. Then it is an affirmative act to make oneself needed. I would not have gone on and on with it, certainly. I had planned to have someone take her back to Florida to her home when she was well enough."

"When did Miss Bowie leave your home?"

"She was becoming more alert and responsive. On Saturday in the early afternoon, a young man came asking to see her. I told my gate man that he could see Bix. Then Bix came to me and asked me if she could go for a ride with the young man. She said he was a friend. I thought it would be constructive to give her a test of her will and her desire to be cured. So she left with him. When she did not return Saturday night I was annoyed and disappointed, and quite alarmed. She had become a likable personality. But I had no reason to report it. One cannot keep a houseguest locked up. Then she did not return Sunday night either. My cook went to market Monday morning and came back and told me of an unidentified girl killed on the mountain road. I had her identification and her belongings at the house. I do not care to be involved in such things. I summoned my attorney, Alfredo Gaona, and explained the situation, and sent him to make arrangements with the police so that it could be done as quickly and quietly as possible. The body was sickeningly damaged, of course, but I knew at once from the chain she wore on her ankle and the red shoe that it was Beatrice

Bowie. The police came to my home and claimed her belongings. And I did not care to stay there in the house longer. It was very depressing. So I came here the same evening. I have maintained this suite since the hotel opened."

"She was over her addiction?"

"She had been addicted intentionally to several compounds, each less powerful. It is a common method of treatment. Perhaps she could have been cured entirely. I do not know. There seemed to be in her a great need to escape herself, to blot out her known world."

Neat blanks, neatly filled.

"What day did Mr. McLeen come to you, asking about his daughter?"

"Let me think. Was Bix there? No, because he wished to question her about where Minda might have gone. I believe that it was quite late on Saturday afternoon."

"Then you must have told him to come back, because at that time you thought Bix would be back from her ride."

"Then I am mistaken, and it was late on Sunday afternoon, because I did not ask him to come back. He is a very tiresome and talkative man."

I was running out of blanks. So there was left only what I expected would be the doorslammer.

"Mrs. Vitrier, did Minda McLeen try to prevent your having an affair with Miss Bowie?"

She stared at me, so motionless I could believe she had stopped breathing. Then she gave a husky, earthy, single bark of derisive laughter.

"Do you wonder that I close the world out, Mr. McGee? There is always some kind of obscene poison, isn't there? Can you look at me and believe that?"

"Well, it isn't easy."

"I have buried four husbands, Mr. McGee. They were all elderly and extremely well off. I respond to older men. Perhaps that is a weakness. I do not know. I loved them. There was poison then, too. Each time. Snickerings about how I had seen to it that they would die in bed. The world is nasty and cruel. Fortunately they left me with all the money I shall ever need, and nasty gossip cannot touch me."

"Maybe the gossip started because you've brought so many big, healthy, pretty maids down there with you, one at a time of course."

"Oh? Yes, I *see*. That could do it, couldn't it? But how grotesque! It is a kind of work I do for an institution in Brussels, Mr. McGee. The rehabilitation and training of disadvantaged young girls. I give them a year of training, and when each one leaves my service, she is competent and disciplined and polite. I must confess that I select ones who are attractive to look at. I select paintings and lamps which are attractive to look at. And I try to see that they are sturdy enough to do a hard day's work. Do you understand? One cannot protect oneself against idle malice. I am a mystery. They seek answers. They will not accept the idea that there is no mystery at all. But I believe you will. You are, I think, an understanding and complex man. You look like the sort of man who is paid to strike a ball with a stick, or to fly to another star. But you have an easiness, an awareness of pleasure, no? And a life style which contents you, I think. You disconcert me. And you intrigue me."

"Which makes us even, Mrs. Vitrier."

"More blanks?"

"If I think of any, I'd like to come back and stand out here in the hall and have a nice little chat."

"Sorry. This is the only chance you will have."

"And. . . . I've run out of blanks."

She smiled, and without another word she closed the door. I stared at it and wondered if she was looking out the little peep hole at me. I walked back down the corridor. Nice going, McGee. Handled it real swell. And besides, you've got a life style which contents you. But not very much right now. You are pure hellfire with an insurance secretary from Guadalajara, but to the pretty French lady you are as impressive as a bag boy at the A & P.

226

Something about her was so vivid and so directed and so strong, it was difficult to think clearly in her presence.

So I adjourned the meeting to a metal table on the wide deck outside Azulejos. One was a quorum.

All right. Meeting come to order. What was wrong? Standing out in the hall. She's alone, she likes privacy, too many people could be on the make for some of that money from those four old dead boys. So she is alone, eh? Where are all the servants? All right, this is one of the great hotels of the world, and they can give you service until you drown in it, particularly if you maintain a suite like that permanently, and if you demand service, which I imagine she would. And it could be the maid's night out.

When I came to the doorslammer, why didn't she slam it instead of explain herself? What would she have to lose? Maybe she has so much pride in being 110 percent woman, she doesn't want anybody to believe she likes girls.

So why hadn't I tried to break up *that* act by bringing in Bruce Bundy? Because I knew she was lying anyway. And how did you know that, McGee, you subtle, clever, complex fellow? Nothing but pure instinct. Don't knock it. Meyer says it is made up of things you saw without knowing you saw them.

So what did I see that I didn't know I saw? Close the eyes. Focus on the room behind her. Whoa! Scan back. Change focus. Something there. Corner of coffee table. Fancy box. Candy box. How do you know it's candy? Because, dammit, there were those things on the floor there. What things? Well, candy litter. Wadded up pieces of that kind of red tinfoil and yellow and blue they wrap up good candy in. And some of those little pieces of brown paper.

So she has a sweet tooth.

And throws the debris on the floor under the coffee table?

Maybe she isn't neat.

But wasn't the rest of the room, what you could see of it, so neat as to be practically sterile?

227

She was sitting on the couch eating chocolates. Why not?

But I'd been aware of two scents coming from that woman. One was perfume, faint and astringent, and the other was gin. Gin and candy? Ech!

So the servant eats candy.

And throws the wrappers on the floor?

Well, it was a big hotel and they would take very good care of the monied guests, and they would make a practice of not handing out information for the hell of it. But a big hotel has to have a big staff, and there are always new people who haven't learned how to keep the mouth entirely closed. And guests have room service, maid service, laundry service, dry cleaning, television repair, dog-walking service. All in Spanish, no doubt.

If you skulk, you attract attention and suspicion. If you have to sneak, be loud and brash and confident about it.

My approach drew a blank with the guest service director's staff, and it drew a blank with the travel agency office, and I struck out with the switchboard girls, and then I started hitting the shops, all open at that time of the evening, on the lower level, showing my white teeth and finding out which clerk had the most English. I varied my pitch to fit the shop situation.

"You do speak English? Good. Golly, I sure hope you can help me out of an awful spot. I just had a drink up in Fiesta Suite D as a guest of Mrs. Rivereta, and she did me a real important favor. Now what I want to do, honey, is send up a couple of little gifts. But I must be losing my mind, because I've drawn a blank on any name except Mrs. Rivereta, and I thought maybe you might have sold stuff and sent it up there and know the names."

So you walk and talk, and it goes clunk, clunk, clunk, and in a little silver shop it goes DING!

She was a brisk, cute little thing and she had pale streaks dyed into her black, black hair, and she frowned and went thumbing through records, and asked questions of the other girl, and then finally pulled a card out.

"Yessss! I *thought* I remember something. But I don't know if this is a guest living there or it is something she is taking outside the hotel to a fiesta, a birthday. These things Mrs. Rivereta signed for and they are put on her hotel bill. Very nice. Let me show you one thing." She scampered off and came back with a thing that at first glance looked like a silver cigarette case, but turned out to be a purse gadget, with space for coins, notebook, pencil, identification.

"Across here, inside, people like the name engraved. We can give two-day service. And here, see, on this copy is the name. Meenda McLeen. Also, many, many sets of our initials for luggage and personal things. M. M. In silver and gold, different es-styles. And also one bracelet with the initials. I can show you the kind of bracelet. Señor? Anything is wrong?"

"No. You've been a big help to me. Yes, you've been a big help, and I certainly appreciate it more than you can know."

She was glad she had helped. Her smile was eager and pretty. I found the door without walking through the glass, and went down a corridor and came upon the coffee shop and sat at the counter and had coffee.

So it sorted out with a dismal and feral logic. Lose the first choice off a mountain road, so pick up the trail of the little brunette and cut the loss by settling for second choice. The door had stayed chained. Maybe second choice wasn't exactly a willing guest? Want to indulge in a dramatic rescue attempt, McGee? Adolescent emotions. The thing to do is talk to Minda, because she was the one who was closest to Bix, and she would know the story and be able to guess how it must have ended.

I did some exterior surveying. I found a place where I could walk from the end of one of the buildings, parallel to it, far enough out to look up and see the night-lighted green of the fourth floor garden patios, and, above them, the narrow balconies outside the fifth floor windows of the bedrooms of the Fiesta Suites. So I got back up to the fourth floor and paced the long straight corridor, counting the strides to her door, took my count back outside and paced from the same basing-point and found that the bedrooms of Fiesta D had to open out onto the seventh and eighth balconies from the end.

EIGHTEEN

The roof areas by the tennis courts and the heliport were too popular as a place to get kissed and a place to gawk at the great humming city. The chill of nighttime at seven and a half thousand feet didn't seem to discourage either pastime.

And there was one of the hotel guard staff wandering around from time to time, on no schedule. I spent almost an hour and a half noodling around, knowing exactly the route I had to take, but unable to make my start because people get very edgy about watching other people go over the edge of a roof.

When the crowd was down to one couple and they moved toward the stairs, I moved to my drop zone, and as I did not know how long the privacy would last, I swung over, hung by my fingertips, kicked myself away from the wall, and dropped, landed on balance, and scuttled over and stood behind a bank of floodlights waiting for somebody to start yelling.

Of course somebody could have been looking out of the window of one of the rooms and might now be phoning the desk to complain about people sneaking around at midnight. So move along, aware of the residual stiffness in the leg where Wally had popped me that good one. Down the cornice, behind the spots and floods, over to the higher one. Jump and grab. Hear the shoulder gristle pop as I pull myself up. No lights on the roof at this level. Angle across. Look down, count the shallow balconies.

Seven and eight. Pick any number from seven to eight. Because seven is lucky, I chose eight. High ceilings in their hotel. Looked like a thirty-foot drop into the fourth-floor roof garden.

Make it fifteen down to the floor of the little balcony. Cement railing maybe four and a half feet high, so call it ten and a half down to the railing. And it was about four inches wide and had a flat top. Drop to the balcony floor and it is not going to sound exactly like a stray birdfeather floating in. And hang by the fingertips and it is going to be a blind two foot drop to the railing.

Shoes off. Tie the laces. Hang around the neck. Check the pockets for any jingle-jangle of keys or change. Take a long long look around to see who might be watching the fun. Wave and see if they wave back. Momma, momma, look at the funny man on the roof!

Get it over with. And, for God's sake, McGee, in the future why don't you try to believe what people tell you? Just pray for a nice landing, drawn draperies, and an unlocked door.

I let myself down, hung, rehearsed it in my head and let go. I turned toward my left to land with feet at right angles to the balcony edge. Less chance of straddling it, which would sting like crazy. Landed, by design, leaning in, off balance. Landed on the railing, then dropped like that birdfeather to the balcony floor. Looked through a screened gap eight inches wide into a room with a brighter focus of light than I could have guessed from above. It did not illuminate the balcony because it was a recessed prism light in the bedroom ceiling. It shone straight down onto a tufted blue carpeted area. Beyond it I could see, in the dim glow, an open door and bathroom fixtures beyond. To my left I could see a low couch, a chair, a coffee table. To my right I could see the bottom corner, apparently, of a bed that was against the wall to the right, said corner perhaps six feet from the narrow opening created by opening the sliding door that far and pulling the draperies open to the same distance.

It seemed a little bright for a night light. But maybe it

232

would serve. More probably the room was empty. I stayed down below the railing height. Less chance of being noticed from a nearby building or from one of the other balconies.

Knelt and found the edge of the sliding screen and gave it a very gentle and cautious tug. It opened silently, a full inch. Another. Another. And somebody made a groaning sigh. Just as I was getting back into my skin, somebody said something, half mutter, half whisper, and I had to steady myself down again. Whoever you are there, talking in your sleep, why the hell did you leave the light on? One small advantage, however. Enough light, maybe, to be able to distinguish one dark head and be able to see whether it was Eva Vitrier. If so, I could then make my well-known death-defying leap across empty space to the other balcony.

I got the screen open as far as the door, and knew I would need a few more inches before I could go through it sideways. Had just put my palm against the edge of the door and the screen when I heard breathing. Not the deep breathing of sleep. This was more like the long distance runner. Bellows, getting deeper and faster, a huffing and a panting, then a cough and then the unmistakably, wide-open-throated, strained, soft, have-mercy cawing of woman in climax. It ended. There were some whisperous murmurings, too faint to catch. Then silence. A new set of rules had just been posted.

The bed creaked and suddenly a pale shape moved past the corner of the bed and stopped in the light, facing the balcony. I had pulled back quickly, but one instant had stamped it into memory for as long as memory would last. Naked, skin so white it seemed to blaze in the downthrust of the ceiling spot. An incomparable figure, simultaneously rich and delicate, without blemish. Nipples of that rare youthful pink, soft pubic bush, a color paler than old pennies. And it did what the picture could not do. It brought her into the focus of memory, of almost a year ago, when Meyer took the wheel and I went forward to bend a line on the new anchor. She was the one who stood at the bow in white shorts and a red top, and had looked

233

out across Lake Worth with almost the same soft, brooding, dreamy, inward expression. The wind had tangled her hair that day as much as bed had tangled it a year later. Welcome back from your damp Florida grave, Miss Bix.

The throaty, French-lady voice from the bed corner said, "Darling? You're too sweaty to stand in that cold night air. You'll get chilled."

"Can we go out on the balcony and look at the stars, Eva?"

It was a little-girl voice, humble and obedient.

"Of course, darling child. But we'll have to put something on."

I wondered if there was a gap at the other end of the draperies, where I could look in through the glass, from a darker area. I moved over and stood up and found a slit just wide enough. I saw Eva come to the edge of the light and hang some kind of floor-length cape or cloak over the girl's shoulders. It was a dark, rich blue, a violet-blue. She kept her hands on the girl's shoulders and I could hear her distinctly as she said, "Did I make you happy?"

The taller, younger girl turned quickly into Eva's arms, eagerly, gladly. Murmurous love-words. A soft, triumphant little laugh. Long kisses. And then Bix went off into shadows while Eva stood in the edge of the light, half-smiling. Hers was a slightly more spare and forthright body, as feminine, but with more of a look of function, so that naked she seemed more naked. Swarthy skin tones, sharp breasts with broad umber-dark nipple areas, long downsweep of muscular belly to the wide, vital spread of curly blackness, a look of compacted sinew along the tops of the thighs.

Bix brought a tailored gray robe and held it for Eva to slip on. My mind had been caroming around amid probables and improbables, bouncing off obstacles, like the shiny ball finding its way down the pinball machine, looking for the bumper that would ring the bells, flash the lights, award me some free games.

As Eva Vitrier looked down to fasten the belt of the robe, taking her first step toward the balcony, I pulled the doors wider and stepped into the room.

"Hate to bust in like this," I said.

Bix Bowie moved back into the shadows and stood staring at me without expression, yet with a kind of market-dog wariness which says that to find out if stones will be thrown, or food, one must wait, ready to run and ready to eat.

Eva Vitrier leaned forward in fishwife fury, backs of her hands against her waist, elbows cocked forward. I think that had I been able to understand French, the words would have chopped out little chunks of my flesh and left smoking craters. As I waited for her to run down, she whirled and dived to grab the nightstand phone. I clapped the cradle back down an instant after she lifted it. She hit me in the middle of the forehead with the earpiece. I clopped her on the side of the head with a cupped palm. It knocked her onto her hands and knees. She rose slowly, touching her hair, and said, "Bixie sweetie, go into the bathroom and close the door."

"I want to watch, Eva."

"Mind me! Or there'll be no surprise tomorrow, and no candy."

The girl turned and went into the bathroom and closed the door. And Eva came after my eyes with ten long nails. A wiry, furious, unrestrained woman can be dangerous to all men who, out of some notion of chivalry, try to quell her furies, hold her wrists and avoid her kicks and bites until she gives up.

Chivalry is pretty flexible. And sometimes it is dead.

So I hooked her a pretty good one in the stomach as she was coming in, and it was on a slightly upward angle, so her heels lifted off the floor, her legs swung up, and the first thing that hit the floor was that rear end which Enelio had found so delectable long ago. Momentum rolled her over onto her back, and her legs went up and over and she ended on her knees, the gray robe forward, and all entangled about her head and arms, which were

235

resting on the floor. Enelio might find that angle even more entrancing. She rolled onto her side, sat up, smoothed the robe down. She reached and caught a chair and pulled herself up and sat on it, making inhalation groans to try to suck enough air back into herself. Hit a woman, would you, McGee? I surely would, now and then.

All the spark and snap was gone. I saw switches by the door and went over and turned on the rest of the room lights. I closed the glass doors and pulled the lined draperies shut. I sat on the foot of the tousled bed.

She straightened herself. "You know, I could have you killed for that."

"If you know where to go and how much to offer."

"I can find out."

"And I can walk you into the bathroom there and try to teach you to breathe underwater, and I might have to do just that if I don't like the answers."

"There won't be any answers."

"Suit yourself, French lady."

"What are you looking for?"

"Something to knot you up with. Nylons are great. Stronger than steel. Then we'll see how much of this Kleenex we can cram into your mouth, and I'll tie that in place, roll you under the bed there, get Miss Bowie into some clothes and take her to the Embassy and phone her father from there. So forget the answers. I don't need them."

"Wait a minute. Sit down. Stop opening drawers, please. Listen to me a minute. I brought her back from living death, Mr. McGee. You don't know what she was like. Even I didn't know how lovely she would look."

"What is she blasting lately? She's way off center right now."

"She can't get along at all without something. I don't think she ever will. She's on charas. An agent brings it in for me from Calcutta. It's like marijuana, but very, very powerful. They use just the resins. I let her smoke three tiny little cigars of it a day. We make a ceremony out of

236

it. Don't you understand? She's been too badly damaged. She can't exist in the real world."

"But your world is just dandy. Best thing for her."

"She gets love and protection, and I keep her in good health. We have silly little games we play. I make her keep herself clean and pick up her clothes."

"And you get her her distemper shots and keep her coat glossy, and some day you can bury her in the foot of the garden and put a mossy little headstone up. Bix. Beloved pet. But that would be a little sentimental, huh?"

"You are certainly a cruel bastard. All right! So maybe I don't want any more challenging human relationships."

"After four old husbands?"

"You meet the simple young ones who can introduce you to the important young ones who can introduce you to the important and rich old ones. And you work at it, you know. You give fair value. All of them use you like a waste bin, a conveniently shaped receptacle, just as males used Bixie. But there is tennis and sailing and all the vigorous games in bed, and the old ones do not last long. The money was earned. The privacy was earned. The freedom was earned."

"I might pop you another one, just for luck."

"I don't think it would astonish me, actually."

"So she gets love. From you."

"I saw her and Minda in the zocalo. I followed them. They had to keep stopping at benches so Bix could rest. There was something about her. I had to know her. They needed help. The word probably doesn't mean anything to you, but do you know that she had never been sexually awakened? Can you imagine how much restraint and patience it took? But now she is more easily stimulated each day. She's very sensual. But she lives on Lesbos forever, because it is the only island she has ever known."

"That's pretty poetic there, French lady. What are you getting at? You want to keep her around the house?"

"She can never endure any contact with any part of her old life without reverting. I arranged to have her tourist permit renewed, in Minda McLeen's name. It was expensive. I am taking her . . . to another country where identities can be purchased. I intend to see that if anything should happen to me, she shan't want for anything."

"So Minda went off the hill in the yellow car. That's why she doesn't need her own papers. And Bix's papers went to Florida with the body and the personal effects. Was it expensive getting Minda bumped off the road, French lady?"

"It wasn't that way."

"What way was it?"

"Minda began to get suspicious after Bixie began to improve. And she began spying on me, and finally caught me . . . caressing Bixie in a way that couldn't possibly have been anything except what it was. She made a very ugly scene, and said some very ugly things. She said she would not permit it. Permit it! Can you imagine the impertinence? She tried to stay with Bix every moment, day and night. I asked Minda to my room to discuss the problem. I tried to seduce her, because I knew that would shut her mouth, but she acted as if I were some sort of sickening animal. She said she was going to get in touch with Bix's father. So as I was afraid I might lose Bix, the next time Minda left the house, I had a trusted friend of mine come at once in her car and pick up Bix and bring her up here to the city; I asked her to stay here in the suite with Bix until I could arrive. I informed the hotel they would be using the suite. I knew I could trust my friend to be careful and discreet, but I knew she would never be able to keep from making love to such a lovely child. But I had to accept that, even though it made me feel wretched. So when Minda came back I asked her if she had seen Bix. I pointed out that all her things were still in her room. I said she had wandered out and that I was worried. Minda knew it was a trick of some kind. She said she would stay with me and I would lead her to wherever Bix was."

The bathroom door opened and Bix came wandering out. "I'm tired of staying in there, Eva."

"Just a little bit longer, dear. Please."

"Well . . . all right." She went back in.

"On Saturday, in the early afternoon, that Rockland person came to my home demanding to see Minda. She did not know of it. She was in her room. I had Rockland brought to me, at the garden house beyond the pool, and I had Ramón and his nephew stay close by. I told you before, it was easy to see he was a low type, crafty and arrogant. One must exploit their greed to find out what plan they have. He was so obviously relieved to find no one else had been there before him, asking about her. It took a little time and a few simple threats, but I found out that Minda's father was in Oaxaca and had looked for Rockland and found him. Rockland had made an arrangement to deliver the girl to her father for money. He thought he could get ten thousand American dollars if he managed the affair skilfully. Nothing could have been more obvious to me than that if he did manage it, Minda would seek aid from her father in taking Bix away from me. One cannot tell how much resource an American businessman has in such matters. It would be obvious that at the very least he would feel an obligation to acquaint the other father with the state of affairs. I would want neither the notoriety nor the legal problems, nor want to take the chance of losing the girl. So I offered him twice what he expected from Mr. McLeen, if he would take Minda away with him on some pretext and leave her far enough away so that by the time she made her way back I could be gone and there would be no way to reach or find me. Then, if he chose, he might be able to continue his arrangement with her father.

"We set the schedule. I gave him five thousand dollars and suggested he take her to Coatzacoalcos on the Gulf of Campeche, on the pretext of taking her to where Bix was. Transportation is awkward from there to Oaxaca. He had a car. He could drive far into the night. It is something over three hundred miles from Oaxaca. He was to abandon her there, without funds, and return quickly. I would wait until a nine o'clock flight out of Oaxaca Monday evening. I would give him the rest of the money then, and he would, if ever questioned, swear he had loaned Bix money to fly back to the states."

But, she related, she had been awakened at midnight on Sunday night to be told that the young American was back, that he was on foot, that he was at the gate demanding to be let in. She dressed and went down to the gate and they talked in the courtyard. He said he had been too tired to drive so far. He thought it would be just as good to take her up into the mountains. She had gone willingly when he said that Bix needed her and he was taking her to where Bix was. But she became suspicious. He had found a place to pull off the road when night fell. He had kept her there with him. He had wanted to wait long enough so that she, Mrs. Vitrier, would think he had taken Minda a long way away. He had not wanted to lose track of her because of her resale value. It was his plan to tie her to a tree or something, out of sight of the highway on Monday, and go down and get the money and come back and pick her up again and make his deal with Wally.

Late Sunday afternoon while she was napping in the back seat of the little car, he had fallen asleep in the front seat. He had slept so heavily that apparently she had been able to work the car keys out of his pocket, put the key into the ignition, silently open a front door, brace her back against the other door, put her feet against him and suddenly shove him out onto the ground, yank the door shut and lock it. As he tried to break in, she got it started and pulled out and headed down the mountain, accelerating. He had picked a spot, after a long walk, where trucks would have to shift way down to negotiate a steep uphill curve. He had to wait hours before one came along with a tailgate he could climb onto. He had dropped off in the city and made his way to Eva's house. When he found that Minda had never arrived, he was certain she had gone off the mountain. And if she had, she was dead.

"I took him to the sitting room which adjoins my bedroom. We discussed the possible repercussions of this event. It had been a car he had taken without permission, but he was quite certain the owner would give very little if any information to the police, and he explained why. By then, you see, I knew that a car had gone off the mountain, and they would look for it by daylight. It sickened me to think of it. She was being very difficult, but I had not wished *that* for her. But it had happened. And in many ways it simplified things. One must be mature and accept facts, yes? So he said he must have the rest of the money because it had been promised. He was looking at me strangely, I thought. He said that in addition, I would give him the ten thousand he would have gotten from the father. I told him that was not my affair. He said it had become my affair. I had given him money to get rid of the girl and he had gotten rid of her. He said it would all be difficult to explain.

"By then I began to see that he could be of some danger to me. He was greedy and crafty and brutal, but not intelligent. It had been a mistake to make an arrangement with him. I knew that to disarm him I had to appear to be . . . manageable. I said I did not have so much in American dollars in the house, but I could make up the difference in Swiss francs. I got it all for him and explained the rate of exchange. I even told him the name I use in this hotel. He counted the money too many times and, also, too many times he told me that it was the last time I would have to give him money. It meant that he was thinking that he would ask again.

"He began looking at me in another strange way and said that we were now associated in this affair. He said he knew from Minda what I was, but that it would please him to come into my bed and use me as a woman, just to verify our trust and friendship. I told him there would be no pleasure in it for me, and he said that it did not particularly matter whether there was or not. At such times one must be very careful. And so I pretended fear and begged him not to, then seemed to accept the inevitable,

241

and asked him if he minded if I had some brandy before all this would take place. He said, as I expected, that he would enjoy some also, and that we could drink a toast and seal the bargain. I got a special bottle kept in a special place, and silver glasses so that he could not tell that I would let it run out of my mouth back into the glass. In a little while he smiled foolishly and his words blurred and soon his head toppled forward and he began to snore. I took the money from him and replaced it in the wall safe in the back of my bedroom closet. I felt as if I were moving through a dream. I had quite a lot of the meperedine left, which we had sometimes given Bix when she became unmanageable. Ten little ampules. I had been taught how to administer hypodermics when my first husband was dying, and of course I had given Bix injections. I prepared him properly, with an alcohol swab, and knelt by his chair. But I could not. One wonders if it is possible to kill a human being. I had a dozen reasons to do this thing. But I could not. I could touch the point to the vein on the inside of his arm, but I could not shove it through the skin, no matter what I told myself."

So in the end she had tied him securely, binding his wrists and ankles to the heavy chair. She had paced the floor until dawn, wondering what to do. When he began stirring, she had sedated him heavily. On Monday morning, early, Wally McLeen had arrived, having at last tracked his missing daughter to her house. She had taken him to the garden house and had given him some of the vivid highlights of Minda's Mexican vacation, throwing in incidents that had happened to Bix as though they had happened to Minda, including how Rockland had taken her into the cornfield to service the men who had showed up out of the night at the campsite. From his reactions she was afraid he was having a massive coronary. When he was at last more normal, she had said that it was possible that Minda was dead and that Rockland was responsible. She did not say more than that. She said that if he would get hold of some vehicle and if he would come to the vehicle gate at ten that night, there was a possibility she might be able to deliver Rockland over to him, so that he could take Rockland to the police. She showed him where the vehicle gate was. She would not answer his questions.

She had then decided, later on in the day, hearing that the body could not be identified, that if she made an appearance and made the identification and then said that the last she had seen of the girl was when she had driven off with Rockland on Saturday, it would help insulate her against any future accusation.

"But when I saw how . . . the terrible condition of the body, I knew that one could identify it as almost anyone. There was the chain, of course, that Minda wore about her ankle. But who could say that Bix did not wear one and it was not that one? Or could say those were not Bix's red shoes? I had the personal papers and personal things of both of them. My mind raced. I stood holding the perfumed handkerchief against my nose. I saw how it could be. If it was Bix who died, she would be mine without question. So I identified her and the police came to my house and I gave them Bix's things. I brought Minda's papers here, and I arranged to have the permit renewed under Minda's name without Bix having to appear. I sent all the servants out that night. I opened the gate for Mr. McLeen. I helped him get Rockland down and into the trunk of an American sedan Mr. McLeen had rented. Mr. McLeen was very strange. He whistled and he walked on his toes, and he said that everything was splendid, that Minda was going to come back to Oaxaca and he would wait around for her until she returned. Rockland was very groggy. When he was curled up in the trunk compartment on his side, Mr. McLeen gave him little pats on the back and called him son and said everything would be arranged properly. I thought I was all right. I thought I was not feeling much of anything. But when I had shut the gate again, all of a sudden without warning, I vomited. Afterward, I felt so faint it took me a long time to finish packing the last few things. I flew from Oaxaca Tuesday on the early schedule. Bix was happy to see me, happy as a Christmas child."

She was watching my face carefully.

Bix came out of the bathroom again. "Please?"

"All right, dear girl. Sit over there on the couch and be quiet. Mr. McGee, does she look abused? Surely you must have the right to make choices in your work. I am fond of her. I cherish her. I will take her to lovely secluded places. Look how splendid that color is for her. It makes those deep blue eyes look almost deep violet. I will dress her in indigo, and in the good blues and greens and grays. Cool tones suit her kind of beauty. I can control her . . . need for escape into drugs. She will not be sick, or lonely, or institutionalized. Can anyone else in the world promise that? Can her own people promise that? What do you return to them if you do your nasty little job, Mr. McGee? A young girl with a drug-retarded mind. A committed and incurable addictive personality. A committed and incurable lesbian. A person the police of your country will be watching closely, as they promised. You will be taking back heartbreak. Isn't it kinder, by far, to let her stay dead?"

"Dead?" asked Bix.

"The kid asks a good question, French lady. So do you."

"Think about it carefully, please."

So I sat and thought about it. It was nice and easy, her way. Let the dead stay dead. Tell a happy story to good old Harlan Bowie. Feed Meyer the story Eva had fed me through the chained door. Go back and romp away the final few days of Elena's vacation. Mission accomplished. But should the father have the chance to undo the damage that he had started and others had finished? He had a lot of money, enough to buy penance, good clinics, sleep therapy.

"I have a wall safe here," she said. "In that closet. I think there is the equivalent of about forty thousand American dollars. I can give you that now, and I can

244

have an additional hundred and sixty thousand here by the day after tomorrow."

"You buy the girl for two hundred thou?"

"That is a clumsy way to put it. I buy her happiness, and mine. I can afford it."

"I know. You earned it. The hard way."

I walked over toward her. She stood up and looked up at me, and I saw the hard mocking confidence in the back of her eyes. She was wearing the small smile of the winner. So I smiled too, and I sighed, and I wondered if it was getting to be too attractive a habit as I steadied her with one hand, chopped the side of that long muscular throat with the other, caught her as she dropped, and slung her onto the bed.

Bix had stood up. "Now what are you doing?"

"I am going to take you for a nice little ride in a nice murderous taxi, sweetie."

"To the movies?"

"Maybe. Why don't you go put some clothes on? Where are they?"

"In there. In that other room in the closet and all over."

"Go get dressed."

"Sure."

She went into the next room. I wanted to fix French lady so she would stay put for a nice long time, but not too long, in case nobody dared unlock the suite unless asked. I yanked the sheets out from under her and took them in and dropped them in the tub and got them sopping wet. I took them out and spread them out on the rug, took her out of her gray robe, put her down at one end of the soaked sheets, and rolled her up in them like a window shade. I put her back on the bed with the last wet end tucked neatly under her. As long as they stayed wet, she stayed still. When they dried out, she would wiggle loose.

I pried her jaw down and found that in spite of the plump little meaty mouth, there was room in there for a hell of a lot of Kleenex, if you packed it carefully. I

245

knotted a nylon stocking in place, webbing it between her teeth and against the Kleenex so she couldn't tongue it out of the way and start yelling.

Then I went in to see how Bixie was progressing. She had lost ground, because she had shed the robe and added one lacy pale-green bra. So I told her I expected her to shape up better than that, which at the moment was the wrong expression, and I started digging around trying to find what you put on a naked young girl to take her to the Embassy in the middle of the night.

I heard some kind of disturbance, but by then I had found where the skirts and blouses and sweaters were. So I took time to match them up reasonably well. Bix had gone back into the first bedroom. I heard a lovely gasping delighted giggling, and I heard some kind of muffled grunting and thrashing.

When I hurried in I saw that Bix was bending over the bed, and she had grasped Eva Vitrier firmly with thumb and first two fingers, right by the Nefertiti nose, thus cutting off all air except what the woman might try to suck through all that Kleenex. French lady's face had turned very, very dark. Her eyes were bulging and blind, and she was spasming and grunting and flapping, looking very much like an oversized, dying whitefish in the bottom of a skiff. And, believe me, she did not have very far to go. Like twenty seconds more, possibly. I snatched Bix's playful fingers off lovergirl's nose, and Eva subsided, breath whistling as she hyperventilated through that noble beak. She opened her eyes and looked up at me, in combination loathing and appeal. Her effort had burst a blood vessel in one eye, and half the white had turned bright crimson.

I tucked her wet sheet firmly under her, patted her on the cheek, took Bixie in, and crowded her into her clothes. She passed inspection. In the elevator on the way down she said, "Wasn't Eva funny? Wasn't she funny, though?"

"She was a scream, kid."

"I wish you hadn't made me stop."

"So do I, sort of."

246

So we taxied to the Embassy, not far down Reforma, and stood on the wide sidewalk as the cab went away. She yawned.

"Is this the movies?"

"Bixie baby, things can get very, very, very rough for you. I don't even know if you can understand how rough they have been, or will get. I would feel a lot better if I thought maybe you could cut it."

"Oh hell yes," she said. "Let's go in."

NINETEEN

Meyer was at the Oaxaca airport to meet me when I came back from Florida via Mexico City five days later.

He looked fit and smug and amused, and he wore a straw hat from the market and a blue shirt covered with zippers with metal rings in them.

I peeled out of the inbound line and said, "Relapse? What the hell kind of a relapse are you having?"

"It's no worse than a bad cold."

"Then you could have all by yourself gotten on a plane and all by yourself flown home, right?"

"But I don't like to travel alone. Anyway, are you paying for the extra trip?"

"No. But this isn't the happiest place in the world to come back to, for me. I guess you know that."

"Oh, I guess I do. But I don't have to get depressed just because you do. That wasn't such a great phone connection. How did Harl take it?"

"How the hell did you expect him to take it? He's bursting with joy and hope and all that, in a good effort to hide the fact that what we took back there to him might be, in his code of values, better off dead. She started coming apart. She was very, very raggedy by the time the reunion happened."

"Nothing out of the Vitrier woman?"

"What could she do? Why should she try to do anything? And they had to buy my story. I saw the girl wandering around near Sanborne's. I was sure I recognized her as Beatrice Bowie, who was supposed to have died. In fact, I was in Mexico at her father's request, finding out how she died. Here you are, Embassy. Straighten things out. They would rather have had me hand them some armed infernal device. They hated it. They kept looking very Princeton and sighing and hunting for new forms to fill out. Meyer, goddamit, pack! I want to be home. I want to be on the *Flush*. I want to go to some island no developer has ever found yet, where no beer can has yet washed ashore."

"Enjoy beautiful Oaxaca."

And she hit me at a dead run, grabbing and laughing and saying if we were going to stand out here all day, she, Elena, could not wait for the surprise.

I told her she was supposed to be back at work.

She told me she wanted a little more vacation, and so did Margarita, and so they took a little more.

"But can they just do that?" I asked Meyer.

"When Enelio Fuentes owns that much of the insurance company they can, buddy."

So we had drinks and dinner at the Victoria, abundant and long and I tried to be festive, but it kept slipping on me. I kept worrying the whole thing. Picking at it. Meyer said impatiently, "Will you kindly get off that tiresome point of no return, McGee? Please? For me? And for these Guadalajara girls, and for your own sake? A grown-up man must make a lousy decision from time to time, knowing it is lousy, because the only other choice is lousy in another dimension, and no matter which way he jumps, he will not like it. So he accepts the fact that the fates dealt him two low cards, and he goes on from there. Or better, why don't you two go on from here. I seem to have been moved into another cottage, and only this insurance friend of mine seems able to find it after dark."

But it still kept nibbling and chewing at me. It kept me just a little apart from all the joy of Elena. And it woke me near dawn, thinking again of that look in Harlan Bowie's eyes, and wondering if the son of a bitch would clap her away somewhere forever, for her own good, of course.

Dawn-thoughts are the bleak ones. And these took me back to T. Harlan Bowie's arena—Garden Suite Number Five in that quietest part of Coral Gables. As a medical precaution they had put him on a tranquilizer and then told him I was on the way, bringing back his only chick, alive. I left Bix with his nurse-therapist, Mrs. Kreiger, while I tried to prepare him for her.

I tried, but I don't think he was listening closely. "Look, Mr. Bowie, she went down there with rotten people. It was a setup. She could put her hands on twenty-five thousand, and they knew it, and they conned her out of it, every dime of it. Some people, Mr. Bowie, have too much of a taste for marijuana. It takes over. They just float and they don't give a damn."

"My daughter isn't that kind of person, McGee."

"She was fogged over, believe me. In the early part of the trip the three men were all banging her, and the other girl too—the one you buried."

"Then they were taking her by force, and I am going to see that they are prosecuted."

"This wasn't kid games. Two of them are dead. She's under suspicion of conspiring to smuggle heroin across the border. She got hooked on heroin, Mr. Bowie. She was an addict, or is an addict. A woman gave her a home cure. She cycled her down through some other opiates and got her over onto something that's not physically addicting. It was a lot of trouble. The woman wanted her."

"Wanted her?"

"And got her, as a girlfriend, as a female homosexual partner."

"Are you out of your mind?"

"I'm just trying to tell you that this is a different girl. She's an addictive personality, and she isn't going to be able to handle any part of this without getting back onto some kind of a high. And you can't reach her because she bombed herself so long and so big, her mind is not on our wavelength anymore. I'm trying to tell you that—"

"McGee, I think I'm a little tired of you telling me things. I want to see my daughter, please."

Bixie was down off the charas high, and was being threatened with all the hard edges of reality, and she wanted no part of it. She was mean, edgy, suspicious, and unpredictable. She was vulgar and sullen and semipsychotic. And she was not about to rush in and kiss dear old daddy and cry tears of joyous welcome, and express any sympathy for his being in a wheelchair.

She came scuffing in, glanced at him, and went over and slouched into a chair. Mrs. Kreiger saw him having problems with the wheelchair and hurried around and wheeled him over to the girl. He reached and grabbed her hand. He was weeping. "Bix. Oh, Bix, honey."

But Bix honey looked narrow-eyed at me. "Is this the big treat, you rotten, dirty bastard? You bring me back to this silly old fart? Where's Eva? What have you done to Eva? Look, I've got to have a surprise. Honest to God, I've got to have a surprise or I'm going to go up the walls screaming."

"You're home now!" he said.

"Somebody get him off me," she said.

"I thought you were dead, honey."

She looked at him with the coldest dark blue eyes in town. "And I wish you were, old man. I wish to hell you were."

Mrs. Kreiger said, "Doctor Kohn wants to have a look at her. Should I . . . take her along now?"

"Yes. And . . . let me know what they suggest, please."

When they were gone he wiped his eyes and shook his head. "It isn't possible she could change so much. What can . . . be done?"

"I think maybe you've got to make her able to live with somebody she despises. She despises Bix Bowie, and always has, but didn't know there was a way to escape. It will take a lot of love, a lot of patience, a lot of motivation to make her ever believe that the Bix Bowie of the real world isn't a total failure. Excuse me, but what else have you got worth doing?"

"It . . . it's a second chance?"

"And very damned slim."

"It's the only thing I can do."

So maybe he would and maybe he wouldn't give it the big try. Or it might last only so long. I wondered about that look in his eye. Maybe I'd only imagined it was there. Second try, second rejection. But maybe, just maybe, he might have the guts for the job.

I heard a rooster crow a long way across the silence of the predawn morning in Oaxaca.

Near dawn, and Elena was curled into me, fists against my chest, round knees pressing against my belly. So I kissed the sleeping eye that was nearest and handiest.

She grunted and came but partway up out of sleep, far enough to begin a slow and determined worming and squirming, trying to work the undermost leg under me, under my waist. When I saw what she was trying to do, I made it easier for her. She slid the leg under, and then hooked her calf back against me. She lifted the other leg over me, the drowsy weight of it coming down across my waist. She uncurled her fists and slid her hands around my ribs, one under me, one on top, and flattened her palms against my back.

So then there was the unseen questing, and a guiding touch, and then a snubbed pressure increasing until— celebrated with a little snuff of sudden insuck of air through her nose—we were suddenly, sleekly, deeply coupled. She hitched herself a little higher, changed her position, moved her hands further around me, and made her small warm sound of contentment.

I slid my hands down her back until they reached and cupped the warm, smooth, solid buttocks. And like some familiar, faithful, trusty, loyal little machine, that touch and pressure was enough to start the slow, rhythmic pumping of her hips, rich and sleepy and demanding.

So with gray at the windows, and her mouth turning upward for the kiss, with the slow deep steady beat that would begin to change only when we neared climax, *this* became the reality, *this* became the life-moment, *this* became the avowal, the communion, the immortality. The

252

private rhythm of our need, a small and personal and totally shared thing, was that special thing in the world and in time which changed the Rockos and Evas, the Jerrys and Wallys and Bruceys and Carls, the Bixies and Beckys to scare-masks fashioned of cardboard and spit, empty things which hang on strings from an empty tree, turning in the parching wind that blows across the empty heart.

"Ah," said the tireless, tawny, loving engine.

Bless all the sisters, wherever they are.

OTHER GREAT ADVENTURES IN THE BRILLIANT TRAVIS McGEE SERIES BY

JOHN D. MACDONALD

Follow the quests of Travis McGee, amiable and incurable tilter at conformity, boat-bum Quixote, hopeless sucker for starving kittens, women in distress, and large, loose sums of money.

"McGee is top-notch MacDonald."—Chicago Tribune

A Fawcett **Gold Medal Book**

Wherever Paperbacks Are Sold

Contents

Introduction

This guide had its beginnings in the summer of 1984. Members of the Preservation Coalition of Erie County met in an Allen St. watering hole to discuss ways of publicizing Buffalo's fascinating industrial archaeology, and by extension, preserving it. (That summer, the Cargill Electric elevator was demolished and steel plants were facing the cutter's torch.)

The result is a modest book which is part architectural description, history, industrial archaeology, and part a book of curiosities. It looks at the High and Mighty (the 1833 lighthouse) and the ordinary (an auto crushing company). We hope it reflects the variety of the waterfront.

There may be mistakes and omissions. We hope knowledgeable readers will bring them to our attention so corrections can be made in future editions.

This guide, for the most part, uses colloquial terms for the parts of grain elevators. For instance, a marine leg is that part of the elevating apparatus which is lowered into a ship's hold to remove grain, but it can also mean the entire marine tower. More often than not, it is called simply a leg. As in, "My, that elevator has a nice pair of legs!"

1758 Daniel Joncaire Sieur de Chabert builds a farmstead on the south bank of the Buffalo River.

1817 An open boat, the "Troyer," brings the first flour into Buffalo from the west.

1820 Samuel Wilkeson builds a pier at the mouth of the then Buffalo Creek.

1825 Erie Canal opens.

1828 First machine shop and foundry in the village of Buffalo established by Beals, Mayhew & Co. at Ohio and Indiana streets. Also, the schooner "Guerriere" brings the first load of wheat from the west, 2,500 bushels, but there was no demand for it and it was sent down to Dunkirk.

1833 Second Buffalo lighthouse completed on stone hillock, or molehead, at end of pier.

1842 Joseph Dart builds a grain warehouse with an elevating mechanism to remove grain from ships. His Evans Elevator is a world's first.

1850 Blackwell Canal, later renamed the City Ship Canal, opens. A smashing success.

1851 Ohio Basin opens.

1852 Main and Hamburg Canal opens.

1861 Civil War period finds dramatic increase in wheat received in Buffalo. Receipts of 1861 double the level of 1860. This, in turn, sets off an 80-year boom in elevator construction.

1897 Steel tank elevator, the Electric, completed and the Great Northern, another steel tank elevator, essentially complete. Both are electrically powered. The Electric has the first movable marine tower.

1899 First reinforced concrete grain bin, "Peavey's Folly," built in Minneapolis. First full scale concrete elevators built in Midwest, 1900-1901.

1900-1903 Lackawanna Iron & Steel complex built.

1901 Concrete superstructure placed on old timber crib substructure on outer harbor breakwater, a world's first.

1902 Dakota Elevator built of steel. Replaces wooden Dakota that burned earlier.

1903 Tile elevator built at Washburn-Crosby site.

1906 By this date, Buffalo's first reinforced concrete elevator, the Washburn-Crosby B, in operation.

1913 Article by Walter Gropius on industrial architecture in *Jahrbuch des Deutschen Werkbundes*, illustrated with seven pages of American grain elevators and factories, among them the Washburn-Crosby and Dakota.

1914 Grain elevator impact seen in the work of Italian Futurist Antonio Sant'Elia and in the sketchbooks of Erich Mendelsohn. Also, the Superior elevator, first elevator engineered by the prolific A.E. Baxter, built.

1923 Swiss-born architect and theorist Charles-Edouard Jenneret-Gris, Le Corbusier, publishes *Vers une Architecture*, or Towards a New Architecture, using grain elevators as prototypes for an industrially rooted style.

1924 Erich Mendelsohn visits Buffalo.

1926 Mendelsohn publishes *Amerika: Bilderbuch eines Architekten*, containing photographs of several Buffalo elevators.

1929 Bruno Taut publishes *Modern Architecture*, the first book on the new architecture targeted to an English speaking audience. Concrete Central is illustrated.

1932 The improved Welland Ship Canal opens. Large ships, particularly those carrying Canadian grain, can now bypass Buffalo.

1940 Electric elevator extension.

1943 Peak of grain trade.

1954 Last elevator construction in Buffalo, the Connecting Terminal extension.

1959 St. Lawrence Seaway completed.

1955-1965 The grain transshipment trade in Buffalo plummets due to navigational improvements in Mississippi and St. Lawrence rivers and changing railroad freight rates.

1965 General Mills closes Dakota elevator. It is later demolished.

1974 Erie Basin Marina opens on downtown waterfront.

1978 Tifft Farm, once a site of coal docks and canals, reopens as a nature preserve.

1983 Bethlehem Steel announces the ending of steel making at its Lackawanna plant.

1984 Electric elevator demolished.

Present The only active grain elevators are those owned by milling or malting companies. Closing of heavy industries has greatly lessened waterborne pollution. Fish return to Buffalo River. Contaminated land and river bottom sediments remain. Leisure use of waterfront increases dramatically; public demands more waterfront access.

1 Buffalo Lighthouse.
Located on the Coast Guard base across from the Erie Basin Marina, the lighthouse is a conspicuous symbol of Buffalo's past and present. Built in 1833, it is the oldest

building on Buffalo's waterfront and one of the oldest lighthouses on the Great Lakes. It is the second of four lighthouses to serve as Buffalo's primary light.The base, up to the cornice, dates from 1833, while everything above it dates from 1857.

The light stands near the end of a long stone pier which can be called the foundation of Buffalo, originally having been laid down by Samuel Wilkeson in 1820. (The first Buffalo light stood at the shore end of the pier.) It created a sheltered harbor along the previously untamed shore.

The lighthouse is

constructed of ashlar limestone and bluestone, and is one year younger than Buffalo itself (chartered as a city in 1832). The tower is 68 feet tall and tapers from a 20-foot diameter at the base, where the walls are four feet thick, to a 12-foot diameter at the top, where the walls are two feet thick.

In 1914 the lens was taken from this tower to one built just behind the outer harbor breakwater. The breakwater light then became the principal, or third, Buffalo light. A fourth light, a 71-foot white tower on the breakwater itself, has been the main light since 1963.

Unused and deteriorating, the 1833 light was almost demolished in the late 1950s. After a proper hue and cry it was saved and restored by 1961. Further restoration in the late 1980s resulted in floodlighting of the tower's shaft and illumination of the cupola.

The lighthouse cannnot be reached by public transportation, but can be seen from the Erie Basin Marina on the north bank of the Buffalo River. A pedestrian path along the south bank from the head of Fuhrmann Blvd. ends at the light and affords a nice view of the skyline. The Coast Guard station itself is occasionally opened to the public for special events.

2 Erie Basin Marina. A welcome sliver of public access, the Erie Basin

Marina is one of the top destinations on the Buffalo waterfront. It was—and still is—the only public access to

the downtown waterfront since at least 1825, the year the Erie Canal opened.

Several small buildings are clustered at the marina's south end and around a lookout/lighthouse at the northern entrance channel. All are of reinforced concrete construction, in the *beton brut* style popularized in the1960s. The massing and the raked roofs of the snack bar buildings at the south end create a very pleasant, accessible, and democratic oasis. A larger restaurant, Crawdaddy's, lies outside the public marina on the old Coit Slip. It looks like something out of *Cannery Row,* but has a nice patio on the slip.

The marina gets a lot of use, particularly since much of the rest of the waterfront has been given back to private developers who have an inordinate fondness for mediocre architecture and discouraging public access.

3 Lake Erie. The lake, once seen as a convenient dumping ground for the industries and farms which line its shores, is now seen as an irreplaceable natural resource. It has recovered to the extent that it has played host to regional and national fishing tournaments. With cleaner water has come a new boom in recreation.

Some Erie facts: It is 9,940 square miles in area, or a bit larger than the state of Vermont. The lake is about 240 miles long and ranges from about 10 miles (at the eastern, or Buffalo, end) to 58 miles wide. The lake is very shallow, with an average depth of only 90 feet. This makes for very turbulent conditions if the wind is blowing just right. In extreme southwest winds, the water has been known to drop eight feet at Toledo in the western end and to rise as much in the eastern end, at Buffalo.

4 Breakwaters. Prior to European settlement Lake Erie's eastern shore was

Lake Erie from Erie Basin Marina

regularly inundated by the pounding waves and shifting water levels of the huge lake. The mouth of Buffalo Creek was an area of mudflats, sandbars, and brush, not given to safe anchorage or permanent settlement.

That changed forever with the building of breakwaters to keep the waves away and bulkheads to direct the flow of the river and keep soil in place. In 1820 Samuel Wilkeson was chosen by early Buffalo moguls to build a municipal pier and make a harbor where there was none. He also channelized the mouth of Buffalo Creek. Together, these improvements led the New York legislature to pick Buffalo as the terminus of the Erie Canal. *That* made the city. (Indeed, Wilkeson's

tombstone in Buffalo's Forest Lawn Cemetery reads "Urbem Condidit"—He Built the City.)

It is likely that much of the stone and rubble south wall of the Buffalo River, opposite the Erie Basin Marina, is Wilkeson's original pier. Here surely lies the foundation of Buffalo.

The current system of breakwaters stretches from opposite the foot of Porter Ave. in LaSalle Park to Lackawanna, over 22,000 feet in all.

Buffalo's early breakwaters were basically a series of timber boxes filled with stones and rock. The side facing the lake was reinforced with a sloping wall of loose rocks (riprap). Wave energy would dissipate on the irregular

Cross sections of various Buffalo breakwaters

surface. The crib tops were originally heavy planking, but concrete shells were soon installed above the waterline.

The leeward side of the breakwaters had very little in addition to the timber cribs themselves, usually just enough riprap (below the waterline) to hold the breakwater in place. Occasionally major storms drove waves over and through the breakwaters, sometimes resulting in great shore damage and loss of life.

As technology advanced, the breakwaters were built more imperviously or improved to new standards. The North breakwater, for instance, was completed around the turn of the century, and was originally built of timber cribs filled

with stone. It later received a reinforced concrete cap. It lies opposite the Erie Basin Marina and connects with the Bird Island Pier. The North breakwater is Buffalo's first defense against storm driven waves. On very windy days, especially in autumn, it is dramatic to see the giant waves crashing and foaming over it.

5 Marine Drive Apartments. The landward side of Erie Basin has changed dramatically since the 1950s, when railroad tracks, coal docks, and waterfront warehouses dominated the scene. The area had what a chamber of commerce might call a "colorful" past. An 1893 map by a group called the Christian Homestead Association, which

SECTION OF SOUTH BREAKWATER -G-
(BUILT 1897-1902)
(SUPER-STRUCTURE 1902-1927)

SECTION OF SOUTH BREAKWATER -E-
(BUILT 1897-1902)

Cross sections of various Buffalo breakwaters, 1903

concerned itself with the area, found 75 "houses of ill-fame," over 100 saloons, and 75 shops and restaurants.

The apartments, originally called the Dante Place Apartments, were a federal urban renewal project. Blocks of houses, shops, bars, and other buildings serving the lake and Erie Canal trade were demolished to make way for the cruciform brick towers.

The new neighborhood had no amenities, period, and was soon cut off from downtown by the Thruway, which went through in the late 1950s. The development flopped, as tenants rebelled against living in such a dirty and isolated environment.

It was not until the mid-1970s, after the railroad trestles and warehouses were removed and the Evans Ship Canal was filled in, that the apartments became desirable. (There is an apocryphal tale that debris from Frank Lloyd Wright's masterpiece, the Larkin Building, was used as

fill.) So sweeping were the clearances that, between the elevated section of the Niagara Section of the New York State Thruway and the Erie Basin Marina, only the Marine Drive Apartments existed in 1980.

Today Erie St. runs along the path of the old slip and a strip of green park runs along the Buffalo River where once a coal trestle stood. The Marine Drive Apartments are now privately run and there is a waiting list to get in.

It is ironic that during the 1980s most of what had been cleared open land, publicly owned, was replaced by an impenetrable wall of private office buildings, condominiums, rowhouses, and towers. More towers are projected, perhaps with a themed shopping "experience."

6 Vietnam Veterans Memorial and Korean War Memorial. At the point where Erie St. bends westward on its path to the marina lies the Vietnam Veterans Memorial. The memorial consists of

Vietnam Veterans Memorial

mahogany colored granite panels in the form of two curved and sloping walls. They flank an octagonal granite post, the top of which is a pictorial relief by a local craftsman. The panels list the 486 people from eight Western New York counties who died in the war and 22 missing in action.

The Korean Memorial is a modest one, located about 50 yards upriver from the Vietnam Memorial along a pedestrian path. The memorial consists of an egg-shaped granite mass, with two soldiers in high relief, and a hexagonal granite post on which are engraved the names of local Korean War fatalities.

The arc of steel mesh benches which borders the memorial, incidentally, is a quantum leap in comfort and design over the area's more prevalent wooden benches.

7 Miss Buffalo Cruise Boats. On the Buffalo River near Erie St. The first Miss Buffalo cruise boat was christened in 1972, signalling a new recreational interest in the waterfront.

The present Miss Buffalo and Miss Buffalo II sight-seeing vessels offer scheduled tours of the Buffalo waterfront. Evening cruises with live entertainment and fishing excursions are also available. Admission charge.

8 Naval and Servicemen's Park. Foot of Pearl St. and Marine Drive. With its sharply thrusting angles and metal cladding, the park's naval museum (1978, Stieglitz, Stieglitz & Tries) bears a resemblance to the vessels it memorializes. The two-level museum contains 6,400 square feet of space devoted to exhibits which highlight the contributions Western New York has made to America's seapower.

The 6.5-acre museum site runs along 1,300 feet of prime water frontage, beginning at the foot of Main St. south of Memorial Auditorium. The centerpiece of the exhibit is the destroyer USS *The Sullivans* (named for five brothers who died during WW II). *The Sullivans* is a National Historic Landmark. The 376-foot-long vessel

Naval Museum

was donated by the Navy to the city, along with the cruiser USS *Little Rock*. They were later joined by the submarine USS *Croaker*. Besides the huge warships, the Naval Park also displays two jet fighters, a minesweeper, and a submarine. Admission charge.

9 Memorial Auditorium. If you can ignore the metal fascia panels, added during a roof-raising and expansion in the '70s, there is an elegant art deco building lurking at 140 Main St. The building (1939, Green and James), with its thin bands of vertical openings and exterior of Indiana limestone, bears a resemblance to the federal and state office buildings on Niagara Square. Little wonder, since Green and James was the successor to

the auditorium.

A major engineering feat took place in 1975 when the 2,000 ton roof was lifted by 24 hydraulic jacks to make room for a 4,500 seat balcony.

Acoustical devices which look like marshmallows were hung from the ceiling to help the poor acoustics, without

Skyway over the inner harbor

Green and Son, which worked on the office buildings.

While the "Aud" has many art deco details, such as the wonderful carved eagles which guard both sides of the Terrace entrance (you may have to peer behind some trees to find them) and geometric designs above the doorways, it also shows the influence of the growing modern movement in architecture.

The interior functions are expressed on the outside of the building. A rectangular three-story entrance hall is flanked by two lower appendages with rounded fronts, housing a lounge and offices. These elements front on the large mass of

noticeable success. The concert lovers and hockey fans who periodically pack the Aud don't seem to mind.

10 Buffalo Skyway. The Skyway, opened in 1955, is the first fixed-span bridge to be built over the inner harbor. Steel and concrete piers lift the roadway far above the Buffalo River and the City Ship Canal. Clearance over the Buffalo River is 100 feet.

The Skyway permits traffic to bypass downtown Buffalo on its way north or south. Prior to its opening, lift bridges were the only means of crossing the City Ship Canal and Buffalo River.

Also bypassed by the

The Americana

Skyway were the Old First Ward's grain elevators and metalworking shops—to be nearly forgotten, until recently, by the outside world.

It is a wintertime Buffalo tradition to listen for reports of the Skyway being closed because of high winds, blowing and drifting snow, and massive auto pile-ups. Sometimes all three at once.

11 The Americana. On the Buffalo River at the foot of Main St. Built in 1926 by Bethlehem Steel, this 150-foot-long vessel was originally christened Fishers Island. The 863 ton ex-steamer initially was used as a ferry on the Block Island and Long Island Sounds. It was later renamed Block Island.

In 1959, the ship was converted from steam to diesel power. It provided regular ferry service until 1986.

A Buffalo businessman bought the vessel in 1987 and refurbished it. In 1988, the newly re-christened Americana began her second life as a nostalgic excursion boat.

On board the 550-passenger ship is a 60-year-old band organ, much like the melodic devices found on merry-go-rounds. Much of the original operating equipment is still intact. The vessel cruises at 11 miles per hour, although it can move at 13 miles per hour. Scheduled trips are made into Lake Erie and the harbor. Admission charge.

12 Irontown. The area bounded Perry St., South Park Ave., Washington St., and Michigan Ave. is virtually Buffalo's last existing link with the Erie Canal and its feeder canals. Here are warehouses and small manufactories with roots deep in Buffalo's past. Clues to its history lie thick along the cobbled streets—from the Oldman boiler works to food storage facilities (Buffalo's major vegetable market and ship's chandlers were located in the area). We'll call it Irontown.

Ironically, as one stands within it, all direct links to the water have vanished. The Erie Canal's extension, the Main and Hamburg Canal, ran where the Thruway now runs, and the Clark and Skinner Canal, connecting the Main and Hamburg Canal with the Buffalo River, ran approximately where Baltimore St. now runs. The Buffalo River is hidden by

Looking east up Perry Street

the NFTA train sheds, used to store Buffalo's rapid transit cars.

This was also the center of Buffalo's small-scale iron-working industry. The first machine shop and foundry established in what was then the village of Buffalo was Beals, Mayhew & Company. In 1828 they set up shop at Ohio and Indiana streets. For the next 100 years, the neighborhood would spawn a profusion of ironworking shops.

By 1920, it is estimated, Buffalo foundries and machine shops employed between one-fifth and one-sixth of all those employed in Buffalo. The number of plants was 258. (These figures do not include steel manufacturers such as Bethlehem Steel.) Many of these could trace their existence back to the small, tight neighborhood in the First Ward.

As the companies expanded they moved mostly eastward, along Broadway and the railroad corridors of the East Side. New, small—in today's terms, entrepreneurial—companies took their place in the industrial lofts of the First Ward. This remarkably fertile process was made possible by three things in proximity to each other: cheap, adaptable building space, an infrastructure of suppliers, and a readily available pool of skilled

No. 41 Perry Street has cast iron Corinthian columns

A manufacturer's ad from the 1882 Buffalo City Directory

workers and aspiring executives. The market for their products—ships, railroads, and factories—was either literally across the street or easily reached via the transportation network.

In the mid-19th century the entire block from Mississippi to Baltimore streets between Perry and Ohio streets was occupied by the Jewett & Root Stoveworks and the Eagle Iron Works. Jewett & Root was one of the largest makers of stoves in this part of the country. The Eagle Ironworks created all kinds of cast iron architectural elements, such as window pediments, columns, storefronts, stair railings, and posts. Nothing is left of these works except the products they made.

The block bounded by Mississippi and Illinois, between South Park and Perry, contains representative buildings and industries that relate to the history of the whole waterfront area. Several good functional reinforced concrete structures remain on this block, one of the few heavily built-up blocks remaining in this once vital area. The building at 89-97 Perry St. (1922) is a handsome loft building with a reinforced concrete frame and brick and tile curtain

The Oldman Boiler Works

walls.

The Phoenix Die Casting Co., at South Park and Illinois, is a long-established company in the area and is located in a complex dating to the mid-19th century. On its South Park facade are some very fine cast iron architectural elements, more than likely made in the locality.

13 Buffalo Blacksmith. 120 South Park Ave. Hard to believe, but a blacksmith still plies his trade in downtown Buffalo. As one would expect, it looks nothing like the sanitized dioramas in museums or life-size museum villages. Instead, piles of scrap metal and all manner of tools, barrels, and gadgets lie about, in a system only discernible to the resident smithy.

The building has segmental arched windows and brick corbelling at the roof line. The rear additions date to c. 1884 and c. 1915. The current rectangular garage door replaced the original round arched carriage entrance.

The building is a good example of an early brick industrial structure and was built by Mr. A. H. Brown around 1872 as a machine shop and brass foundry. Ghost lettering from its

Buffalo Blacksmith

original use is still visible below the third story windows.

Mr. Brown carried a full line of water and steam gauges, engineers' supplies, copper, and sheet iron. He did work for tanners, brewers, and others, and made a specialty of railroad and steamboat brass castings.

14 DL&W /NFTA Train Sheds. The two-story reinforced concrete train sheds on the Buffalo River at Washington St. are virtually all that is left in Buffalo of the old Delaware, Lackawanna and Western Railroad. The sheds, completed in 1917, were part of a passenger, freight, and commodity complex that gave the railroad practical control of the inner harbor from the westernmost point of Erie Basin to Ohio and Michigan streets, a distance of almost three-quarters of a mile. The rights of way, and previous DL&W warehouses on the site, dated from the 1880s.

Train tracks were actually elevated, with freight storage and a Railway Express office located in the ground-level basement. The train sheds end abruptly with a mirrored glass wall where the old passenger terminal was attached. The terminal was closed in 1962 and razed in 1982 to make way for ground-level entry into the train shed basement, which currently serves as a storage and maintenance facility for the NFTA's light rail rapid transit

cars. A brick addition by the NFTA dates to 1982.

15 Malamute Bar. The Malamute, at the corner of South Park and Michigan avenues, is a workingman's

bar constructed of cinder blocks with a brick facing. The Malamute and the building next to it on South Park Ave. have curious concrete stairs leading from street level to the main floor. The structures had been built when this stretch of South Park was an approach to an elevated viaduct over a railroad spur. After the track was abandoned, the viaduct was removed and the street brought to ground level. The stairs were built so the building entrances wouldn't be left high and dry.

16 Fireboat Edward M. Cotter. Engine 20 of the Buffalo Fire Department is the fireboat Edward M. Cotter. The Cotter is named for a long-time firefighters' union president and sits in a slip under the Michigan Ave. Bridge.

Launched in 1900 from Elizabeth, New Jersey, the fireboat is the only firefighting apparatus that can reach much of Buffalo's waterfront. While it is the slowest moving piece of equipment in the Buffalo

The Fireboat Cotter

Fire Department (11½ m.p.h.), it can pump 15,000 gallons of water per minute, 10 times the capacity of an average fire truck. The Cotter could fill an average backyard pool in 42 seconds!

The bright red 118 foot boat was nearly destroyed in 1928 when an oil barge and oil tanker caught fire and severely damaged the fireboat, which was docked at a wharf alongside the river, and killed its engineer. The boat was promptly rebuilt, and the coal-fired steam engines were converted to oil at that time.

In 1953, the boat underwent another overhaul and its engines were converted from oil to diesel.

When not fighting fires during the winter months, the Edward M. Cotter works as an icebreaker on the Buffalo River.

17 Michigan Ave. Bridge. This bridge is one of a long line of bridges spanning the Buffalo River at this point. The first recorded bridge was built in 1873, while the current vertical lift bridge was opened in 1960, replicating a 1933 design that was destroyed in a shipping accident.

The bridge affords a fine view of the rotting remains of wooden wharves which once lined the north bank at this point. They serviced a New York Central Railroad warehouse and grain elevator.

The Swannie House

18 Swannie House.
According to the current owners, the Swannie House was first opened as a bar in the 19th century by the Swanerski family under the name "Swanerski House" (the building dates from 1892). Ethnic tensions between the majority Irish and East Europeans were high in the First Ward at the time, and the owners thought it prudent to modify their name to Swannie.

At the time, the first floor served as a tavern, the second as a boarding house

Buffalo native Roger Dooley mentioned the tavern several times in his fictional accounts of life in the First Ward.

In 1983, Timothy and Marlene Wiles purchased the historic tavern. The building was in great need of restoration. The floors of the tavern were replaced with those from the old Plaza Suite Restaurant, a 1970s landmark atop the M&T Bank building.

During exterior rehabilitation, a new coating

Inside the Swannie House

for ship captains and their officers, and the third (the attic) housed seamen of lower rank. The letting of rooms above taverns was common at the time.

The tavern, at the corner of Michigan Ave. and Ohio St., has a vivid past. Records show James Swannie, sailor and saloonkeeper, operated next door since at least 1882. Noted author and

of paint threatened to obliterate a large painted sign from the waterfront's heyday advertising Kentucky whiskey. The firefighters aboard the fireboat Cotter, docked in a slip across Michigan Ave., managed to convince the owners to restore the sign instead.

19 St. Mary's Cement Elevator. Originally the

St. Mary's Cement Elevator

Kellogg elevators A and B, it was pictured in Erich Mendelsohn's influential book, *Amerika: Bilderbuch eines Architekten* (1926). The St. Mary's complex, on the river at S. Michigan Ave., is, at first glance, odd. It consists of a large set of bins joined at the top through a transfer system to a small collection of bins on the south, with a gap of perhaps 150 feet between.

Looked at from the Michigan Ave. lift bridge, the reason for this begins to reveal itself: there is a break in the metal bulkhead lining the river at this point. A slight indentation in the shoreline reveals rocky fill. There was once a slip here, which had

a brick and wood elevator on either side, Kellogg A (south) and Kellogg B (north).Two vessels could be handled at once. Somewhat before 1917 the B elevator was demolished and replaced by the reinforced concrete elevator which survives today. The enclosed transfer mechanism was also built at this time. For reasons unknown, the A elevator was demolished but never replaced, except for the desultory collection of bins on the site today. Instead of storing grain, the complex is used to store cement .

20 Agway/GLF Elevator and Mill. An irregular, picturesque, and

Agway/GLF Elevator

A Greek Revival rarity: the NY Central's old freight warehouse

incongruous complex of shapes and materials gives the Agway complex its other-worldly appearance. The combination of geometric shapes and vernacular architectural elements is accentuated by the intermix of concrete corrugated metal and brick materials. The complex is on the river south of the St. Mary's elevator.

Part of what makes the complex so romantically appealing is the very tall work houses on either end of the "A" elevator (the latest storage section, built in 1941, and largest, with a 1.75 million bushel capacity,). The east works, on the river, is 194 feet tall; the west works 199 feet tall.

The complex was begun in 1929 for the GLF Exchange, with construction of the feed mill and ancillary structures. The so-called elevator "B" was probably inherited from the Wheeler firm. It was built in 1908 and is the present middle elevator, 550,000 bushel capacity, with a fixed, or stiff, marine leg. Three 600,000 gallon molasses tanks were built on the northern edge of the property, next to the St. Mary's/Kellogg property. The 170,000 bushel "C" elevator was built in 1936.

The site is now used to shred and store rubber tires and to store lumber and, recently, recreational boats.

21 New York Central Freight Office and Warehouse. At the corner of Moore and Ohio streets is a rare instance of the late Greek Revival style adapted to an industrial building. It was constructed in the 1860s for the New York Central RR. At the turn of the century it was owned by the Buffalo, Rochester & Pittsburgh Railway, the New York Central having built a huge freight depot on the river from Moore to Chicago streets. The brick detailing, including cornice dentils, identify it as one of the oldest surviving waterfront structures. There is a block-long one-story-high continuation of the building containing the original loading docks for this waterfront terminus of the freight line. The one-story section was later bisected by a railroad viaduct, now removed, leaving granite buttresses to interrupt the original brick wall along Moore St.

22 Harbor Inn. This bar and restaurant fills a wedge formed by the intersection of Ohio and Chicago streets. The three story brick building is commercial Italianate in style. Insurance records indicate the building was erected in 1874 as a saloon and boarding house by a certain Patrick Kane, who had operated a similar establishment on the site since 1870.

The semi-hexagonal corner of the building has cast iron Corinthian columns flanking the central bay on the ground floor and a piece of 20th century kitsch—a one-and-a-half story representation of a lighthouse, complete with neon lettering (inoperable), standing on a platform over what probably was the original entrance.

The establishment is presided over by the genial Ed Malloy.

23 E&B Holmes Machinery Co. This is reputedly the oldest business in Buffalo which has operated in the same location under the same name. Founders Edward and Britain Holmes were the first, and sole, saw millers for 12 years in Lancaster, New York. The brothers moved to Buffalo and the corner of Michigan Ave. and the Main and Hamburg Canal in 1852, where they opened E&B Holmes Planing Company.

Four years later, they bought the Chicago Iron Works Building at 59 Chicago St. They began specializing in the design of machines used by cooperages to make

Harbor Inn

E & B Holmes

wooden barrels. Previously, all wooden barrels were handmade.

Much of the the present structure dates from the early 1880s, after a fire devastated much of the original construction in 1879.

As times changed and wooden barrels were replaced by fiberboard drums and plastic containers, cooperages became a thing of the past. Liquor companies are the main users of wooden barrels and cooperage equipment today. E&B Holmes still produces an occasional cooperage machine but, for the most part, it is a general machine shop.

24 Numbers 60 & 62 Chicago St. Across from E&B Holmes are a pair of tiny 19th century houses. They indicate the modest living standards of many of those who worked on the waterfront at the time. Heat was provided by a single coal-burning stove. A privy was attached to the rear of the house.

These houses and a larger one at 64 Chicago St. are all that are left of a series of houses and shops which occupied this block as late

Nos. 60 & 62 Chicago Street

The Ohio Basin Area, circa 1930

as the 1950s. The people who lived here did so amid the tumult and grime of a New York Central freight warehouse along the river, the E&B Holmes shops, and the King Iron Works on the north side of Mackinaw St. (which formerly extended west from Louisiana St. to Ohio St.).

With the advent of streetcars, buses, and higher wages, the more prosperous workers moved to neighborhoods a bit more accommodating.

25 Sam's Truck Stop. This mid-'50s truck stop at 300 Ohio St. typifies the change in shipping from rail and water to truck.

This filling station and restaurant was built on the site of the Central Manufacturing Company,

Buffalo's first manufacturer of top of the line burial caskets. Occupying a site at the corner of Chicago and Ohio streets and extending east to the Ohio Basin, the complex consisted of large offices, four extensive warehouses and manufacturing shops, and a large planing mill.

The current filling station accommodates the milling and trucking industries located nearby.

26 Conway Playfield —the Old Ohio Basin. Now filled in for playing fields, the Ohio Basin was part of the Main and Hamburg Canal system, which extended the Erie Canal from Main St. to Hamburg St. Near the present Louisiana St., a branch, the Ohio Slip, cut south to the Ohio Basin. The

Basin was connected to the Buffalo River via a short channel called Dead Creek, and to the Main and Hamburg Canal via the Ohio Slip.

The Main and Hamburg Canal and Ohio Basin network proved to be a boondoggle. Many existing businesses around the Ohio Basin area were cleared out prior to construction, and work was slowed considerably by a cholera outbreak in 1849 and various legal wrangles. By the time it opened, railroads were making deep inroads into the local transportation market.

The canal was begun by the city in 1836, taken over by the state in 1848, and completed in 1852. The conditions failed. In 1898 enabling legislation was passed to fill in the canal, work which was completed in 1901. (The land was later sold to the Lehigh Valley Railroad, thence to the New York State Thruway Authority.)

The filling in of the canal made conditions in the Ohio Basin even worse. In 1901 it was recommended that it be abandoned.

A 1939 act of the state legislature authorized its transfer to the city for park use, but it wasn't until 1953 that the basin was filled. The playground was dedicated in 1954 as the Father Thomas Conway Playfield in honor of a neighborhood priest who died in World War II.

Carmen's Bar

Ohio Basin was finished in 1851. Unfortunately, the new canal and basin had little current, and the water quickly became stagnant and foul. The whole mess was declared a public nuisance in 1855. All attempts to improve

27 Carmen's Bar.
Carmen's, at 64 Louisiana St., is a popular watering hole for sailors and nearby factory workers. Owner Carmen Calabrese believes this humble wooden building was originally a barn, but was converted into a tavern

some 50 years ago. The neighborhood bar serves a variety of sandwiches, but is best known for its Italian sausage sandwich.

28 Huron Cement Elevator. This elevator, unlike the St. Mary's complex downriver, was built in 1928 expressly to handle cement. Tall, reinforced concrete cylinders are an economical way to store a variety of commodities, not just grain.

The structural cement for Orchard Park's Rich Stadium, Niagara Falls's Convention Center, and Buffalo's Marine Midland Center, M & T Plaza and Main Place Mall was supplied by Huron Cement.

Cement is drawn for shipment by truck or bagging from the bottoms of the bins by a basement screw conveyor system which has six openings for each bin. This allows for rapid refilling of the packaging and bulk storage bins. Bags are filled to 84-pound weight by an automatic packer.

An adjacent steel tower, 85 feet high, is a bulk loading station and is designed to load a truck in three minutes.

The complex is on Ohio St.

Huron Cement Elevator

Ohio Street Bridge

on the south bank of the Buffalo River.

29 Ohio St. Bridge. This bridge was completed in 1962 and is "tower driven." The machinery to move the cables attached to the counterweights is located at the top of towers at either end, shrouded in a metal covering.

The first public Ohio St. Bridge was built in 1866 and was, like its downstream cousins, a swing bridge. The bridge swung about a turntable on a pier built in the middle of the stream. This sufficed as long as boats were small and the shoreline adjacent to the swinging span was clear of any dock space or building projections.

Soon swing bridges became a liability on narrow rivers lined with expensive real estate, such as in Buffalo and Chicago at the time.

With vessels getting wider and riverfront property getting more valuable, the city of Buffalo was forced to replace the old swing bridge to keep up with economic forces. In 1904 the city built the world's first bascule of the Brown design (bascule, French for seesaw, meaning a bridge so balanced that when one end is lowered, the other is raised).

The Brown bascule was ideal: it freed up adjacent

First Ohio Street lift bridge was the world's first Brown bascule, an important design advancemant

The Standard, Buffalo's most approachable elevator

real estate for development and it leaped the river in a single span, eliminating the need for a dangerous pier in midstream and allowing larger ships to pass. A companion bridge, the Hamburg Turnpike bridge, was built over the City Ship Canal about a mile south. The operating machinery was different, but the method of balancing was the same as in the Ohio St. design.

After almost 60 years of use, the Brown bascule was replaced by the current vertical lift span. The vertical lift bridge offers significant advantages over bascules, the major one being cost. The counterweights merely have to equal the weight of the span, whereas bascule counterweights generally weigh two to three times the weight of the roadway to be lifted. Further, since the floor of the span always remains horizontal, any kind of pavement can be used (the Ohio St. Bridge's is steel deck). Lastly, should the grade level of the approaching roadways be changed, it is a relatively simple matter to adjust the draw to fit the new grades, without having to move any machinery or the towers themselves.

30 Standard Elevator. This grain storage elevator on St. Clair St. is the largest operating in the city. The elevator was built in 1926 and later acquired by Standard Milling of Seneca and Hamburg streets in Buffalo, a family-owned factory that grew into one of

At the time Standard was shutting down, Buffalo had six milling plants which produced 10 million pounds of flour daily. The loss of Standard cut the capacity by 1.4 million pounds.

With the closing, Standard sold its grain elevator to Pillsbury. It is now known

Electric Elevator, 1940 extension

the city's largest flour mills. The elevator was erected by James Stewart & Co., A. E. Baxter, architect.

The Standard is the most accessible elevator in Buffalo and can be seen from all angles. It is not as architecturally pure as some of the others, having modulation of wall surfaces, brackets, and roofline articulation that is not structurally necessary.

Standard Milling could not survive a period of intense competition from national millers like Pillsbury and General Mills, nor the relative lowering of railroad shipping costs. It closed in 1981. It was Buffalo's first major flour mill to close; nine grain elevators had previously closed.

colloquially as the Pillsbury Standard.

31 Electric Elevator Extension. The 1940 extension of the original 1897 Electric Elevator is all that remains of a powerful riverfront assemblage. The Electric originally consisted of low, large-diameter steel cylinders with tremendous double gabled marine legs, black as an obsidian cliff. The Electric was the first elevator to be designed to use electricity rather than steam power. The use of electricity, which removed the need for on-site burning of coal for steam power, reduced the chances of grain dust exploding and other mishaps.

The Electric had one stationary, or stiff, leg, and

the world's first loose leg, mounted on rails and powered by electricity. It also featured freestanding cylindrical bins without exterior cladding. Within a few years other elevators would have tall, thin cylinders of reinforced concrete: the "classic" elevator form which borders the Electric on all sides. Sadly, it was demolished in 1984.

The Electric extension is not what it seems, a collection of rather squat bins. It is far the largest elevator in Buffalo. Together with the original Electric, capacity was 7.55 million bushels.

According to architectural historian and critic Reyner Banham, the Electric extension is the prototype of the latest generation of modern grain storage facilities. These are simply large boxes in which front-end loaders can move the grain about (instead of men and draglines or gravity and conveyor belts). Almost 100 years after Joseph Dart's

The Grain Shovelers Union Local 109

actually six huge rooms measuring 150 feet by 90 feet. The design used the self-buttressing properties of cylindrical shapes, as well as the local knowledge of rapid slip form construction, to build a huge and cheap storage facility.

The extension has a capacity of six million bushels. That makes it by invention of the bucket system (p. 56), Buffalo still led the world in an important design type. This new type of elevator has in some ways rendered obsolete the "classic" elevator of tall ranked cylinders so familiar around the world.

32 Scoopers Union. Chances are, there are few union halls as charming as

View downstream from the foot of Hamburg St.

this humble home of the grain shovelers,' or scoopers,' union—the men who toil in the holds of ships, feeding the voracious marine legs.

Many of them were Irish, living in modest accommodations much like that surrounding the current union hall. The Irish established the first true ethnic neighborhoods in Buffalo, settling in "The Flats" on Lake Erie, near the mouth of the Buffalo River. Their main source of income was loading and unloading lake and canal boats.

Eventually, the Irish settled in the First Ward and South Buffalo. The First Ward encompassed an area roughly from Main and Exchange streets east to Seneca and Fillmore, then southwest along railroad rights of way to Hamburg St. and the Buffalo River, then along the river to Lake Erie. Defined as it was by natural features and almost immutable railroad barriers (and now highway barriers), the First Ward took on a distinct character

coterminous with its political boundaries which long survived the breakup of the old ward system.

Many Irish men continued to be active as grain scoopers, shoveling grain from the holds of lake boats. They were at the bottom layer of society in Buffalo: they were the newest immigrants, had the poorest housing, and held jobs on the lower end of the ladder. The union movement became the means of economic mobility. 110 Louisiana St.

33 The Foot of Hamburg St. This is perhaps the best vantage point to view grain elevators as a "streetscape," as well as individually. Looking downstream toward the Ohio St. Bridge, the first elevator on the left is the Lake & Rail (with a large flat wall on the river), followed by the Perot Elevator and plant, the American Elevator (with easily visible marine legs), and the Electric Elevator extension. On the right is the Standard Elevator. This group of elevators, and the Marine A Elevator just upstream, can

Lake & Rail elevator from Childs St.

also be approached along Childs St., which runs south of the elevators from Ohio St.

34 Lake & Rail Elevator and Mill. The Lake & Rail, now owned by the Con Agra company, was built in four stages between 1927 and 1930.

For reasons unknown, the newest section, the Northwest Annex of 1930, was built with flat walls enclosing the cylindrical bins. The pie-shaped spaces between the wall and the area where adjacent cylinders meet, the interstices, are also used for storage. Every other elevator in Buffalo, as well as the other parts of the Lake & Rail itself, uses semi-cylindrical interstitial bins.

The North Annex, at the inside of a 90 degree bend of the Buffalo River, was built in 1928, at the north end of the Main House (1927). The South Annex, the base of which roughly

describes an attenuated triangle, was built to the Childs St. lot line in 1929. A dramatic view can be had of this section from Childs St.

The mill produces 2,700,000 pounds of flour per day, enough for a like number of loaves of bread. According to the elevator superintendent, the Con Agra mill is the second largest in the country, after only a Nabisco plant in Chicago.

With four working elevators in such proximity, there is a good chance to see a lake freighter being unloaded here. The Lake & Rail, for instance, gets visited about once a week during shipping season by a typical 600-foot lake freighter.

Such a freighter will carry perhaps 630,000 bushels of wheat. Even with two marine legs that can scoop up 17,000 bushels per hour, it takes over 18 hours, minimum, to unload such a huge freighter at the Lake & Rail.

With that 630,000 bushels it is possible to produce 252,000 hundred-pound sacks of flour. At one pound of flour for a loaf of bread, that's over 25,000,000 loaves' worth of raw material in the typical lakes freighter.

35 Perot Elevator. Currently operated by the Fred Koch Malting Co., the complex consists of two

Perot Elevator

parts, the grain elevator and a plant containing germinating compartments.

The Perot elevator, named for the malting company for which the plant was built, never had marine legs. It is connected to the adjacent American/Peavey elevator and its marine legs by an overhead conveyor.

The Perot was built in two stages. A set of nine bins without interstitials was put up in 1909, some distance back from the river, followed by a set of bins with interstitials built on the river in 1933. From a distance this can be easily seen by the slightly different shading of the metal-sheathed work

area above the bins.

36 American Elevator. Also known as the Peavey, the American is another elevator which has the distinction of being printed in the influential work of Erich Mendelsohn. The European modernist published a head-on photograph of the freestanding legs in his 1926 tome, *Amerika:*

Bilderbuch eines Architekten.

The northern part, on the river, was built in 1907. This makes it the second oldest reinforced concrete elevator in Buffalo, after an annex of General Mills (then the Washburn-Crosby). The first reinforced concrete elevator, actually a single test bin, was built in 1899 in Minneapolis and is a National Historic Landmark.

The American is placed almost perpendicular to the river, with two marine legs on the short river side. The unusual angle leads to a unique seperation of its marine legs. The marine legs, of course, must follow

American Elevator, with "legs" that Erich Mendelsohn adored

the path of the concrete dock, away from the elevator.

Marine legs, tall and thin as they are, had a history of blowing down. Later designs held the legs to rails running along the elevator tops, as at General Mills, retrofitted after a storm in 1922. Evidently, despite their exposed position, such a fate never befell the American towers.

The complex consists of three parts: the flour mill visible from the Ohio St. bridge, the 1907 elevator (on the river) with a capacity of 2.25 million bushels, and at the rear, facing Childs St., the 1931 elevator with a capacity of 1.5 million bushels. They are separated by the workhouse.

37 Marine A Elevator. South of the Lake & Rail elevator at the foot of Childs St., this elevator had a fairly short active life, about 40 years from its construction in 1925. Without an associated mill, it closed during the collapse of the transshipment business in the 1960s.

All interstitial bins in Marine A are square steel tanks bolted to the convex concrete walls around them. In addition, the outer interstitials have fan-shaped steel tanks divided into five segments.

Very few elevators in Buffalo survived unaltered from the date of original construction. Marine A, with a pure and simple form, is one.

38 Tugboats. More likely than not, the visitor will find two tugboats tied up at the

Marine A Elevator

old Union Furnace dock. The dock runs south along the river from near the foot of Hamburg St.

The tugs are the "Delaware" and its twin, the "Alabama." They are owned by Great Lakes Towing of Cleveland (hence the large G on their smokestacks). The two tugs handle all the shipping traffic in and out of the inner and outer harbors, or about 200 movements per year.

39 Airco. Anyone wandering about the neighborhood around the Katherine St. peninsula (a

neck of land formed by the serpentine Buffalo River) will hear a distinctive "whoosh" at regular intervals. This is the sound of excess air escaping the "reversing heat exchanger" at Airco Industrial Gases, after it has broken down air into carbon dioxide and moisture at the 101 Katherine St. plant. Airco separates air into its basic components, primarily oxygen, nitrogen, and argon. The business began in the 1920s on Hydraulic St., about a mile east of the present location. The company occupied the

Airco Industrial Gases, from which the "woosh" emanates

Concrete Central, east elevation, from the foot of Smith St.

present site in the 1960s, after it had been abandoned by Hanna Furnace. The tower on the property is a 165' tall distillation column.

The site across Katherine St. was formerly occupied by Union Furnace's steel operations.

40 Concrete Central Elevator. Stretching along the Buffalo River for more than a quarter of a mile, the Concrete Central Elevator stands abandoned in silent magnificence amid flat grassy fields. The sight of the immobilized marine legs, slowly decaying, against the monumental wall of ranked bins is humbling.

The bins were built in stages from 1915 to 1917. Concrete Central's three marine legs were the largest ever built in Buffalo. Their skeletal construction is easily appreciated since much of the sheet metal covering has fallen away. The western elevation with marine legs is visible from Katherine St., while the eastern elevation— and the elevator's isolation—is best appreciated from the foot of Smith St.

The elevator was illustrated in Bruno Taut's *Modern Architecture,* perhaps the first paean to modern architecture to originally appear in English, in 1929. Concrete Central hasn't been altered since Taut's visit.

The complex has more than 250 bins, some of which tower 150 feet high. At the time it was built it was the city's largest elevator, with a capacity of 4.3 million bushels. In its heyday, the structure allowed crews to load and unload 20 railroad

"I was looking at one of the great remains of a high and mighty period of constructive art in North America, a historical monument in its own right."

—Reyner Banham on approaching Concrete Central, from A Concrete Atlantis, 1986 cars an hour, shipping at a rate of 85,000 bushels of grain per hour.

Built of reinforced concrete (hence its name) by the Mouaren Engineering Co., the facility was used for grain storage until 1966. At its closing it was reported that Concrete Central employed 18 men during the winter and 23 during the navigation season. An office, in the Marine Trust building, employed two people. It was only in the flour and feed mills that large numbers of people could find work. Elevators by themselves employed few people.

Lawrence Seaway or to the Gulf of Mexico via the much improved Missouri-Mississippi waterway

In the mid-1970s, the city of Buffalo took over the abandoned elevator in lieu of back taxes. After two children fell to their deaths while playing on it in 1976, there was talk of tearing down the complex.

The fact that Concrete Central and other elevators still stand has more to do with an impoverished municipal budget—the well-built behemoths are very expensive to demolish—than enlightened municipal management.

The Cargill Superior Elevator

The Concrete Central was bought by the Continental Grain Company in 1944. In 1955 Continental began buying old Great Lakes freighters for use as floating warehouses in Buffalo. By 1959 it had 13 of these, with a total grain storage capacity of 3.2 million bushels!

The ships were sold for scrap in 1962, with the Buffalo grain trade in a downturn as shippers went straight through the St.

41 Cargill Superior Elevator. Cargill Superior, opposite the foot of Katherine St. on the river, was Buffalo's first reinforced concrete elevator to be designed by local engineer A.E. Baxter, who would go on to design several other elevators and mills in Buffalo and, reportedly, scores across the country.

It was begun in 1914. The first section became known as elevator "A" when a second section, "B," was added east of it in 1919. The easternmost section, "C," was added in 1925.

The elevator, and probably all reinforced concrete elevators in Buffalo, used a method of construction called "sliding form" or "slip form." The same method, incidentally, was used in the construction of Toronto's CN

Ward. The bar and restaurant, at 73 Hamburg St., is a neighborhood haunt, of course, but is also popular with the Irish powerbrokers downtown, who never forget the old neighborhood.

43 Our Lady of Perpetual Help. 115 O'Connell St. The only Catholic parish left in

Our Lady of Perpetual Help

Tower, the world's tallest free standing structure.

In early sliding-form construction forms only four feet high were used in pouring concrete. When a level of concrete had cured sufficiently, the form was raised and another measure of concrete poured. In a matter of days a grain elevator could be structurally complete. Later, forms of only two feet in depth were used. It all added up to shocking speed and a landscape that could literally change overnight.

42. Gene McCarthy's. This is probably the best place to experience the flavor of an Irish saloon in the Old First

what was once a solidly Irish-Catholic neighborhood, Our Lady of Perpetual Help is still a center of Old First Ward activity. The parish was founded in 1897 with a Reverend R.C. O'Connell as pastor. The cornerstone for the present church was laid later that year on reclaimed swampland. Most of the original parishioners were Irish, with a smattering of Germans. The men were mainly grain handlers and shipyard workers.

The church is a Gothic Revival-inspired structure of Medina sandstone. A brown frame rectory which is adjacent to the church was completed in 1900.

Ad from 1882 city directory. For almost 100 years, the First Ward was the center of Buffalo's wholesale food trade

44 Commodore Perry Housing. This housing project is one of the oldest federally funded projects in the city, having been completed in 1940. It lies roughly between South Park Ave. and I-190 and Chicago and Hamburg streets. Over 300 houses were demolished to make way for the project, which provided 772 units of housing.

The block north of Perry St. between Louisiana and Chicago streets was

mid-1800s, the Elk Street Market, predecessor of the Elk Market Terminal, was one of the most efficient and important wholesale markets in the United States. Through this market passed the bulk of the food consumed in the city, and large quantities were shipped throughout the adjacent territory.

The original Elk Street Market stretched from the present intersection of

The Elk Market Terminal

formerly occupied by the five long sheds of the Elk Farmers' Market, where local farmers sold their produce. The Farmers' Market was associated with the Elk Market Terminal across Chicago St.

45 Elk Market Terminal. Established by the city in the

South Park (this section of which was formerly called Elk St.) and Michigan avenues northward to Scott St. East Market and West Market streets are the sole remnants of this early market. The blocks formed by the two streets, all of perhaps 40 feet wide, are the shortest in Buffalo.

In 1914, the New York Central built a food terminal nearby and called it the Elk Market Terminal. The last version of the city-built Elk Street Market burned in 1922 and was not rebuilt. Tenants moved to the Terminal instead.

The area surrounding the newer market declined in the early 1930s when the Niagara Frontier Food Terminal was built by two

Fulton St. near Perry was used to make two kinds of oat cereals. During the early 1950s, the plant was producing nearly 6,000 cases of cereal per day.

Lured by Buffalo's superior shipping facilities, the H-O company, begun in New York in 1893, moved to Buffalo in 1895. The Fulton St. mill was the largest of several local H-O mills.

The packing and mixing plant, situated at the

The H.O. Oats Elevator and Mill

railroad companies at Bailey Ave. This attracted many of the wholesale grocery and produce businesses, and remains the main food terminal for Buffalo.

46 H-O Oats Elevator and Mill. The 134-foot-high H-O Oats complex towers over the porches of the few nearby houses. One longtime resident on Marvin St. fondly recalls the days when the complex at 54

southeast corner of the complex, was built in 1912. This four-story brick-faced building has a rusticated stone foundation, a common occurrence in Buffalo industrial buildings of the time even with the widespread use of steel and reinforced concrete framing.

The warehouse and storage plant were built in 1929 and the grain elevators were built two years later. The structures consist of 35 steel bins with a capacity of 585,000 bushels. The elevator has a five-story working house.

The cereal plant closed in 1975. In recent years, the sprawling complex has been used as a warehouse for tires and other goods.

In the summer of 1987, flames swept through portions of the complex, causing extensive damage. After the fire was doused, one could still spot a sign on the building's charred facade, a boast from H-O Oats's heyday: "Pan Toasted For Flavor."

47 General Mills Plant & Elevator. The General Mills Elevator, or more accurately those parts of it that—when it was known as the Washburn-Crosby—were documented by European visitors, exercised enormous influence on the developing Modern Movement in architecture. Washburn-Crosby photographs taken in 1909 were publicized by Walter Gropius. Later, Erich Mendelsohn personally visited. Although the original elevators have been added to, parts of the original Washburn-Crosby can be seen within the General Mills complex.

The rapidity of change in the storage of grain is apparent in the General Mills complex and the neighboring Great Northern elevator. The Great Northern, completed in 1898, has steel bins inside a weatherproof brick container. Soon after, tile and reinforced concrete bins were constructed at Wasburn-Crosby.

In 1903 the Washburn-Crosby company built a set of nine grain bins next to its flour mill on South Michigan Ave. The bins were made of earthen tiles, a system of construction that was developing concurrently with steel and reinforced concrete construction. The design of various

Elevator C annexes   Stiff Cylindrical leg   Elevator C   Milling block   1903 Tile bins

The General Mills Elevator and Mill

components and methods of assembling them were patented, and the patent information of the General Mills bins is presented on a specially molded tile placed at knee height on each bin.

The motive force behind the development of the tile bin was its fireproof nature. Insurance rates for the prevalent wooden types were nearly ruinous.

A three-story milling building with base was designed by A. E. Baxter in 1922, and has many fine Modern details, such as the three narrow bands of windows along its taut western facade. This building occupies all the available space between the tile bins and the City Ship Canal. A four-story addition atop the southern end of the milling

block was added later. (The only place to view the complex properly is from the west, across the City Ship Canal, at what was once the western approach of the South Michigan Ave. lift bridge. Access is from Fuhrmann Blvd.)

Another elevator, B, was added no later than 1906 and was of reinforced concrete. This was the first reinforced concrete elevator built in Buffalo. The advantages of concrete were evidently so persuasive that, thereafter, no other type was built in Buffalo. The tile bins of elevator A were to be the first and last of its kind.

Elevator C and its various annexes (beginning with annex C of 1912) were originally the Frontier

Details of Barnett-Record, or Johnson-Record, bin at General Mills (Ketchum, The Design of Walls, Bins, and Grain Elevators 1919*)*

Great Northern Elevator

Elevator, which was always attached by conveyor to the Washburn-Crosby mill and elevators.

It is surmised that Daniel Joncaire's farmstead, the first enterprise by a white man in what later became Buffalo, was constructed in 1758 at the future General Mills site.

48 Great Northern Elevator. This one-of-a-kind elevator represents an important advance in the application and aesthetics of elevator technology. It was begun and virtually completed between February and September, 1897—an astonishing pace for an elevator that briefly was probably the world's largest, with a capacity of over 2,500,000 bushels.

The Great Northern and the Electric elevators, both built around the same time, were important not only for their use of electricity as a power source but for cylindrical steel bins for storage. Prior to this, probably all but one of the grain elevators in Buffalo consisted of square wooden bins sheathed in corrugated metal or wood. (A "fire-proof" elevator, the Plympton, at Chicago and Ohio streets, was built in 1868 of iron and brick. It must have been very expensive to build, for no other elevator in Buffalo followed its example. It was demolished to make way for an expanded New York Central freighthouse, probably in the 1890s.)

A typical wooden bin could hold 5,000 bushels of grain. The Great Northern's primary bins could hold

Layout of Great Northern bins, enclosed by brick shell

74,000. In addition, wooden elevators had the disturbing habit of burning down, often within only a few years of having been built. In fact, so many burned during the 1860s that some suspected it to be the work of Confederate saboteurs!

Steel bins, apart from the odd structural defect, can last considerably longer: those in the Great Northern are original. They can, however, deform in the heat caused by fires. The Great Northern's narrow cylindrical bins were an important engineering advance that would determine the "classic" shape of grain elevators all over the world.

The first steel elevator in the U.S. was the Washington Ave. elevator in Philadelphia, started in 1859 and completed in 1866. For some reason, steel wasn't seriously considered again until after 1895.

Then, the Electric and Great Northern were built in 1897, both of steel, both powered by electricity. (It is believed the Electric was completed first.) For six or seven years there was a spurt of steel construction, with the Dakota, Pioneer, and Lake Shore and Michigan Southern (LS & MS) all built of steel in Buffalo. After 1906, however, all major Buffalo elevators were built of reinforced concrete.

The Great Northern is the

The hemispherical bottoms of the Great Northern bins

Auto shredder, Advance Metals Recycling

last of Buffalo's major "working house" elevators, in which the storage bins, work spaces, and conveying apparatus were all located within a single structure. In this respect it was much like the old wooden elevators.

There are 30 bins, 38 feet in diameter, placed in three rows of 10, and 18 bins, 15½ feet in diameter, placed in the interstices of the larger bins in two rows of nine bins each. The bins can withstand stresses of 17,000 pounds per square inch. A 2½ -foot brick wall encases the bins.

The elevator's brick skin serves strictly as weatherproofing and does not carry the weight of the cupola or the grain bins.

Originally the elevator had three marine towers on the City Ship Canal. These were destroyed by a storm in 1922. The present two towers were replacements built between 1923 and 1928. The elevator still has four spouts sticking out of the north wall. These served to load grain into canal boats, which docked in a slip which was cut for that purpose.

The Pillsbury company bought the operation in 1921 and demolished a warehouse south of the elevator and erected a concrete framed flour mill, which opened in 1924. Partial renovation of the plant occurred after a devastating explosion and fire in 1972. The mill is the largest of the 30 plants in the Pillsbury system.

As this book went to press, citizens' groups were trying to prevent demolition of the Great Northern by its owners.

49 Advance Metals Recycling. This recycling operation was begun in 1976 on land which once was the site of the Archer-Daniels-Midland elevators.

The company devours approximately 135,000 car bodies a year with its auto shredder. An entire car body, sans the tires and gas tank, can be shredded in 45 seconds. The remains of what once was someone's pride and joy is reduced to chunks of steel the size of a fist. The resulting steel is then sold directly to mills for melting and the making of new steel.

There are four separate buildings on 18 acres of land owned by the company.

50 Skyway Marina and South Michigan Access Point.
Unknown to all but a handful of boaters and the stray fisherman is one of the most compelling panoramas in Buffalo. From the old jumping off point of the South Michigan Ave. lift bridge, the adventurous tourist can see, during sailing season, a long stretch of water bordered on one side by the lined up masts of a multitude of sailboats and on the other by the heroic bulk of the Great Northern and General Mills elevators.

With luck, a huge lake freighter will be docked at one of the elevators. It is likely such a freighter will belong to the Kinsman Lines of Cleveland. The ships of the Kinsman fleet are all nearly 600 feet long and sport a large S on a green field on their smokestacks. (The S is for Henry Steinbrenner, father of George of New York Yankee infamy, and a long-time principal of Kinsman.)

The west bank of the City Ship Canal is also the only place, besides the water itself, where the earthly remains of the great Dakota elevator can be seen.

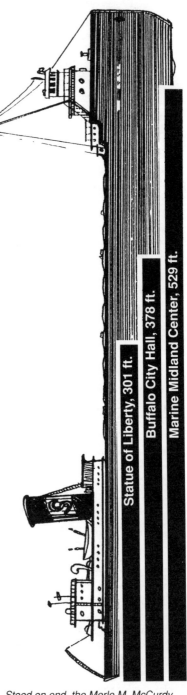

Statue of Liberty, 301 ft.

Buffalo City Hall, 378 ft.

Marine Midland Center, 529 ft.

Stood on end, the Merle M. McCurdy would easily top Buffalo's tallest building, the Marine Midland Center.

Part of the concrete and wooden dock upon which the marine legs moved still exists, directly south of the Skyway, running south for several hundred feet.

51 City Ship Canal. Soon after Joseph Dart's invention of the marine leg caused a boom in Buffalo shipping, a need for more protected docking space became apparent.

The city began acquiring land for a new canal south of the Buffalo River in 1847. Construction began in 1849 and the canal was completed in 1850. It was perpendicular to the canal, connecting it with the Buffalo River. The slips more than doubled the available docking area. Later, two more slips were cut, bringing the total to six.

In 1883 the Buffalo Creek Railway Company was permitted to extend the canal 5,000 feet southward into its own land. This connected to property owned by the Lehigh Valley Railway Company, which built canals and coal docks on the old Tifft farm.

After the turn of the century individual grain elevators

Connecting Terminal Elevator

named the Blackwell Canal after the contractor.

Unlike the ill-fated Main and Hamburg Canal of the same period, the Blackwell Canal was a smashing success, attracting grain elevators, warehouses, and railroad commodity terminals.

In 1853 the canal was renamed the City Ship Canal. In the early1850s the canal was lengthened twice. Four slips were also cut grew to enormous size, as did lake freighters. The slips, less useful than before, were partially or fully filled in as the old wooden elevators they served were burned or demolished. The Watson slip became part of the Buffalo River in 1920, after the city bought the island on which the Watson elevator had stood and removed the island.

52 Connecting Terminal Elevator. This is the last in

a line of Connecting Terminal elevators around this site. The previous incarnations were of wood and, inevitably, met their fate at the hands of Lucifer. The site is now owned by a private marina, but the elevator is easily viewed from Fuhrmann Blvd.

The Connecting Terminal consists of two sections. The first, or northern, section was completed in 1915. It has a raised basement, the early signature of the engineer A.E. Baxter. The bins are carried by a reinforced concrete frame which rests on the foundation at grade level. In this sense Baxter's elevators imitated the steel construction of the Great Northern and the Dakota, as well as the LS & MS elevator, which had steel bins above a concrete frame.

The southern section was built in 1954—the last grain storage facility to be built in Buffalo. It, and every Buffalo elevator built after about 1930, had cylinders which rested directly on a below-grade foundation. Openings for the necessary conveyors and chutes were placed at the bottom of the cylinders.

Bell bouy

The steel bin bottoms were placed about 12 feet above the bottoms of the concrete cylinders.

The workhouse above the bins was partially dismantled in the early 1980s.

53 Coast Guard Base and Lighthouse Point Park.

The Lighthouse Point Park is essentially a pathway along Coast Guard property to the lighthouse. Informative signs dealing with waterfront history line the path. The route ends at the 1833 lighthouse around which various buoys and an old lighthouse lens are

Bouys at Coast Guard Base

Bouys at Coast Guard Base

displayed.

Of particular interest, besides the 1833 lighthouse itself (described in this guide's first entry), is the 40-foot-tall "Milk Bottle" light. This metal structure was built and installed on the North breakwater in 1903. It was replaced in 1985 by a simple light pole. The light was restored in 1988-89 and put on display.

54 Times Beach. This area, a partially built diked disposal site, is south of the mouth of the Coast Guard Base. It is one of the city's most valuable wildlife areas and lies on an important flyway for migrating water and land birds.

The littoral, or shore zone, and the shallow water zone are the key habitats at Times Beach that make it exceptionally attractive for wildlife, especially waterfowl and shore birds. Two-hundred-twenty-two species of birds have been recorded there, most being migrants and visitants.

Times Beach was originally a tree-and-shrub-bordered sand beach, fronting the Buffalo Outer Harbor. It was opened as a public beach in 1935 by the *Buffalo Times* newspaper. The city health department soon condemned it due to pollution from nearby factories.

In later years the area was enclosed by a dike and was used as a disposal area for dredging material from the Buffalo River. Needless to say, the muck contained some toxins, but during the 1970s nature reclaimed the site to the extent that the city designated it a nature

"Milk Bottle" light prior to restoration

The Canada Goose is often seen at Times Beach

preserve in 1978.

The diking and filling altered the ecosystem greatly. This has not only affected the area's flora and fauna, but has combined with long- and short-term fluctuations in Lake Erie levels acting through the porous parts of the dikes to create even more alterations in these ecosystems.

Rare and spectacular birds are among the many species recorded at Times Beach. The American Wigeon, a duck which has been known to breed here, is classified as an irregular rare breeding bird in Western New York. No less than six broods totaling at least 30 young have been observed there within recent years.

Birds that can be seen include the mallard duck, Canada goose, various hawks, mute swan, various herons, pheasant, osprey, and warblers, to name a few.

The site is not open to the public.

55 Shooter's Waterfront Café and Seaway Piers. Shooter's, part of a national chain of waterside restaurants, was completed in 1989 on the old Seaway Piers. The piers were actually built as part of the Outer Harbor development in the early part of the century, but were renamed in the hopes of drawing St. Lawrence Seaway traffic.

The glitzy restaurant and its large patio is Party City in the summer, drawing huge crowds evenings and weekends.

56 Freezer Queen and Port of Buffalo Buildings. The Buffalo Outer Harbor, completely protected by modern breakwaters since 1905, never developed the

brick. Two steel framed extensions were added later.

The Ford assembly plant, a handsome, brick-faced building, was completed in 1931, just in time for the Depression. Until recently it was the Port of Buffalo site. That has recently moved to Lackawanna and the old Bethlehem Steel slip. The building currently is a foreign trade zone.

57 Small Boat Harbor. The Small Boat Harbor, owned by the Niagara Frontier Transportation Authority, was begun in 1950 by the city. The original 60-foot

Freezer Queen Building

industrial infrastructure that the Inner Harbor did. The buildings of a defunct cold storage company (now the Freezer Queen building) and an assembly plant for the Ford Motor Co. (Buffalo Port Terminal) are among the few ever built on the Outer Harbor.

The Freezer Queen building, the southernmost of the two, was built in 1925 of reinforced concrete and

wide breakwater was constructed of blast furnace slag from nearby steel mills. Fill was dredged from the resulting enclosure and dumped in the southern end, where it now forms a treeless asphalt and gravel plain used for parking.

An expansion in the mid-1980s added more berths, a board and batten service building, and fortified and extended the breakwater.

Small Boat Harbor Service Building

The capacity of the marina is 612 vessels. During winter when the ice is sufficient, usually January to late March, the area becomes Buffalo's mecca for ice fishing.

The service building contains a snack bar with a deck overlooking the anchorage of hundreds of sailboats and motorboats. The high breakwater, which hides views of Lake Erie, and noise from the adjacent frozen foods plant make this less pleasant than it could be.

Better to take your food through the oceanic parking lot at the southern end of the marina and follow the footpath along the lakeside. Plenty of seating on the riprap, and great views, too. Perhaps you can contemplate the practical genius of Col. T. W. Symons of the Army Corps of Engineers, who designed the great breakwater you see in front of you.

The breakwater is the Stony Point extension. It is over 7,000 feet long and is the longest continuous wall on the harbor. Work began in 1898 and continued for several seasons.

Like an iceberg, over 90% of this breakwater is under water. The base rests 30 feet under the mean lake level and is 135 feet wide. The top of the breakwater is 12 feet above the mean lake level and is 14 feet wide. There are three layers: a gravel core, covered by rubble stone, which in turn is surmounted by the stone revetment, made up of huge roughly shaped blocks. The breakwater has lasted almost 100 years with little damage.

Cross Section of "Stony Point Extension" Breakwater

The southern 1,000 feet or so of this breakwater was timber crib with plank decking. This was to provide a place for ships to tie up close to the harbor entrance, which couldn't be done easily with a stone breakwater. Storms in September and November 1900 smashed the decking to pieces, and a concrete cap was installed the next season.

58 Cargill Pool Elevator. The Cargill Pool is the only

The city acquired the grain elevator for back taxes in September 1984. A clever partnership bought it a few years later for only $10,000 for use as a marina and boat storage facility. It is doubtless worth many times more now, in light of the explosion of interest in the waterfront.

59 Independent Cement Complex. This small elevator and processing complex was built in 1926 and has had a succession of

The Cargill Pool Elevator

grain elevator on the lake itself. This allowed it to service ships with a larger draft than those on the Buffalo River. A Canadian cooperative, Wheat Producers Ltd., built the structure in 1925 with a storage capacity of one million bushels. One year later, the facility added a section to the east, or landward side, of the existing elevator, doubling capacity. It currently has 135 bins, stands 200 feet high, and is the length of approximately two football fields.

owners through the years. It is now owned by the Independent Cement Corp.

Two elevators on the site are active: a squat set of 24 bins, in two bundles of 12, set on a muscular concrete frame under which trucks are loaded, and a taller and narrower elevator for rail service, which is connected to a packing house.

The rest of the site—an administration building, a three-binned elevator (1928), and various other buildings, is abandoned and forms an interesting bunker landscape of reinforced

Indepent Cement Elevator and Truck Loading Facility

concrete.

The old administration building, domestic in scale, has a molded concrete monument in front of it commemorating a perfect safety record in 1929. On it, a modern worker and an ancient centurion stand in relief under the slogan "Safety Follows Wisdom."

The abandoned three-bin elevator is interesting for its one interstitial "bin" on the east side which in fact contains a stairway with windows at each landing. This is yet another example of form *not* following function (counter to the image European polemicists bestowed on Buffalo's elevators). Rather, here and elsewhere in Buffalo, it seems to be a case of form following economy.

60 Union Ship Canal. The Union Ship Canal, close to the city line at the Route 5 bridge, began its existence as the Goodyear Slip, begun in 1903. The slip was built to service Frank and Charles Goodyear's new iron plant, The Buffalo & Susquehanna Iron and Coal Co.

The Goodyear Slip was completed in 1905 to a length of 4,000 feet. Its wharves serviced the plant and provided for the unloading and shipping of iron ore and limestone to other points on the Goodyears' Buffalo & Susquehanna Railway.

The Buffalo & Susquehanna was the last railroad built in Buffalo and the first to be abandoned (1916). Eventually the iron plant itself ended up in the hands of Hanna Furnace, which produced pig iron at the site until 1982. The entire plant was scrapped over the next several years.

The canal was formerly crossed by the high-level Father Baker Bridge. With that bridge deteriorating and no viable industry on the canal, it was determined to build a lower, shorter span. This would appear to limit future use of the canal to barges and pleasure boats.

61 Tifft Farm Nature Preserve. Where at one time belching locomotives trundled along coal docks, wildfowl, muskrat, and the occasional fox have

ownership is of the Holland Land Co. in 1796. The land was eventually acquired by certain Pratt and Coe families for farming.

In 1834 it was bought by O.H. Dibble & Co., which attempted to dig a canal and develop the site. These efforts failed, and in 1848 local iron man George Tifft bought the land, now "Tifft Farm," and provisioned merchants with dairy products. Tifft added a stockyard in 1855 and a lumberyard in 1861.

Brown Bullhead, a hardy denizen of Tifft Farm Nature Preserve

reclaimed part of their former waterfront domain. The 264-acre Tifft Farm is a heartening example of formerly industrial land reverting back to nature.

Over 250 plant species, 250 bird species, and dozens of fish, reptile, amphibian, and mammal species have been observed at Tifft Farm. Lake Kirsty, the largest body of water on the preserve, is connected to Lake Erie via a 48-inch culvert, and so has seen rainbow trout and other game fish.

The first humans on the site were Native Americans; signs of their presence date back 5,000 years. The first record of European

In 1881 the Lehigh Valley Railroad bought the land for the purpose of building a series of canals, ore docks, and coal trestles. This came to fruition in the later years of that decade, as the City Ship Canal was lengthened to connect with the Lehigh Valley's West Canal (now the western arm of Lake Kirsty). The development, called the Tifft Basins, apparently had a hard time developing traffic (partly because of legal anti-monopoly measures), for only about half of the planned canal system was built. The eastern end of the site was and remains a marsh.

Tifft Farm then (1903)...

The Depression finished off much of the traffic at the site, and the Tifft Basins became known as a haven for the "idle fleet" — vessels that moored at the site during the lean years when Great Lakes traffic had ebbed.The site also evolved into a popular dump. Finally, the city purchased the land from the railroad in 1946 and filled in a section of the West Canal connected to the City Ship Canal, effectively forming Lake Kirsty.

In 1955, the city sold the site to Republic Steel, which is probably responsible for the slag flat at the old West Canal's north end. The city repurchased Tifft Farm in 1972 to rebury garbage from an old dump. Officials were persuaded of the value of the wildlife habitat which had developed, and mounded the fill in the southwest quadrant of the property. The mounds were covered with soil taken from what is now the Beth Pond area.

Tifft Farm was opened as a wildlife preserve in 1976. Today it is a popular waterfront attraction. Visitors can best appreciate the six trails during fall and spring when muskrats, pheasants, ducks, and a variety of birds can be spotted in the woodlands, marshlands, and brushlands. There is a visitor center on the grounds, where several excellent guides can be purchased. Guided tours are offered Sundays at 2PM. Admission is free. Telephone: 896-5200.

...and Tifft Farm now

G rain elevators play a central role in the history of Buffalo, socially, culturally, and economically. They also play a seminal role in the history of modern architecture.

The grain industry, contrary to popular belief, did not explode into existence with the opening of the Erie Canal in 1825. Although the theoretical cost of shipping a ton of Ohio grain to New York City fell from $100 to $10 or less, there was little grain to be shipped initially. Secondly, eastern cities were served by local farmers. The opening of the canal, though, probably did stop the expansion of acreage devoted to grain in the east. Any increase in demand would fall to the midwestern farmer.

Gradually, the flat, fertile land of the midwest yielded to the settler's ax and plow. Grain surpluses followed. Shipped east, they found incrementally larger markets. The marginal farms of the east, on wrinkled topography and poorer soils, either shifted to more specialized crops or went out of business entirely.

Buffalo was the chokepoint on the route of western grain to the east coast and beyond for the simple reason that the ships used on the Great Lakes were too big for the Erie Canal. The lake ships had to unload in Buffalo, where smaller canal boats took on grain or flour (in 1835, almost 80% of foodstuffs received from Ohio was in the form of flour) and hauled it farther eastward. The loose grain was scooped into baskets and hauled onto the dock by block and tackle. Sacks of grain, and barrels and casks of flour, were also laboriously removed by human muscle. With luck, the cargo could be transferred to a waiting canal boat immediately. Usually, however, the foodstuffs had to be stored in a warehouse for a time.

This system was tolerable for relatively small amounts of grain, but by the late 1830s, when Buffalo began receiving grain from Michigan and Illinois, it was clear to observers that soon congestion on the docks and the sheer volume of grain would overwhelm the harbor's ability to handle it.

One of those observers was the Buffalo businessman Joseph Dart. He hit on the idea of adapting a system of belts and buckets, first implemented earlier in

"Bird's Eye View of the City of Buffalo 1888," shows a number of timber crib elevators, the most prominent of which is the Bennet Elevator, a successor to Joseph Dart's original elevator of 1842. Reprinted from the *Buffalo Courier-Express*, April 1970

the century by Oliver Evans for the Ellicott grain mill in Maryland. In the fall of 1842, Dart arranged a series of buckets 28 inches apart on a leather belt and mounted the belt on a contraption which could be pulled out of his warehouse and into the hold of a ship. The contraption came to be known as a marine leg. Dart quickly refined the system until the buckets were 16 inches apart and his elevating system could handle 2,000 bushels an hour—an amount that formerly took a full gang of men, working in ideal weather, a full day to unload and store.

Other businessmen were slow to follow Dart's lead. It was only after 1846, when Dart expanded his elevator—a term now describing his grain warehouse—and therefore offered incontrovertible evidence of its success, that other elevators were built. Seven elevators were built in two years. There was a lull until 1861, when four large elevators were built and the amount of grain going through Buffalo exploded, going from about 30 million bushels in 1860 to over 60 million in 1861. The world had never seen anything like it. After that, Buffalo became famous for its grain trade and grain elevators. The ungainly wooden elevators became tourist attractions.

Ever increasing volumes of grain and almost ruinous insurance premiums on wooden elevators caused engineers to seek more durable and efficient methods of construction. This led, after 1900, to structures built of steel, tile, and reinforced concrete. The resulting elevators were monstrous in scale: huge, monolithic, technological wonders.

The American engineer had clearly created something new. Progressive European architects took notice:

> Thus we have the American grain elevators and factories, the magnificent FIRST FRUITS of a new age. THE AMERICAN ENGINEERS OVERWHELM WITH THEIR CALCULATIONS OUR EXPIRING ARCHITECTURE.
>
> —Le Corbusier, *Vers une Architecture* 1923, quoted in Banham, *A Concrete Atlantis* 1986.

In Europe a small group of theorists was rebelling against the florid excesses of the Art Nouveau and the constraints of the Beaux-Arts, which had mined historicism to its limits. They had a slogan: Ornament is Crime (coined by Adolf Loos, who favored stripping all decorative accretions). What they didn't have was a universal solution to their depraved architecture. They needed concrete proof that their ideas were correct. They needed credibility.

The grain elevator provided it in spades. It was everything Europe was not. New. Big. Progressive. Confident. Rational. The meaning of the elevators was clear. Technology would liberate architecture. It would liberate society. It was heretical.

It is significant that people outside the architectural profession, engineers, sounded the death knell of the old order. They were almost totally free from concern for form and appearance. Their mandate was strict economy. The result was an utter reduction of form to its basic meaning, structures totally shorn of embellishment.

Engineers had produced what architects had not, could not: totally unself-conscious architecture. Having no pre-conceived notions of form, the forms the engineers did produce were true to the physical laws of nature—pure, cerebral, and honest. The engineers, in their innocence, had re-invented architecture. Gropius recognized this at once.

This was architecture serving a higher purpose, truth, not mere human whimsy or predilection. Rooted in the laws of nature, laws that were the same everywhere, this was an architecture which had as much credence in Berlin as in Buffalo. Here was the seed of a universal, international style. Gropius, having collected photographs of American elevators, Buffalo's Washburn-Crosby and Dakota prominent among them, had them published in the *Jahrbuch des Deutschen*

Werkbundes in 1913.

The pictures were a sensation. Erich Mendelsohn, of Berlin, was fired by the Gropius illustrations. He took to sketching grain elevator forms as early as 1914. So did the Italian futurist Antonio Sant'Elia. After World War I, Le Corbusier published some of the photographs in a series of magazine articles. In 1923 he published *Vers une Architecture*, probably the most influential book in the development of modern architecture. Again, the Dakota and Washburn-Crosby are featured.

The Dakota was built of steel, north of the Washburn-Crosby, in 1902 to replace an earlier Dakota of wood. The steel Dakota was an idiosyncratic design with an unusually tall basement and working house, both apparently sheathed in corrugated steel.

The most striking feature of the Dakota may have been the immense pressed metal skins hung in front of its cylindrical bins. In flat light, from a distance, they looked like quilted batting. At the four corners a seg-

Joseph Dart's concept is evident in cross section of Marine A

"It could be argued, and with very little exaggeration, that Elevators A, B, and C of the Washburn-Crosby complex constitute the most internationally influential structures ever put up in North America."

Banham, *A Concrete Atlantis*, 1986.

ment of rounded grain bin appeared. It was a rational building, designed only to fulfill a certain function as cheaply as possible.

The Dakota's unabashed rationality, writ *very* large, produced very romantic notions of powerful technologies harnessed by man.

In 1924 Mendelsohn made the pilgrimage to Buffalo, the now legendary home of the monolith monsters. He had to see these otherwordly constructions himself.

Mendelsohn went gaga. He wrote of the scene to his wife:

> Mountainous silos, incredibly space-conscious, but creating space. A random confusion amidst the chaos of loading and unloading corn ships, of railways and bridges, crane monsters with live gestures, hordes of silo cells in concrete, stone and glazed brick. Then suddenly a silo with administrative buildings, closed horizontal fronts against the stupendous verticals of fifty to a hundred cylinders, and all this in the sharp evening light.
>
> I took photographs like mad. Everything else so far now seemed to have been shaped interim to my silo dreams.
>
> —Mendelsohn, as quoted in Banham, 1986

The die was cast. Modernism had begun its march around the world.

Operationally, grain elevators have not changed much since 1861, when the English author Anthony Trollope visited Buffalo. He, like Mendelsohn, saw them as almost living creatures, terrible dinosaurs preying on lumbering ships. (For convenience, the following passage has been divided into many paragraphs. One existed in the original. Trollope's term for grain is corn, a usage common in England.)

An Elevator is as ugly a monster as has yet been produced. In uncouthness of form it outdoes those obsolete old brutes who used to roam about the semiaqueous world, with their great hungering stomachs and huge unsatisfied maws. The elevator itself consists of a big moveable trunk, moveable as is that of an elephant, but not pliable and less graceful than an elephant's. This big moveable trunk, the head of which, when at rest, is thrust up into the box on the roof, is made to slant down in an oblique direction from the building to the river.

When its head is ensconced within its box, and the beast of prey is thus nearly hidden within the building, the unsuspicious vessel is brought up within reach of the creature's trunk, and down it comes, like a mosquito's proboscis, right through the deck, in at the open aperture of the hole, and so into the very vitals and bowels of the ship. When there, it goes to work upon its food with a greed and avidity that is disgusting to a beholder of any taste or imagination.

Its long trunk, as seen slanting down from out of the building across the wharf and into the ship, is a mere wooden pipe; but this pipe is divided within. It has two departments; and as the grain-bearing troughs pass up the one on a pliable band, they pass empty down the other. The system therefore is that of an ordinary dredging machine; only that corn, and not mud is taken away, and that the buckets or troughs are hidden from sight.

Below, within the stomach of the poor [ship], three or four laborers are at work, helping to feed the elevator. They shovel the corn up towards its maw. Thus the troughs, as they ascend, are kept full, and when they reach the upper building they empty themselves into a shoot, over which a porter stands guard, moderating the shoot by a door, which the weight of his finger can open and close.

Through this doorway the corn runs into a measure, and is weighed. By measures of forty bushels each, the tale is kept. There stands the apparatus, with the figures plainly marked, over against the porter's eye; and as the sum mounts up to forty bushels he closes the door till the grains run thinly through, hardly a handful at a time, so that the balance is exactly struck. Then the teller standing by marks down his figure, and the record is made.

The porter touches the string of another door, and the forty bushels of corn run out at the bottom of the measure, disappear down another shoot, slanting also towards the water, and deposit themselves in the canal-boat. The transit of the bushels of corn from the larger vessel to the smaller will have taken less than a minute, and the cost of that transit will have been— a farthing.

Rivers of corn are running through these buildings night and day. The secret of all the motion and arrangement consists of course in the elevation. The corn is lifted up; and when lifted up can move itself and arrange itself, and weigh itself, and load itself.

Over and beyond the elevators there is nothing specially worthy of remark at Buffalo. It is a fine city, like all other American cities of its class. The streets are broad, the "blocks" are high, and the cars on tramways run all day, and nearly all night as well.

—Trollope, *North America*, 1862

The "Old First Ward" is unknown to most Buffalonians, even though it is only a few blocks from downtown and borders much of the waterfront. Bounded by Lake Erie to the west, Interstate 190 to the north, and the Norfolk Southern Railroad tracks on the east, the area is most easily recognized by the grain elevators that line the Buffalo River. Outsiders who may have wandered into this neighborhood are likely to have been bewildered by the dead-end streets, intersecting waterways, and huge and often abandoned industrial sites. Yet this is the most historic area in Buffalo, and well worth exploration to uncover its hidden treasures.

The isolation of First Ward has made it a small town unto itself.

The isolation of the First Ward is nothing new. A combination of geography (wedged between Lake Erie, the Erie Canal, and the Buffalo River) and ethnic prejudice and preference (for years the neighborhood was dominated by the Irish) have always kept this section of Buffalo a small town unto itself.

Traditionally, water defined the area. The site of the first white settlement in the area, the First Ward was the natural focus of development in Buffalo because it was, and remains, the location of the city's harbor. With the opening of the Erie Canal in 1825, intense commercial activity transformed the area into the largest grain port in the world. Buffalo was a great inland port because, in the time before the Welland Canal and the St. Lawrence Seaway, Great Lakes shipping could go no farther.

At the terminus of the canal at the Buffalo River, canal boats unloaded their cargo of manufactured goods from the Eastern Seaboard to be reloaded onto lake vessels, which would in turn unload their cargo of grain and lumber from the Great Lakes region onto the canal barges. This area was known as "The Flats" to distinguish it from the higher ground on which the rest of the city was built. (The drop of elevation from the "upper town" is still quite apparent while traveling down Main St. past the Marine Midland building.) Although proximity to the water was the neighborhood's reason for existence, the marshy, poorly drained soil made it susceptible to water-born diseases, especially cholera, which swept through the neighborhood at regular intervals.

Although the lake and the Buffalo River still define boundaries, many of the waterways that once gave the area its character and its economic basis are now gone. The Niagara Section of the Thruway runs on the filled bed of the Erie Canal and continues on the path of the old Main and Hamburg Canal that once linked the Erie Canal to the Little Buffalo River.

On the south bank of the Buffalo River, a peninsula formed by the Buffalo River and the City Ship Canal was once a series of six islands, separated by slips, providing direct access and maximum wharfage. It is possible to imagine the scope of the waterways by visiting Father Conway Park at Louisiana and Mackinaw. This park follows the exact boundaries of the old Ohio Basin, a major loading dock for canal boats. Walking from the southern end of the park across Ohio St., you can still see the slip that once led from the river into the basin, now cut off by the street.

Before streetcars or automobiles, laborers had to live within walking distance of their jobs, and nowhere in the city is this more apparent than in the First Ward. Huge grain elevators and industrial sites lie next to modest single family houses and corner grocery stores. The tightly knit Irish neighborhood that fits into the triangle formed by Louisiana, St. Clair, and Hamburg streets preserves its nineteenth century character almost entirely. This

Huge grain elevators lie next to modest single family houses and corner grocery stores.

mixture of residential and industrial buildings, so uncharacteristic of the suburbanizing city, was typical of many urban areas in the nineteenth century. The corner of South and Vandalia streets is an excellent vantage point to view both the elevators and the neighborhood that was spawned by them.

The Irish have always dominated the First Ward. They came to work on the Erie Canal in the 1820s and in the wake of the great Potato Famine of the 1840s, settling in Buffalo where unskilled jobs were plentiful and their countrymen had established a presence. In the 1855 census, the First Ward was 73% Irish-born, and was the home of 35% of all Irish in the city. They clustered in this part of the city, and in the area along the Niagara River to the north, partly because of discrimination against them in other parts of town, and because it was close to the harbor, where they worked as laborers loading and unloading boats.

It was backbreaking and poorly paying work. Typically, a lake boat would dock, grain would be scooped into barrels that would then be hoisted onto the backs of Irish laborers. They would carry them into the grain warehouses for storage until the process was repeated in reverse to load the grain onto canal boats. The exploitation of Irish labor was apparent in the phrasing of naysayers in the 1850s, when Joseph Dart developed the first automatic grain elevator: The new-fangled elevator would fail because "Irishmen's backs are the cheapest elevator ever built."

Dart's elevators were in fact a spectacular success, becoming tourist attractions in the mid-nineteenth century. Far from replacing the Irish, the elevators created the need for more workers in related industries, especially in flour milling. The mills and grain elevators that dominate the neighborhood today are from a later period, but are a continuation of the industry that was once the foundation of Buffalo's economy.

The Irish did the scooping, backbreaking and poorly paying work.

The Irish in the First Ward lived in small frame houses that were considerably cheaper than those of native born citizens ($1,000 vs. $3,854 in 1855), but, perhaps surprisingly, a large number owned their own home. An example of the small size of many of these houses can be seen at 60 Chicago St., near Ohio. Unlike many other cities, tenement housing was never common in Buffalo, and large boarding houses were the exception. Most Irish lived with their families or as single boarders in another family home.

For men, work almost always meant the waterfront, either directly as a stevedore or in the mills that were dependent on water transport. Men usually left the family at age 18 to become boarders for a few years before marrying and setting up their own household. Irish girls left home earlier, almost always to become live-in domestic servants in the homes of native born citizens. However, this was not a permanent occupation for most women; by age 21, over half were married. Thus, while men of the First Ward had very little contact with other Buffalonians outside their ethnic and geographic area, women usually spent several years learning the values and ways of life of the native born Buffalo elite.

The local parish remained the focal point for most people of the First Ward.

Given the concentration of Irish, it is little surprise that the Catholic Church was such a prominent factor in the life of the area. At first, the Irish had difficulty in mingling with other Catholics who were predominantly Germans. The arrival of the first bishop of Buffalo in 1848 changed that forever. John Timon began a line of bishops of Irish descent that continues to this day.

Timon was a champion of the Irish, and made the First Ward his headquarters. He antagonized both Catholics of other ethnic groups and the local Protestant elite with his aggressive advocacy for better working and social conditions. The local parish remained the focal point for most people of the First Ward, providing not only spiritual, but social and economic support to the growing population. St. Brigid's at Louisiana and Fulton streets, is an example of one of the earliest churches in the area.

Another landmark Irish church was Bethel Church, formerly located in what is now a parking lot for Memorial Auditorium, more than a mile from St. Brigid's. This underscores the former extent of the neighborhood's residential component.

Social change came slowly to the area. The opening of the Seneca St. Trolley in 1896 allowed families to move out of the shadow of the elevators into less crowded and more "rural" surroundings in the South Park area.

The First Ward came to be less residential and more industrial. As this process took place, much of the immigrant housing was torn down to build warehouses, train sheds (including the Delaware, Lackawanna, and Western station of 1917, refurbished as the NFTA subway shed at Washington and South Park avenues), and other commercial structures. This was especially true in the heart of the historic area closest to downtown ("Irontown" and the Elk Market area).

With the decline of the port, the First Ward went into a decline. The filling of the canals and the building of Interstate 190 (the Thruway) on their beds ironically preserved the boundaries of the neighborhood in exactly the same place the canals once did. Water once separated the city from the neighborhood; the approaches to the Thruway now have the same function.

The times may be hard, but much remains to fascinate in the First Ward.

The First Ward has fallen on hard times, but much remains to fascinate. The remaining grain elevators are the largest and most significant collection in one place in the world. Driving by on the Skyway gives no impression of the immensity of these structures. Standing at the foot of the Great Northern elevator (1897) on Ganson St., one of the last "brick box" elevators still standing in North America, it is possible to imagine the work of the mill hands of the late nineteenth century. Looking out upon the Buffalo River from the Michigan Ave. bridge, the flavor of Buffalo in its heyday, when barges were jammed from shoreline to shoreline, and laborers roused themselves from beds above tap rooms, is still apparent.

John Feather, Ph.D.

Bethlehem Steel, on the Lake Erie shore south of Buffalo, occupies a site first proposed for a grand waterfront park in the 1890s by the renowned landscape architect Frederick Law Olmsted. The huge integrated mill soon came to represent Buffalo in the eyes of the nation. Twentieth century Buffalo is seen as blue collar, grimy, gritty, and tough because of the huge plant and the other heavy industries attracted by its presence. Today that reputation, if ever accurate, is less so. Most of the steel plants and their workers are gone.

When Bethlehem ceased steel making at the site in the early 1980s, plans were implemented to demolish structures rendered unnecessary. The landscape has changed drastically and will continue to do so for the next several years. In the interest of keeping this guide up to date, descriptions of the site will have to await future editions, when the stability of the Bethlehem site is more certain and a guide to the site will have lasting value. We offer here a brief history of this most important part of Buffalo's heritage.

The decline of heavy industry in Buffalo has been wrenching, especially by those who lost their jobs. Still, it has made for much cleaner air and water, and intensified the longing for meaningful public access to the lakefront. Perhaps Olmsted's park dream, a dream that has been deferred for 90 years, can come true. Ed.

The sprawling Bethlehem Steel Plant complex dominated Buffalo for more than 80 years. Today, this once third largest plant in the country, employing over 22,000, is only a shadow of its former self. As the vast steel giant is slowly dismembered and the land leveled, plans are being made to use this vacant property to build new businesses and recreation areas.

The idea for a steel plant on the shores of Lake Erie goes back to the 1890s and the Lackawanna Valley of Pennsylvania near Scranton. There, the Lackawanna Iron & Steel Company was looking to

In its heyday, the steel plant employed over 22,000 people.

expand operations to meet the needs of a booming nation. The demand for steel seemed insatiable, but the company was hindered by a pre-Civil War era plant and the unfavorable topography of its narrow and twisting home valley. It searched the country for a suitable location for a new plant.

Meanwhile, rich new sources of ore were being developed at the far reaches of the Great Lakes in Minnesota, and new coal mines in Pennsylvania were coming on line. Buffalo, at the eastern end of lake navigation and with excellent rail and canal links with the coalfields, and huge tracts of level, undeveloped land, became a desirable location for a steel plant.

In addition, Buffalo had abundant fresh water and the promise of cheap hydropower from Niagara Falls.

In 1899 a site south of Buffalo known as Stony Point was chosen by Lackawanna Iron & Steel as the site for their new plant. It was the same site renowned landscape architect Frederick Law Olmsted had recommended for use as a waterfront park. The steel plant won out and the park, now called South Park, was moved inland, east of the main-line railroad.

The new plant was hailed as the eighth wonder of the world, dwarfing all others.

Buffalo business-man John H. Albright was authorized by the Lackawanna Iron & Steel Company to purchase property at Stony Point, south of Buffalo, for the pur-pose of building a new steel mill. The Stony Point Land Company was formed for this purpose. The new steel plant was incorporated in New York State as the Lackawanna Steel Company and construction was well underway by 1902.

Engineers were encouraged to take advantage of the latest technology to develop this new plant. The site consisted of a 1,500-acre tract, huge when com-pared to the largest steel plant at that time—the Homestead Works with its 156 acres. The new plant was hailed as the eighth wonder of the world and attracted the attention of steel men throughout the world.

The new plant was extremely modern for its time, employing all of the latest technology. Its massive and extensive use of electricity, for a steel mill, was unprecedented. Waste gasses from furnaces were reused to run machinery, another innovation.

Some equipment for the plant was transferred to the site from Scranton. Two blast furnaces and the blowing engines were relocated. A huge forge and even an entire building was moved. The plate shop building once stood in Scranton, Pennsylvania.

To move raw materials within the plant and the finished product to market, the company built a railroad called the South Buffalo Railway. The railroad connected to all the major trunk lines in the Buffalo area. Besides general freight, steel and raw materials, the railroad hauled passengers—workers who commuted between the plant and downtown Buffalo.

Being on the lake gave the plant certain advantages. A harbor slip was dredged to handle lake freighters carrying ore, coal, and limestone, some of which the steel company owned. The Lackawanna Slip was 200 feet wide and, after being lengthened three times, a full 4,000 feet long. It was said that the Lackawanna Slip was the best harbor on the Great Lakes.

To house workers and their families, two housing developments totaling 600 dwellings were constructed. These developments were known as Ridge Road Village and Smokes Creek Village. They still stand, along Route 5 between Smokes Creek and the huge rolling mill. The tiny community of Limestone Hill grew to become the city of Lackawanna.

Fresh water, electric power, and flat land were in abundance on Erie's shores.

The Lackawanna Steel Company was purchased by the Bethlehem Steel Company in 1922. The plant was now called the Lackawanna Plant of Bethlehem Steel. Many improvements were made throughout the following years. In the mid-1930s the strip mill was built and between the mid-1950s and the mid-1970s, a huge building program was taking place. The Slab Mill, the Basic Oxygen Furnace, the Bar Mill and a new administration building were built. The future for Lackawanna looked very good. In 1970, Bethlehem's chairman, Edmund F. Martin, declared the Lackawanna Plant was the best in the country.

In the 1970s the world steel industry underwent increased competition at the same time that the overall

The coke ovens still make coke, the Bar Mill still rolls bar, and the Galvanizing Mill still makes galvanized products. People, 1300, still make a living.

U.S. market declined. The domestic automobile makers, always major consumers of steel, lost a big chunk of market share to imports from Europe and Japan.

In the United States, Bethlehem Steel's own new plant at Burns Harbor, Indiana, completed in 1970, was more efficient in manufacturing and shipping steel. The Lackawanna Plant, and steel, in general, was in big trouble.

Big layoffs came to Lackawanna in 1977. The rail mill was shut down, as was the structural mill. Then, in December of 1983 Bethlehem chose to close the entire steel-making facility at Lackawanna. Although steel is no longer manufactured at the site, there still is a Bethlehem Steel in Lackawanna. Coke ovens still make coke, the Bar Mill still rolls bar products, and the Galvanizing Mill still makes galvanized products. There are about 1,300 people in Western New York making a living working at Bethlehem Steel.

Paul V. Pietrzak

Credits & Bibliography

ILLUSTRATIONS: Front cover **Ed Sobala**; pp. 4, 27, 38, 45 **Penny Wyatt**; pp.5, 10-12, 14-20, 23, 24, 25 (top), 26, 28, 32, 33 (bottom), 36, 41 (top), 43, 44, 46, 47, 50 (top), 51, 52 **Daniel Haskin**; pp. 6, 7, 22, 59 **City of Buffalo**; pp. 18, 21, 29, 37, **Dorothy Markert**; pp. 30, 31, 33 (top), 34, 39 **Matt Rollwagon**; p. 35 **Timothy Tielman**; pp. 54, 55 **Tifft Farm Nature Preserve;** pp. 25, 41 (bottom), 42, 50 (bottom) *Engineering News.*
ACKNOWLEDGMENTS: Buffalo Fire Department, Thomas Choinski, City of Buffalo (Department of Planning, Office of the City Engineer, and Office of the City Survey), John Conlin, John Feather, A. Scott Field, Peter Filim, Wayne Gall, Gary Pools (Annette), Eion Gordon, Carol Henry, Greg Jandura, Steven Janke, Karen Kaptur, Marilyn Kihl, Mark Kohan, Mary Langdon, Ed Malloy, Dorothy Markert, Deborah Mattice, Susan McCartney, Brian Meyer, Pam Meyer, Lynn Newman, Paul Pietrzak, Carolyn Schaffner, Albert Spears, David Thiel, Tifft Farm Nature Preserve, Tom Toles, Elmo Weatherspoon, U.S. Army Corps of Engineers, Mike Vogel, Tom Zyskowski

BIBLIOGRAPHY
Banham, Reyner. *A Concrete Atlantis.* Cambridge, 1986
Banham, Reyner. "Buffalo Industrial: An Introduction." Little Journal 1 (1979) 2-19
Baxter, Henry H. *Maps: Buffalo Harbor.* Buffalo, 1965
Baxter, Henry H. *Grain Elevators.* Buffalo, 1980
Buffalo, City of, Division of Planning. *Buffalo—The Place: Preserving Its Identity.* By John Conlin. 1982
Buffalo Architectural Guidebook Corp. *Buffalo Architecture: A Guide.* Cambridge, 1981
Buffalo City Directory for the Year 1882. Buffalo, 1882
Buffalo City Directory for the Year 1884. Buffalo, 1884
Buffalo Courier-Express
Buffalo News
Engineering News, 1896-1906
Goldman, Mark. *High Hopes: The Rise and Decline of Buffalo, New York.* Albany, 1983.
Hatcher, Harlan. *Lake Erie.* Indianapolis, 1945
Hill, Henry W. *Municipality of Buffalo, New York: A History 1720-1923.* New York, 1923
Hovey, Otis Ellis. *Movable Bridges.* Vol. 1, *Superstructure.* New York, 1926
Jandura, Gregory. Letter to editor, July 7, 1986
Ketchum, Milo S. *The Design of Walls, Bins and Grain Elevators.* New York, 1925
Kohan, Mark. Letter to editor, May 3, 1987.
Scully, Vincent. American Architecture and Urbanism. New York, 1969
Scully, Vincent. Modern Architecture: *The Architecture of Democracy.* New York, 1974
Trollope, Anthony. *North America.* 1862. Reprint. Edited by Donald Smalley and Bradford Allen Booth. New York, 1951